ALL'S FAIR
IN LOVE
AND
TREACHERY

Also by Celeste Connally

Act Like a Lady, Think Like a Lord

ALL'S FAIR IN LOVE AND TREACHERY

CELESTE CONNALLY

MINOTAUR BOOKS
NEW YORK

First published in the United States by Minotaur Books, an imprint of St. Martin's Publishing Group

www.minotaurbooks.com

Design by Meryl Sussman Levavi

Map by Liane Payne

The Library of Congress Cataloging-in-Publication Data is available upon request.

ISBN 978-1-250-86760-5 (hardcover)
ISBN 978-1-250-86761-2 (ebook)

First Edition: 2024

10 9 8 7 6 5 4 3 2 1

For my cousins Elizabeth and Amy—
for whom Lady Elizabeth and Lady Sloan
were named—with love

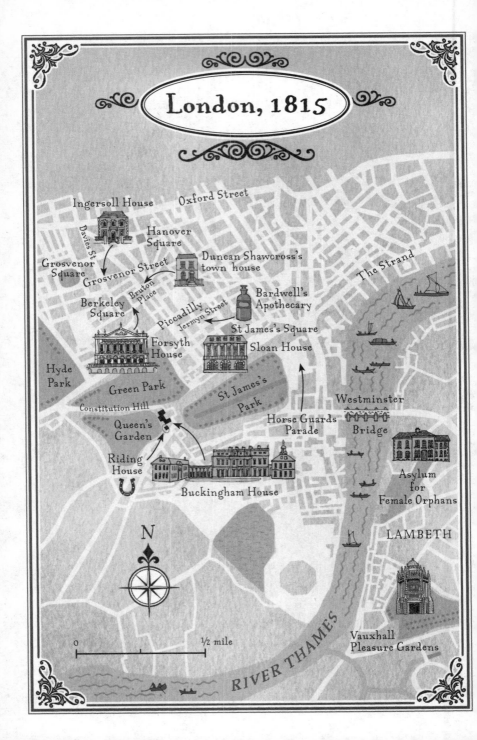

ONE

Wednesday, 21 June 1815
3 Bruton Place
Mayfair, London, England
The four o'clock hour of the morning

THE DAMNING WORDS FOLDED IN ON THEMSELVES AS THE PAPER crumpled in Lady Petra's fist. Flames danced merrily in the fireplace until one log split under the crushing heat, sparks flying like the spitting of an angry cat.

From beyond the window shrouded in heavy curtains came the rumble of thunder. Numbly, Petra pulled the tartan blanket tighter about her body, her mind crowded with too many thoughts. Her gaze fell to the handle of the fireplace poker, the brass glowing in the firelight as if beckoning her.

You could be an avenging angel, it seemed to say.

The implement was long and well crafted, ending in a point almost as sharp as a dagger. She crushed the paper tighter in one hand and reached out with the other to close cold fingers around the warm brass handle, casting her eyes to the ceiling and the bedroom above.

Would he deny the veracity of the words she had just read?

A crack of lightning made Petra start, her hand reflexively loosening, then tightening on the poker. Outside the small, warm library in which she stood, the resulting bright bolt speared the transom window above the heavy oak front door and lit up the foyer of the town house.

In that moment, she could see the foot of the staircase clearly, and her memories flared just as brightly to that horrible early morning three years earlier when she came down a very similar set of stairs. Ones located west of Hanover Square, on a street called Chaffinch Lane, when she made the terrible discovery of her betrothed—her darling Emerson—his neck at an unnatural angle, all life gone from his body.

Petra had been assured it was an accident. That the young, handsome viscount must have missed a step as he rushed downstairs. Or slipped in his stockinged feet, perhaps, as he went to answer a knocking at the door that Petra had not heard. She had been cocooned in their bed, slumbering as only one who was blissfully exhausted from lovemaking can.

The explanations for Emerson's fall had been believable—all too easily so, in fact. For the theories had come from a man she trusted with her life. The man who had helped her slip away into the darkness of London before anyone could bear witness to Lady Petra Forsyth, the unmarried daughter of the Earl of Holbrook, emerging from a bachelor's lodgings, half-dressed and with her reddish-blond curls hanging loose down her back.

Petra lifted her eyes to the ceiling and the bedchamber above, imagining that man as she'd left him a mere half hour earlier. Green eyes, so startling, hidden behind lids closed with deep sleep. His thick, wavy hair, mussed from her hands, would look black as night against the white linen pillow. Duncan Shawcross was the man who had helped Petra that fateful morning. The man whom Petra had more recently realized she had always loved; whom she had known and trusted since they were both children. Even some months earlier, when she feared their friendship lost, Petra's faith in him had never truly wavered.

Now it seemed to be crashing down around her.

She whispered an agonized oath, stumbling backward until her shoulder blades rested against the bookshelf. The fireplace poker was somehow still in her hand, its pointed edge having dragged through the thick blue carpet with swirls of rust, cream, and goldenrod.

Petra unfurled her fingers that held fast the small piece of paper. Being of fine quality, it retained some of its integrity despite being compressed. Slowly, it began to open like the petals of a night-blooming jasmine flower. Not fully, but enough so that she could read the words once more.

It was but one page in a ledger full of information gathered for the purposes of blackmail. The handwriting was of a man named Drysdale, a sham physician who was as cruel as he was clever.

At the top of the page was written *Duncan Shawcross (Honorable)*. Beneath were a few sentences regarding his background and minor vices. Then followed a mention of Duncan lending his lodgings to Emerson, Viscount Ingersoll, and Lady Petra Forsyth for their scandalous premarital liaisons. And how, three weeks before the nuptials, Emerson had died of a broken neck after falling down the stairs of Duncan's town house. Then came two short, final sentences.

Am told no accident. Contrived by Shawcross himself.

A hot tear Petra had not realized had formed dropped down to the page, landing atop one word. She watched as the letters blurred, the ink retreating and swirling, bleeding out Duncan's name.

Thunder came again, so loud and close that Petra felt it deep within her, saw how it made her fingers tremble. Or were they already trembling?

Clenching the page once more, Petra lifted the fireplace poker. Her knuckles whitened as she gripped the handle, the spear blackened from stoking fire after fire. Despite the intense heat it faced, the sharp point had never bent. And neither would she.

The tartan blanket began to fall away, but she stopped it at the last moment. Lifting her chamberstick, its candle lighting her way, Petra made her way up the stairs, lethal poker at the ready.

Silently, gently, she pushed the door open, eyes darting across the bedchamber to the mahogany four-post bed.

Her lips twisted with vexation. The fireplace had long gone dark and cold, but a finger lamp burned atop the round carved-marble table at the far corner of the room, next to the bed. She had not lit it before going downstairs, but now it gave her all the light she needed.

Hangings of moss-colored velvet that had created Petra and Duncan's nightly cocoon, and from which Petra had earlier slipped for some reading in the library, were now open and tied back at two of the four corners. She saw rumpled linens, but the bed was empty. As was the bedchamber itself, with its dark oak-paneled walls on which hung evidence of Duncan's penchant for landscape paintings, including Runciman's *A View near Perth.*

She took two quick steps to the right and peered into Duncan's dressing room. The wooden valet stand holding his breeches, shirt, and coat had been freed from every bit of clothing. His haversack no longer sat on the wooden stool in the corner.

Duncan was gone. Only the scent of him lingered, a mixture of saddle leather, green grass, fresh air, and lemon drops.

No doubt he would have escaped her by using the hidden staircase at the corner of his dressing room that wended down to the servants' entrance at the back of the house. It was the same way she would exit in an hour when the prearranged hackney arrived, the driver having been paid handsomely to keep his eyes averted and his mouth closed.

Still, even with her face concealed by a poke bonnet and her attire by a full cloak, the drivers of London's hackneys were canny men. The driver would know he was collecting Lady Petra Forsyth from the town house of Mr. Duncan Shawcross, the son of the late Marquess of Langford and the grandson of the Duke and Duchess of Hillmorton.

If word of where she spent her nights began to infiltrate society, it would not matter that Lady Petra had declared herself as never wishing to marry, or that she had a fortune of her own. Most of society would simply ignore the fact that Duncan and Petra had known each other—even loved each other—for the bulk of their lives. Society's view would be harshest on her. They would say that Lady Petra Forsyth was still an unmarried woman risking an illicit liaison with a handsome, rakish gentleman. She was staking her reputation, and that of her family's name as well.

But was she now risking her life, too? Was she having a scandalous affair with a man who was not only a liar, but also a killer?

Though she had indeed known Duncan her whole life, for the past three years, as she mourned Emerson's death and slowly healed her heart, Duncan had been traveling around the Continent at the behest of his grandfather, the duke. In truth, however, he had all but fled Petra's presence and England the very day after Emerson's funeral.

Realizing she'd had her back to the staircase when she made her discovery only minutes earlier, she had to wonder: Had Duncan witnessed her accidental uncovering of the accusations against him? It was easily possible. Duncan had more than once slipped down the stairs before without her knowing, always in search of her touch, her kisses, her body.

If so, did he at first watch with languid amusement as she opened her book and the long-forgotten page from Drysdale's ledger fell out?

She could imagine his eyes widening with apprehension when she read the page, watching her go still and pale, whispering in anguished tones, "No, no. *No!* This cannot be!"

And had it been then that he had fled like a coward?

She felt a vexing swoop of emotions. Duncan Shawcross had never been a coward, ever. Yet only someone guilty would act as he had.

With a sigh, Petra set her chamberstick atop Duncan's chest of drawers. Then a movement made her start; in the pool of candle-light, a shadow began to grow from the far side of the chest.

Instinctively, she shrugged off the tartan blanket and raised the fireplace poker with both hands, aiming it like Diana about to spear the stag that was Actaeon.

"Make yourself known, whoever you are," she said, her heart thudding in her chest.

Someone was rising from the chair set against the wall. Petra squinted as the form—a small man or a boy—moved better into the light.

It was indeed a boy. A street urchin, by the frayed trousers, bare feet, and dirt-stained shirt. Yet his face remained in darkness, as if he had no face.

She blinked twice. Were his hands shielding his eyes? They were, presumably from her state of wearing nothing but one of Duncan's own shirts.

The fingers of one of the boy's hands splayed to reveal a sliver of an eye.

"'Allo, and good morning, my lady."

The end of her fireplace poker tipped and fell to the marquetry floor.

"Teddy? Is that you?"

TWO

Some minutes later and properly dressed in a simple cotton day gown that required no buttoning, Petra poured Teddy another cup of tea. She added sugar and milk, and watched with satisfaction as he finished a generous slice of the chicken and ham pie she'd brought from Forsyth House. Then she held out a ginger biscuit. Teddy's blue eyes brightened and more color returned to his cheeks, which had been much too pale for Petra's liking when she finally got a proper look at him.

She had sent Teddy back down to the library with the tartan blanket to warm up, for his thin shirt and too-short trousers had been soaked through by the rain outside. She'd also insisted he exchange his dirty and nearly outgrown shirt for one of Duncan's— albeit one with a stained cuff, as she knew Teddy would be wary of taking one that was too new or too clean.

Petra used the brass poker for its proper job and stoked the fire with it, relieved at not having had to use it for any other purpose. Then she replaced it alongside the other fireplace implements and returned to sit next to the young boy on the sofa.

"Drink up, love," she said. "And finish that biscuit. Because once you have, it is time for you to tell me how you came to be in Mr. Shawcross's bedroom, especially as he himself seems to have disappeared without a word."

Teddy obeyed and Petra glanced at the mantel clock, then out into the hallway. It was a quarter past four. Though the sun had been rising for one half hour already, no light was yet filtering through the transom window. Yet the carriage would arrive soon to take her home to Forsyth House.

There, Annie would be waiting at the little-used boot room entrance on the west side, nearest Berkeley Square. Petra's new hound, an all-brown pointer named Sable, would be there, too, sitting with lovely manners and wagging her tail ecstatically. No other servants would witness any of this, for the eastern side of Forsyth House was their general domain. As such, it had become the easiest way for Petra to leave for a night in her lover's arms and return in the early hours without the house any the wiser.

She was not so silly as to believe those she employed did not have their suspicions, however. Yet if any disapproved to the point of commenting on her rather scandalous behavior, Annie had never let on.

However, Forsyth House had run smoothly with only a small complement of servants for many a year. That meant all but the newest underfootman and two of the younger housemaids had known Duncan Shawcross since he was a lad, and Petra doubted they would have a negative comment to profess. Especially as all of them, including the three newest, were as under the influence of Duncan's charm as Petra was.

Or had been.

She pressed her lips together while looking Teddy over once more. Now that the boy had been fed and watered, she could see tiredness stealing over him.

"When did you last truly sleep, Teddy?"

"Yesterday 'bout midnight, my lady," he replied, attempting to stifle a yawn.

"Then you shall come home with me and get a proper nap and some food to take with you to the other children."

"Nay, my lady," he said, though with a brief return of his cheeky grin. "I'm ever so grateful, I am, but I 'ave to be gone. Mum's expecting me at seven o'clock. But you asked how I came to be in Mr. Shawcross's rooms, and I'm obliged to explain, and pass along his message."

Though the smile remained in place, Teddy's vibrant blue eyes seemed to shutter with the brief mention of his mother. Petra longed to know where his mother was on a daily basis that caused Teddy to sleep rough on the streets of London instead of in a warm home. But the few times Petra had asked, he had evaded her questions as deftly as Petra herself could use a simple hairpin to unlock Mrs. Ruddle's pantry down in the kitchens of Forsyth House.

"All right, then," she said, stifling her resignation. "For I should like to hear his message as much as you would like to impart it."

"He sent for me four days ago, Mr. Shawcross did," Teddy began. He tilted his head in the direction of the back of the town house. "He's been waitin' on a message, and was told the man would deliver to the stables, not the house. Mr. Shawcross's groom is old and a mite deaf, as you know, and Mr. Shawcross 'imself ain't got no servants, as you know as well, so he hired me to collect it when it came."

In truth, Petra was not surprised at the idea of a message being delivered under odd circumstances. Since his return from the Continent, Duncan had been placed in charge of security for his grandmother, the Duchess of Hillmorton, and was at the constant disposal of his grandfather, the duke, as well.

"I've been sleepin' in the mews hayloft every night since then," Teddy continued. "He offered me a bed in the groom's quarters, but I like the open air. And I was 'appy to 'elp in whatever way he required. I like Mr. Shawcross, I do, ever since I met 'im that afternoon in the Green Park. When . . ."

"When we discovered the murder of the poor footman, yes," Petra said soberly.

"'Struth, my lady. Well, I'm sure you knows Mr. Shawcross has paid me to do jobs for 'im ever since."

Petra's eyebrows briefly raised, but her tone was light. "No, I did not know."

"Pays well, he does," Teddy said. "Always gives me an extra copper or two for some sweets to share with me mates, too."

"And do you go to Bardwell's Apothecary to buy your sweets, like Miss Frances bade you?" asked Petra with a smile brought about by thinking of her new friend. Serious by nature, Frances Bardwell had the generosity of a healer, and such a way with herbs and flowers and the crafting of them into oils, waters, medicinal draughts, and even foods.

Teddy's head bobbed up and down with enthusiasm.

"Occasionally Miss Frances gives me more than I pay for, and I overheard one day that it's Lady Caroline who pays for 'em, along with some tinctures and whatnot when they're needed. It were ever so kind of her to do that, my lady."

He leaned forward, the smile on his own face infectious.

"An' did Miss Lottie tell you I've been helping her walk the dogs she's been trainin', my lady? She brings me biscuits, too."

"Miss Lottie did indeed tell me," Petra confirmed, her own smile growing at the mention of her dearest friend, Lady Caroline, and her other new friend, Miss Charlotte Reed.

Lady Caroline had as much heart as she had influence in society, though she generally hid her kindnesses behind a sharp wit and a studied indifference. Caroline also hid her prowess with a bow and arrow, pretending to have only the small level of talent with archery that was acceptable for a gently bred lady.

Lottie, on the other hand, exuded an open heart and warmth, along with an extraordinary ability for training dogs to do everything from sitting patiently to retrieving downed birds to, on command, leaping up to set their teeth into the buttocks of someone wholly deserving of it.

Petra poured herself another cup of tea, adding, "And Miss Lottie says you have been so helpful that she now has time to concentrate on a new commission of finding a dog for my friend Lady Vera, the Dowager Countess Grimley."

Teddy's face glowed with pride, and the thornlike feeling that had wedged in Petra's heart eased.

"Now," she said, after sipping the strong, malty China tea, which she took just as it was, "we have little time until my carriage arrives. Do finish telling me what Mr. Shawcross told you to pass along, Teddy."

"Well, my lady," he began, his elfin face screwed up with seriousness, "the man finally came tonight, bearing a letter. I took it, as arranged, without the bloke even gettin' off his horse. Mr. Shawcross must've heard the horse, for he met me at the back door. He then asked if I would wait and deliver a message to you." Teddy then looked sheepish. "I already knows you was here, my lady. After what happened to you with that Mr. Drysdale, I confess I've kept an eye out, see? I hope that don't offend you. But I ain't told no one, I swear it. And to my knowin', no one else has seen you."

"Excellent news, Teddy," Petra said faintly. Then she offered him a smile. "I am most honored you would look out for me."

Relief softened his features again, and he suddenly looked very young and earnest. "Mr. Shawcross had me repeat the words I was to tell you as he packed, my lady. He said they were of the utmost importance, and that he had planned to tell you himself, but he could not risk you hobbling him when he must away without a moment to spare. He also said you are to begin an assignment for the Queen today in Lambeth, at the Asylum for Female Orphans, and you must concentrate on your task."

Teddy then stopped, beaming with delight at the expression that had come over Petra's face.

"He knew you would look confounded—just like you are, my lady. *A bit all-a-mort,* is what he said. And that you'd give me the cutty-eye, too!"

"He might have simply waited until he returned and then told me," Petra said, staring peevishly into the leaping flames of the fire, entertaining the idea of setting one of Lottie's dogs onto Duncan's firm backside. He deserved the pain for using Teddy and his innocence in such an ill manner. Furthermore, if the information she found were true, he would deserve it for using her, for making her believe in love again, only to then crush her heart.

"When he does return, I shall hobble him in punishment, relishing every moment of it."

When she realized Teddy had gone silent, Petra straightened her shoulders.

"Forgive me, Teddy. I am not myself this morning, and I thank you for agreeing to pass along this message. You are doing well. Carry on, do."

"It's not that, my lady . . . ," Teddy said. Much like Petra had earlier, he glanced up at the ceiling, as if Duncan might still be there, listening to ensure Teddy did not stray off the topic of whatever balderdash he had been entrusted to repeat.

"What is it, then?" she asked, feeling suspicion rising.

"It were only that . . . I don't know where Mr. Shawcross is going, or what he is doing, but the man deliverin' the message tonight bade me to take it to Mr. Shawcross as fast as I could. If I didn't, the man said he'd find me and thrash me. His horse were a mite skittish, and he thrashed it for not standin' still, and he said he'd take the same whip to me."

At the very idea of this, Petra was outraged. "Is that so? Well, I should like to see the blackguard try to hurt you, or indeed his horse, for he shall have to contend with me first. What did this man look like?"

Though his responsorial shrug was blithe, pink spots formed in Teddy's cheeks, and he suddenly looked embarrassed to meet her eyes. "I ain't afraid, my lady. And the man were all in black, his face covered by a kerchief, and a hat pulled low. I only heard his voice, which was rough, like his manners. But it were Mr. Shawcross I thought about. The man said Mr. Shawcross had but a short time to be where he were expected, and that . . ."

"And that what, Teddy?" Petra asked.

Teddy's eyes widened and the worry in them was like the rippling of an otherwise pristine blue lake. "That Mr. Shawcross might not be comin' back."

A shot of cold apprehension ran down Petra's spine. What did that mean exactly? Was this Duncan's way of escaping the justice that would come to him for Emerson's death? Or was it something more?

Asking Teddy to shoulder further concern will not do, she told herself sharply. Then she reminded herself that this man on the skittish horse, rude as he was, was merely a messenger. That he likely was part of Duncan's own team of men, and knew little, but enjoyed frightening young street urchins like he enjoyed mistreating his horse.

Petra forced her exasperation with both Duncan and the unknown messenger down enough that her voice came out with a semblance of normality, for it was clear Teddy was in a state of genuine concern.

"I thank you, Teddy. You are as kindhearted as you are resourceful, but I assure you that Mr. Shawcross is quite capable of taking care of himself."

"That's what Mr. Shawcross said, too, my lady, even when I said I didn't care for the rusty-guts fellow."

"Indeed?" said Petra, briefly arching an eyebrow at his dark tone. "You said you could not see this man, which I do not doubt— but do you know him just the same?"

Teddy hesitated, then shook his head. Yet Petra saw a flash of something washing over the lad's face. It seemed a mixture of the protective nature she'd often witnessed in him, and something counter to it as well. She felt she'd seen a bit of the wiliness young Teddy possessed that had allowed him to survive, if not thrive, on the streets of London.

"All right then, Teddy," she said. Suddenly, she was exhausted, and she settled back into her seat. "Let me hear the message Mr. Shawcross bade you to impart."

At this, Teddy threw off the tartan rug and stood. Clearing his throat, he closed his eyes, blowing out a slow breath as if he were an actor on the boards at Drury Lane about to deliver a monologue. Despite herself, Petra nearly grinned, feeling a rush of warmth for her young friend.

"Lady Petra," Teddy said, deepening his voice and speaking in grave tones that contained a hint of Duncan's own Scottish burr. "I beg of you to trust the compass within you, and those most worthy. For both they and you have knowledge unrealized, and memories unsurfaced."

Teddy's cheeks puffed out as he blew a sigh of relief mixed with pride that he had done as he had pledged, seemingly unaware that Petra's lips had parted and then closed, or that her eyebrows had knitted together. Was this the whole of the message?

Damn and blast, Duncan Shawcross, she thought. *You used poor Teddy to keep me here for no bloody reason other than managing your escape!*

"My lady?"

Thoroughly nettled, Petra focused once more on the bright clarity of Teddy's eyes.

"You're also to never be without your lockpicks."

THREE

"IT IS RATHER A PITY THAT MEN CAN BE SUCH ROTTEN CREATURES, is it not, Lady Petra?"

The guttural echoes of Queen Charlotte's native Germany added an extra bite to her already peevish tone, jerking Petra from her wool gathering. The porcelain cup she was lifting to her mouth wobbled in consequence, causing a splash of the steaming coffee to leap over the rim and land with burning precision atop her knuckles.

Repressing an oath, Petra managed to return the cup and its saucer to the table full of elegantly displayed breakfast dishes without further mishap, and hurriedly dabbed her table napkin over her hand. If the coffee had dripped on the delicate embroidery of her new silk day dress, she felt Annie would somehow know, even though her lady's maid was currently waiting for her belowstairs, in the servants' hall of Buckingham House.

As if a force were compelling her, Petra glanced up and found herself meeting the narrowed eyes of her godmother, the Duchess of Hillmorton. Her heart began to beat with intensity. Yet the duchess merely pursed her lips, her indigo gaze flicking toward the Queen.

"Yes—yes, indeed, it is a pity, Your Majesty," Petra hastily responded.

But what had she missed? To what man had Her Majesty been

referring? Could these two venerable women possibly know why her heart was breaking?

Selecting a piece of toast and biting off a corner, Petra hoped an indelicately full mouth would deter any conversation that might pertain to Duncan.

Not that Her Grace would tell her where he was. No, the duchess never discussed Duncan's whereabouts as they pertained to his role as her man of security. But, damnation, she did delight in teasing Petra and Duncan both about their attachment to each other.

And how would I possibly respond now? Petra thought wildly as she chewed. *"Well, Your Grace, if the incriminating page I discovered this morning is true, your grandson—my friend, my lover—took the life of my darling fiancé three years earlier, and he has lied to me ever since. And now Duncan has disappeared, and I know not why, or where he is. Indeed, I am both furious and terribly worried, and the only reason I am able to sit so calmly across from you is because I have not yet fully comprehended all that has happened in recent hours. Yes, Your Grace, I am truly in a state of shock. Have you some aromatic vinegars, by chance? For I am so frightfully overwhelmed that fainting does seem like a lovely option at present."*

She nearly let out a dark laugh even as thunder rumbled outside the Queen's private breakfast room and rain began to beat against the windowpanes.

No, that would not do. And neither would a swoon. I have never done so from shock before, and I certainly shall not start now.

But as much as she wished to distrust the words the odious Mr. Drysdale had written, there was little reason to do so. For one, by the date at the top of the page, it was penned well before Petra had become a threat to the despicable man.

No, his words could not merely be a cruel trick played on her in retribution. Petra had realized this earlier at Forsyth House, as she'd rushed to hide the paper in the first book her fingers found on her bookshelves in her bedchamber, determined not to let Annie see it. For Annie, who loved Duncan as if she were his older sister, would be devastated by such knowledge.

The delicious toast had turned to something akin to paste in her mouth with these thoughts, and Petra hurried to take a sip of her coffee, earning her a suspicious look from her godmother.

The Queen, however, appeared to have noticed none of this. She was studying a set of snuffboxes situated on the small table next to her chair, finally lifting a gold one with an enameled top. Petra and the duchess both politely averted their gazes as Her Majesty gave the top three brisk taps. There was one quick inhalation followed by a second. A heady scent of tobacco mixed with the marzipan-like scent of bitter almonds and the deeper, musky aroma of ambergris permeated the air. It overpowered the scents of fresh bread, strawberry jam, three kinds of eggs, and rashers of bacon, all of which had been laid upon the table by a series of footmen. Two of which remained in the Queen's breakfast room, standing ramrod straight, their backs to the large windows and red velvet draperies.

And the one in Petra's field of vision? Lawks, was he perspiring?

Petra glanced to the other, catching him looking equally nervous. That was when she realized Queen Charlotte's narrowed gaze was focused on the two footmen. And the food upon the table, it seemed. Seeing Her Majesty transfer her glower to the dishes, Petra slowly put her toast back on her plate. Even the duchess—the Queen's closest ally and friend—hesitated in the act of choosing a soft-boiled egg, which Her Majesty noted.

"No, no, you must go back to your enjoyment of Chef Carême's breakfast spread," said the Queen with a thin veneer of gaiety before her tawny eyes focused on Petra. "Lady Petra, I have invited you here to discuss your assignment today at the Asylum for Female Orphans, but it may wait a bit longer as we are all clearly in need of morning sustenance. So let us enjoy our coffee and this delicious toast, made from what Chef Carême calls his *pain ordinaire*.

Yes, we must enjoy it while we can, for I am hearing rumors that Chef wishes to leave the royal household and spread his culinary wings. Thus, we may soon be eating plain British bread instead."

Ah, Petra thought with some relief, *so this was the real cause for her ire.*

"If he chooses to leave, I will not stop him," Her Majesty continued, looking to Petra, but clearly speaking to the footmen, and by extension, to the French royal chef. "But until then, I will enjoy the right to ask my chef to create the type of foods the King and I wish to enjoy." With a tight voice, she focused on the enameled top of her snuffbox, on which was painted a crystalline blue sky. "The foods that I wish to enjoy, at least."

The duchess and Petra exchanged the swiftest of glances, and Petra received an encouraging look.

"May I ask after the health of our beloved King, Your Majesty?" Petra asked.

Queen Charlotte was still staring at her snuffbox. Petra wondered if, in its hue, she could see the color of the King's eyes. Bright blue and cloudless, as they once used to be.

"His Majesty has been in better health, Lady Petra," she replied in a voice that seemed far away. "But his recent days, I have been assured, have been . . . not as fretful. And for that, I must be grateful."

"As we all are, Ma'am," Petra said.

"More coffee?" the Queen asked. Without waiting for a reply, she smoothly topped off all three cups, her eyes not straying from her task as she commanded, "Leave us."

The two footmen made hasty, silent exits to the sound of another grumble of thunder. Then the Queen glanced at the small ormolu clock upon the side table.

"We have but a half hour before the duchess and I are due to be whisked away to the safety of Kew Palace, and there are details you must know for your investigation before we board our carriages." Then Her Majesty's mouth turned down and her eyes sparked with irritation. "Do not gape, Lady Petra. It makes you look like a carp. Duchess, I thought you said Shawcross was to inform Lady Petra of the most recent events and our travel plans."

He bloody well did not, thought Petra hotly. Yet it faded just as quickly, for she *might* have been partially to blame.

She had very literally leapt into his arms last night when he opened the back door to Bruton Place, hadn't she? Kissing him before he could even utter her name, running her fingers through his dark hair, she had then pulled back just long enough to rasp out, "If you do not take me to your bed this moment, Duncan Shawcross, I shall never speak to you again."

Yet while his attentions were as weakness-inducing as always, had she not sensed a hesitation in him? Was the light in his green eyes dimmed somewhat, or had it been a trick of the candlelight? Was he already planning his escape from having to admit to what treacherous things he'd done, even as his mouth trailed down her body?

Petra reached for the pitcher of barley water and poured herself a cooling glass. She risked a glance at the duchess through lowered eyelids as she drank, and found Her Grace looking only mildly perturbed by Duncan's lack of communication.

"Then I suspect Shawcross was detained elsewhere last evening and could not stop by Forsyth House as intended," the duchess said with a lift of one shoulder. "I know he had important business of some sort, for he sent his new deputy to me last night with details for today's move to Kew."

Not wishing to have the duchess dwell on Duncan's whereabouts the past evening, Petra looked to the Queen.

"Forgive me, Your Majesty, but you spoke of being taken to the safety of Kew Palace. Has something happened?"

"Indeed it has, Lady Petra," replied the Queen, who eyed her snuffbox again before turning away from it. "But I shall let the duchess explain."

As the duchess stirred more sugar into her coffee, her voice was brisk, almost as if going over the menu for a dinner party with her head housekeeper.

"Lady Petra, you, of course, were tasked with attending today's opening of the new dining hall at the Asylum for Female Orphans as a representative of Her Majesty." Pausing to taste her coffee, she gave a satisfactory nod and continued. "This was to give you sufficient reason to speak with anyone in attendance—including the guardians, the patronesses, the orphan girls themselves, and the new matron. Indeed, your ultimate task was to inquire about the untimely death of the former matron, Mrs. Huxton, who was found in the chapel with a wound to her head. Lady Petra, why do I have the feeling you are about to ask a rather impertinent question?"

"More of a bold question, Your Grace," Petra replied with a brief grin at hearing the mixture of asperity and amusement in her godmother's tone.

"This breakfast was designed for just such questions, Lady Petra," the Queen said smoothly. "You may proceed."

Petra acknowledged this with a grateful nod, then asked, "Your Majesty, does your intelligence officer believe the matron died of some natural cause, or does he think she was, well, killed?"

"The latter, Lady Petra—and now my man has confirmation," she replied before giving another impatient wave to the duchess to continue explaining.

"I was here with Her Majesty when word arrived of the matron's untimely demise," said the duchess. "Though we felt it wise to withhold any news until the royal physician could confirm what was relayed by Lady Vera."

"Lady Vera?" Petra repeated. "It was she who discovered the matron?" All but feeling immune to surprises at this moment, Petra canted her head thoughtfully. "But I cannot claim much astonishment. Her ladyship is one of the most dedicated patronesses of the orphanage, and has been for years."

"Nearly thirty years," said the duchess. "Though it is not widely known that Lady Vera often met the matron for a private breakfast to discuss the state of the orphanage. It was when Lady Vera arrived for one of their meetings that she went to the chapel and found the body of Mrs. Huxton beside the altar. A silver candlestick was found next to the matron's head. Upon confirming the matron was beyond help, Lady Vera ensured that the body was moved and the area scrubbed before the orphan girls could discover the tragedy and become upset. The girls know their matron passed, but they believe it was peacefully, and in her own bed."

The Queen used her fork and speared two raspberries from a heaping bowl of summer fruits and examined them as she spoke.

"Lady Vera also rightly alerted the palace to the matron's death after sending for Sir Bartie's girl to confirm the death was not natural," she said. "Lady Vera is of the belief, and I agree, that an apothecarist is often as knowledgeable as any physician. And as she did not wish for the girls to know that something was amiss by bringing a man into the orphanage, she called for my apothecarist's daughter. I understand the girl is quite as talented as her papa." She dipped her forkful of raspberries in some clotted cream. "Yes, I am certain had it been anyone other than Lady Vera and Miss Bardwell, London would be rife with gossip and the orphanage would be in an uproar."

This time, Petra closed her mouth before either woman saw her gaping. It was possible she was not yet immune to new shocks. "Do you mean Miss Frances Bardwell, Your Majesty?"

"Of course that is who I mean, Lady Petra," the Queen snapped. "Does Sir Bartie have another daughter of whom I am unaware?"

"No, indeed, Ma'am," Petra replied, but her mind was whirling. She had seen Frances at least three times in the past week, and her friend had not said a word. Not even a little hint that she had news to share—not even when Petra said she herself was tasked with representing Her Majesty at the orphanage today.

For that matter, Petra had encountered Lady Vera out on Rotten Row just yesterday, driving her hackney pony while Petra rode sidesaddle, skillfully keeping her chestnut gelding at a sedate trot. She and Lady Vera had even chatted for several minutes about the brilliant Gold Cup win of the Earl of Holbrook's prize stallion at Royal Ascot earlier in the month. Petra had not considered for a moment that Lady Vera was harboring a secret.

Is everyone I care about concealing truths from me? Petra thought testily. And then, to her horror, she felt a slight prick behind her eyes.

The duchess, seemingly reading Petra's thoughts as she was often wont to do, said, "Now, now, Lady Petra. I know Miss Bardwell is your friend, and you have been a favorite of Lady Vera's since you were a small girl, but they were instructed to keep their counsel until we knew more."

"They would be in the Tower of London at present had they not," the Queen drawled, taking up her knife and cutting through a rasher of bacon with one swift move.

Across the table, the duchess caught Petra's widened eyes, and gave the merest placid shake of her head as if to say, *Do not worry, my girl, I would have talked her out of it.*

Forging ahead, Petra asked, "Your Majesty, as I understood it when I was initially set this task, your intelligence officer believes the matron's death is a signal that something untoward is happening at the orphanage. Will any of your men of security be investigating as well?"

"They most certainly will, Lady Petra," the Queen replied, "but not at the orphanage itself. I believe the situation there requires a woman's touch rather than the often brutish actions of my men—as useful as they are at other times."

"Yes, a woman's touch is key," agreed the duchess. "This is an asylum for young orphaned girls. All below the age of fifteen, and it is an open secret that most are the illegitimate daughters of soldiers and the gentry. Whilst the governors of the orphanage are all men, as well as many of the patrons, they have little interaction with the girls—except for at events like the one today. If one of Her Majesty's men began asking them questions, especially with little finesse as is their general habit, these girls may be frightened into silence, or hysterics. But you, Lady Petra? With your station, youth, and the particular affinity for making those around you feel at ease? Yes, you would have been quite perfect for the task."

"I thank you, Your Grace," Petra said. Then she blinked, realizing that certain words took on a stronger meaning. "But forgive me, I do not understand. You have been speaking in the past tense. May I ask why that is?"

She watched as the Queen and the duchess exchanged glances. The Queen then lifted her chin.

"My intelligence officer has come forward with additional news, Lady Petra," she said. "Whilst he has not determined the specifics yet, my man believes that there may be a connection somehow between the orphanage—and therefore the matron's death—and a ring of radicals that wish to do the King and I, and indeed the entire royal family, harm." Then, almost as an afterthought, she added, "And members of Parliament as well, so I understand."

"You are being threatened?" Petra said, aghast, then quickly added, "Your Majesty."

"Yes, Lady Petra," said the Queen on an exasperated sigh. "The royal family is no stranger to threats, of course, so I would not be much bothered by it were it not for the fact that my man believes some bad business will take place quite soon."

Petra had many questions all of a sudden, but none immediately issued forth. It was the duchess who supplied more information.

"Her Majesty's intelligence officer believes something is afoot with these radicals, who call themselves the Bellowers," she explained. "It seems they fancy themselves town criers, and seek to bellow out to the people the need for reform—that is, the abolition of the monarchy, and the desire for Great Britain to become a republic. They believe strongly in doing so by force rather than peaceful means. It may be possible that a recent theft of hundreds of cannonballs can be attributed to them, in fact."

"Most distressing indeed," Petra said. "And does the intelligence officer know when or where this bad business will take place?"

"He does not, but he feels something of a violent nature will occur after news arrives of our defeat of Napoleon." A patriotic gleam came to the duchess's blue eyes. "And we, of course, are anticipating the complete defeat of the upstart general and his forces any day now."

The Queen then said, "What you must understand, Lady Petra, is that my son, the Prince Regent, will declare three days of celebrations once the news of the war's end is delivered. And my intelligence officer believes—and rightly so, I expect—that whatever nefarious doings these radical Bellowers have planned is likely to occur within those three days. And thus, knowing the connection between the orphanage and the Bellowers has become much more important."

Petra nodded, though her mouth felt a bit dry. "Is anything else known, Ma'am?"

The duchess's mouth pursed. "But little. All he could tell us is that the Bellowers are not the usual sort of ruffians, at least not all of them."

"Yes," mused Her Majesty, her eyes darkening. "Some are members of the aristocracy."

"Truly?" Petra said, feeling a slight shiver at this knowledge. Naturally, she understood that members of England's nobility were just as inclined to be unhappy with the monarchy and Parliament as anyone else. Yet to think some of her acquaintances—gentlemen she danced with at balls, peers whom she greeted at Hyde Park, those she conversed with at dinner parties—might be a part of a potentially violent radical group was chilling.

"Yes, truly, Lady Petra," the duchess confirmed. "And because of this danger, Her Majesty is being taken to Kew Palace in Richmond, where she can be best protected, and I will be accompanying her."

"Of course," Petra said, nodding. "Most sensible."

The duchess then gave Petra a surprisingly maternal look, saying in a softer tone, "And also because of this danger, Her Majesty and I did not feel as if it would be right to have you looking into the matron's death, and the orphanage, without knowing this information. After all that you experienced at the hands of that odious physician recently, we felt you might wish to decline the task. We would not be disappointed in you if so."

"But it is not my wish, Your Grace." Petra looked to the Queen and leaned forward in her seat. "Please tell me you will not keep me from making inquiries, Your Majesty."

I must have this distraction, Petra thought fiercely. *And now I am certain it deserves my attention all the more.*

Yet the slowness at which the Queen arched one eyebrow left Petra wondering if Her Majesty were now considering relegating *her* to the Tower of London. And when the Queen spoke, her voice was stony.

"You are indeed as impertinent as your godmother tells me, Lady Petra."

The Queen then looked away, out toward the window, where the gray skies were clearing, hinting at a beautiful, warm day to come. Indoors, absolute silence reigned for three long heartbeats. Petra sat back slowly, ready for further rebuke.

Then the Queen snapped, "But what vexes me most is that the duchess wagered me that you would not back down. And now I am out two shillings!"

The Queen leveled a glare at the duchess, who did her best to look as if she were not enjoying being correct, and did not entirely succeed. Petra had to curl her toes to keep from actually grinning herself. Knowing her godmother was confident in her abilities was surprisingly helpful in soothing her fractured nerves.

Then she realized she was still missing information. "Your Majesty, if I may ask. What led your intelligence officer to believe there is a connection between the matron's death and the safety of the royal family?"

"I have been waiting for you to ask, Lady Petra," the Queen said. "And now that you have confirmed you wish to continue, I shall tell you." She took up her snuffbox once again. "When the matron's body was moved, a note was found beneath her head. Would you like to know what was written on it?"

"Yes, Your Majesty," Petra said eagerly, but the Queen did not seem to hear as she gave the top of her snuffbox three raps, each sounding like the crack of a grouse gun.

"It read: *Those who protect the Queen shall find an early grave.*"

FOUR

THE BRISK KNOCK UPON THE BREAKFAST ROOM DOOR BROKE
the silence. "Enter!" commanded the Queen. A steward stepped into
the room, bowed, and his words were calm, yet urgent.

"Your Majesty, Your Grace, your carriages are ready and we must
away immediately. We have reports of citizens beginning to con-
gregate on certain roads as they await news from Flanders and the
Duke of Wellington. This includes the road toward Richmond and
Kew. The rumor is that news is to arrive late tonight, and crowds
will be massive. The staff and all provisions are leaving now. Lady
Petra, your lady's maid is already waiting in your carriage."

"The duchess and I require another minute with Lady Petra,"
the Queen snapped, and made a shooing gesture to her steward. He
looked uncertain, but bowed and backed from the room. The door
shut, and the duchess wasted no time in speaking.

"Regarding the threat to Her Majesty," she said, "the note discovered after the matron was killed was the first time such a threat
had been found in such a manner, but not the first time such language has been used."

The Queen nodded, truculence etched into every line on her
face.

"Those who are opposed to the monarchy—the republicans, as
they are called for their desire to have Great Britain turned into a
republic—have used similar rhetoric for years. My men whose job it
is to know such information have kept the royal family alerted to such
groups and the battle cries they use to stir up hatred for the monarchy
amongst their followers. The language changes somewhat, but it is always the same: support the monarchy at your peril. Utter rot, I say!"

Petra had questions on her tongue. The duchess, however, had given her a preemptive quelling look.

"Now is not the time for a discourse on the matter of politics, Lady Petra," she said. "What is different this time is these devious Bellowers have specifically referenced our Queen, but we do not know why. And due to the circumstances in which this note was found, it has been deemed possible that one or more of them have a connection to the orphanage."

"And you suspect Mrs. Huxton may have discovered this connection and attempted to stop it?" Petra asked. "Or do you believe she may have been complicit in whatever misdeeds are being conducted at the orphanage?"

The duchess sighed. "It is another aspect we do not know, and hope to discover."

"Of course," Petra replied, nodding. "Though if I may ask, how do you know it is the Bellowers who may be connected to the orphanage and not some other radical group?"

"You ask the pertinent questions, Lady Petra. I like that," the Queen said. "Yet beyond the fact that my men have all the known groups in their sights and were able to rule most out, a letter was recently intercepted that all but confirmed the Bellowers' involvement. However, my man who managed to procure it was seen and chased, forcing him to take a swim in the Thames and rendering the letter quite damaged."

She then turned to the table holding her snuffboxes, produced a key from around her neck, and unlocked the lone drawer, pulling from within a wrinkled piece of paper filled with residual smudges of ink.

"The letter was declared unreadable except for a few words that seemed to reference another member of the peerage. To my surprise, when it dried completely, I felt some of the letter might be read after all. I have sent word to him to come collect it later for further deciphering."

She tipped the letter from side to side, displaying the black wax seal and its imprint, as well as the blurred wording. Petra felt she might be able to discern the words if the Queen had let her see the page for a few moments longer, but it was returned to the drawer.

"Though it is a cheap wax, the seal remained intact," the Queen said. "Shockingly, it also bears the coat of arms of a well-known family—though I shall not reveal the family until my man has thoroughly investigated their involvement."

With uncharacteristic haste, the duchess added, "The family, such as it is now, has not had direct ties to London in some time. There is little in their family coffers, so we are told, and they live in genteel shabbiness in some quiet little village."

"Indeed . . . ," the Queen replied, and she shared a brief look with the duchess that had Petra feeling like the two older women had deliberately withheld something from her. Then both rose, and Petra hurried to do so as well, sliding the strings of her reticule over her wrist as the Queen spoke.

"I am relying on you, Lady Petra, for good intelligence. Both in regard to the late matron's death, and in connecting it to the threat we received."

And then the room brightened with a sudden clearing of the skies outside, emphasizing the lines on Her Majesty's face, and the exhaustion that could not be hidden by the best cosmetics available.

"I know how my subjects see me, Lady Petra. As a Queen who enjoys power and excess. And in some cases, they are correct. However, they will likely never know that I take no issue with those who do not believe in our divine right to rule. Or that the monarchy should not make decisions for the people. What I do not tolerate, however, is those who wish to use violence to make their points known." Her eyes all but sparked with fiery determination. "I simply will not abide by it!" There was a heartbeat of frustrated silence, and then her self-possession returned. "Regardless, it is not your duty to protect the royal family—that is for my men to do. I only wish you to do your utmost to assist them with any knowledge you gain so that we may prevent the United Kingdom from descending into lawless violence."

"Of course, Your Majesty. That is my wish as well," Petra replied fervently, and sunk into a curtsy. When she rose, the Queen was striding toward the door, but the duchess had held back. Her smile seemed strained, but she gave Petra's cheek a gentle pat.

"Your ability to trust and take the measure of people will serve you well, my girl. It always has, even when you have not liked what you found. You know, we women excel over men in many ways that often go unnoticed and unheralded, but one is our ability to accept help. Especially from our confidantes." Her tone became more insistent. "Lady Caroline, for one—and your other friends—tell me you will not eschew them for the sake of wanting to take everything upon your own shoulders."

"I promise, Your Grace," Petra said dutifully, though she suppressed a frown at hearing advice that sounded quite similar to that which Duncan had conveyed through Teddy this very morning.

"Good," replied the duchess. "Now, the Queen's intelligence officer will make himself known to you as soon as he is able, and you and I shall have tea when I return."

Petra curtsied, yearning to ask about Duncan while she had the chance. To ask what her godmother knew of the night Emerson died, and if Duncan was as guilty as the words she had read this morning claimed. When she rose, however, Her Grace was already too far away.

Petra's eyes trailed to the table with the Queen's snuffboxes, and the lock that stood between herself and the letter. After Teddy's warning this morning, she had slipped a thin roll of leather dyed a peacock green into her reticule. Inside were several carefully stitched slots, just right for thin implements. It was a smaller version of her set of lockpicks, gifted to her by Duncan only a month earlier. She could have the drawer open in a trice.

"Lady Petra? If you would?"

Damn and blast. She moved toward the door and the steward waiting for her to take her leave.

As the trees of Hyde Park flashed past the window of her landau carriage, shafts of sunlight peeked through the clouds, making the leftover raindrops sparkle upon the leaves.

Petra half listened as Annie recounted bits of gossip she'd obtained in the servants' hall of Buckingham House, yet her mind was on the mysterious letter locked away in the Queen's breakfast room. That and the idea that a member of the peerage—even if one who rarely came to London—had sent it.

I could name at least five or six families of the peerage, and two additional baronets, who have come down in society in recent years, she thought. *In each case, their extended family's links to the respective titles are sadly well on their way to being dormant or extinct.*

Emerson slid into her memories once more. He'd had no brothers or sisters himself and had spoken often of his wishes to have a son to secure the continuation of the viscountcy. It had been her dream as well, but the only thing now left of the title was Emerson's gold signet ring with the celadon-hued stone carved with the Ingersoll coat of arms. Though it, along with Emerson's other possessions, was now in the hands of his remaining family in Dorset.

Petra could still recall the moment she saw the signet ring on the stairs that awful morning, winking up at her with each erratic flicker of the candle shaking in her hand. After confirming her worst fears, that Emerson was indeed gone, she had scooped up the ring, pulled on Emerson's coat, and rushed out into the mews, barefoot, to wake the stable lad.

"Mr. Shawcross, you must find him," she'd cried out to the sleepy young boy. "Bring him to me. Go, now!"

Less than a quarter of an hour later, Duncan was holding her to his chest as she sobbed, Emerson's signet ring, icy without his life heat, around her first finger.

Even now, with her fingers ensconced in silk gloves, Petra could still recall the cold of the ring and the feeling of Duncan's fine linen shirt in her hands as she gripped it, aching to hold on to something real. Desperate to feel warmth and a heartbeat. Wanting to sink into oblivion with her pain.

Within two days, however, she had stood on the doorstep of a handsome house on Grosvenor Street that, if the remodeling had continued, would have become Ingersoll House. Would have become Emerson's and her house. Petra did not cross the threshold— her grief made it impossible—but placed a box containing the signet ring and a few other items of little consequence in the hands of Emerson's valet. He would deliver them along with her letter of condolence to a widowed aunt of Emerson's, Mrs. Garretson, whom Petra once had the pleasure of meeting before the older woman had decamped permanently for the fresher air of Dorset.

Petra still had Mrs. Garretson's warm letter of reply, writing that she would treasure the signet ring, even if the Ingersoll viscountcy was no longer. And she had agreed with Petra in that they each took some solace that both Emerson's mama and the kindly governess who had raised him were no longer alive to be informed of his sad outcome, or to see the title fade from society.

In the end, the only items Petra had left of her fiancé were a small leather folio containing charcoal drawings from his travels and a portrait she had commissioned of him, which now hung in her dressing room. While it was a handsome rendering showing his kind blue eyes and a gentle, closed-lipped smile, she now wished she had insisted that his truest smile be captured, the one that seemed to rise up farther on the left, charmingly exposing more teeth on one side than on the other.

"My lady, it is unlike you to sigh as if I have said something pitiable when I have just told you that Chef Antonin gifted me the recipe for his *pain ordinaire*. For I am certain Mrs. Bing will make my favorite dishes for a week once I present it to her."

Pulling herself back from the past, Petra focused on Annie, whose lips were set in playful disapproval while holding up a piece of paper with some triumph. On it was clearly written a recipe, the ingredients and directions easily readable due to the bold penmanship.

"Chef Antonin, is it?" Petra said, eyebrows lifting. "Not Chef *Carême*? Goodness, should Charles be jealous?"

Annie scoffed as she carefully rolled the recipe into a scroll and stored it away in her reticule. "Of course not, my lady. Besides, if Charles were a jealous man, then he would not be the right man for me."

Petra agreed, privately grateful for the absolute steadiness in conduct and character of her head footman, for Annie deserved nothing less.

"Did you ever feel that Duncan was jealous of Emerson?"

The thought had felt voiced of its own accord. Yet Annie did not look as if it were a shocking question. In fact, she grinned.

"*Of course* he was, my lady. From the moment you returned Lord Ingersoll's affections, Mr. Shawcross was all but miserable with jealousy. For he had loved you for so long, but you had not yet seen him as your own heart's desire."

The sun was now beaming brightly through the windows of the landau, further warming the space. Petra pulled her fan from her reticule, suddenly needing the cooling air.

"And then he was forced to insert a respectful distance between himself and you when you and Lord Ingersoll became betrothed," Annie continued. "Oh, my lady, do you not recall how Mr. Shawcross would look pained when Lord Ingersoll would slip his hand about your waist? Or how he would hurry to leave the breakfast table, claiming he had business to attend to, after Lord Ingersoll arrived and greeted you with a kiss to the back of your hand? And even the way he became much more formal in your presence once he knew . . ."

Annie blushed, which was a rarity, so Petra spoke for her.

"That I had given myself to Emerson? Even though Duncan had known that would be my intention when he offered up his town house for Emerson and I to . . . enjoy our liaisons?"

"Yes, my lady. Though I always felt his formality was more out of respect for your relationship with Lord Ingersoll, not out of disregard for your choices."

Then the landau met a pothole and Petra was lifted off her seat for a moment with the jolt. Annie instantly had her head out of the window.

"Do take care, Rupert! Her ladyship nearly struck her head!"

"My apologies, my lady—and you as well, Annie," came the deep, amiable voice of Petra's head groom and coachman.

Petra tsked. "I did not come near to striking my head. And Rupert is the best coachman in all of London. He never drives over a pothole unless it cannot be avoided."

Annie gave a merry shrug. "Sometimes it is best to keep a man on his toes, my lady."

"And sometimes I do believe you do enjoy stirring the pot," Petra returned on a laugh, whisking her fan open again with a dramatic flourish. While Annie's recollections did little to ease her mind, somehow the discussion of them felt a good thing.

Glancing out the window, this time Petra registered they were on St. James's Street, and inspiration struck her. She might not be able to look at that intercepted letter, but she need not wait to begin her investigation, for someone who could provide some answers was already close by.

"As we have time before we are expected at the orphanage, let us tell Rupert to take us to Jermyn Street and Bardwell's Apothecary to visit Frances," she told Annie. Thinking on the moment this morning when she opened her book and out came that horrid piece of ledger paper, she added, "That is, until Hatchards opens on Piccadilly. For I do not care for the bookmark I have been using and therefore I require a new one."

FIVE

Wednesday, 21 June 1815
Bardwell's Apothecary
Jermyn Street, Westminster, London
The ten o'clock hour

PETRA KNOCKED UPON THE DOOR OF BARDWELL'S APOTHECARY, frowning when she noted the curtains that shielded its windows were fully closed. Frances normally made certain to open at eight o'clock in the morning to accommodate the housekeepers, valets, and lady's maids needing supplies before those they worked for awoke and another day began in earnest.

She knocked harder, with more insistence. "Frances? It is Petra. Are you in there?" She began fumbling in her reticule for her lock-picks, ignoring Annie's curious glance.

Just as her fingers closed over the leather roll, however, Petra saw the curtains twitch open and Frances's dark eyes peeking out from beneath even darker, straight fringe. Her expression was one of suspicion until locking onto Petra and Annie. Then it eased into a smile and the locks receded with a deep *thunk*.

"Why, good morning. What a lovely surprise," Frances said as she pulled the door open. With it came a whoosh of scent, a mixture of herbs and flowers, both dried and fresh, mingling with handmade sweets and casks full of herbal syrups to help with a variety of ailments. The top note was the heady fragrance of the lemon oil that kept the wood shelves clean and shined.

Wearing a dark blue dress covered by a full apron with straps crossing at the back, but no bonnet or mobcap, Frances gave Petra a quick embrace, bade Annie a good morning as well, and waved them into the shop. As she did, she looked down the street before setting the locks and pulling the curtains closed once more. The only light inside came from the transom windows atop the door and a sliver from the bay window.

It was enough, however, to see that Frances had written a new sign with her excellent penmanship to indicate her latest concoctions. BARDWELL'S TINTED BALMS FOR THE LIPS AND CHEEKS. Annie eagerly rushed to view the options.

"Frances," Petra said, turning to her friend and indicating the curtains. "Whatever is the matter? Why are you not open yet?"

Frances gave Petra an assessing look, and a tinge of her mother's native Spain could be heard mingling with the teasing in her voice. "Is it mere concern for my safety that has you looking as if you have had two days put together in one morning? Or is it Duncan's safety, too?"

"How do you mean?" Petra said, her voice a bit too high and sharp, causing Frances to look mildly taken aback.

"Only that, when I saw him early this morning at Borough Market, he was conversing with several unsavory types. But as you yourself told me the first time I witnessed this, it is part of what he does in the name of security for the duchess." Her eyes narrowed in thoughtful fashion. "Oh, you two did not have a row, did you? I hope that is not the case."

Though the duchess—and Duncan himself, through Teddy— had encouraged Petra to confide in those she trusted, she only pressed her lips together. Suddenly she felt mulish about discussing Duncan and how her heart was hurting. Instead, she affected a queenly raised eyebrow.

"Whilst you *may* be correct that we are at odds, I am still brooding on the matter. Beyond that, I am not certain which I dislike more, finding my friend's shop uncharacteristically shut tight, or having that friend say I look quite careworn in my pretty new day dress."

Frances laughed and held up her hands in surrender.

"All right. You will talk when you are quite ready. As for why the shop remains closed, have you not heard of the preparations for celebrations all throughout London?" She moved to a set of bins filled with dried flowers, and took up a small wooden scoop. "I have a delivery of ready-made transparency screens scheduled to arrive any minute, and I have already had customers eager to purchase them. They were most disgruntled my stock had not arrived yesterday, I can tell you that. And thus, I am not opening until my order is here and ready to be sold to any customer wishing for a pretty screen to illuminate."

Flicking a glance toward Annie and finding her holding up two balms in rosy hues to compare the differences in color, Petra lowered her voice.

"I saw you looking down the street as if ruffians were after you, Frances. Are you feeling unsafe after confirming the nature of the matron's death at the orphanage?"

"Ah, so you have had your meeting with Her Majesty and Her Grace," Frances said calmly, using the scoop to swirl a bin full of lavender. "Good, for that means I may now finally speak freely with you. I do hope you are not cross with me that I could not tell you before."

"Of course not," Petra said, brushing aside the residual irritation. Glancing again to be certain Annie was not listening with pricked ears, she added, "Though I must say, my questions are growing by the moment."

"As I expected they would," Frances said. She then called across the room. "Annie, I am experimenting with more colors of my tinted balms, and I would quite like your opinion on them. They're on the trestle table in the stock room, if you are willing."

It took no convincing, and Annie disappeared into the back

of the apothecary before Petra had even set aside her reticule and gloves. From the pocket of her apron, Frances pulled some empty linen sachets to fill. When Petra reached for them to help, Frances insisted she put on an apron first to protect her dress.

"You will not see me risking Annie's wrath if something damaged your dress, which is quite pretty indeed."

In no time, Petra had shrugged into an apron that rose high enough to protect even the delicate strand of sapphires at her neck, and then took up her post as the holder of sachets. In return, Frances began recounting the previous week's events without having to be asked.

"To ease your mind, only Lady Vera and three others are aware I was at the orphanage. Lady Vera said she would not have sent for me at all had they first moved the matron's body and found the threatening message beneath her head. For once they did, it was apparent something malicious had happened, not just a horrible accident."

"Malicious, indeed," Petra said darkly. "Who were the three others?"

"One was Mrs. Yardley, the undermatron, who you shall no doubt meet today. The tragedy meant she has ascended to the role of matron, of course. Then there was the cook, whose acquaintance I did not make as she had been sent back to her duties, with no one questioning her innocence. Lady Vera was certain—and rightly so, I believe—that the death had occurred not long before her ladyship entered the chapel at six o'clock. The cook is always in her kitchens by half four and does not leave, with kitchen maids who can attest to it."

"And then who was the third woman?"

"She is a girl of fifteen, actually, and goes by the name of Nell Parker. She came to collect me and it seems she was sent because she is the oldest girl in residence, knows a bit of London, and is not afraid of the cart pony. I was given the impression that she almost acts as a secondary undermatron, for she has quite a bit of freedom. For instance, it is she who is in charge of making certain the girls are all in their beds by ten o'clock. Their dormitories are then locked until half six the next morning." As if reading Petra's worries, she added, "Nell assured me the other orphan girls know nothing of what happened."

"I am glad," Petra said. "And no other person saw you whilst you were at the orphanage?"

"Not one other soul. With the message Lady Vera found, her ladyship made certain of it."

Tipping some fragrant lemon balm into the sachet, Frances explained that she had entered through the chapel door at just before seven o'clock, and exited the same way an hour later, during which time the entire orphanage was at their morning meal. "I met no one as I took my leave, either—except for Nell, who had fetched Lady Vera's carriage to take me home."

"Did Lady Vera actually show you the message she found?" Petra asked.

Frances nodded, looking grave. "Shocked, we all were. A threat to Her Majesty? And we all could not help but ask, what was the late matron's involvement?"

"You mean was she friend or foe to the Queen? Mm, yes, that is the question I am to answer for Her Majesty and Her Grace," Petra said. Then she explained about the Bellowers and a connection to the orphanage that needed to be discovered. Frances was not inclined to be agog, but her dark eyes did blink in surprise.

"I wish I had seen something that might help you, for I don't care for the sound of a radical plot one bit. Yet all I saw was the chapel and the bedchamber belonging to the late matron, Mrs. Huxton. I could hardly even tell you what it looked like, I was so focused on determining the nature of Mrs. Huxton's death."

As Petra tied off the sachet, she asked to hear the account Lady Vera gave of finding the matron, and Frances's tale was all but a copy of what she had heard at Buckingham House.

"I understand Lady Vera then quickly found Mrs. Yardley, who recruited the cook, and then sent Nell to fetch me, all without fuss and with great haste. The matron's body had been moved to her bedchamber, and the chapel cleaned of any blood, by the time I arrived but one hour after the discovery."

"That is what happens when Lady Vera takes charge," Petra said. "She always goes like a ship in full sail, and suffers no fools—and yet she manages to do so with great wit and kindness."

"On that I agree, and I found I respected her more when Mrs. Yardley became overly distressed as I began my examination of the late matron." She grimaced, saying, "The smell of blood did become a bit overpowering at that point, so I could not blame her. But Lady Vera began telling an amusing story of her three Labradors, and by the end of it, Mrs. Yardley had recovered herself."

"Yes, her naughty Labradors always make for a diverting story," Petra said, smiling briefly. "Will you tell me what you saw in your examination? And I may remind you that I grew up around my papa's racehorses and stable lads, and I have seen my share of unsightly injuries. So do not be concerned that I shall feel faint."

"Yes, you are made of sterner stuff," Frances said, as she used her scoop to make slow swirls in the dried lavender. "Well, Mrs. Huxton's wound was to her head, but near the back of the ear." She touched the area behind her ear on the left side of her own head to show Petra the exact placement. "You were told that a silver candlestick was used to strike her, yes?"

When she nodded, Frances continued, "Indeed, the mark upon her matched the candlestick on the altar to perfection." She then ceased swirling the flowers, and the calming scent of lavender began to dissipate. "Yet as I sponged the area, I could see something else—a different indention, much smaller, and within it was a bit of twisted string. Silk, I would guess, and a shade of green. Petra, there was a second wound."

"Lawks," Petra said, horrified. "The poor matron was struck twice?"

"She was, though I do not believe the other blow would have been a fatal one as well. It seemed too shallow."

"Could you tell which one was inflicted first?"

Even as Frances shook her head, there was a banging to be heard, and a man shouting, "Delivery, Miss Bardwell!"

"That must be Mr. Fife with my transparencies," she said, and disappeared into the back of the shop.

A moment later she returned, followed by a tall, burly, smiling man who was lugging a crate and sporting a flatcap and side-whiskers in unruly tight curls. Behind him were two boys with another crate between them, with Annie trailing behind.

Then Petra pressed her lips together to stop a giggle when she noted Annie had four spots of tinted balm on her cheeks, each one darker than the next. As Annie attempted to step around the crate, a smiling Mr. Fife looked up into her face. Then his eyes widened at the sight before flicking across the room to meet Petra's and affecting a bow.

Frances, catching sight of Annie's overly painted face, hurried to whisper in her ear. With flaming cheeks, Annie turned and fled behind the curtain once more.

Chuckling, Mr. Fife used a crowbar and levered open both crates, then wiped sweat from his brow. Between protective sheets of silver paper were painted screens ranging from six inches by eight inches to twelve by sixteen inches—perfectly proportioned to fit either one pane of a sash window or spread across two panes. Made of paper and elaborately illustrated and varnished, they arrived ready to be put in the front windows of Londoners of all walks of life. By placing a lit candle behind the screen, the painting would be illuminated, producing a glowing painting for all those on the street to see and wonder at as they passed by.

Petra helped Frances remove them from the crate. There were images of the British flag, one of Wellington astride his brave chestnut stallion, and various other battle scenes. She also noted beautiful country landscapes, horse racing and hunt scenes, as well as views of waterfalls and vistas of famous mountains and hillsides such as Box Hill and the Peak District. There were even a few portraits of the royal family, and a handful of paintings featuring puppies and kittens.

"Children love them," Frances explained, picking up one of a gray tabby kitten batting at a ball of pink yarn, then proceeded to tell Petra if she saw a transparency she liked, to put it behind the counter.

Petra picked up one of Box Hill in Surrey. Turning toward the transom window, her foot caught an uneven spot in the wood flooring and she wobbled. Mr. Fife graciously held out his forearm and she used it to steady herself, her fingers briefly gripping the top of his arm and soft, well-worn coat.

"I thank you, Mr. Fife," she said as she angled the transparency up to the light and marveled at how close the painting was to the real thing. Then she nearly felt as if she would wobble again for a different reason. Looking at the scene made her recall a sunny day, loads of strawberries and cream, and a laughing party of twenty people who had been invited to Surrey by Lady Caroline and her husband, Captain Smythe. And with sudden clarity, Petra remembered Emerson, pacing in a little copse that was just visible on the left side of the painting.

"He did not understand me! I must speak with him again, for I know I could make him see, and then he shall come round to what we are trying to achieve!"

"See what, my love? Who were you talking to?" Petra had said, looking about and finding none of their party. Emerson had whirled, his flaxen hair tumbling over his forehead as he searched the little grove. Finally stilling, he muttered an oath, then turned to her with a smile.

"Do not concern yourself, my darling. Merely some dashed incon-
venient MP business to attend to, nothing more. Must do my duty to
my constituency and all that nonsense."

Frances's voice cut through her thoughts, abruptly ending
the memory, but not the recollection of seeing Duncan walking off with Emerson toward that little copse only a few minutes
earlier.

"I'm sorry, Mr. Fife, but I did not place the order for these other
ten—no, eleven larger transparencies," Frances said, leafing through
a grouping from the bottom of the second crate. "Why, they appear
to be scenes of fireworks over famous sights in London." She held
up one from the lot, both she and Mr. Fife narrowing their eyes as if
unfamiliar with the landmark. Petra noted it was a house but could
not quite place it, either, before Frances shrugged, returned it to the
crate, and picked up another. "They are all lovely, to be sure, but I
did not order them, and thus I will not pay for them."

"Beggin' your pardon, Miss Bardwell," Mr. Fife said. "But I's got
me orders, and I was told to bring these two crates of transparencies here. Checked twice, I did, that all scenes ordered were accounted for. No, I ain't tellin' no porky pies, Miss Bardwell. I ain't
due to collect no money, either, so seems to me them extras are
yours to sell for a nice little profit."

He dug about in his pocket and came up with a shilling.

"In fact, the wife told me to come home with one of 'em to
amuse the little 'un, who's cuttin' his first teeth and fair miserable.
You give me one—nay, I don't care which one and neither will my
boy—and you'll have your first sale."

Frances took his coin and told him to take whichever one he
pleased as she moved to the back corner and selected a jar. Mr. Fife
shrugged, looking bewildered at all the choices, but gamely sifted
through them, finally handing one to his delivery boy, who trotted
out with it and the crowbars while Petra gently put the painting of
Box Hill back in the larger crate. The memory of that outing stirred

in her both happy and unsettling thoughts. She felt she would be better off with another transparency altogether, and chose a small one that reminded her of Buckfields instead as Frances returned.

"Here, Mr. Fife," Frances said, handing him a small jar. "For your little 'un's gums. It'll help soothe them while his teeth come in. No, no, you've already paid me for it." And she held up the shilling.

Mr. Fife seemed moved by this gesture and thanked her profusely. Finally, he tipped his hat to her with a genial smile, saying he had other deliveries to make, bowed to Petra with a murmured "My lady," and was gone.

Frances gave the smaller crate of transparencies a wry look. "Well, Petra, you shall be my witness if anyone comes looking for payment of these, and you will not have to tell any 'porky pies' when you say I offered to send them back."

She held two of the transparencies up to the light to show one was fireworks exploding over St. James's Palace, the other over Regent's Park. Then she traded them for another showing colorful explosions over the Theatre Royal at Covent Garden, and another over the Palace of Westminster. Each bit of fireworks was painted almost like a colorful galaxy of stars than a true explosion, as if one of the bands of the Milky Way were shooting out from one part of the edifice or another, some curving up, some down, some gently undulating like a country path.

"They're rather breathtaking," Petra said, shuffling through the others still in the crate, "and each is slightly different. They will be beautiful in someone's window, and I expect they will sell easily enough for you. Come, let me help you arrange them in the window, and then you can open for business." Peeking through the curtains, she added, "Heavens, there is already quite a crowd."

She grinned at Frances, who had glanced out as well, and found her friend looking uncharacteristically flustered.

"So many people," Frances said faintly. "I am used to a busy shop, but that is usually only five or six customers at a time." She pulled in a shaky breath. "There are easily thirty or more out there. I do not know how to handle that many."

"It will be all right, Frances, do not worry," Petra said, grasping her friend's hand. "I had forgotten you told me you do not much like crowds."

"No, I do not like them," Frances said, backing away from the window. "Not at all."

Goodness, she was even shaking her head. Petra had never seen her friend like this before. At a sound, she looked over her shoulder. Annie had come back, her face now scrubbed of every speck of tinted balm. She was checking the time on her watch fob.

"My lady, we must leave for the orphanage immediately. You are to be there at eleven; we will only make it in time if there are no crowds blocking Westminster Bridge as they wait on news of the war. Rupert has brought the landau round back and is ready to set off."

A smile was stretching over Petra's face. "I have the solution," she declared to Frances. "Annie will stay and help you."

"What?" Frances looked perplexed, and pushed her fringe from her eyes. "I could not. It would not do to leave you without your—"

"Do not mention propriety to me, Frances Bardwell," Petra interrupted with mock disdain, "for I am now quite known for flouting the rules, and I do believe I like it. Besides, no one is better at managing people than a lady's maid. Annie here is the best of them all, too, and she has been here so often that she already knows every product you make and offer—do you not, Annie?"

Within a moment, Annie had taken in the situation, the look of fear on Frances's face, and the growing murmur of the crowd outside.

"Of course I do, my lady. Miss Frances, I should enjoy helping you today, if you would allow it."

"If you are certain, Annie . . . ," Frances began, her dark eyes wide with hope.

Annie nodded with enthusiasm and Petra gave her a grateful look before pulling Frances toward the front counter. She took up her reticule, gloves, and a sachet filled mostly with lavender as she did. The weight of her reticule from her lockpicks gave her another idea, too. One for later, though. One that would be easier if Annie were safely somewhere else.

"You will not regret it, Frances. Now, I must go do my duty to the Queen at the orphanage." She put the sachet in her friend's hands. "Breathe this lavender in to calm you like you are always telling others to do, and take up your post at the till until your strength returns. Good; I shall return later. Annie, please open the doors!"

"My lady, you are still wearing an apron!" Annie called out, but Petra was not deterred.

"Not to worry!" she sang as she hurried out the back door. "I shall keep it safe until this afternoon!"

SIX

"LADY PETRA, WELCOME! YOU ARE MOST WELCOME INDEED! I am Mrs. Yardley, the new matron of the Asylum for Female Orphans. We are so grateful to have you here, representing Her Majesty, the Queen, at the opening of our new dining hall!"

At this overly enthusiastic pronouncement, the heads of several ladies and two gentlemen turned to stare. All then inclined their heads in a gesture of greeting, save one.

Blast. I had forgotten Duncan's waspish stepmama is a patroness of the orphanage, Petra thought.

She had never wished for the good favor of the Dowager Marchioness of Langford, though. Not since a young age, when she realized Lady Langford was as cold as she was beautiful, cruelly acting as if Duncan did not exist. Or outright speaking to him with vicious disdain, tossing out barbs regarding the circumstances of his birth.

What was more, her ladyship endeavored to do all she could to keep her own son, James, at odds with Duncan. Even after James inherited the title of the Marquess of Langford after the death of their father, his mama had not ceased to take every opportunity to make Duncan feel belittled, driving the wedge between the two brothers deeper.

Each time she bore witness to it, Petra fumed and threatened to give Lady Langford a piece of her mind, but Duncan always wearily encouraged her to leave the situation be. It seemed to matter to him that she not bring contempt upon her own shoulders as well by defending him.

Over the years she had acquiesced to his wishes, yes, but that had never meant she had not waged her own private, silent war with the dowager marchioness. Thus, despite her conflicted feelings toward Duncan at present, Petra did not refrain from returning Lady Langford's icy gaze for a long moment. Then she focused her attention once again on the matron, who seemed happily oblivious to the entire exchange.

"My new undermatron is readying things in the dining hall," explained Mrs. Yardley with a little titter before turning to the girl of fifteen standing at her side. "And this is Nell—one of our oldest girls here. She will be acting as my maid now that I am matron of this fine charity."

By the way Nell's mouth briefly tightened, Petra felt that maid was not the title the young woman had hoped to receive, yet her "Good morning, my lady" was quite polite.

Both Nell and the new matron wore dresses of dove-gray cotton along with necklaces holding a thin silver cross. While the hairs at Mrs. Yardley's temples had begun to whiten, the straight brown tresses beneath her lace cap gleamed like the fine silk ribbon that came down and tied snugly under her chin.

By contrast, Nell's dark ringlets were carefully framing her face. Indeed, she wore only a small mob cap that did not detract from her efforts, along with a white apron that began beneath the bodice of her dress. The girl's intelligent blue eyes held both a violet hue and a spark of defiance, and Petra reminded herself that Nell should be queried about the night of Mrs. Huxton's death.

Several more girls, all much younger than Nell and wearing simple gray dresses, stood against the wall in a room a few steps away. Petra realized the room was, in fact, the lobby of sorts of the building, which had once been the Hercules Inn. The girls bobbed curtsies in tandem when men and ladies of rank passed by, excitement mixed with awe on their little scrubbed faces.

Mrs. Yardley glanced at them, too, and lowered her voice to a whisper. "We are happy to have you here for the other reason as well, my lady. Oh, yes, Lady Vera told us to expect you to be making some inquiries." She shook her head, using her thumb and first finger to gently rub the base of her silver cross. "Such bad business indeed. Mrs. Huxton is quite missed, she is."

"I am honored to be here for both reasons, Mrs. Yardley," Petra said. "And Her Majesty, the Queen, and Her Grace, the Duchess of Hillmorton, bade me to send their very best wishes and compliments to you and the entire charity."

"I am delighted they would say so. Do you not agree, Nell?" Without waiting for a response, the matron said, "We continue to be most grateful for Her Majesty's patronage. Most grateful indeed. She has been kind and generous to us, as has our president, Prince Adolphus." Mrs. Yardley looked around Petra's shoulder. "Is His Royal Highness to attend today, my lady? We were hoping he would grant us his charming presence . . ."

"I must deliver the regrets of Prince Adolphus as well, Mrs. Yardley," Petra said. "Though he very much would have liked to be here, he had to attend to a matter of great military import."

She knew not if it were the truth, but it was what Her Majesty's steward had told her to say as he escorted her through an eerily quiet Buckingham House to her carriage earlier this morning. Nevertheless, the answer seemed to satisfy and impress, even eliciting a widening of Nell's eyes.

"I expect it has something to do with Napoleon and his ridiculous belief that he can thwart Wellington and our forces," Mrs. Yardley said, determination and British pride shining in her eyes. "But Napoleon will not succeed! And no doubt our brave princes are making certain our country remains safe from French invasion."

"Quite so, Mrs. Yardley," Petra said, not wishing to dampen the matron's enthusiasm by reminding her that Their Majesties' seven living sons were all in their fortieth decade or older and were likely doing little more at present than being dressed by their valets.

"My lady?" began Nell, an eager look in her eyes. "Did Miss Frances happen to say she found a document when examining the body of—?"

"Hush, girl!" Mrs. Yardley snapped. "How dare you speak out of turn to Lady Petra and ask her such questions! Now go. Be off with you to the dining hall and check that all is ready for the recital for our honored guests."

Nell muttered an apology, bobbed a curtsy, and turned to go, when Mrs. Yardley clutched her arm, eliciting a frown from the girl.

"Mr. Fife is here with the delivery. That man! I told him we would have the finest names in London here for our little party and he should arrive this afternoon."

Mrs. Yardley pulled a coin from her apron pocket, and Petra glanced over her shoulder to see the genial Mr. Fife filling an arched doorway leading to a hall. Seeing her, he smiled as he used his neckerchief to mop his brow and gave a bow at the neck.

"Give him his coin, girl," said Mrs. Yardley. "I expect he brought the varnish I ordered for the girls to make their own transparencies. No, simply have him put the box in my quarters so it is not distracting to our esteemed guests."

Nell's murmured "Yes, Mrs. Yardley" seemed a bit sulky to Petra's ears, but the new matron merely looked on the girl with a measure of indulgence.

"Do forgive Nell, Lady Petra. She was quite distressed by what happened to poor Mrs. Huxton. The girl is claiming that Mrs. Huxton told her she was to inherit seven thousand per annum upon coming of age. That was the document to which she was referring when she spoke so impetuously. Yet there was nothing of the sort on Mrs. Huxton's . . . well, we have found no proof of such a claim." She touched her cross again as she glanced over all the young orphaned girls in the room. "Oh, if I had a penny for every time one of these poor girls was certain they'd been left a fortune, that their mother or father was someone of rank . . ."

"And if I had a penny for how many times it might be true," came an amused voice, lowered to sotto voce.

"Lady Vera," Petra said with delight, reaching out to clasp her friend's hands. At twice the age and half a head shorter than Petra—whose own head barely topped the strong pectoral muscles in Duncan's chest—Lady Vera, the Dowager Countess Grimley, somehow managed to seem taller and more vibrantly alive than most women of Petra's acquaintance. "You are looking well, as always."

"And you are looking thoroughly in the pink, Lady Petra. One could wonder if a certain towering gentleman with the most delectable Scottish burr you were seen laughing with at Hyde Park might be the reason . . ." One of her silver eyebrows raised, and a chuckle erupted from her that shook her entire body.

Then before Petra could find her voice—or a shocked Mrs. Yardley could find her composure—Lady Vera pulled Petra's arm into her own and led her away.

"I shall take her from here, matron," she called back. "Lady Petra and I have much to discuss before all these ladies and lords rush out to their carriages once more."

"You are as naughty as ever, Lady Vera," Petra chided as she allowed herself to be guided through a throng of guests walking through the narrow corridors of the orphanage, no doubt to the dining hall. As per usual, however, she was unable to sound convincingly put out. "Sometimes I feel like you and Lady Caroline could be in a competition for those who say the most outrageous things in public."

Her friend let out another laugh. "Oh, my dear, I would trounce

Lady Caroline in spectacular fashion. In fact, we practiced bandying about shocking commentary yesterday when I saw her whilst paying a call to your friend Miss Lottie Reed."

"Oh, yes, Caroline was rather surprised to learn she quite likes spending time with Lottie's canine charges, especially when her captain is away at sea."

"And she mentioned Lord Whitfield had been away recently as well," Lady Vera said, waggling her eyebrows. "He is a handsome one, is he not?"

If it had been anyone other than Lady Vera, Petra might not have dignified such a comment. Yet her friend was one of a select few who were aware that Caroline's husband, Captain Smythe, approved of the match between his wife and Whitfield. An unusual stance, to be sure, if it were not for the fact the marriage between Lady Caroline and her captain was one of deepest friendship and platonic love, and nothing more. Both lived their separate lives with each other's blessing, retaining the semblance of a marriage in society for the sakes of their respective powerful families, and no other reason.

Petra laughed. "Yes, he is quite handsome, but you will not get any further gossip on that subject from me. Now, tell me why you visited Lottie. Are you in the market for another cheeky Labrador?"

"Heavens, no," she said loudly, causing heads to turn again. "I have enough dogs to be going on with already. This time, I am giving one to the orphanage. I contracted Lottie to determine what type of dog would be best, and to train it to behave better than mine. It shall be a surprise for the girls."

"That is a lovely idea," Petra said. "And such a kind gesture."

Lady Vera waved this off. "I was forced to clear it with all the blustery guardians, of course." She leaned in, her eyes going pointedly to one portly gentleman. "Had to hint to a certain baronet that I knew his daughter might not have the dowry she hopes come her time on the marriage mart." She then jutted her chin to a man in army regalia. "And one retired colonel had to be reminded that he promised his wife he would stop taking snuff. Yet I frequently see him at Fribourg & Treyer, sampling their latest blends and buying a tin *or three*."

Petra chuckled at this. "You are too clever by half, Lady Vera." Looking around, Petra whispered, "And is this dog to help protect these girls after what happened to the matron?"

"It certainly would not hurt, my dear," said Lady Vera in a rare sober tone. "I cannot imagine who would have done such a thing to the matron. She was a good woman, our Mrs. Huxton. She was strong-willed and kept these young girls constantly working toward bettering themselves, but she was also kind. However, with that message I found that threatened our beloved Queen? The idea that radicals may be using this fine orphanage in some way?" She shook her head sadly. "Well, I am glad you are here to ask questions, Lady Petra. For this is a conundrum we must solve."

"I agree most heartily," Petra said, giving Lady Vera's arm a quick, bolstering squeeze. Lifting her chin, she added, "In fact, since I have declared myself as never wishing to marry, I have often heard others saying I wish to be a nosy busybody instead. And that means few will think twice when I ask all the questions I like."

SEVEN

STANDING BY THE FIREPLACE IN THE FRONT ROOM MORE THAN an hour later, watching the number of the orphanage's patrons and patronesses gradually lessen as carriages pulled away outside, Petra contemplated two truths.

One, that a cup of tea would be welcome after endeavoring to interrogate so many ladies and gentlemen of rank without their knowledge, subtly guiding the conversation first to the late Mrs. Huxton and then the royal family to ascertain their views on the monarchy.

And two, that despite her efforts she was fairly rubbish at the art of interrogation, subtle or otherwise.

A Bow Street Runner, I would never make, she thought while watching one of the younger orphan girls pick up a handkerchief dropped by an elderly baroness, who smiled graciously and gave the little girl a boiled sweet. Seeing the yellow hue made an unexpected lump form in Petra's throat. Would she forever associate lemon drops with Duncan?

You must not think of him now, she chided herself as the lobby cleared save for the elderly baroness, Lady Vera, and the group of girls lined up to see their guests off. Mrs. Yardley stood outside with some of the older girls, waving merrily as the carriages pulled away. Lady Vera, however, was staring at the new matron with a disapproving frown.

Petra thought back to the festivities in the dining hall, when a chorus consisting of girls of varying ages were singing a Scottish folk song. Everyone had been giving their polite attention to the girls, but Petra had seen Lady Vera having a whispered conversation with Mrs. Yardley at the back of the room. Both had looked nettled, and Mrs. Yardley had glanced down pointedly at something in her hand, which had caused Lady Vera to briefly recoil, her face then hardening in a way Petra had never seen.

Concerned, she was about to make her way to Lady Vera's side when the singing stopped, and clapping took over. When Petra looked again, the new matron was gliding up to the head of the room with a smile that seemed a bit smug, and Lady Vera was sipping her tea as if nothing had happened. Yet did her hand not shake as she lifted her cup?

"Ah, Lady Petra," came a honeyed voice that sent her out of her reverie and had her backbone stiffening. "It was *such* a delightful surprise seeing you here today. Have you attended in hopes of becoming a patroness of this fine charity?"

Petra turned to meet the clear brown eyes of the Dowager Marchioness of Langford and added some sweetness to her own reply. "Why, yes, I have been considering it, your ladyship, and I think I may do so."

Lady Langford pulled on one silk glove in a pale blue that matched her dress and complemented the curls of palest flaxen peeking out from her fashionable bonnet. While almost painfully thin, she had undeniably retained the swanlike beauty that, over five and twenty years earlier, had led her to be singled out by Robert Shawcross, the roguishly handsome, dark-haired, green-eyed Marquess of Langford.

"Mm, yes." She let her eyes roam down Petra's own dress, a slight twitch of her upper lip indicating she could see the quality and resented it. "Indeed, that will make it easier."

"Easier, Lady Langford?"

"Why, for when you and my stepson are in need of its services yourself, of course," she replied gaily, at a level just loud enough that the elderly baroness a few steps away turned with an inquiring look.

Thankfully, Lady Vera was with the baroness in a trice. "Why it has turned into quite the lovely day, has it not, your ladyship?" she chirped while helping the baroness to shuffle outside to her carriage.

Petra turned slowly back to Lady Langford, a cold retort on her lips mingling with the still-innate instinct to protect Duncan, and nearly stepped back at the venomous look she received.

"Twenty years ago," Lady Langford hissed, "when the marquess brought him back from Scotland, I sent that sideslip away from Langford House, never to return. And now his presence has polluted the sanctity of my home *twice* in a fortnight, including this very morning. You will tell him—either in your drawing room, or whilst being the strumpet you are in his bed—that he is not welcome in my home, and never shall be."

She went to turn away, dropping her second glove as she did. Petra swiftly moved to pick it up, effectively blocking the dowager marchioness's path.

"And yet," Petra said softly while letting all politeness drop from her voice, "you no longer hold sway over Langford House, do you? No, for it is your son, and Duncan's own brother, who is the rightful Marquess of Langford, and who now has a wife who supersedes your authority as mistress of the house, if not in precedence. Thus, should the marquess allow his brother across the threshold, then I believe your opinion comes to naught." She held out the glove.

"You will tell him to leave us be," Lady Langford snapped, snatching the blue silk from Petra's fingers, her eyes now almost bulging with anger, yet her voice was lower and more vicious than ever. "I will not have that . . . that *scapegallows* on my property, putting my son . . . my dearest James . . . the *only* legitimate heir to the duchy of Hillmorton, under suspicion."

Chin at a defiant angle, Lady Langford sailed away before Petra could ask her what she meant. She merely stood there, breathing like one of her papa's thoroughbreds after a hard race. And yet her thoughts continued at a gallop.

If what the dowager marchioness had said was true, Duncan and his brother James had begun spending time together, and yet Petra had no knowledge of it. What's more, the two had never been known to seek out each other's company. If they had suddenly begun to do so, did that make the situation more or less suspect?

In truth, Petra had always felt James was honorable at his core, but too rakish, arrogant, and easily swayed by outside influences. If Duncan were more wicked than she ever knew, was it feasible he had convinced James to go along with some plan, such as one to harm the royal family, or disrupt Parliament? Lawks, could Duncan and James have taken up with the radical group known as the Bellowers?

If possible, her heart sped up further. For Her Majesty's own words were in her ears, relating the details about the letter connected to the Bellowers that was intercepted on its way to the orphanage.

"Shockingly, it also bears the coat of arms of a well-known family—though I shall not reveal the family until my man has thoroughly investigated their involvement."

Petra bit her lip, recalling how the Duchess of Hillmorton had then quite hastily added that the family in question had no direct ties to London anymore, and little money in their coffers. Petra had to admit, she'd felt the details had almost sounded forced.

No, that was not quite right, she mused. It was more as if Her Grace had hastily cobbled together an explanation that Petra would not question in order to disguise something else of importance.

Could it be that the duchess had told a falsehood to draw Petra's attention away from a more painful truth? Was it possible the family in question with radical views was named Shawcross? Specifically James Shawcross, the Marquess of Langford, and his half brother, Duncan?

Petra's skin began to prickle. If this were the case, was it Duncan who managed to sway his brother's views? Or did James support reform as well, and the two found a common ground in wishing to change the political landscape of Great Britain, but they felt they must do so in secret?

If so, what better way to cover up an alliance between the two brothers than the acrimonious relationship they already had?

Petra's mind once more strayed to that locked drawer in Buckingham House, and her trembling fingers all but itched to go back and unlock it, to look at the seal upon the damaged, intercepted letter, and to attempt to read what it said. For she felt certain it might contain some answers, or at least direct her in a better direction.

By the very bollocks of Pegasus, if the truth is in that letter, I must get to it before it disappears!

She knew her cheeks were pink, for several reasons now, and could only feel grateful to Lady Vera, who was busy drawing the attention of the few curious young girls left in the lobby. Petra heard her telling them what a brilliant job they had done today and watched as she handed out sweets from a small tin marked with the stamp of Bardwell's Apothecary.

Petra's eyes moved to the arched doorway that Mr. Fife had filled earlier. This time it was Nell standing there and the girl's gaze was going back and forth between Lady Vera and Mrs. Yardley, who could still be seen through the front windows. With a frown seemingly directed at both women, Nell turned and hurried away.

"Tea, my lady?"

Petra looked down to find the little girl who had received the lemon drop from the baroness. She was holding up a cup of tea with both hands and had ginger hair plaited down her back. The little bulge in her cheek said she had the lemon drop in her mouth, but it was her two front teeth that were just growing in that caused her charming lisp.

"Lady Vera thaid you might be needing a cuppa," she said. "I'm ever tho thorry, my lady. I forgot the thaucer."

"That is quite all right, my darling. Thank you," Petra said, feeling her heart start to calm with the girl's bright smile and the warm cup she took in her hands. "This is rather perfect."

The girl beamed, bobbed a curtsy, and ran off to join her friends, who were all being herded away by one of the other older girls. Petra sipped her tea, letting the warmth soothe her throat and allow herself to feel centered again.

A moment later, Lady Vera was standing before her, staring thoughtfully out the windows to where Lady Langford was last seen berating her footman as he hastily fumbled to let down her carriage stairs.

"You do know I have long called her the Dowager Viperess, yes?" And when Petra nearly choked on her tea, Lady Vera grinned. "I do not know what she said to you, my dear, but I will advise you to act as if it is a mound of what horses leave in the streets, and step around it instead of in it."

Looking into Lady Vera's wise face, seeing a warm smile mixed with a hint of residual concern in her eyes, Petra nodded. Determinedly, she told herself to put her worries about Duncan into a compartment in her brain, lock them away, and hide her lockpicks.

Just until I complete my task here. Just until I am able to think clearly once more.

EIGHT

GATHERING HER WITS ABOUT HER, PETRA GAVE HER ATTENTION to Lady Vera and where it was most needed. Namely, investigating the untimely death of Mrs. Huxton.

"Well, then, how did you fare during our time in the dining hall?" she asked her friend. "I appreciate you offering to interview the older orphan girls and the staff. Were your talks fruitful, by chance? I, for one, discovered little or nothing of substance from the available members of the *haut ton*."

"And I discovered nothing I did not already know," Lady Vera replied. "Amongst orphans and staff alike, Mrs. Huxton was respected and most are sad she is gone. A few cared little, but their reasons were just as small. A kitchen maid said Mrs. Huxton was prone to complain if her food was even a mite cold. One of the older orphan girls did not like that Mrs. Huxton forced her to learn Latin, that sort of nonsense."

"Was this Nell, by chance?" The girl's countenance had been all but surly throughout the festivities that officially opened the new dining hall, and Petra had twice caught her sidling away when Mrs. Yardley floated near. No doubt to keep from having to perform more menial tasks for the new matron.

"Nell? Oh, no. She was terribly saddened by Mrs. Huxton's passing. She had been in training to become Mrs. Huxton's undermatron, you know. For Mrs. Yardley had previously voiced her desire to leave the orphanage and move to the country within the year."

"Indeed?" Petra said. "I felt Mrs. Yardley is quite happy to have ascended to the rank of matron."

"Oh, but she is . . . now. Prior to the unhappy event of last week, however, she had been saying she knew of a small girls' school somewhere—in Somerset, I believe—that would like to bring her on as headmistress. She had been all but counting the days until Nell's sixteenth birthday, when the governors agreed Nell would be able to formally apply for the position of undermatron. Nell has a way with the youngest girls in helping them adjust to life here." Lady Vera then frowned thoughtfully. "But the governors quickly brought on a new undermatron—a very experienced one out of York named Miss Stebbins—and poor Nell has been relegated to being Mrs. Yardley's lady's maid of sorts."

"I was briefly introduced to Miss Stebbins and she does seem a kind and capable woman to serve as undermatron," Petra said. "But I cannot fault Nell for being disappointed that she was not promoted." She glanced about for the girl. "I never managed to speak with her earlier. I wonder if I should do so now?"

"I think there is no need to take up your time with her," Lady Vera said, waving off the notion. "She will only work her tongue and complain that she is concerned someone will take her inheritance before she reaches one and twenty. Though I have not yet determined if the tale of a fortune is true, I have assured her that any monies these girls are to inherit are kept safe." She punctuated this with a decisive nod of her head before asking Petra if she had yet interviewed Mrs. Yardley.

"I managed but a few minutes with her—this was before I saw the two of you conversing at the back of the dining hall, of course." Petra said this with what she hoped was a look that invited Lady Vera to offer explanations as to why she and the orphanage's matron had argued earlier.

All she received was a most innocent expression from Lady Vera in return, which she did not entirely believe. She had known Lady Vera for the whole of her life; her ladyship rarely ever looked entirely without guile. Still, half-amused and half-impatient, Petra went on.

"I found Mrs. Yardley to be properly shocked at the fate of her predecessor. She also spoke warmly of her, saying that though she and Mrs. Huxton had their differing opinions on occasion, they got on well together in her nearly four years as second in command."

"True enough, I suppose," said Lady Vera.

"I also believe Mrs. Yardley might well be enamored with Prince Adolphus and Prince Frederick, who she claimed are her favorites of the Queen's sons," Petra said with a little chuckle. "When I told her Frances's delivery of transparencies arrived this morning and I spied a portrait of Their Royal Highnesses, I felt as if she might swoon right in front of me."

Petra followed this with an overly exasperated roll of her eyes, hoping an indication that she thought Mrs. Yardley a bit silly might finally encourage Lady Vera to express her own feelings about the new matron.

Once more her hopes were dashed, however, when Lady Vera merely snorted. Thus, Petra drank the last of her tea, placed the cup on a nearby side table, and forged on.

"Though as for my intelligence otherwise, whilst a handful of patrons and patronesses were willing to admit they were concerned for the political state of Great Britain, most said little about the royal family—and if they did, it was hardly radical views."

Then she said that if her attempt to discover potential radicals amongst the guests proved relatively fruitless, her questions regarding the murdered Mrs. Huxton had produced almost nothing.

"Well, that is not entirely true . . . ," she amended. "I suppose I learned that two governors did not care for Mrs. Huxton. Whilst they felt she was quite dedicated in her duties, they blustered on about her intractable way of seeing the world. I felt it meant little as neither man could be our murderer. Oh, no indeed. I overheard both their wives talking. One gentleman was ill with a summer cold last week, and the other was in Bath to take the waters. But I have thought more upon what it might mean for the two to see Mrs. Huxton in such a poor light."

"I am intrigued. Do tell, my dear," said Lady Vera at the particular knowing inflection in Petra's voice.

"Well, I have recollected from my knowledge of politics, slim as it may be, that both of these gentlemen are quite staunch Tories," Petra said. "And one has even been known for disliking how Parliament is structured, claiming the powers of the monarchy should be *increased*. Thus, if they found the late matron so intractable, I do wonder if she held the opposite view politically?"

"Are you saying it is possible the matron was a reformist? Maybe even a radical one?"

Petra shrugged. "Yes? It is a possibility, I suppose."

Lady Vera paused. "Mm, yes, it is."

Petra responded by giving her second cutty-eye of the day. "Lady Vera . . . what are you not telling me?"

With a sigh, her friend tilted her head toward the back of the orphanage. "Have you yet been to the chapel? Come, let us talk there."

As they walked past the dining hall, Petra looked in to find the girls scurrying about like little mice in gray dresses with brooms and mops. Mrs. Yardley stood in the middle of the room, overseeing the cleanup, a smile of satisfaction on her face as she spoke with the new undermatron, who was a tall woman of middle age with a narrow face and kind eyes. Nell, however, was nowhere to be seen.

The chapel was open and the two girls sweeping the center aisle bobbed a curtsy and exited quickly when Lady Vera politely asked for the room. Yet she did not immediately begin her explanations, but clasped her hands tightly together and walked solemnly up to the altar.

Petra followed, finding the altar was a simple but sturdy wooden affair, with two silver candlesticks on top, both with fresh candles waiting to be lit. She picked up the candlesticks, one after the other, but there was no indication which one had been used to make the fatal blow to Mrs. Huxton's head. Both were shiny and blemish-free. And there was nothing she could see that might have made the secondary cut to the matron's head that Frances had spoken of, causing a bit of twisted silk string to become embedded in the wound.

In truth, the entire chapel was spotless, as was the area around the altar. The only thing that indicated a life had been taken at the base was a small dark stain no bigger than her own index finger. It was as if someone had merely spilled the dregs of a cup of coffee instead of a woman's lifeblood—and though she had never met Mrs. Huxton, Petra felt a pang in her heart for the late matron just the same.

As Lady Vera seemed to be in her own thoughts, Petra then walked to the back entrance of the chapel. If anyone knew the signs of a lock being picked, it was she, and she dug in her reticule for a small quizzing glass to look for signs of telltale scratches on the brass plate. There were none, however. Only those regular nicks and scratches that come over time from someone fumbling to insert a key into the lock.

"How many doors are there for one to enter and exit in the entire orphanage?" Petra asked.

Lady Vera explained there were three in total, not including the front doors. The chapel door, one on the north side of the building by the staff quarters, and another at the kitchens. The latter two were kept locked for the safety of the girls. It seemed the kitchen staff attested that no one came through the kitchen entrance, and the door by the staff quarters was known to be particularly loud and creaky, awakening everyone in the staff corridor when it was opened. As no one had heard the door, it was safe to say it had not been accessed.

"May one assume you came to the same conclusion as I did, my dear?" Lady Vera asked, taking a seat in the first pew. "That whomever murdered the former matron did not break in? They either had a key of their own, were let in by Mrs. Huxton herself or another member of staff . . ." Something flickered in her eyes. "Or, they were already inside the orphanage because they live here."

"Indeed, and each one is a more distressing thought," Petra said, frowning. "Tell me, where are Mrs. Huxton's things? Her books, property, letters and such? And may I see them?"

There was the slightest pause, then Lady Vera smiled, and patted the seat next to her.

"Come, sit. The items are in the matron's dressing room—which now is in use by Mrs. Yardley, of course. Though there was little of any interest except for a wooden box containing a few trinkets and a miniature portrait of a child from her early days as a governess." When Petra sat, Lady Vera looked discomfited, then gathered herself. "I must apologize to you, my dear, for I have not told you the entire truth."

"Ah, I surmised as much," Petra said with gentle teasing, and Lady Vera rewarded her with a brief, self-deprecating smile.

Lady Vera went on to explain that some fifteen years ago, at the turn of the century, when Mrs. Huxton applied to be the matron for the Asylum for Female Orphans, it was because Lady Vera herself had recommended her. Miss Huxton—as she'd been then—had worked for Lady Vera for a time as governess to her daughter.

"Yet it was clear she could do more. She was quite keen to apply for the matron position here, too. Until I explained it would require more letters of recommendation beyond the excellent one she'd had from another lady of rank." Then she gave a dismissive wave of her hand at Petra's inquisitve look. "But I shall explain who said peeress was later, for it is the *gentleman* employer Miss Huxton worked for prior who is the subject of my story."

Lady Vera went on to explain that when she asked Miss Huxton to provide additional recommendations, Miss Huxton became distressed, claiming she could not ask the widower gentleman who had previously employed her as a governess. But Lady Vera would not be deterred on knowing the reason why.

"In the end, Miss Huxton only revealed the details to me on the condition that she not be forced to confess any names, for she wished his child to not be burdened by any scandal." Lady Vera's lips pursed thoughtfully. "I complied, and I have kept my word for fifteen years. Now I wish I had insisted on knowing."

"Do not leave me to beg you to continue," Petra said, turning in her seat to better face her friend.

"It is very compelling, I must say," Lady Vera said. "It seems that Miss Huxton had a liaison with the gentleman who was the father of her young charge—though if the child was a boy or a girl, she never said, and the miniature we found gave little clue. As for the gentleman, if he were a peer or simply part of the gentry, she never let that be known, either.

"Nevertheless, the gentleman had recently inherited a fortune and became interested in political reform. Yet, his interest quickly grew into the believing of wild conspiracies, and to the use of violence. From what I was told, he became instilled with this ideology due to the influence of a relative—his cousin, I believe—who was an occasional lodger at his home."

Lady Vera went on to explain that Miss Huxton, too, quickly came to believe what was sermonized. She helped write pamphlets that suggested brutal force should be used against those who supported the monarchy, and assisted in distributing them. Miss Huxton was completely taken over by reformist zeal, and passion of the age-old sort as well.

"Yet, when she began seeing the violence with her own eyes, she soon became disillusioned. And when her paramour became cruel toward *her,* she fled to London, absolutely broken at having to leave her young charge behind." The fierceness of a protector then came into Lady Vera's eyes. "Once she took the position of matron here—gaining the honorific of Mrs. along with it—I watched her like a hawk. I would have had her arrested tout de suite if I'd seen any sign of untoward behavior. I never did, however, and these girls thrived under her care."

"From what I have heard, she was an exemplary matron," Petra said. "However, it must be conceded that Mrs. Huxton did have some reformist views, even if they were in her past. Do you believe they had some connection to her death a sennight ago?"

"I wish I knew," said Lady Vera on a sigh. "As I said, I have watched her closely over the past fifteen years, and have met with her regarding this charity on a weekly basis. She has never given me any reason to believe she has reverted to her radical ways." Lady Vera's shoulders then slumped a fraction. "Yet if I am being truthful, I suppose it is possible. I always felt she was never quite willing to share the workings of her heart or mind. I am sorry to say I cannot attest I ever really knew her to those depths."

Petra thought briefly of Duncan, wondering how much she really knew of his heart, of his true feelings, but then forced her concentration back to the tale of Mrs. Huxton's past.

"What became of the gentleman and the child?" she asked Lady Vera. "The child would now be anywhere from one and twenty to, oh, a year or two older than I, yes?"

"I should think so," Lady Vera agreed. "As for the gentleman, it seems an illness of some sort began to afflict him, and he died in 1801, saving him from being known for his political views. The child was then sent to live with relatives and was saved from being tainted by association. I understand the child—now quite grown, yes—sought out Mrs. Huxton a few years ago, and was reported to be intelligent and good-humored. Mrs. Huxton would not say more on the matter than that."

"I expect seeing her former charge happy must have brought her great solace," Petra offered.

Lady Vera's graying brows tilted inward. "It did . . . and yet, I recall it also made her quite despondent thereafter. I would say her demeanor ever since was tinged with melancholy. Still, as it did not impact how she treated the girls here—she seemed to be even more protective of them, if possible—I offered my assistance if she required it, and then let her be. And now I feel a bit melancholy myself that she did not confide in me about what ailed her."

Lady Vera then rose stiffly to her feet, gazing at the floor beneath the altar as if offering up a silent prayer, an apology, or both. Petra stood as well, tucking Lady Vera's arm through hers. Then they turned and walked slowly out the chapel doors.

Turning north, they soon reached a hallway running perpendicular to their current path. Lady Vera explained that to the right were the staff quarters, including Miss Stebbins's room and one that would have belonged to Nell if she had been allowed to begin her training as undermatron. They then turned in the opposite direction, where Mrs. Yardley, as the matron, had a bedroom, a small sitting room, and a dressing room. As they approached, a low rumble of voices could be heard from the bedroom. Before Lady Vera could knock, however, Petra stopped and turned to her friend.

"Forgive me, but I must ask. I saw you and Mrs. Yardley arguing in the dining hall earlier. She showed you something that startled you as well. What was it that distressed you so?"

Lady Vera's arm stiffened in hers. "It was nothing, my dear." Then she sighed. "Oh, that infernal woman—"

It was Petra who held up her hand to silence her friend. She turned toward the matron's door as the sounds became clearer. Raised voices, sounds of a struggle, and a crash.

Petra went to the door and tried it, but it was locked. She banged on the door. "Mrs. Yardley? Are you well?"

There was a yelp, and more crashing. Lady Vera was shaking the door handle, but Petra had dug into her reticule. "Please, let me, Lady Vera."

"My dear, are those lockpicks?"

Petra did not reply. Inside there was another crash, and a guttural sound of frustration mixed with one of pain. But she had already sunk to her knees, not caring for the state of her fine silk dress, and felt herself calm a bit as she always seemed to in moments of crisis. This lock was a type she had opened many times, and—"Huzzah!"

She pushed the door open and was on her feet, then rushed after Lady Vera into the room.

NINE

THEY BOTH HALTED JUST INSIDE THE DOOR, LADY VERA'S GASP echoing about the small bedchamber. Petra's eyes swept the room, finding a bed against the far wall, a window with the sash thrown open, a washstand, spindly side table, and a chair toppled on its side over a thin woven rug. Mrs. Yardley lay crumpled upon it, eyes closed, her bonnet thrown back off her head and a thin trickle of blood running from her hairline.

Petra dropped down to her knees once more, her fingers to Mrs. Yardley's wrist, and found the pulse remained strong beneath them. The matron's eyes fluttered and she moaned.

"She is alive, just in a bit of shock, I believe," Petra said to Lady Vera. "If you would bring a damp flannel, I will help her sit up."

As Lady Vera rushed to the washstand, Petra helped Mrs. Yardley to come to a sitting position against the bed. As she did, the matron's hand fell open and a square of linen dropped to the rug, opening as it did and disgorging something small in a celadon hue. Petra picked it up, recognizing it instantly as a tassel. What's more, the tassel's neck was wrapped in a braided silk thread of bright gold.

She stared at it, realizing the tassel was just like the handful that had adorned a reticule she'd gifted a friend quite recently. Petra glanced toward Lady Vera, then turned the tassel over.

What the deuce? She quickly transferred her grip so that she was holding it up by its golden neck. One side of the pale green tuft of silk was stiff with dried blood.

Plucking the scrap of linen Mrs. Yardley had used, she placed the tassel within it once more, then looked up to find Lady Vera, stopped in her tracks at the edge of the rug, holding out the wet flannel. Her blue eyes had widened, and her face had lost all color.

At seeing her friend sway, Petra rocked back, tucking the toes of her silk shoes under her, and was on her feet. She lunged for the fallen chair, righting it moments before Lady Vera's knees buckled.

"Heavens, that was lucky," Petra exhorted, tucking the linen-wrapped tassel into her reticule, for she had no pockets in her fine yellow day dress. At the washbasin, she poured a glass of water from the pitcher. "Drink this," Petra insisted.

Lady Vera gave a weak chuckle as she took the glass. "I have never admired your strength and litheness more, my dear. It is all that time with horses, riding astride, and jumping hedges and fallen logs on your papa's lands at Buckfields. Most unladylike, as some would say, yet I would say most useful. Now, do not fuss, I am well. Go, tend to the matron."

Petra leaned in, whispering tightly, "I will, but then we shall discuss the tassel that is the very match for those adorning the reticule I gifted you but two months ago."

She had never seen Lady Vera look cowed or afraid, until now—yet she nodded, but without meeting Petra's eyes.

Taking the flannel, Petra went to the matron, gently dabbing at the cut on Mrs. Yardley's temple and eliciting a hiss from the older woman. "Whatever happened here?" Petra asked when the matron scrunched up her face, indicating her senses had fully returned.

"Nell . . . ," Mrs. Yardley said in hoarse tones. "She attacked me, my lady. I came in to find her in my dressing room . . . going through my things. When I confronted her, she leapt at me like a wild thing." The matron brought one shaking hand up to gently touch her temple, the space beneath her short fingernails already stained with her lifeblood. "We struggled and then she struck me." With effort, her eyes went to the window, where the slightest of warm breezes was ruffling the thin curtains. "She escaped out the window when she heard you at the door."

"But why would Nell attack you?" Petra asked, helping Mrs. Yardley to rise and sit atop the bed. "And what did she strike you with?"

"It was a box, my lady," said Mrs. Yardley, sounding weak. "A wooden box, very pretty, with carvings of a woodland field. It belonged to Mrs. Huxton and held a few pieces of jewelry—all paste, she once told me—and a miniature portrait of a child."

"From her days as a governess," Lady Vera explained, but if possible she looked even paler.

Petra poured water into the only other vessel, a tooth mug, for Mrs. Yardley and brought it to her, watching with concern as the matron touched her head again with her fingertips. Something about that gesture seemed odd, but Petra could not quite place what it was.

Draining the tooth mug full of water seemed to revive her, for Mrs. Yardley's eyes sparked with indignation. "Nell also stole some of Mrs. Huxton's clothes we were planning to give to the poor. She has absconded from this orphanage, my lady. The very charity that took her in as a girl. And now she is a thief and an accoster! Oh, I cannot believe the girl would do such a thing."

"Have you any thoughts as to why?" Petra asked.

Mrs. Yardley sighed. "She continues to go on about a possible inheritance. That Mrs. Huxton promised her there was proof she was due one, but I heard no such thing from the late matron. Nell is also claiming that two of the orphaned girls she came up with—girls who are now in service or apprenticed elsewhere—were due an inheritance, and never received it. And those two girls say they know of three more. Poppycock, I say."

Petra looked at Lady Vera for confirmation, and received a weary nod. "It is unlikely, I agree. No girl is admitted here without a guardian or benefactor petitioning the governors first, and the matron meets the girl only once she is accepted to the orphanage. Any documents for her future are drawn up beforehand, by the governors, and kept under lock and key. Why, the matron never even knows the details and the girls are never told of any monies due to them until they turn fifteen and leave this charity. This is done to keep all the girls on equal footing whilst in the orphanage's care." Lady Vera's lips twisted briefly. "But also because, occasionally, the monies supposedly left for the girl . . . shall we say, never come to fruition."

Petra caught Lady Vera's look and knew her friend meant that the monies were likely gambled away before the girl had the chance to claim them as she aged out of the orphanage.

Mrs. Yardley, a disgruntled note in her voice, added darkly, "Indeed, the matron receives the orphan, and it is we women who raise her, but as with everything in a female's life, whether she is a wee babe or a woman fully grown, it is the men around her who dictate her world. Especially when it comes to her money, which they give and take at their own whims, always thinking of themselves first."

"Then Nell will need to be found, and have her misconceptions corrected regarding any inheritance," Petra said firmly. "I am certain once she understands, she will be most horrified with the way she acted, and she will want to beg your forgiveness, Mrs. Yardley."

The matron's lips quivered. "You are most kind, Lady Petra. I shall, of course, forgive her if she shows contrition for her actions." She patted the pocket of her apron, then looked about on the floor, before shooting a surreptitious glance toward Lady Vera. "I seemed to have dropped my, ah, linen handkerchief. Did you see it, Lady Petra?"

Petra, however, pretended not to hear, instead asking a question of her own. "Do you know where Nell might have gone, Mrs. Yardley?"

The matron's disdain was thick in her voice. "Into the streets of London, no doubt. Nell Parker—for that is her full name—lived as a street urchin for a year after her mother died, before her benefactor found her and placed her here. She was but a child of ten, but she's never forgotten her streetwise ways." The matron's upper lip briefly curled. "I've known her to steal some of my writing paper, so what else might the girl be up to? Yes, I've always felt Nell would go bad one day. Pains me to say so, but I cannot deny those are my feelings. In fact, I've had my concerns that she was the one to kill Mrs. Huxton on Wednesday last."

Lady Vera rose from her chair like a wave cresting, and declared, "You cannot be in earnest! Why did you show me that tassel and accuse *me,* then?"

"Because it was Nell who said she felt *you* had done her in," retorted Mrs. Yardley, standing up just as quickly, a flush upon her cheeks. "It was Nell who found the evidence of the tassel and gave it to me. Oh, but I knew something was not right. That girl is prone to telling untruths, she is." Her voice softened somewhat as she conceded, "And, well, that morning, when you came and fetched me in my room, seeking my help after Mrs. Huxton was found dead, I felt you to be genuinely in a state of shock."

She rubbed the base of her cross again, pulling the cotton fabric at her breastbone up as she twisted the bit of silver between her fingers. Her brows knitted as she thought back.

"Yet Nell seemed in such a state as well. Thus, when she gave me the tassel, several of which I had seen decorating your reticule, at first it only seemed logical that you could be the guilty party."

Petra whirled to face Lady Vera—though her friend, instead of looking frightened as she had before, was suddenly the strong-willed titan of a woman Petra had always known. Standing up to her fullest height, Lady Vera pointed to Petra's reticule, as if in doing so the purse would open on its own volition and the linen-wrapped clue would leap out.

"Lady Petra, that is indeed my tassel Mrs. Yardley dropped after being attacked by Nell, and I shall dispense with any more nonsense and tell you the truth." She raised her chin even higher. "I shall tell you what I did not earlier." Then Lady Vera began to pace the small area to the door and back again, her words coming with certainty. "That morning one week earlier, I did not come into the chapel and find Mrs. Huxton dead. She was quite alive when I arrived."

"Hah! Then Nell *was* right," crowed Mrs. Yardley, a look of satisfaction passing briefly over her face as she bent and snatched up her bonnet, placing it back on her head with nimble fingers.

"You will be quiet, please, Mrs. Yardley," Petra said, sounding like the Duchess of Hillmorton when in high dudgeon. "We shall hear what Lady Vera has to say."

Mrs. Yardley looked briefly surprised, then cast her eyes downward, murmuring, "My apologies, my lady."

Lady Vera, however, was not cowed by the interruption. Instead, it seemed to bolster her resolve.

"Indeed, I met with Mrs. Huxton that morning—but she was agitated and angry. Like I had never seen her before. She was stalking about the chapel, saying she had proof that something untoward was happening and she was going to go to the governors."

"Untoward?" Petra repeated. "Was she referring to the inheritances? Was Nell correct?"

Lady Vera all but gritted her teeth with agitation. "I know not, Lady Petra. I insisted Mrs. Huxton calm herself, to explain more clearly, but she would not. She seemed quite incapable of settling, and I could not have her storming up to any of the governors with baseless claims. Oh, do not misunderstand me. It was not about propriety, no, indeed. More because I know these men who govern this charity and she would likely be sacked for acting hysterically. For speaking what they would consider to be out of turn. I did not wish for the orphanage to lose her."

"And she gave you no clue as to what she felt was happening that was wrong?" Petra asked again.

"No, she did not," Lady Vera replied sharply, but her heat seemed to be directed at the memory of the late matron. "Indeed, Mrs.

Huxton would not calm. She was insistent that she go to the governors then, for she knew they would be gathering for their monthly meeting in the assembly rooms but a minute's walk from here. She was becoming untethered from her normal, calm ways. She walked up to the altar, ranting of dangers to these girls if she did not act. And when I attempted to take her arm to lead her to a pew, she threatened to strike me with one of the silver candlesticks if I did not let her pass."

Lady Vera's chest was heaving by this time. Then, suddenly, her voice lost all its strength. Indeed, she seemed to wither slightly before Petra's eyes.

"But I did not do as she asked. And when Mrs. Huxton turned to grab for the candlestick, I confess I reacted out of fear. I raised my reticule and struck out at her, simply to buy myself some time. To hopefully shock her back into her senses." Lady Vera looked down at the reticule that was on Petra's wrist, and her voice went to a strangled whisper.

"In the pretty, tasseled reticule you gifted me, Lady Petra, I had a small tin of boiled sweets. I often bring them, and I give them to Nell to distribute amongst the girls when they do particularly well. I always have to hide the tin lest the girls see it, you understand. Thus, it made my reticule quite heavy. I had been clutching it in my hand already, for letting it dangle from my wrist by the strings was unbearably awkward."

She stopped, swallowing hard. Petra went to her side. "And what then, Lady Vera?"

Her friend's voice was hollow. "And when I struck poor Mrs. Huxton . . . the blow held more force than I anticipated. I wounded her, and as I did, one of the tassels broke free, and it seems one of the silk fibers came off in her . . ." She raised one trembling hand up to the spot behind her ear, in exactly the place where Frances said Mrs. Huxton had been struck.

"I quite take your meaning," Petra said gently. "Please, continue."

Lady Vera swallowed hard, then returned to her chair, but did not sit.

"When Mrs. Huxton fell . . . I regret to say she hit the floor harder than expected, her head made such an awful sound as it hit the stone, and she lay there without moving." Lady Vera looked imploringly at Petra. "But she was alive, I swear upon my own good name. I could see her breathing, and I felt for her heartbeat and found it slow, but steady. Then I hurried to the kitchen for help, knowing the cook would have reviving salts, and gauze for her wound." Her voice went almost to a whisper. "Yet when I returned, Mrs. Huxton was dead, the candlestick by her head."

"You are saying she never actually managed to take hold of the candlestick before you struck her?" Petra asked, and Lady Vera nodded with such vehemence that her whole body seemed to bob up and down.

"It is the truth. She never touched the candlestick, or the altar, when she collapsed."

There was silence for a moment, then Lady Vera's mouth thinned into a grim line.

"And there is something else that I did not tell you, or Miss Bardwell, or the Queen's men who came to interview me. When I returned from the kitchen, I observed Nell running from the chapel." Then once more, her voice grew in strength. "Lady Petra, I believe Nell is accusing me, because I may just as easily accuse her in return."

Mrs. Yardley nodded sagely at this, then stopped as Lady Vera's eyes slid to her.

"But whilst Nell brought evidence of my misdeed to you, matron, the girl also came to *me* with something she saw as well."

Mrs. Yardley sank back down onto the bed, clutching at the cross at her neck. "What did that girl say?"

"That you were not truly asleep when I went into your room to ask for help," Lady Vera snapped. "Indeed, matron, Nell saw you.

She said you were skulking about the hallways, in fact. And when you heard Mrs. Huxton speaking to me in the chapel, it was because you were listening at the door."

"That devious little brat!" spat Mrs. Yardley, jumping to her feet once more. "How dare she accuse me of such things!"

"Maybe she dared because it was true," returned Lady Vera with narrowed eyes before swiveling them Petra's way and throwing her shoulders back. "Well, my dear, it seems you have three suspects now. For the matron here had as much opportunity as Nell and I to deliver the final blow."

The room went suddenly silent. Petra could hear the ticking of a small clock hanging upon the wall. It was now after one o'clock, and if the Queen's intelligence officer were correct, word would come tonight about the war's end. Then tomorrow, three days of celebrations would be declared, with something deadly already planned for one of them.

Brilliant, she thought as exhaustion washed over her. *I have three suspects, one who is missing, and three days at most to discover who is telling the truth and who is not.*

TEN

PETRA RUBBED THE SPACE BETWEEN HER EYES WITH ONE HAND and used her bonnet to swipe away the high-growing grass as she tramped along an overgrown path at St. James's Park.

Upon boarding her carriage at the orphanage, she'd asked Rupert to lower the forward half of the landau's roof. She'd wanted more air as the day had grown ever more sweltering. Yet now she regretted not having had a darkened carriage in which to rest for the nearly half-hour ride from Lambeth to the park. For her eyes felt as if someone had sprinkled sand into them, and her mind felt like congealed porridge.

Still, at least she'd had time to breathe, to be alone, and to think on all she'd learned. As her carriage bumped along, Petra had made a mental list in her mind of what she knew.

Mrs. Huxton, the late matron, had a background as a radical from her time as a governess—though for the last fifteen or more years, she had shown no signs of such behavior.

Then, seven days ago, Mrs. Huxton was killed in the orphanage chapel. While she had sustained a nonfatal blow from Lady Vera that rendered her unconscious, someone had then used a candlestick to make certain she never awoke.

Thus far, Lady Vera was quite right in that Petra had three suspects: Mrs. Yardley, the new matron; Nell Parker, the fifteen-year-old orphaned girl; and then Lady Vera herself.

Was there also still a possibility it could have been someone else?

She didn't know, but for the time being, she had utilized her status as agent for the Queen and ordered Mrs. Yardley to be confined to her rooms, with the new undermatron, Miss Stebbins, taking charge of the girls. She'd then bade Lady Vera to return to her house. Neither was to leave their respective premises for the next two days. Both women were unhappy with this directive, but agreed that Petra should be allowed time for her investigations.

She now thought for a moment on Nell. The girl had attacked Mrs. Yardley before escaping with a wooden box once belonging to the late Mrs. Huxton. It seemed the box contained nothing of value, so why did she take it?

As her carriage went into a tight left turn to enter Westminster Bridge, so did Petra's mind as Duncan's handsome face seemed to swim before her eyes in the warmth of the afternoon.

Vexation washing over her, Petra once more thought of the note she had found this morning that seemed to prove Duncan had been the one to kill Emerson—or he had him killed, which to her was one and the same. Then, if the Dowager Marchioness of Langford was to be believed, Duncan had brought his half brother, James—the current Marquess of Langford, no less—into some sort of nefarious dealings.

She wondered again about the seal on the letter intercepted by Her Majesty's intelligence officer. A letter that was still in the locked drawer in the Queen's breakfast room in Buckingham House. Might its seal contain the coat of arms of the Shawcross family?

Petra's hand had strayed to her reticule, which was next to her on the carriage seat. Within its silk confines she could feel the leather roll containing her lockpicks. A plan that had been slowly germinating since this morning at the apothecary was now blooming in her mind. She knew what she wanted to do, and just how to go about it, by the time her carriage had crossed Westminster Bridge.

One part of her plan involved Teddy—likely the one person she knew who might be able to find Nell Parker.

And the other part? *Well, it might have some thinking me a bit mad,* she thought with an ironic twitch of her lips as she lifted the apron she had been wearing at the apothecary this morning. She held it up to her dress, again noting how the apron would conceal nearly the entirety of her pretty frock, making her look like just another shopgirl. Or nearly, at least.

Both parts of her plan, however, would start at St. James's Park, and she thusly directed Rupert to take her there, explaining that Teddy would be with Lottie, helping to train some of her canine charges. As the carriage rattled along, she had another idea. One that might help protect the girls at the orphanage without anyone being the wiser. She tore out a piece of paper from the small notebook she kept in her reticule before using her pencil to craft a short note.

Rupert drove her to the southeastern side, near George Street, but without trespassing onto Birdcage Walk. He was unable to place her any closer, not with the growing number of Londoners congregating on the northeast side, along the Strand and the Horse Guards Parade, waiting on news of the war's end. Once she had alighted from the landau, however, she sent Rupert off again with the note she had just written.

"I am sorry I did not think of doing so sooner," she told him, "for it requires you to return to Lambeth. I've written the direction on the reverse side. Do not worry," she said at seeing the look of concern in his brown eyes. "I will have Lottie take me back to Forsyth House in her dog cart."

"Very good, my lady," Rupert had said, tipping his hat to her.

At least Annie, in her ever-intelligent way, had made certain Petra's walking boots were in the carriage. For when she finally began making her way down the overgrown path, rubbing at her growing headache and batting away high grass with her bonnet, she was at least not ruining her shoes along with the hem of her dress on the still-damp ground.

Still, with each swipe as she walked in the direction of the park's canal, where the ornamental Chinese pagoda still stood on the footbridge, she felt tiredness threatening to weigh her down.

"I need tea, and something other than cake if I am to think clearly," she groaned aloud, taking aim with her bonnet at the leaves of a low-hanging tree branch, just because. Then she did it again, even harder, because it felt good. Then she felt guilty, for the poor leaves had done nothing to deserve her wrath.

"Would some cold chicken, bread, and cheese do?" came a voice from the other side of the tree. "I expect those leaves and your bonnet would both tell you to stop faffin' about and accept."

Petra tipped her head back and heaved a grateful sigh. "*Lottie.* How good it is to hear your Yorkshire vowels."

Then another voice drawled, "Dearest, do come and sit with us and the dogs. The tea has gone cold, but it is quite refreshing on such a sultry day."

Stepping around the tree, Petra exclaimed, "Caroline! What are you doing here with Lottie? Is Teddy not with the two of you? And how did either of you know it was me? I know I was grousing, but I was not quite that loud."

Lottie and Caroline both sat on a blanket in the tree's shade, picnic things all about them as Lottie's dandelion-like head of pale-blond curls tilted to an all-brown pointing dog with a bit of white on her chest sitting next to Fitz the terrier.

"Your Sable, of course. The only time I ever see her whole body quiver with excitement, and that tail of hers beat like a field drum, is when she hears your voice—or Duncan's."

Lottie then spoke a word in Gaelic, and Sable dashed to Petra's feet, wiggling all over, saving Petra from a reply and finally putting a smile on her face.

"Hello, my darling," she cooed, rubbing Sable's silky brown ears as the hound looked up at her with adoring eyes. Yes, it was just what she needed.

"It is rather Shawcross's cross to bear, making females quiver with excitement, is it not?" Caroline said with a grin as she held out a piece of bread folded in half and containing cold chicken, watercress, and a thick slice of cheese.

Petra was too hungry to even form a reply. She took a huge bite, and the well-seasoned roasted chicken made her emit a small moan.

"I expect Shawcross and his quiver-inducing ways means he hears quite a bit of that from our Petra, too," Caroline said to Lottie with a wink, and both friends giggled as Petra gave them a mild look of exasperation.

She simply did not have it in her right now to explain what she had found this morning in Duncan's town house, or to feel the same intense hurt. Besides, Caroline's teases were never meant to harm; she knew this from so many years of friendship. And after listening to Lady Vera and Mrs. Yardley sniping at each other earlier—to the point that Petra had finally been forced to bellow, "Enough!"—the idea of any kind of confrontation made her wish to smack a hundred more tree limbs with her bonnet.

"Come, sit, dearest," Caroline said, pushing a dark curl from her eyes and patting an empty spot on the blanket. "I was just telling Lottie the latest deliciously underhanded move Lady Elizabeth played against her sister in their never-ending game of who shall best whom in the running of their houses. It involved the swapping of an entire cask of excellent red wine with *vinegar*. And you and I are to attend Lady Sloan's dinner this very night, with the Prince Regent expected to attend!"

Lottie had poured tea into a pewter mug and Petra drank some down even as she shook her head.

"I do not have time to sit, I'm afraid. I came to give Teddy a job. Is he off running one of the dogs?"

"He has taken the two I was working back to their homes, I'm afraid," Lottie replied. "Is it important? And did you give him that new shirt? We saw him earlier at Bardwell's—yes, Frances and Annie are both doing quite well, selling transparencies and half the apothecary, it seems. Anyway, Frances told him he looked quite handsome in it, and his little cheeks turned the color of beetroot."

"The shirt is an old one of Duncan's. Teddy had quite outgrown his other one," Petra said absently as she gave Sable a bit of her chicken. "And the matter is one of great importance, I'm afraid. I was also hoping he might help me with another small matter right now as well."

"And what would that be?" asked Caroline, who smiled at Fitz as he laid down and rested his head on her knee while Lottie put her hands on her hips, pretending to be jealous her faithful terrier was so enamored with Caro.

"Oh, it is simple really. Just a bit of breaking into Buckingham House to get a good look at a letter before the Queen's intelligence officer does."

When Lottie and Caroline gaped up at her in twin expressions of astonishment, Petra's lips curved up and she took another big bite of chicken.

"Why are we hiding behind trees at the old Riding House and not Buckingham House?"

Lottie asked this from the side of her mouth as she, Petra, and Sable watched Caroline stroll with Fitz on a lead. They heard Caroline laugh, clearly delighting in the terrier's antics as he picked up a stick three times his size and proudly trotted along with it.

"Because my papa used to take me here as a child," Petra said, "and there is a door that leads straight from the stables onto the grounds of Buckingham House. From there, as I recall, there is another door that takes one into the library—which would keep me from being seen by anyone in the service wings. From there, I only need to make my way to the Queen's private breakfast room and have a few minutes with that letter. For I am certain it will tell me what I need to know."

"And you believe that wearing one of Frances's aprons will make anyone believe you are a delivery girl for Bardwell's Apothecary? You, in your fine silk dress and looking like . . . well, an earl's daughter. You believe this is going to help you if you're caught?" Lottie's eyes shone with mischief as she took in Petra's attempt at concealing herself with an apron.

"I have let my hair down as well," Petra protested, pulling at the plait now hanging over her shoulders. "I also have the half-used tin of sweets Lady Vera left behind as my supposed item to deliver. And do not worry. I shall replace it for the girls with two tins of Frances's best sweets when this is done."

Lottie lifted one blond eyebrow. "I did not doubt it for a moment. However, I should like to reiterate that Caroline and I think this is a foolish endeavor."

"And yet both of you are willing to help me. Why?"

"One reason is because we trust you, Petra," Lottie said, as if this should have been obvious. Then she grinned. "And another is because I, and Frances, too, have learned in the short time we've known you that you do not stop when something is important to you. And Caro has confirmed this. Annie, too. And Duncan and your papa were both quite vehement on the subject, I must say. Even Lady Vera has said so as well. And—"

"I think you have painted quite the portrait of those who think me impulsive and headstrong, dear Lottie," Petra interrupted, though with amusement thrumming in her voice.

"Oh, Caro is giving the signal!" Lottie breathed.

Walking in a deliberately sedate manner, Caroline passed the lone guard in the Queen's livery who stood at the gates of the now-deserted riding school once used by the king before his health took a turn. Conveniently, a harried nursemaid passed by in the opposite direction, pulling along a little boy and pushing a pram with a squalling child. Using this distraction, Caroline leaned down to pet Fitz. No one but Petra and Lottie saw her slip his collar off. Or heard her say a command that had the little dog dashing off into the thicket of trees beyond the Riding House. A moment later, Caro ran up to the guard, distress painted all over her face.

"Oh, dear! Oh, heavens! Guard, my precious little doggie—he has run off! Would you be so kind as to help me locate him?"

"'Fraid I can't, miss. Cannot leave my post," said the guard.

Then he stood straighter, looking flustered as he became aware of Caroline's statuesque beauty, shiny mahogany hair, and fashionable white muslin dress that was exceptionally low at the bodice. It left no one to imagine the curves of her body when standing in a shaft of sunlight—which Caro had expertly managed to do.

Caroline could be heard giving another bit of pleading, no doubt with some extra widening of her coppery, doe-like eyes. Then she clapped her hands together. "Oh, you are too good! His name, you say? Why, it is Darcy."

Lottie giggled. "I tried for five days to get the daft thing to answer to Darcy when he was a pup—but he preferred Fitzwilliam instead." Then, "Oh, the guard is away! That is your cue, Petra. Go! I have taught Sable a new trick, and we shall utilize it and do our part if and when needed."

"I adore you both for helping," Petra said, flashing a grin, then made herself stroll casually out, looking for anyone who might see her. Finding only Caroline motioning her forward, she broke into a run, lockpicks at the ready.

"You were brilliant, Caroline," she said as she found what she had expected, the same sort of padlock she'd been opening at the Buckfields stables in Suffolk since she was a young girl.

"Sometimes I believe I should have been a thespian," said Caroline. "Now do hurry. I should not like to have to flirt again with that guard, as sweet as he did seem. And he did have those delicious shoulders—now only if the Queen would let him grow a beard . . ."

"Here," Petra said, handing her the padlock. "And thank you for being willing to stand in the sunlight for me, Caro, darling." She blew her friend a kiss, slipped through the wooden door, and heard, "Anytime, dearest, and *do be careful*," as there came the sound of the padlock being clicked back in place.

She was in, and wasted no time, not even bothering to lament how empty and derelict the once opulent riding school now looked. She raced into the stabling area, slowing whenever she saw an opening that might lead to a door. Most looked to be for drainage of water and muck, stopping at a wall covered in ivy.

Lawks, did I misremember the door that Prince George once led Papa and me through? she thought in a panic. Then she skidded to a halt at finding a proper walkway to another ivy-covered wall, this one where part of the greenery seemed disturbed.

Pushing aside the leaves, she saw there was indeed a ring-style door pull. Rusted, yes, but the keyhole itself was in good working order. In fact, her lock picks were not even needed, which she discovered when the door swung inward with hardly more than a touch of her hand.

"May it all be this simple," she whispered, and stepped into a small courtyard with pathways leading in three directions. One was clearly to the service wing, and she scooted behind a tree when she saw the back of a footman in a window. The second pathway seemed to lead to the west side of the house—often called the garden front—and exactly where she needed to be as the Queen's breakfast room faced the gardens. However, the path was long and curved around the house, increasing her chances of being seen. That left the path straight in front of her, to the library.

She was there in a few steps, and found the lock to be a bit trickier, but eventually it gave way. Inside was a ground-floor boot room with a circular staircase leading up directly into the first-floor library.

Transom windows giving her much-needed light, silently she made her way up the stairs. She was met with the heavenly smell of books, all leather and old paper and dust, and it produced a familiar, warming feeling in her heart. *The magic of a library,* she thought, even as she dashed to the door that would lead her toward the back, or west, portion of the house.

Having grown up with Duncan at Buckfields, where they often wagered as to who could sneak down to the kitchens first to pilfer sweets without being detected, Petra had more experience than most at moving silently about a palatial house. She managed to open most doors with nary a creak and her bootheels never touched the floors. She used connecting doors, relying on her instincts as to where they might lead, and only had to pick the locks of two before she was certain she was close to the breakfast room.

Yet the prickling sensation that she would get when either Duncan or some unwitting servant was close by had not yet left her, it seemed. For just as she was about to open a connecting door, she stopped, and then two beats later, she heard the voices. Men's voices, but she could not make out what they were saying.

Bollocks, she thought. Was this the Queen's intelligence officer, coming to collect the letter, or just two footmen walking down the hallway?

She flattened herself against the wall, holding her breath, as they walked by the drawing room and she heard a guffaw.

"Don't let ol' Reg see you takin' a nip of Her Majesty's brandy. You'll be out on your ear before you can say 'Prinny the Ninny.'"

"I only wanted to know what it tasted like," protested the other one, who sounded quite young. "If I don't know, how can I serve it to others?"

Petra heard the first one teasing the younger one about being ol' Reg's protégé as they walked away, and she allowed herself to breathe again. They'd been heading in the opposite direction from where she needed to be. She stayed, tuning her ears until the sound of receding footsteps faded away completely, and then gently opened the door.

Peering out into a main hallway, she knew exactly where she was. The Queen's breakfast room was but a few strides away, just past another hall containing a staircase. Next to it was a side door to Her Majesty's private sanctum, and it might not be locked . . .

Petra started at a noise from behind her, then recognized the sound had come from the floor below. Still, she scurried down the hall, whipping into the darker staircase hallway and rushing for the door. Taking hold of the ornate doorknob fashioned with the Queen's own coat of arms, she turned it and breathed a sigh of relief when it proved unlocked and she was able to slip inside the breakfast room.

Since the room had dark paneled walls and red velvet . . . well, nearly everything . . . Petra braced herself to find an almost pitch-black room from the curtains being firmly shut. Instead, she found herself blinking in the bright afternoon light coming through large gaps in the velvet hangings. They'd all been loosened from their tiebacks, but had not been fully closed, likely because the windows faced the private gardens, which would give the expected Queen's man all the illumination he needed to collect the letter.

Was it only a few hours ago that I was here with the Queen and the duchess? Petra thought, her heart speeding up with the idea of finally getting a good look at the letter she'd seen this morning—and that wax seal.

She turned to lock the door, one hand already clutching her lockpicks, when a man's large hand slammed over her mouth, and another snaked around her waist.

ELEVEN

FEAR HIT HER FIRST, AND BEING RESTRAINED MADE HER FLY into a panic.

She fought against the steel bands of the man's arms, and raised up the metal pick in her fist, aiming for any part of flesh she could reach. Yet before she could make contact, she was spinning. Or being spun, rather, as the man turned her to face him.

His hand released her mouth, but for only a moment, then his palm was covering her lips once more. He'd clearly felt it necessary when her eyes flew open.

"What in the name of Zeus's cods are you doing here?" Duncan hissed, his Scots burr thickening his words. "And do not dare bite my hand like you did when we were children, Petra. Ow! Petra, you *will stop*."

He jerked his lower body away from her just in time, then caught her wrist, eliciting a cry from her throat, but she managed to hold on to her pick. He was facing the windows and she saw the flash of regret in his eyes at the sound, and his hand loosened on her wrist.

"Forgive me," he panted. "But will you please cease this nonsense!"

She stilled, and nodded, and he slowly released her.

He was wearing dark brown trousers tucked into half boots, a muslin shirt with no cravat, and a brown coat with a matching waistcoat. A tweed flatcap pulled low barely helped to shade his green eyes. With his hair worn long, dirty, and curling over his collar, he cut the figure of a workman or a gardener. It was the perfect outfit to blend into the shadows, and look as if he belonged back in the wilds of Scotland on his maternal grandfather's sheep farm instead of sipping the best whisky in crystal glasses with his paternal grandfather, the most powerful duke in England.

Petra looked up into his handsome face. That angular jawline, roguishly accentuated by a day's worth of stubble. The full lips she had never wanted to stop kissing once she'd felt them on hers, and those waves of dark hair that felt so good in her fingers. His eyes, that startling green mixed with flakes of gray that marked him as a Shawcross, were glittering like emeralds under moving water. And it all made her so angry.

Without warning, her hand formed into a fist and she slammed it into his hard stomach, making pain shoot up her arm.

Yet she could not stop. Her other hand did the same and she punched his arms, his stomach, and his chest. Why could she not see him clearly anymore? Was it because her face was screwed up with rage? Then she felt the hot tears, which only made her angrier. A guttural sound came from deep within her belly, but her throat was so tight that it barely went above the whispered grunts Duncan had emitted only a few moments earlier.

"Why?" she cried—and it was tearful, not a yell. Damn and blast, why could she not scream the words?

Her fists now stinging with pain, she went to a flat palm, dropping her pick as she beat her palms against his chest, her throat hoarse from its inability to shout.

"Why did you kill him? He was . . ." She could not say the words "my fiancé," and only managed to ground out, "And your closest friend. Why? Tell me, Duncan. Why did you do it? Why did you make me love you when you are a liar, a traitor, and a man who would take away what was important to me for his own selfish reasons?"

It was then she realized he had not fought back. Hadn't moved a muscle, but had let her beat on him. She saw his lips parted in surprise. And she stopped, and stepped back, shocked at what she had done. Still, she lifted her chin, letting the hot tears fall down her face. "Why?" she whispered.

"How? How—when did you . . . ?" He raked a hand through his hair, looking wildly around as if he could not bear to accept that he had been unmasked. Her heart, if possible, shattered into a thousand new pieces.

She bent and retrieved her metal pick, saying in a flat voice, "Your grandmama, she trusted and loved you as much as I. How will she survive knowing what you did to Emerson?"

"Petra . . ." His voice was rough and the streaks of sun coming through the windows into the Queen's breakfast room were all but in his eyes, showing her clearly just how astounded he was.

Then there were shouts from outside, a soldier's voice, commanding and intense. "Her Majesty's house has been breached! Find them!"

There were sounds of boots entering the house. Before Petra could but put two thoughts together, Duncan grabbed her by the hand, pulling her across the room so fast that the chinoiserie vases and patterned Axminster carpet swam before her eyes. Then he spun her around once more before propelling her into a corner between a tall casement clock and a thick set of red velvet curtains. One arm went around her back so that it took the brunt as she stumbled backward, slamming against the wall. Before she could move, he'd pulled the curtain completely around them both and his arms pinned hers to her sides.

"What are you doing?" she snapped. "Get off of me."

"No," he grunted back as she attempted to lift her leg between his. But her dress—confound it, her *dress*—was too heavy and well made, keeping her jab from landing as high as it needed. Though it came close enough for Duncan's stomach to pull in, and his muscular thighs to further bunch as they slammed closed over her knee.

"Damn you, Duncan—"

She stopped as they heard the rattling of the door. Then another man saying, "I have the key, Colonel!"

Duncan tilted his head and she could see one blazing green eye as he hissed in her ear, "These men were trained by the Swiss Guard, Petra. They will kill first and look into your face after, all in the name of the Crown. There are but six of them here at present, but that is damned enough. Now stand still, by the bloody bollocks of Pegasus!" And it was with that oath in her ear, sending an unexpected frisson down her spine, that they heard the doorknob turn.

Suddenly, she could feel Duncan tucking her in, cloaking every part of her he could with his own body, and yet, she realized, somehow barely touching her. Her fingers found his shirt and gripped it, her metal pick still in her hand as she closed her eyes and touched her forehead to his chest. She concentrated on breathing in the scent of him as her heart slammed against her rib cage.

She heard the creak of the door, and then footsteps on the wood floor. She felt Duncan tensing his muscles, almost as if he were creating a protective shell out of his own body. His hand slowly went to his leg, and it was then that Petra vaguely recalled seeing a scabbard tied to his thigh. He had a knife, and was willing to use it to protect her. But she could not help but think, was he doing so as the man of honor she had always known? Or as the political ruffian she was so deeply worried he had become?

Boots tramped across the floor in confident strides, blocking any further thoughts from her mind except for staying still and quiet. She heard the low, thick rustle of the heavy curtains being moved about. Petra feared she had stopped breathing for a moment as the curtains at the very next window were pushed aside.

"Make certain that door behind you is locked—yes, of course the one leading to the Kings's quarters. And check the door leading to the stairwell, too!"

The order came from the guard across the room, and Petra stood, frozen against Duncan as they heard another guard come near. By the sound of it, he was just a few feet from where they hid as he checked the door that led to the King's quarters. More footsteps, then she nearly let out a hysterical laugh when the guard tried the door she had locked just a minute earlier and declared it secure.

"The main door was locked as well," the first guard said. "They're not in here."

There was a shout from down the hall, and the two men ran out of the Queen's breakfast room, all but slamming the main door behind them. And as soon as the footsteps faded, Duncan swiped the curtains aside and backed away, leaving a rush of suddenly cool air between them. He looked down at her, breathing heavily, and his eyes went flat. Then he grabbed her hand.

"We're leaving, now." Jutting his chin, he indicated the door nearby, leading to the King's quarters. "Down through that stairwell is our way out. There is a secret tunnel that leads to the Riding House—"

"No," Petra said, balking. "I came here for a reason."

Duncan whispered another oath, then asked, "Whatever for? And where is Annie?"

She pointed to the table that had not moved from its place next to Her Majesty's chair. "Annie is assisting Frances at the apothecary. But I have come for what is in the drawer of that table. I must see that letter, and what it proves. For I am certain it will be the link to many things."

It will help me prove once and for all whether you are a traitor or not, too, she thought grimly.

He looked momentarily astounded, and then pulled her toward the door, even as she was already opening her leather roll containing her lockpicks.

"Duncan!" Petra said, a little too loudly, and saw his teeth grit. They both froze, waiting to hear the sounds of boots coming their way.

When none came, he threw the lock and swung the door wide, saying through clenched teeth, "If you would, my lady."

Petra lunged to the side, determined to get into that table. She tried to go around him, but he lifted her easily off her feet—*damn and blast, it was frustrating to be half his size*—then he carried her over the threshold, plucking the metal pick from her hand as he did.

"There is nothing in that table for you to find, my lady," he said as she struggled, and it was not with the warmth in which he often teasingly called out her rank. It sounded formal, tight, angry. He set her on her feet with gentleness, and she bared her teeth with a snappish response.

"And how do you know, Mr. Shawcross?" If he could switch to formalities, so could she.

Once more, when he turned slightly, she tried to dash back through the door. But he blocked her way handily, then—*blast it all again*—with his arm outstretched, he palmed her forehead and stepped forward, compelling her to back up. It was a tactic from their spirited childhood moments, usually after she had already issued several laughing taunts.

Yet there was no wide grin on his face this time. And she could not stamp on his toes now like she did then, when she'd had one of her few spurts of growth, making her legs almost as long as his . . . for possibly a week.

She slapped his hand away instead, making a low growl of annoyance, the only thing keeping her from screaming being the sound of bootheels somewhere above them, indicating the guards were still searching.

He closed the door, not bothering to lock it, and started down the stairs, pulling her after him with one hand, using his other hand to yank his flatcap low over his eyes as he spoke.

"I know because I came for the letter, too, and it was already gone."

TWELVE

"WHERE ARE YOU TAKING ME?" PETRA SAID, ATTEMPTING TO set back on her heels once they had made it through the ivy-covered door to the Riding House grounds. Duncan shut the door and locked it. Then, instead of walking her out the gate from which she came, he was leading her toward the far side of the stables.

In the back of her mind, Petra realized she had been in Buckingham House for only a matter of minutes. Possibly ten at most. She had told Lottie and Caro to give her at least twenty before beginning to wonder if something was amiss. Would they still be outside the grounds near the Riding House, playing with the dogs? If she shouted, would they hear her?

Somehow, she doubted it, and frustration swirled within her once more. She attempted to pull her hand from Duncan's. His grip, which had not been tight, still managed to hold her own fast. "Where. Are. You. Taking me?" she said again, her words coming staccato through clenched teeth. "I do not wish to be anywhere near you! Ever again!"

Duncan stopped in his tracks, his hand immediately loosening further on hers. The look that passed over his face was as if she had punched him again. Then he scowled and turned back, pulling her with him once more. Petra realized she was not actually frightened, though. Furious and galled, yes. Determined to learn the truth in whatever way she could, no doubt. But she did not fear him—nor did he seem to want her to. And despite the logical side of herself telling her that she should just wait to see where they were going, his refusal to answer her only made her want to nettle him into talking.

"How did you know the Queen's intelligence officer was coming to collect the letter tonight?" she asked, lengthening her strides to keep up. Then sarcasm filled her voice when he did not even attempt to answer. "Oh, no, you do not need to tell me. Your grandmama would have told you, wouldn't she? Because the duchess trusts you implicitly. Because she felt you were good from the moment you were that little scruffy boy, speaking unintelligible Scots and with hair that had never seen a comb. And now you are betraying her by coming to steal the evidence? Why, does it link you to the threats to the Queen, and the group they call the Bellowers?"

Duncan's scowl deepened, but he did not reply. They reached the second gate of the Riding House and Duncan only had to shove a rock aside for it to swing open. She realized immediately they had ended up on a path that skirted the Queen's private gardens, and thus, not so far away from the spot where she'd left Caroline and Lottie.

Petra's fit of pique was rising to a crescendo. He had not answered even one of her questions, and though some part of her recognized his silence was making her unable to hold her tongue, she did not care.

"Do you know, I was recalling Caroline's house party from three years ago," she said. "I saw you and Emerson walking off together that day on Box Hill. I heard him insist that if he could only make you see, that you would change your mind. I did not know what he meant that day, only that it involved something political."

She saw him blink at that, but nothing more. Inwardly, she said some very unladylike oaths.

Emotion was in her throat now and her accusations felt like they were coming wildly, as if all her pain from different places within her were rising to the surface at once. It felt like a jostling herd of horses trying to burst through a too-small pasture gate. Chaotic, and with the occasional one leaping the fence in order to be set free first.

"I've known since we were children that you supported Scottish self-rule, Duncan," she continued. "But now I know that it has gone much further, sir. You have killed a good Englishman, and why? Because he tried to make you see sense regarding political reform? And now, instead of using your influence to bring about change in a peaceable way, like he would have wanted, you have chosen to align yourself with a group that advocates violence?"

Weeds and tall grasses whipped at her skirts, and still Duncan remained silent.

"And me?" she asked, using the only barb she had left. It filled with the acid from her tongue and she let it fly. "Did you push Emerson down your own staircase when he attempted to block your path, both politically and to having me? Oh, I had not admitted it to myself then, but all day long I have been recalling little things. Buried memories. And I knew, somewhere deep down, that you have wished me for yourself since we were both young. But to kill the man who was to be my husband so that you could finally accomplish it? How could you?"

She saw a muscle flicker in his jaw. Good. And a new thought came to her lips just as a landaulet—a smaller, two-seat version of her own landau—came slowly into view.

"Was being sent to the Continent for three years after Emerson's death by your grandfather—was it His Grace's way of helping you evade justice? That must be why the Dowager Marchioness of Langford called you a scapegallows earlier today!"

The coachman of the landaulet pulled the matched bay horses to a halt.

"Everythin' all right, sir?" he said.

"No, it is not," Petra jumped in huffily. She pointed to Duncan with her free hand. "This man is abducting me and I beg of you to help me!"

But Duncan was already pulling open the door, and Petra was lifted into the dark carriage before she even knew what was happening.

"Lady Petra is with me," she heard Duncan say. "Were you seen coming this direction? Good, then let us be off. No, nothing of the plan has changed. But we must make one stop first."

The horses were set in motion before she could even sit up after flopping like a sack of flour onto the plush carriage seat. Though as she did, Petra managed to see through a gap in the curtains behind her head. Something small and brown was frozen into a familiar stance some distance away. And just as Duncan settled in beside her, closing the door, she saw what looked like a walking dandelion puff. It was Lottie, and Sable, who was literally pointing her out.

They had seen her. The landaulet gained in speed, making calling out to Lottie a rapidly pointless endeavor, but at least she'd been seen. Now she could only hope her friends could find some way to follow her, too.

Petra resorted to fuming in silence, crossing her arms over her chest, her head turned toward the side window, not caring her view was blocked by curtains of the darkest blue velvet. Asking questions had led her nowhere. Goading him had only made her cease to act rationally, which she loathed. She would simply have to wait until they arrived at their destination.

In truth, she was becoming rather curious. Despite everything, she remained innately certain Duncan would not hurt her or bring her to harm. *Though he is doing a rather good job of disrupting my investigations at present,* she thought irritably. Still, what was this so-called plan he referenced? Was it something to do with the Bellowers? Would they end up in some dank back alley in the East End? Or would it be somewhere closer to home?

Sod it. She reached for the curtain and was just about to yank it open to see which way they were heading when Duncan spoke in a weary voice.

"Though I have sadly taken a life before, Petra, it was not that of Lord Ingersoll."

Her hand dropped. For a second her heart briefly soared. Then it plummeted again into a conflicting battery of emotions, every other thought in her mind dropping away as she faced him.

"I do not believe you. Even if you did not kill Emerson, you contrived to do so. The information I discovered said so, and there was no reason for it to contain falsehoods."

When Duncan finally spoke, his voice was soft and a bit ragged.

"There was a moment where I thought I would be forced to do so, yes, or to order it done. In the end, however . . . Where did you hear this, may I inquire?"

Astounded that he would admit it so freely, any other questions ceased momentarily and she could do little but answer with equal soft finality, telling him briefly of Mr. Drysdale's ledger page that had dropped out of her book this morning.

"Ah," he said, with the smallest huff of a laugh. "That would explain young Teddy's tale of finding you looking like Boudica with a fire poker, and speaking of ways of hobbling me with rather too much dark glee."

Petra wanted to ask after Teddy, and inquire about the shadowy man who had made the lad feel so uncomfortable. She wanted to insist Duncan tell her why he had left this morning if it were not because of what she had found. But all she could think of was Emerson. Anger was filling her again, but Duncan seemed to read her thoughts before she could form a coherent sentence.

"You are wondering why I never told you that Ingersoll had been murdered. You are wondering why you believed for three years that he had merely slipped going down the stairs, and broke his neck. Well, the latter is what I told you because it was quite a plausible thing for you to believe. It was also closest to the truth, and I felt it the kindest thing to do."

"Kind?" Petra spat. "*Kind?*" But Duncan broke back in before she could enter into a diatribe.

"If I had told you Ingersoll had been murdered, what would you have done, Petra?" he returned with heat. "You have always been strong, but you were different back then. You were one and twenty, sheltered beyond belief, in a state of shock, and grieving. And even if you would have known he had been murdered and searched for the culprit, you would have found nothing. For there was precious little to find."

He pulled the flatcap from his head, his eyes intense, jaw tight.

"Indeed, you did not even notice the clue that would have told you Ingersoll was murdered. If you had, maybe I would have insisted you help me when I spent the next week searching like a bloodhound, using ways you did not have at your disposal, until my grandfather barricaded me in my rooms at Hillmorton House one night and forced me to take a dose of laudanum so that I could sleep."

Petra's fists were clenched, but curiosity formed a temporary barrier to her anger. "What was the clue I missed?"

Duncan groaned, almost as if he wished he hadn't spoken the words. Yet he did not attempt to deflect her.

"Ingersoll was fully dressed, Petra. Down to his cravat—which you know he spent nearly an hour tying each morning. He had staved off wearing his boots so that he could sneak down the stairs without waking you. It was an ungodly hour of the morning, and he was fully dressed, leaving to meet someone." And before she could respond, he added, "In fact, you may recall his boots were a bit too neat at the base of the stairs, were they not? That meant he had left them there as he let someone into the town house—*my* bloody town house. Someone he clearly knew."

"Oh, but of course," Petra said, her tone thick with sarcasm, "because he would have simply led the blackguard upstairs again, only to allow that man to shove him down a set of stairs?"

Through the little chinks of sunlight coming through the carriage curtains, Petra saw a flash of pain in Duncan's eyes.

"There was another clue. One you might have noted if I had not sent you back to Forsyth House with such haste," he said. "There were signs . . . bruises upon his neck and face . . ."

"From the fall, yes," she said impatiently.

"No, Petra." He rushed a hand through his hair. "There were bruises that showed up a bit later, of fingers that gripped his face hard enough to twist his head . . . and break his neck. The only answer after that is that the blackguard, as you rightly called him, then put Emerson over his shoulder and walked up to the landing. It would have been easy, for Ingersoll was tall, but slight. And then he would have—"

Suddenly, Petra felt bile in the back of her throat. She began shaking her head to clear it of the image of Emerson, his neck broken so that his head swung like a wild pendulum as he was thrown over a man's shoulder. Of having some faceless, hateful man position Emerson on the treads so that his lifeless body could then be slid down the stairs. Like she and Duncan used to do at Buckfields when they were children, a blanket beneath their backs. For amusement.

"Do not say it. Do *not* complete your thought," she cried.

Then suddenly she could not breathe. Duncan threw open one of the windows, allowing in fresh air, and only when he put his hand on her back, rubbing it as he murmured soft words in Gaelic, did she begin to calm. Yet when she could finally speak again, tears streaking down her face, her chest heaving, she glared at him.

"I do not believe you. It was your town house. How do I know you were not the man to let Emerson in? I may not have noticed everything, but the one thing I do recall is that you were lodging at Hillmorton House then, nearly a half hour's walk from your town house on Chaffinch Lane. And not much less on horseback, unless you gallop through Hanover Square. Yet the lad I sent found you with exceptional haste and you managed to be at my side in less than ten minutes' time, without the aid of your horse. So how were you so nearby?"

She wiped angrily at her tears with the back of her hand, too many thoughts coming at once. "And even if you did not commit the horrid deed, you have admitted you would have arranged to have Emerson killed. In one manner or another, it is clear you considered taking his life, and you have given me no excellent reason as to why."

"I have not answered you, no," he said slowly. "And I do not wish you to believe me simply because I say so. You have always questioned bloody *everything*, Petra, until you could see that what someone was telling you was true with your own eyes, ears, and heart. And that—*that* is what I loved about you from our earliest days at Buckfields."

A brief smile touched his lips. "I remember the day we met. Those blue eyes of yours narrowing, silently but brutally assessing my character. And even though you consented to be polite, to ride ponies with me, and even share your food when our nursemaid was not looking and you could tell I was still hungry, you did not even begin to trust me until that summer had turned to fall in your presence. And it is one of the things I still love best about you. That *you* decide what you believe after you have gathered the facts."

Yet he shook his head, a bit sadly.

"No, you must determine what is the truth about Ingersoll on your own. For your questions will never cease until you verify the facts to your satisfaction, as you always have done. Of who Ingersoll was, of who I am, and of what and whom you feel you can trust . . . or not. And I respect that as much as I respect you, and myself. For I will not beg you to believe me, Petra. Nor will I live in a constant state of vexation and turmoil that you will never trust me again."

Then he leaned in and she saw a flash of pure anger in his eyes, even if his voice remained low and calm.

"But remember this: I have never sought or *contrived* to trick, convince, or even encourage the heart of any woman who does not wish me to know it. And your heart has been the only one I have ever wished to know intimately. Think of me what you will and I will accept it, but that is one truth you have always known, and it has never altered."

He sat back, even as she felt frozen in place. He was right, of course, and she was humbled by it.

"Yes. That, I do know," she whispered after a long moment, looking him in the eyes.

Then, realizing she was still wearing the Bardwell's Apothecary apron, she yanked it over her head, not caring that her curls were likely coming loose from her plait and falling all about her face. To keep from having to reply to all that he had told her about Emerson's death—no, his murder—when she simply could not find room in her heart or her brain just yet, she changed the subject.

"There is more that is vexing me at present," she said crisply. "I have been investigating the murder of the orphanage matron, Mrs. Huxton. For she was indeed murdered, and I have three suspects. One of whom is an orphan girl on the run, one is Lady Vera, and the third is the current matron—and none of whom I can imagine being a murderess."

"Lady Vera?" he repeated, looking surprised.

"Mm, yes, but do not change the subject," she replied. "It is possible that one or more of my suspects could be proven guilty through the information in that letter the Queen's intelligence officer found—the letter you and I were both seeking at Buckingham House. Yet it was you who broke in before me, so how can I trust it was stolen by someone else? How can I be certain it is not actually upon your person now?"

Duncan held up his hands, and a bit of amusement tinged with challenge was in his voice. "You may search my person, my lady."

Perhaps she should have had qualms, but she did not. She searched every pocket, opening his coat, lifting his muslin shirt and feeling around every corner of his hard chest and stomach, causing him to emit a little grunt, but found only a few coins and two paper twists containing lemon drops.

After checking that the scabbard tied to his leg contained nothing but a blade, her hands expertly undid the buttons on the fall of his dark breeches. He wore no smalls, but again, she did not hesitate, for he always had a secret pocket sewn into his trousers, did he not? Thus, she stuck her hand in and felt about for the pocket, recalling how, a fortnight earlier, she had watched him use it to hide a naughty love poem she'd written.

She found the pocket quickly, yet it contained no hidden missives, naughty or otherwise, and she sat back against the seat, crossing her arms with a frown. But when he shifted a bit, she glanced at his undone trousers and rolled her eyes.

"Ye canna expect me to not respond when your hands are all over my person, my lady," Duncan said mildly, his burr doubly thick as he kept his hands up. "And especially when you handled it the way you did, even if it were to make certain it was not helping to conceal a Thames-soaked letter. I rather think the wax seal would have chafed if I had, pocket or no."

"Do up your buttons, if you please," she ordered, averting her eyes because she very much wanted to take another glance herself. "After that, take off your boots and shake them out."

He did as instructed, putting his boots back on again when there was clearly nothing hidden inside, and afterward lazily untwisted a lemon drop, popping it in his mouth.

"Then who came and took the letter?" she asked in exasperation. Then, just as his broad shoulder lifted in a shrug, something he said earlier finally permeated her brain.

"How did you know it was soaked in the Thames, that the seal remained intact, *and* where the Queen had placed it for retrieval?" She narrowed her eyes, then more so when she saw the tiny flash of wry humor in his. "Unless it is you who is the Queen's intelligence officer."

"That is another thing you must determine for yourself, my lady," he said with an infuriating wink that clearly confirmed her thoughts even as the carriage came to a halt. "Now, if you will, we are here."

"Wait," she said, "what was in that letter? I understand you were chased, and forced to go into the Thames before you were seen, but you must have read at least some of it before you dove in. What did it say?"

"Ah, but I did not," he said. "Or not enough, I should say. That is part of the problem—and why I am doing things that have made you so suspicious. And my dear stepmama, too, or so it seems. Yet you have long been aware I hold my tongue in the name of my grandparents' interests, as well as that of the Crown, so frowning at me the way you are at present will get you nowhere, even if I should wish your hands on me again."

He opened the door, letting down the stairs, and alighted, offering his hand. A moment later, she was blinking in the sunlight on the less crowded street that ran directly behind Jermyn Street, with the back door of Bardwell's Apothecary in her sights.

"You have brought me *here*? Why?" Then she realized Duncan had not been abducting her at all. He had not been about to take her to some shadowy place connected to the Bellowers. As usual, he had taken her to a place of safety.

She turned to find Duncan already back in the carriage, the door closing, and the landaulet's horses were being told to walk on. As the wheels turned and Petra felt the urge to stamp her foot, Duncan stuck his head out of the window. "Lady Caroline will know, my lady."

Petra stood flummoxed. "How do you mean? What will she know?"

Duncan then threw something out the window, which Petra caught easily. And she heard his voice as she realized it was Frances's apron.

"Why it took me but a few minutes to be at your side when you sent for me that night three years ago."

THIRTEEN

Wednesday, 21 June 1815
Bardwell's Apothecary
Jermyn Street
The three o'clock hour

"HE CLAIMS I WITHHOLD MY TRUST, BUT THAT IS FAR FROM the truth," Petra grumbled as she stomped the remaining steps to Bardwell's. "I am bloody well *too* trusting by half! Especially when it pertains to that frustrating man!" She was still muttering to herself when she pulled at the door. Then cursed, finding it locked.

Knocking once, then twice produced no joy. Though it was not surprising as Frances and Annie were likely still inundated with customers. A slight panic took hold when Petra instinctively went for her reticule and found it not about her wrist. Then she remembered she'd left it in Lottie's care so as to not be bogged down when she broke into Buckingham House. Only her lockpicks had not been in her reticule, had they?

Frantically, she clutched at the apron, rummaging in the pocket— it was empty, except for the sole pick that she had attempted to stab her attacker with before she'd discovered he was Duncan.

She groaned again, turning to lean back against the wall. When she had pulled off the apron in the carriage, she had vaguely registered a dull sound, but had thought little of it. It had been her lockpicks, and now they were gone. She would have to go all the way around to Jermyn Street to the front doors of the apothecary. And then she and Annie would have to hail a hackney to go back to Forsyth House to retrieve her older, larger set of lockpicks. Until, that was, she could find Duncan again and retrieve the ones of which she had grown so fond.

Then she heard a sound of rapid galloping—but it was not hoofbeats. Turning her head, she saw Sable racing toward her, ears flapping, something peacock green in her mouth. Farther down the street she saw a carriage, with Lottie's and Caroline's distinctive heads sticking out, and heard Fitz's excited bark.

"Oh, my darling, my clever girl," Petra enthused as Sable came to a halt at her feet and offered up the leather roll. Taking it, she bent to kiss Sable's head. "I can only assume you found Duncan and he gave them to you, yes?"

Sable's silky brown ears lifted at the sound of Duncan's name and her panting increased.

"Of course," Petra said dryly, watching Sable quiver and look about, as if she could find him once more. "If only he did not have that effect on both of us, my darling. If only."

Down the alley, Caroline and Lottie were heading her way, Fitz trotting at Lottie's side. Petra unrolled her picks and chose the ones best for the lock on the apothecary door. By the time her friends were halfway to her, she had the door open and was pulling it to her.

The door was rather heavy, however, and she had to stand aside to pull it back, which is the only thing that saved her from being struck by the whizzing, scented thing that flew just past her shoulder and hit the ground, and a voice called, "Take one more step, and you will wish you had not!"

Then suddenly, the air was filled with a dusty haze, and the smell was enough to make Petra gag after she managed to shout, "Frances! It is I, Petra!"

She felt someone grab her arm, and then she was being hauled into the back room of the apothecary. Sable leapt in after her, sneezing repeatedly. There were shouts and squeals from outside.

"Caro . . . Lottie . . . outside . . . ," Petra said through her coughs. "Lawks, what was that horrid-smelling thing?"

She heard rather than watched Frances go into a tirade of Spanish and then vaguely saw her cover her face with an apron and rush outside. Moments later, Lottie and Caro, coughing and gagging, were ushered into the safety of the back room.

Throwing the lock, Frances said with a grim smile, "It was my homemade flower bomb . . . with some ingredients in the middle to produce a foul-smelling haze upon impact. You do not wish to know what those ingredients are, trust me, but I've made them for years and keep them about for protection."

Through her watery eyes, Petra saw her friend's dark eyes looking fierce. Otherwise, the darkened room inside was making it impossible for her to make out more than several crates and what looked to be a pile of linens on the floor.

Caro and Lottie had both whipped out their fans, desperate for some air. Petra, having no fan at present, used her hand. "Flower bombs, indeed. Well, they do make for an excellent, and foul-smelling diversion if one is required. But why?"

Frances, however, had rushed toward the linen pile and dropped down beside it. Petra had to blink several times, her eyes still adjusting to the dim light, and then gasped, realizing it wasn't linens, but a person.

"Annie!" she cried out. A moment later, she, too, was down on the floor as Frances laid a damp cloth on Annie's forehead.

"I threw one of my flower bombs because someone broke in," Frances said, "and I fear they mistook Annie for me, and attempted to kill her."

Annie had not yet awakened, but showed signs that she would imminently. From out in the shop came the sounds of irritable customers, with shouts for someone to come take their coin so they might leave with their purchases.

"I am only grateful Teddy was already here," Frances said. "He is making certain no one attempts to leave without paying, but I have been back here in the storeroom for too long."

Lottie, fully recovered now from her run-in with the flower bomb, handed Petra her reticule and then held her hand out for Petra's apron. "Right, let me. It has been an age since I helped my uncle in his cheese shop in Thirsk, but I expect I won't be complete rubbish."

"And I shall help," Caroline said, glaring past the curtain, where a man was becoming loud and surly. With Lottie and Fitz following her, she marched out, trilling, "Will you please calm yourself, sir. Miss Reed will assist you, but only if you recall your manners."

"Will Annie be all right?" Petra asked worriedly, holding Annie's hand with both of hers as Frances gently checked Annie's scalp. "And what happened?"

"We had been having a lovely day," Frances said as she used nimble fingers to ascertain other injuries. "Annie here has been nothing short of a miracle all day. And Lottie and Caroline came by not long after you left for the orphanage. They helped me do some more arranging of the extra transparencies to take my mind off the swarm of customers. But it was Annie who kept things going until I found my strength again and felt myself once more."

"She is quite adept at that," Petra said through a tight throat.

Frances, seemingly satisfied to find no broken bones, folded a cloth and slid it beneath Annie's head for comfort as she continued. "As expected, things slowed down to a more reasonable pace after a while, and when Teddy came in, I insisted Annie take a tea break. Teddy then told me he thought he saw one of the customers slip into the back. But when I stuck my head in, I saw no one at first, though I heard the back door close." Frances met Petra's eyes. "It was when I looked down that I saw her here. I locked the back door in case the person who did this attempted to come back in. That was but a minute, no longer, before you picked the lock. Did you not see anyone?"

Petra shook her head, rubbing the back of Annie's hand. "There is more to explain, but let us just say that Duncan brought me here in a carriage with the curtains drawn—all but booting me out unceremoniously. I saw no one, and if Duncan did, he gave no indication of it when he drove off."

Frances nodded with a sigh. "There are several shops the man who assaulted Annie could have entered if he heard a carriage coming. He is long gone by now."

Frances rose to her feet and brought over a small bottle of reviving salts, waving it beneath Annie's nose, eliciting an immediate response. Petra watched as Annie's hazel eyes flickered open and, after a few seconds of blinking, focused on her.

"Oh, my lady," she said groggily. "I am terribly sorry, but I have quite the headache."

"I expect you do," Petra replied with a soggy grin. "Do you remember what happened?"

Annie frowned, which turned to a grimace of pain.

"Of course I do, my lady. I was struck upon the head by some odious man—though I never saw him. He came up behind me as I was having a cup of tea. His arm went round my neck and pulled me back against him. He asked where the gardens were. I thought it quite odd." Annie blinked again, adding thoughtfully, "And somehow, he knew I am a lady's maid, for I am now remembering that he called me an 'abigail.'"

Petra's brows knitted. "How strange. What exactly did he say?"

Annie recounted the words, wincing slightly as she did. "He said, *Where are the gardens, abigail? Who has it?* And rightly confused, I said, *I don't know what you mean, sir.* And then I felt a sharp pain on my head and everything went black. Though now I am wondering if in asking about the gardens, he meant the transparencies."

"How strange," Frances said. "It is possible, of course, but I saw no less than six transparencies that featured gardens."

"I did as well," Petra said. "Was there anything special about any of them?"

"We were so busy today, I only saw them for a moment," Frances said helplessly. "And whilst normally I take meticulous notes on what my customers purchase, with how quickly the transparencies were selling, I only noted it in my ledger as the item sold. I did not make the effort to write down the type of painting featured. Selling them will be a rare occurrence and have nothing to do with my customer's apothecary needs, so I did not think it necessary."

It was decided Annie's health was more important at the moment. Frances asked Annie to answer some questions, count to ten, and to confirm the number of dried marigold flowers she pulled from a bin. Only when Annie answered all correctly did Frances heave a sigh of relief.

"I am happy to report, Annie, that I do not believe you to have a concussion, and all you need is rest, and maybe some of my headache powders."

Caroline appeared then. "Dearest, my carriage is off on an errand, but should be returning quite soon. You both will ride with me to Forsyth House."

Lottie stuck her head in. "I did quite well at the till, if I may say so, Frances. There're only two customers left, both young hall maids on their afternoon off, going daft over your new tinted balms. I've told them they can stay, but I've locked the doors and closed the curtains for the time being. I thought a bit of peace and quiet might be helpful."

Then Teddy was there at Lottie's side, an apron about his waist hiding the frayed trousers that would mark him as a street urchin, his face breaking into a smile at seeing Annie being helped up and into a chair against the wall. "I'll look after Miss Frances when you leave, my lady. Won't let no 'arm come to 'er."

Petra's mind was suddenly feeling as sluggish as it seemed Annie's was, but she had not yet forgotten her mission.

"I thank you, Teddy, but it is most important that you do something else for me, if you can. I need you to locate a girl who has run away from the orphanage."

She told him only the pertinent facts about Nell Parker, including that she had once been a rough sleeper like himself and was thus familiar with London's streets.

"No matter what time you find her, even if it is the earliest hours of the morning, please bring her to me." Opening her coin purse, Petra insisted Teddy take some coins, explaining that he may require assistance from his friends and they should all be compensated.

"Do not forget, Petra, you and I are to attend Lady Sloan's dinner tonight," Caroline said as Petra poured Annie a glass of water. "Her ladyship's housekeeper was just here buying some peppermint syrup, in fact, and she informed me that both the Prince Regent and Prince Frederick are unwilling to leave London until after the dinner tonight. It will be truly an important evening, such that Lady Elizabeth is now helping her sister as hostess. Thus, we must be in attendance, and be scintillating."

Petra groaned, feeling more exhausted than ever. "I will go, but you must be scintillating for the both of us."

Then she realized the dinner party would be the perfect opportunity to speak with Caroline about the night Emerson died. *Indeed, I shall finally find out what Duncan claims I missed that night.*

"I should like to hear an excellent report of the evening," said Lottie, "and the dogs and I shall stay here with Frances and take good care of her." She then addressed Teddy. "Before you leave, do tell Lady Petra what you said about the man you saw. The one with the brown hair and wearing a Corinthian coat, who may have hurt Annie."

Teddy explained he noticed a man—"Wearing quite a dapper coat, 'e was"—who walked straight to the transparencies at the back of the apothecary.

"Acted a bit dodgy, 'e did. Looked about to see who noticed 'im as he took a gander at them transparencies. None of them screens seemed to be to 'is liking, though." Teddy shrugged. "Then the man were there one moment, and not the next. 'E just disappeared."

"Tell Lady Petra what you found strange about him," Lottie encouraged.

"Well, he wore a fine coat, yes, but his buckskins were ill-fitting," Teddy said in disapproving tones. "He would have cut a flash had it not been for them baggy bucks, he would."

"I meant the other thing," Lottie chided, giving him a gentle nudge with her elbow.

Now Teddy's blue eyes seemed hesitant. With a worried glance toward Petra he said, "I confess I did see a bit of him when he walked in, my lady. I couldn't be for certain, but he looked like one of Mr. Shawcross's men."

Petra's mind immediately sharpened. "The shadowy one from early this morning, Teddy? The one who threatened to thrash you?"

But he shook his head emphatically. "Not unless this bloke today could widen himself at will like frightened moggy," he said, giving a rather humorous impression of a puffed-out cat with its claws out and back arched, explaining the shadowy man was much bigger. Even Annie chuckled, which made Teddy smile.

Yet when Petra asked why he thought the man who had attacked Annie might be one of Duncan's men, Teddy became a bit subdued again.

"When Mr. Shawcross summons me for a job, I meet 'im outside a pub or in an alley," Teddy explained. "Once or twice, I seen Mr. Shawcross talkin' to a gentleman who looked much the same as this bloke today. Called him Rushton, he did, though Mr. Shawcross always sent Rushton away without making introductions. Can't say for certain it's the same man, though, my lady. The one from today—I only saw 'im for a moment, and I wouldn't want to accuse one of Mr. Shawcross's men, if you take my meaning."

"Of course. I won't mention it to him unless we know more," Petra said, but she did not like the sound of this. She also felt she had once known a Rushton, but could not recall any families in town for the season with that name. She looked to her friends for signs of recognition.

Lottie shook her head. Frances said she knew a family with that name. "But the Mr. Rushton I know has very little hair on his head, and is quite short in stature. As are all the Rushtons he is kin to, or so claims Mrs. Rushton."

"I cannot say I am acquainted with any gentlemen called Rushton," Caroline mused, "but I feel the name does sound familiar. I shall consult my diaries to be certain."

Teddy then was off like a rabbit, promising he would find Nell and bring her to Petra. Lottie returned to the till to allow the hall maids to pay for their purchases before ushering them out of the apothecary. Seconds later, Lady Caroline's carriage arrived, and Annie was bundled in, falling asleep with the help of Frances's headache powders almost instantly. Petra was about to step in when Frances held her back.

"Everything happened so quickly, I had almost forgotten," she said, digging in her apron pocket. "Do you remember that I said I believed Annie had been mistaken for me when she was attacked?"

Petra began to apologize for not asking sooner, but Frances waved her off.

"I can tell you have had a very long day, my friend. And I hope you will take some brandy in your tea and sleep before your outing tonight. But that is not why. I did not wish to alarm Lottie and Caroline—especially as I did not have time to ask what you told them about your investigation—"

"You may speak freely with them," Petra said, though she knew she had not entirely done so herself.

"Good," Frances said before continuing. "While I do not yet

know the significance of a transparency depicting gardens, I found this on the floor next to Annie."

She held out a small piece of paper that had been folded in half, and her eyes looked troubled.

"Petra, my father is the apothecary to Her Majesty, and I am the one who confirmed Mrs. Huxton's death at the orphanage. I am thinking it is possible the man saw Annie, who is dark-haired like me, working with the customers with such confidence as I usually do, and assumed she was me."

Unfolding the paper, Petra read what had now become a disturbingly familiar refrain.

Those who protect the Queen shall find an early grave.

Petra thought back to her three suspects, who were the only people besides the Queen and the duchess to know Frances had confirmed Mrs. Huxton's death as murder. Any one of them—even Nell, with her familiarity with London streets—might have had the ability to hire a man to attack Frances.

Then Petra recalled Annie saying her attacker had used the informal term for a lady's maid, calling her an "abigail." Taking in Frances's worried countenance, Petra knew her own must look similar.

"If Annie's attacker knew she was my lady's maid, then I think it is also possible this note was meant as a warning to me."

FOURTEEN

PETRA ACCEPTED A GLASS OF LEMONADE FROM A SILVER TRAY carried by a footman and then whisked open her pierced-ivory fan. "Lawks, it is a sultry night. I'm rather glad our hostesses allowed for all the windows to be opened."

Caroline waved her own fan lazily, causing the mother-of-pearl blades to sparkle in the candlelight as the two friends moved slowly through the crowd of dinner guests at Sloan House, well-situated on the western corner of St. James's Square.

"I insisted upon it, telling Lady Elizabeth that it would be a far better thing for the perspiring to begin after the dinner, when we move to the ballroom for the dancing." And when Petra giggled, Caroline looked her over with an accomplished eye. "I must say, that particular shade of hyacinth pink quite becomes you, dearest, and would likely still do even if we end up with reddened faces from the heat. You look quite yourself again, too, and I am happy to know Annie is on her way to recovering from her ordeal."

"Sleep and one of Mrs. Bing's excellent teas will do that for any person, as Annie and were happy to be reminded. I am grateful Annie is better, too, and I thank you for the compliment on my dress."

She barely recalled arriving at Forsyth House, however. Or assuring her butler, Smithers, and her exceedingly concerned footman, Charles, that Annie was well but needed looking after.

And she could not recall at all asking that her young housemaid, Enid, wake her in time to be readied for Lady Sloan's ball, but she must have. Regardless, she fell onto her bed and was in the throes of sleep without even the help of the brandy Frances had advised.

Poor Enid had quite the time waking her, too, for she did not yet know all of Annie's tricks to keep Petra from falling back asleep. These included throwing open the curtains with a flourish and making far too much noise gathering items in Petra's dressing room. And, as of late—marking Annie's most diabolical ploy to date—throwing a stick for Sable in Petra's bedchamber and feigning shock when the stick—and, thus, Sable—happened to land squarely on Petra's backside.

Nevertheless, Enid eventually accomplished her task by using one of Annie's time-honored schemes of nattering on incessantly until Petra finally roused herself, begging for some silence while secretly appreciating the housemaid's tactics.

Caroline, in a lovely dress the color of thistle flowers, turned in a slow arc in Lady Sloan's dining room, appreciating the decorations as she kept one eye on the arriving guests.

"Do be careful, dearest," she said under her breath, "but the Dowager Marchioness of Langford has just arrived—and on the arm of her son, the marquess, no less. I do find it odd sometimes how much Duncan and James resemble one another, yet they are quite opposite in color."

Using the pretense of sipping on her lemonade, Petra let her eyes casually move in that direction, then nearly spit out her drink, hissing through nearly closed lips, "You did not tell me she was staring right at me. She is even ignoring our hostesses!"

"What do you think 'do be careful' meant?" Caroline said out of the corner of her mouth as both inclined their heads graciously toward the dowager marchioness.

In return, Duncan's stepmama gave them both a rather icy look, and did not reciprocate until James, noticing the two, smiled and graced them with a bow. Finally, and with nearly palpable dislike—much to the obvious concern of Lady Sloan and Lady Elizabeth—the dowager marchioness finally gave Petra and Caroline each a stiff tilt of her head.

"Did you know Lady Vera calls her the Dowager Viperess?" Petra asked as they turned away.

Caroline bit her lip, but one of her throaty laughs escaped nonetheless, turning the heads of several men, including her paramour, Lord Whitfield.

Broad of chest and slim of hip, he was standing next to portly Prince George, who was telling some story that had everyone dutifully looking enthralled. Petra all but heard Caroline start to purr as Whitfield's intensely blue eyes locked onto her.

Caroline had never been short of admirers, but Lord Whitfield seemed to have captured her friend's heart, which made Petra glad and concerned in equal parts.

On one hand, the two were well-matched, and Whitfield seemed as besotted with Caroline as she was with him. Yet Caroline and Whitfield could never marry, and he had recently confessed he both wanted and needed an heir. They both knew Caroline could not legitimately provide him with one, though Petra was aware that her friend secretly wished she could.

At least Caroline had not seen what Petra had just a few minutes earlier, when an eager mama pulled her daughter over to make Whitfield's acquaintance, and it was clear the pretty, fresh-faced young woman was more than willing. While Whitfield's smile was tight as he bowed to the girl, Petra felt it would likely be only another social season at most before he took a wife and Caroline's heart would be badly broken. Until that happened, though, she would encourage her friend's happiness. Especially when Whitfield looked at Caroline the way he was now.

"Goodness," Petra said with a smirk. "I have never seen a man who can express such naughty behavior without saying a word. And from across a room as well."

"Have you not?" replied Caroline, scandalously refusing to look away, even when one of the ladies in the group noted where Whitfield was staring. "Then you clearly stopped noticing the way Shawcross looks at you."

"No, you are correct. Duncan's gaze could light that fireplace in a trice," Petra said, nodding to the huge fireplace fronted with two lovely flower arrangements instead of a blaze as the weather was so warm.

Caroline broke eye contact with Whitfield in order to give her attention to Petra.

"I am not certain I have ever heard such a romantic statement spoken in such a melancholy way. And you have been rather irritable all day when anyone has mentioned Shawcross. You have not gone off him, have you?"

"I do not think I could ever go off Duncan," Petra said, then felt surprised she had said it, and knew it to be the truth. "Not entirely, at least. I think my heart has been linked with his from our first meeting."

"Then whatever is the matter?" Caroline's eyes widened. "He is not insisting the two of you marry simply because you two are doing rather naughty things every night, is he?"

"No, it is not that," Petra said hastily. She hesitated, stopped a footman carrying glasses of wine. She took two, then looked at Caroline. "You may wish for one as well."

"It is that bad, is it?" Caroline drawled, and took a glass for herself.

Tucking themselves in an alcove behind a large potted plant while a small orchestra played Bach's "Air on the G String," Petra tossed back her first glass of wine, placing the empty glass in a niche holding a painting of a little copper-colored dog being held by Lord and Lady Sloan's young son. Then she reached into her reticule and pulled out the incriminating piece of paper that had dropped from her book this morning. Like habitually touching a bruise even though she knew the pain it would bring, she could not stop herself from reading the last two sentences that referenced how Emerson had come to be murdered.

Am told no accident. Contrived by Shawcross himself.

She began at the beginning, telling Caroline everything. Her friend paled, gasped, clutched Petra's free hand, and said, "Oh, dearest. How unbelievably horrid!"

But as the tale went on, she was forced to shush Caroline when her friend said, "He found you when you broke into Buckingham House?" a bit too loudly.

And, later, she began to feel as if giving the cutty-eye might be her new lot in life when Caroline's eyes still managed to light up after hearing how Petra had searched Duncan's person.

"Dearest, how did you not ride astride when his fall was down and the rest of him was up? I've done so with my Whitfield in his carriage; it is delicious fun."

"*Caroline*," Petra said before tipping half her second glass of wine down her throat.

"Well, why not?" Caroline said. "You know Shawcross is innocent of what you are suggesting, and we all know you two are desperately in love, so what is the problem?"

"How?" Petra said. "How do I know he is innocent? I want so badly to trust his word, but with everything that has happened, I feel as if I need more proof."

Caroline swirled her wine as she regarded Petra.

"You are already aware Shawcross handles business of a sometimes less-than-clear nature. Of likely a less-than-lawful nature at times as well. You did not seem to have an issue with it before."

"That is because I never knew it had anything to do with me before."

"Indeed," Caroline said, her words heavy with meaning.

Petra's tone was a bit mulish. "You are saying I willingly accepted it before, but now that his duplicitousness, warranted or not, is directed at me, I am suddenly saying he should not be allowed to be so."

"I think it is only natural to feel as such, but it is the truth," Caroline replied. "Though if I may be allowed for a moment to defend Shawcross . . ."

Petra first took another gulp of wine, gesturing with her glass to proceed, adding, "Mm, yes, he said I should ask you about the night Emerson died. That is, how it was Duncan was able to be at my side within minutes even though he was lodging across Mayfair at Hillmorton House. Do tell."

Caroline's brown eyes suddenly softened. "You clearly do not recall. But I did tell you the reason. I told you the day after Emerson's death. It was a small detail at the time, and considering your state, I am not surprised you do not recall our talking of it."

When Petra could do little but look confused, Caroline reminded her that, three years earlier, she and her captain were remodeling Smythe House and had thus rented a town house on Great Swallow Street, only one street over from Duncan's previous lodgings on Chaffinch Lane. On the fateful night that changed Petra's life, Caroline had arranged a small supper party. Duncan had attended, but Petra and Emerson had never arrived.

"*Everyone* could guess why—well, except my captain's niece, who was visiting and far too innocent at the time. But that is neither here nor there. What is pertinent is that Shawcross—miserable as he was at your impending marriage—began drinking . . . and kept drinking."

"He did?" Petra asked, giving her head a little shake as if to clear out a memory cobweb. "But no, your supper was *two* nights before, was it not?"

"I can show you my diary, if you like," Caroline teased, though not unkindly. "Speaking of, I discovered through perusing my diaries that we *did* once make the acquaintance of a Mr. Rushton. He was a guest at one of my house parties, in fact. It was quite some time ago, so I am not surprised we do not recall him. He was a friend of both Emerson and Shawcross from Oxford."

"He was?" Petra felt a mixed surge of hope and apprehension, but Caroline quickly dashed both.

"Indeed, but I think he is unlikely to be the man who hurt Annie—if our Teddy was correct and that was the hateful man's name in the first place. For one thing, Teddy said the man he saw was thin and brown-haired, and I wrote in my diary that the Mr. Rushton of our acquaintance was both fair of hair and rather shaped like an egg with arms and legs."

Petra sighed and sipped her wine, giving Caroline an expectant look over the rim of her glass.

"Right. It seems I have digressed. Though do remind me to tell you what I found in my diary, for there was scandalous behavior involving Rushton and the companion of—"

"Caro, darling. I do adore you, but if you would be so kind as to finish your story about Duncan . . ."

"Fine, dearest. Now where was I? Oh, yes. My captain and I were most concerned about Shawcross, neither of us ever having seen him drink so much wine. He attempted to take his leave and ride back to Hillmorton House, but when he could not even stand atop the mounting block without swaying, we prevented him from leaving."

Petra was still attempting to reconcile this in her mind. She was certain Caroline's dinner, which she had been scheduled to attend with Emerson, had been two nights before his death, not the very last evening she would ever spend in the arms of her fiancé.

"In the end," Caroline continued, "I convinced Shawcross to stay and drink tea with me until he could walk ten steps in a straight line. My captain eventually retired to his rooms, yet Shawcross and

I talked in my drawing room until three o'clock in the morning, and then we both fell asleep. Both still impeccably dressed and on separate sofas, you understand."

"That was the reason Duncan was able to come to my aid so quickly? Because he was at your rented town house, and not at his grandmama's?"

"It was," Caroline confirmed, nodding. "When you sent his stable lad for him, the boy knew Shawcross was only a street over." Caroline took her hand and squeezed it. "Petra, I can account for his whereabouts from nine o'clock the previous evening until nearly four the next morning, when he raced to your aid. Whatever he may have done, Shawcross could not have taken Emerson's life."

Petra nodded, though still getting used to the idea, she asked the first thing that came to her mind, "What did you two talk of that night, Caroline?"

"Why, politics," Caroline replied. "Well, we did later. When he was still foxed from wine, we spoke mostly of our days at Buck-fields. How both of us—he the by-blow of a marquess, and I the daughter of a loving duke and a horrid duchess—could have found ourselves entangled with a spoilt, headstrong, stubborn, pony-mad, intelligent—did I already say obstinate?"

"You chose a synonym, yes," Petra murmured dryly.

"Bloody wonderful ray of strong and utterly loyal sunshine that is Lady Petra Forsyth. The whole conversation was rather sicken-ing, I must say," Caroline said with a grin, adding, "but as he sobered we moved on to equally sobering talk."

"But of what specifically?" Petra pressed.

"Well, we spoke of Parliament, and MPs, and of the royal family, and how our country was best governed." Caroline's full lips twisted to one side as she recollected. "I remember feeling as if he might be wondering where my loyalties lay—and yours, too, which sur-prised me a bit. I remember feeling as if he thought Emerson was influencing you in a way he did not like."

"He did?" Petra's brows tilted inward. "He never said as much."

"Dearest, you were so besotted with Emerson, would you have listened?" Caroline said gently. "Nevertheless, I told him that you and I felt the same. That we are loyal to our King and Queen, but did not believe in a divine right to rule. That if we were gentlemen who could vote, we would both be torn between the Tories and the Whigs, for both had their good points and bad points, and that we both highly doubted that would ever change. That overall, we are glad we have a Parliament, but wished there were many, many more rights for women, if not rights equal to men."

"Hear, hear," Petra could not keep from saying, then asked, "And what did he say about his own loyalties? I know what he has professed to me over the years, but I should like to hear what he told you." Caroline did not even hesitate in her answer.

"I was rather shocked at how much he sounded like us—at least in his loyalty to the King and Queen, if maybe not the Crown in general. Though he, too, wanted much better things. He wished for more rights for the common man, and for women. Home rule for Scotland and Ireland, naturally. That the Tories and Whigs would come together more often and compromise. That our monarchs should better educate themselves as to the way the rest of London lives and such. We've talked about it several times since, actually. Mostly when we are having a game of cards and you are curled up on the couch, asleep, snoring with your mouth open."

Petra lightly swatted her oldest friend with her fan, insisting that she did not snore while marveling at how much better a friend who managed to say the right things could make one feel.

A weight seemed to lift from her heart. She had what she had been yearning for ever since the moment this morning that had shattered all that she had held as the truth. She had absolute proof that Duncan had not taken Emerson's life.

And what of the idea that he had ordered someone to do so? asked a contrary part of her mind. However, it was quickly deflected, if not wholly answered, with the memory from being in the landaulet with him earlier today. By the way Duncan had confessed the truth of that night from three years ago.

"There was a moment where I thought I would be forced to do so, or to order it done, yes. In the end, however . . ."

Petra still did not entirely understand what he had meant, but she had come to believe one thing. That deep in her gut, she did not believe Duncan would have sent someone else to carry out such an order on a man who had been his friend.

No, if he'd been forced in his capacity as an agent for the monarchy to do such an odious deed, he would have done it himself. He would not have allowed another the chance to induce needless suffering, whether by accident or a cruel heart. And the fact that Duncan had not sent a proxy meant that the evil man responsible was someone else entirely.

Petra finished her wine, deciding that, if the questions remained in her heart and mind, she would think more on them after dinner. She would also soon confront her feelings of mistrust, which she knew would not go away so easily, despite her wish that they would. But for now, she simply allowed her heart to feel a bit of peace.

Caroline linked their arms and they left the alcove just as the dinner gong was sounding.

"What I shall never forget is when the stable lad arrived, Shawcross thought Emerson had attacked you, which my captain and I both thought preposterous. But I recall Shawcross grabbing the stable lad by the collar and bellowing"—Caro lowered her voice to a deep whisper marked with a rather terrible Scottish accent—*"Did Ingersoll or his bloody associates hurt Lady Petra? Did they, lad? Tell me!* And when the poor, frightened lad couldn't say, I have never seen a man run so fast as Duncan ran to you."

"Associates?" Petra repeated, as a few steps away the Prince Regent offered his arm to Lady Sloan while Prince Frederick did the same with Lady Elizabeth to escort them into dinner. Lord Whitfield was striding toward Caroline, looking intent. "What could Duncan have meant?"

"I could not tell you, dearest. But what is that noise? Is there a mob in St. James's Square?"

Suddenly, the music stopped and everyone was rushing to the open windows to look outside. Petra, Caroline, and Whitfield managed to take one of the windows directly over the front door of Sloan House.

"There!" shouted someone, and Petra saw the mob moving—no, running alongside—a post-chaise and four bearing two somewhat tattered French eagle standards, the flags whipping as the horses trotted at a fast clip. It pulled up to Sloan House, and the carriage door was flung open from the inside. Without waiting for the stairs to be let down, a man leapt from the carriage, dusty and haggard, carrying a French flag in each hand.

"It is Major Percy, Wellington's man!" shouted Whitfield, and the crowd turned as one as the sounds of a man running upstairs could be heard.

Moments later, Major Percy burst through the doors with a veritable swarm of footmen and servants following, though they stopped at the threshold, their eyes popping with excitement. Percy pushed past a couple of well-dressed men and strode up to the Prince Regent. He dropped to one knee and laid the French eagles at the Prince's feet as he cried out, "Victory, sir! Victory!"

FIFTEEN

THE CHEERS WERE DEAFENING. EVERYONE WAS KISSING, embracing, and jumping up and down as the orchestra broke into a jaunty military march.

"Come, dance with us, dearest!" Caroline said. "The war is over! We have won!"

Petra pulled her eyes away from Major Percy to the doorway in which he had come through, finding the servants were dancing and embracing as well. One, however, was not dressed in livery. Instead, he looked to be a delivery man, and he indulgently accepted a handshake offered by the butler.

"Why, it is Mr. Fife," Petra said. "He has been rather busy today."

Lady Elizabeth was passing by and heard this. "Oh yes, he was good enough to deliver a new cask of wine—and not tell my sister I was the one who ordered the cask of vinegar earlier." She then put her finger to her lips and let out a merry laugh as she was borne away by a handsome viscount to join in the revelry.

Briefly, Petra thought to cross the room to ask Mr. Fife more about the extra transparencies he had delivered this morning, but then thought better of it. Especially as, from the other doorway, she witnessed James, Lord Langford, listening with a vexed expression to his mother, the dowager marchioness.

Whatever his mama was saying, she was angry enough that the tendons on her neck stood out. She put her hand on James's arm, and he jerked it away, silencing her with a few words. Her face blanched in return. James then pushed through the door, which Petra knew led out to a staircase, and left his mama standing there, looking about to cry. Everyone else was celebrating and did not notice the interaction, or James slipping away.

"I cannot believe it," Petra said. "Someone was actually able to silence her." Then she sighed. "And I cannot believe I am feeling badly for the viperess now."

"What was that, Lady Petra?" Whitfield shouted over the growing din, a wide smile upon his handsome face. Caroline was on one arm and he offered her his other.

She took it with both hands, instantly feeling the hard muscle beneath his coat, and the combination of such a handsome specimen of a man, the elation of winning the war, and two glasses of wine on a nearly empty belly made her giggle.

On any given day, she might briefly take the hand or arm of a man who helped her up a set of stairs or out of the carriage, but today she had touched three men enough to truly remember that their sex was most definitely not created equal. Mr. Fife's arm was soft as a pillow, Whitfield's was hard and thick like a tree trunk, and Duncan's arm—well, the entirety of him was all lean muscle, like a splendid, powerful racehorse. The thought made her teeter a bit.

"No, no," Petra said, releasing Whitfield's arm and waving him off with a laugh when he gallantly tried to re-persuade her. "I had rather too much wine, and I fear I may fall over. Off you go, then."

Turning back toward the windows, she found herself semi-hidden behind another large potted plant, and through the leaves she caught sight of the servants again. They were all chattering away and embracing each other without reserve, and with the wine in her giving her extra bonhomie, she looked upon the scene with soft eyes.

At the back was the tall Mr. Fife again, a half smile on his face as he watched the members of the ton celebrating. Now that she was truly observing him, Petra found herself thinking he looked familiar when he smiled like that. Indeed, he'd had a recent shave and his curly sideburns had been slicked into submission with some pomade, reducing his scruffy appearance.

Then he turned and moved off, passing a rather large candelabra that made his brownish hair glint a golden hue. *Goodness, he looks almost handsome,* she thought, then covered her mouth with her gloved hand to try to stop her fit of giggles, complete with snorts.

Then one of the housemaids attempted to stop Mr. Fife and kiss his cheek, and Petra's eyebrows raised at seeing his face briefly harden with disapproval, as if a young woman should not be so forward. The housemaid, too, was taken aback as Mr. Fife walked away, but was soon being happily pulled into a jig by a handsome footman.

But Petra herself could not quit the thought that seeing Mr. Fife walking off alone was an opportunity to ask him about the transparencies, specifically those painted with garden scenes. Glancing about and seeing the rest of the servants were craning their necks to catch sight of both princes offering a toast to Major Percy, she took her chance.

She slipped down the hall Mr. Fife had taken. Upon finding a door closing slowly on silent hinges, she was certain she was close behind, and was soon lifting the hem of her skirt to faster take the stairs.

The cheers and singing from Londoners outside Sloan House were thunderous as she opened a servants' entrance leading to a short alley. Peeking around the door, the light being cast from Lady Sloan's dining room above gave enough visibility that she could see the shadow of a man walking away, toward the square.

Before she could consider a more judicious action, she was out the door and following, her pink silk reticule swinging from her wrist. Her soft shoes meant she made little sound, and soon she could see the back of Mr. Fife just before he reached the end of the alley, turning right, away from Sloan House.

"Mr. Fife?" she said, just as the music came to a loud crescendo upstairs. She lifted her hems again and trotted after him, only to stop when she heard a familiar voice a few feet away, speaking just loud enough to be heard above the din.

"Bloody hell, man. I told you not to risk it."

Duncan.

Petra flung herself back against the stone wall of what she realized were the mews of Sloan House and did not dare move upon hearing the menacing tone in his voice. One that rounded his vowels and clipped every word, making him sound more English than she had heard in some time.

Petra felt he must be talking to Mr. Fife, for the delivery man had just turned the corner moments earlier. But how strange. Did Duncan know Mr. Fife? And was it conceivable the genial delivery man was a part of the radical group called the Bellowers? Or was Mr. Fife secretly one of Duncan's men? Oh, the vexation at not knowing what to fully believe!

From where she stood against the wall, she could see groups of happy Londoners celebrating in the square. Most carried lanterns, which twisted and flitted about like dozens of giant fireflies as revelers moved in and out of crowds, with the level of sound rising and falling at the same time. As such, she had to strain to hear Mr. Fife's reply.

But it was not Mr. Fife's East End voice she heard, though. Instead, this voice was just as clipped as Duncan's, and she recognized it just as quickly.

James, Lord Langford. This is why his mama was so upset, Petra thought. *The dowager marchioness knew James was leaving the party to meet Duncan!*

She reminded herself too that the brothers would not wish to be seen speaking in front of Mr. Fife. The delivery man would not have lingered, either. He no doubt would have rushed past the marquess and Duncan with some haste.

"Yet I learned excellent intelligence whilst there," James said. "They trusted me, Shawcross. Even more so than you."

"But what you did?" Duncan retorted. "It was an unnecessary risk. You've always been impulsive, but this was—"

The response came so quickly, it was like the strike of a snake.

"We may share our father's name and blood, Shawcross, but I am the marquess. The *legitimate* heir, and thus I will thank you to show me the respect I am due. If our access to ready coin is being compromised by this unexpected development, especially now that the war is won, then we must act, and with haste. For we have three days at best, and likely fewer. And if you will not, Shawcross, then I shall. Now bloody well move out of my way so that I may return to Sloan House."

Petra had gone still, shrinking back as best she could against the stone wall, feeling its roughness against her back. As lanterns bobbed in the square, she witnessed James striding across her field of vision, looking smug and confident.

"I say," came another voice. "That was nearly the limit."

Petra edged sideways a bit in an attempt to better hear over all the celebrating in the square. Someone else—a man—was there with Duncan. Or had he just arrived? Nevertheless, by his diction and the slightly lazy delivery of one born to the upper classes, it certainly was not Mr. Fife. Petra held her breath, waiting for Duncan's reply.

"Mm, yes. I may be the bastard by birth, but he has always been the one to earn the sobriquet."

"Yet Langford rather has a point, do you not agree?" said the other man. "About the unexpected development hindering our action—not about you being a bastard, of course."

"He is not wrong, no. We must act, and soon, to secure our ability to obtain the blunt we need for our cause to succeed."

Wanting desperately to see the man who was speaking to Duncan, Petra went to peek around the corner, then stopped abruptly when some heat came into the other man's voice.

"It has been three years since our last attempt, and shall likely be three more if we cannot advance our cause. Yet I shall allow London to celebrate tonight. Thereafter, we will use our might to make significant change to our country."

"Three years ago, the cause did not have *me*," Duncan said.

"Not that I did not attempt it, Shawcross," the other man retorted. Then his voice eased. "Though I do admit that it was rather silly of me to try when we were all having such a pleasant afternoon. I did tell my cousin that later, when he was certain I had mucked it all up with my eagerness."

"Your cousin was the one to pike off," Duncan said bitterly. "If not for his cowardice, Great Britain might already be a republic."

At this pronouncement, Petra felt a trickle of sweat run down her temple even as the rest of her went cold.

"True," said the other man. "But if our plan goes as we think it will, then it will be much better. Swifter. More powerful."

"Then why are you keeping the details secret from all but a handful?" Duncan asked, anger biting off his words. "I can understand not wishing to tell the entire association at present, for too many cannot keep their lips from becoming loosened after the slightest amount of ale. But to keep those in your highest ranks from knowing your plans? Especially one such as I? Have I not proven myself worthy of our needs?"

"You have," the man replied, and it was then that Petra realized the man she could not see must be the leader of the radical reformists known as the Bellowers, or one of them, at least. "What you have procured for us has been invaluable. However, you have been part of our cause for less than a twelvemonth. And the marquess only one month and a fortnight at best." His voice turned thoughtful. "Though how keen he became after we opened his eyes to what could be. It was quite gratifying."

"Indeed. And legitimate marquess or not, my brother and I are one of but a handful with connections to the ton," Duncan said, a growl beneath his voice. "And the others, though they may be able to move votes in the House of Lords, they cannot give you the access to the highest levels of the Crown like we can. One of us, my brother or I, should know the time and place, especially as time is of the essence."

"I shall think on it," mused the other man. "You are aware, just as the others are, that there shall be a sign—a pathway to follow to the righteousness that will be doled out upon those with royal blood."

He paused, as shouts of "Victory!" could be heard in the distance, and then bonhomie threaded his voice.

"I must be off, Shawcross. Tonight, we enjoy ourselves. And then the true victory shall be *ours*."

Though Petra heard Duncan make a reply of agreement, noted with a frown a level of zeal in his tone, she heard not his exact words due to a sudden swell in the cheering within the square. When it died down, the other man was chuckling.

"I could not agree more," he said. "Now, as Lady Petra is likely enjoying pheasant and some excellent red wine at the moment and therefore you cannot enjoy *her*, I have arranged for a lovely lot of Cyprians to offer us their favors. Or so the ladybirds wearing their Sunday finest would like us to believe. You'll find them on the north side of the square. Tell them their suitor sent you—it is the code."

Duncan's reply was unintelligible, but sounded amused. *The rakehell,* she thought hotly.

"Speaking of the beautiful Lady Petra," the man said, the same easiness still in his voice, with something new added in that sent a slice of apprehension straight into Petra's belly, "she is getting too close. We agreed to leave the Earl of Holbrook's daughter alone so long as she acted like a lady should and stuck to making social calls and embroidery. But she is acting on behalf of the Queen, *my* lady tells me, and has discovered too much."

Petra's lips parted. *His lady?* Could this radical have a wife, or simply a paramour, within the ton?

It rather seemed Duncan was curious too, for she heard him say dryly, "And yet you keep her as secret as your plans."

The man chuckled, but when his voice grew fainter, as if he had moved off, Petra's curiosity shifted abruptly as she just heard him say, "You will keep her on a lead, Shawcross."

"Oh, should he indeed?" Petra muttered darkly. "Well, I should like to see him try it."

SIXTEEN

SOMEWHERE IN THE BACK OF HER MIND, PETRA KNEW THE
wave of anger that swept over her made her reckless. Yet it did not
stop her from following after Duncan into St. James's Square.

*My trust in him has only just returned, and now I hear him
talking about radical activities? And what is just as vexing is that the
Dowager Marchioness of Langford was correct. Duncan has pulled
his brother into such perverse notions!*

"Blast it all," she said aloud, though the din was so loud that no
one heard her.

Duncan was heading toward the north side of the tree-filled
square, where the Cyprians were supposedly stationed, and she
was not about to allow him to partake of their so-called favors. Just
like she would not let any man put her on a lead.

Normally, a woman walking alone at night, even in St. James's
Square, would be looked upon with great suspicion at the very
least. Would be the subject of derisive gossip, to be sure, and very
likely run the risk of meeting someone unsavory who wished to
harm her. But tonight was a different matter.

Petra followed Duncan, the lantern lights bobbing about helping her keep him in her sights. She wended her way through celebrating men, women, and children, plus more dogs than she could
count, and even a few rather brave cats. The Londoners were from
all areas of the city, and all classes, it seemed.

Had she not been on a mission, determination straightening her
spine, she would have been in delighted awe at the incredible lack
of adherence to societal rules. She even saw few women wearing
their bonnets, and thus knew she would not be seen as strange for

not having one on her at all. Indeed, everyone was smiling, and singing, and dancing about. Some musicians had set up in the square and were playing country dances. It was a wonderful sight, with the always moving lantern lights making for a magical illumination of their own.

And then Duncan moved behind the musicians, looking about for someone. No one was paying them any attention, so she ran the last few steps and whirled around, planting herself in his path with her fists upon her hips.

"Keep me on a lead, Duncan Shawcross? You could no more do so if you tried. Who was that man you were speaking with?"

While several curse words issued from his lips, he somehow did not entirely look surprised to see her. And then, suddenly, there was cheering, and a line of people forming to Petra's right side. A familiar jaunty tune was being played on a scratchy violin. Then Duncan was reaching for her hands, pulling them from her hips to hold them outstretched.

"Are you in jest? We are dancing?" Petra shouted over the music.

"It rather seems we must!" And then they were galloping sideways down a line of clapping dancers that had seemed to appear out of nowhere.

Reaching the end, Duncan did not release her hands and help form the end of the line as they should. Instead, he folded her hand into his, and then she was running alongside him down another mews alley, her reticule grasped in her other hand to keep it from banging at her side.

Once in nearly complete darkness save for the light coming from the square, he pulled her to a stop and turned to face her.

"How did you find me, and how much did you hear?" he asked, with surprisingly little irritation in his voice. The clip was gone, replaced by the rolling *R*s of his mother tongue.

"I wished to speak with the man who delivered the wine to Sloan House," she said, somewhat absently, for her mind was concentrating on a realization. While there was always some evidence of his birthplace in Duncan's speech, there had been almost no sign of it when talking to the unseen leader of the Bellowers. And the only time she ever heard his burr nearly completely absent was . . . when he was lying.

"You were not being truthful with that man," she said, half impressed, half accusingly. And then she thought on the moment that she'd witnessed James stalking away. He'd been smirking, yes, but was it at Duncan's expense? Instead, she replayed the moment in her mind, and understood James's expression was the self-satisfied look of someone who felt they had convincingly played a part. "And you and James—the horrid way he spoke to you—that was all a farce?"

To her wonderment, far from causing Duncan to be cross that she hadn't come to this conclusion earlier, his lips twitched up and the bit of light that came down the alley emphasized the crinkles at the edges of his eyes. But it didn't last.

"I have spent over one year infiltrating this group, Petra. First whilst still on the Continent, and then here. I have slowly walked the finest of lines to make them believe I was falsely true to my grandparents, whilst still keeping Their Graces' good favor—and whilst keeping any involvement away from the prying eyes of the ton as well. And yes, that meant keeping the secret from you as well, for it was important that you were believably, blissfully unaware." His voice went rough with emotion. "Though it all but brought me to my knees every time I knew I must deceive you."

Petra was silent for a moment as she digested this. "And your brother?"

"Going to James for help . . . well, at first I would have rather strolled over hot coals—and it rather felt like I was. Until he finally realized that working alongside me for the greater good would be something that might actually give him a proper purpose." Now a growl finally came into his voice. "And you could have very nearly undone all of it if you were seen following me."

"I do not believe anyone saw me," she retorted.

"You would not even know if they did," Duncan said, arms akimbo. "Some of the more dangerous of the Bellowers have had years keeping to the shadows and blending in so that they are unseen. Until they are ready to strike out, that is. This association, as they call themselves, is otherwise made up mostly of men of the working class, as are most reformist groups. But they have also managed to recruit a dozen or more from the peerage and the gentry. Petra, you could be sitting directly next to a Bellower tonight at Lady Sloan's and not even know it."

"I—" she began, then Duncan took her hand again.

"I must return you to Sloan House safely nonetheless."

He turned to lead her back out into the square, then stilled. He looked down the alley, then back down at Petra.

"What is it?" she said. She heard voices, but not ones she recognized.

"Forgive me," he said, and for the second time that day, he maneuvered her back against the wall.

He pulled on his flatcap again, dragging it low, then yanked down the sleeves of her dress so that her shoulders were bared, and the top of her bodice just barely covered her modesty. Then, before she could breathe, her skirts were in one of his hands and the other was bringing up her right leg to hook it around his upper thigh. Two fingers slid beneath the silk garter holding up her stocking, making her arch involuntarily as his rough fingers found a bit of her soft skin.

Then his mouth was on her neck as he used his forehead to encourage her to turn her head away from the street. At the same time, he took her left hand, sliding it underneath his coat, down his hip, and wrapping her fingers around something very hard.

It was the handle of his dagger, in a scabbard still tied to his person, but higher up so that she had not seen it. Its handle had been wrapped in soft suede ribbon, giving her excellent grip.

And then she heard what Duncan must have. The sounds of a man who was drunk, cocky, and leading a group of other men from the square right down their alley.

"Oh-ho-ho! Look who we found, chaps," slurred one of the men. "She's a pretty thing, ain't she? 'Ow 'bout I 'ave a go after you, Shawcross?" His words then dissolved into a drunken guffaw that seemed to get closer.

"Only if you don't want to have to explain to your wife why you came home with your tallywags stuffed in your mouth, Caufield," Duncan snarled, his lips barely leaving Petra's exposed throat and his hand tightening on her thigh. "There're more like this to be had on the north side of the square. Code word is 'suitor.' Now be on your way and let me finish showing this one my mettle."

There was a pause that was filled with tension, then Petra could hear the man backing away, saying, "Were only a jest, Shawcross. North side of the square, you say? C'mon, lads, ain't likely ta be no other night we can mix giblets with a fancy piece in St. James's Square . . ."

When the whoops of the other men died away and the sound of general merrymaking returned, Duncan released her, pulling up her sleeves with a gentleness that belied the harsh anger on his face, and pushing a loose curl behind her ear. Before she could even utter a word, though, he'd taken her by the hand again and led her down the alley, away from the square. This time, she let him, lifting her hems and trotting to keep up with his long strides.

Halfway down, with little light to be had, Petra could only hear the frustrated strain in Duncan's voice.

"That man, Caufield? He likes killing, Petra, and had he not been enough in his cups to want a woman instead of bloodshed . . ."

"If you wish me to apologize, I will not," she snapped, the tension from moments earlier still coursing through her. Then she bit back any further retorts, reminding herself to have a little sense. "Though I am cognizant I put us in undue danger and I thank you for protecting me. Thus, you may stop chastising me now."

They had found a corner, with a greenish light coming from a window up ahead. When Duncan pulled her to a stop, she realized it was a transparency—a pastoral scene with grazing cows she recognized from Bardwell's Apothecary. And the verdant luminosity only added another layer of intensity to Duncan's blazing green eyes.

"I will not stop chastising you, Petra. I expect you left that dinner without anyone knowing where you were going. You followed a man you did not even know. You ran the risk of being seen by him, of ruining what my brother and I have worked so damn hard to do. We are trying to stop a group of violent people—trying to determine when and where the Bellowers' show of force will be. But you followed me in the square, for anyone to see. And after that? I had to treat you like a cheap ladybird, and very nearly had to attempt to fight off five drunken men who enjoy violence. Do you have any idea what they would have done to you if I could not have deterred them?"

Yanking off his flatcap, he rushed a hand through his hair, breathing hard. And then he was leading her again, down another alley, through a mews, and down yet another street until they were once more nearing Sloan House. Under his breath, he kept up a Gaelic-infused tirade about it being his fate in life to not be able to refuse impetuous, headstrong women with freckles across their nose in the pattern of Cassiopeia.

Then, somehow, he had led her back to the servants' door she had exited earlier. As the musicians were still playing a jaunty tune in the dining room, her absence might not yet have even been noticed.

"Locked," he said, pulling at the door with another curse.

"Let me," Petra said quietly, and pulled out her lockpicks from her reticule.

Duncan waited with hands on his hips for her to work, and when the lock clicked open and she stored her picks once more in her reticule, his shoulders dropped a bit. Then he reached out again, his fingers just touching another of her loosened curls before he pulled away.

"Petra, please be careful," he said softly, the particular deepening of his accent that came when his emotions ran high sounding in her ears. "Something is to happen before the third day of celebrations is complete, and I cannot be worried about you putting yourself in danger when I have so many lives on my shoulders as it is."

She went to protest, then closed her mouth. She nodded, and he did so in return. He paused, then turned on his heel and walked off.

Then she heard Teddy's worried warning in her ears—about the rusty-guts, shadowy man laughing and saying that Duncan might never return home. Petra wondered if she had met the man tonight, even if she had only heard his voice.

She knew she still had much to discover about Emerson's death, but right then the idea of Duncan never returning to her was worse than anything she could learn. She was ashamed of what her thoughts had been all this morning, all brought on by a piece of paper with lies upon it, written by an odious man who had likely received the information from some cowardly member of the peerage.

She still had questions, yes, but they were no longer about her ability to trust Duncan. And all she knew right then was that she could not let him go, not like this.

In a dash of three strides and lifted hems, Petra grabbed his hand and jerked, forcing him to turn around.

"What is it? Petra, I must away," he said, his brows coming together.

She began backing up, pulling on him. He hesitated, then stepped forward. When her back was once more up against stone, in the privacy of the nearly pitch-black doorway, she whispered,

"I have always known you were an honorable man, Duncan Shawcross—about everything. I have always known it, and I am sorry I lost sight of that for a bit."

She saw one side of his mouth quirk up and she brought his hand up to her collarbone, shivering as his thumb gently traced it.

"However, I have a job to do as well," she said, "and I fully intend on continuing."

She expected his hand to drop, for some of the chastising to begin anew. Instead, she heard the deep rumbling of his voice and a bit of a laugh.

"I never doubted it, my lady. You never do anything by halves, and trying to break you of it completely would only break me, not you." He caught a curl of her hair with his other hand, gently winding it about his finger, his voice becoming serious. "Just promise me again you will be careful."

She moved his hand down, her breath hitching with his as his thumb caught in her bodice, pushing it lower.

"I shall endeavor to be careful," she promised. "I should like to help you wherever I can. And I want to help my country to avoid bloodshed, to look toward reforms in a peaceful manner instead. But right now . . . ?"

His voice went hoarse when her fingers began working the buttons of his fall. "Truly? Here? Where we might be seen?"

"Truly," she said. "Most ardently."

And then her hands went up to his face, bringing it down to hers. Making certain his lips would be as reddened and swollen as her own. That her teeth would leave a slight mark on his neck, and that his fingers went into her garter once more as he lifted her hips to his.

SEVENTEEN

Thursday, 22 June 1815
Forsyth House
Berkeley Square, Mayfair, London
The six o'clock hour of the morning

SOMETHING LIGHTLY SMACKED HER BACKSIDE.

"Duncan, do behave," she mumbled into her pillow, which turned into a yelp as her bed dipped with the weight of a dog who deftly lifted the stick off her bum and then proceeded to lie across the backs of her legs.

Petra's one blearily opened eye witnessed Sable chewing the stick with some gusto, and with the jubilance of a dog who is normally not allowed on a bed, but has been given temporary reprieve of the rules.

She wedged open her other eye and turned to the terrified-looking maid a few feet away from her bed.

"I'm ever so sorry, my lady," quavered Enid, clutching at the apron she wore over a crisp cotton dress.

Petra sighed, which turned into a yawn. "Shall I guess that Annie feels well enough this morning to inform you of this tactic?" Using one hand, she pointed to her dog, who was keeping her from being able to turn over. Yet she could not resist Sable's silky ears and smiled when her dog leaned into her touch with those adoring coppery eyes.

"She did, my lady. I'm ever so sorry. It's simply—I tried to wake you three times already."

"Three times?" Petra went up on her elbows, realizing her room was filled with light from the curtains being opened. There was also a tea tray with evidence of dishes having been clattered about. And her chemise-covered backside had been all too visible because her counterpane had been pulled away.

And she had noted none of it. Though after her long day yesterday plus a dinner that went until one in the morning—and a certain interlude outside a darkened doorway that even now made a tingling sensation erupt all over her person—she had been thoroughly exhausted. "Whatever for? And pray tell, what time is it?"

"It is half six, my lady. In the morning, that is."

"That, I see," Petra mumbled, shielding her face from the light, and then emitted a giggle when Sable belly-crawled over her to land kisses all over her cheeks.

"But it is young Teddy, my lady," said Enid. "He is here. Brought with him a girl not much younger than me. Teddy said you told him to come no matter what the time. I didn't believe him, and the girl tried to run, but . . . have you seen Sable's newest trick Miss Lottie taught her, my lady?"

Petra rolled over and sat up, Sable happily springing out of the way. "He found her? He found Nell?"

"Yes, my lady. We have left her, tied up, in the servants' hall."

Swinging her legs over the side of the bed, Petra stood, horrified. "Tied up? Whatever for? I do not wish Nell to be hurt. Whose decision was it to tie her?"

Enid paled, then spoke in rushed sentences as she dashed to help Petra with her dressing gown.

"She tried to run, my lady. And grabbed one of Mrs. Bing's knives. Teddy gave some command to Sable, who Charles had on a lead as he was to take her with him to Bardwell's Apothecary for some more salve for Annie's cut. You know how Sable loves to visit Miss Frances, my lady. And when Teddy spoke this command, Sable raced about the girl's legs. The lead, it wrapped about her ankles and tripped her. Oh, I can see that you didn't know, my lady.

She's quite good at it, Sable is. And Miss Lottie is *most* impressive in her skills in training dogs to do such things."

"I must agree to the latter, and have no doubt of the former," Petra said faintly, having stopped in her rush to her dressing room at this news, all of which she could envision with little help. "But why on earth did you keep Nell tied?"

"She was very angry and brandishing Mrs. Bing's knife, my lady," Enid replied. "Of course, it were just a little paring knife, and Mrs. Bing jumped out, holding the big cleaver she uses to carve up a side of beef, but that didn't stop the girl from wiggling about like a wild animal caught in a trap. Even Smithers, demanding she stop in that tone he can get that sends shivers down my own spine, didn't help, my lady."

"And Mrs. Ruddle?" Petra had never seen her housekeeper unable to handle any situation.

"Oh, yes, the girl calmed right down when Mrs. Ruddle stood over her. Didn't say a word, our Mrs. R. Just stared until the girl quieted and dropped the knife." Enid's voice was filled with awe. "I hope to be like that someday, my lady."

"She is most worthy of admiration," Petra agreed. "Well, then let us get me dressed quickly—yes, the green cotton chintz will do quite well. Just twist my plait up into a chignon like Annie taught you, and pin it. We can prepare me properly for the day later."

"The entire house is yours, my lady?" Nell said. She looked around Petra's drawing room with its pretty damask sofas in a silvery blue, paintings of horses all about the walls, windows looking out over the gardens, and both a large fireplace and a larger set of bookshelves. A mixture of anger and envy swirled in the girl's violet eyes.

"It belongs to my father, the earl," Petra said, "but he entrusts the care and running of it to me."

A half hour earlier and finally dressed, she'd rushed downstairs to the servants' hall to find a disheveled Nell sitting in a chair. Her ankles were tied by Sable's leather lead, and she mulishly ignored Teddy and Allen, the underfootman, as they played a game of cards while drinking tea and eating toast and jam. Petra had apologized to Nell with formality, untied the girl herself, then asked Allen for tea and breakfast to be sent up to her drawing room.

Teddy had run up, presenting Petra with the ornately carved wooden box Nell had stolen from Mrs. Huxton's effects. Then he said he would wait outside Petra's drawing room, in the garden, should Nell attempt to escape. Allen and Charles would remain on duty inside.

Petra had tried to insist this was not necessary, but acquiesced when Teddy leaned in and whispered, "More wily than she looks, she is, my lady. Took me and six of me mates to corner 'er."

Once in her drawing room, Petra had planned to begin her questions straightaway out of eagerness, but something about Nell's demeanor said she would not be likely to answer truthfully until Petra had proven worthy of it.

Thus, she had poured tea and waited politely for the girl to speak. Nell, once in the presence of eggs and rashers, succumbed to her hunger. Petra ate in silence along with her, contentedly watching Teddy outside her windows as he threw sticks for Sable. It was when she let her mind wander back to the events of yesterday that Nell spoke, and it was clear from the start that she intended to provoke Petra.

"And you think you deserve it, I suppose, all this," Nell now said as she used her left hand to carefully adjust the right sleeve of her ill-fitting brown calico dress, as if wanting to smarten herself despite it all. "People at your beck and call. A lady's maid, butler, footman, cook. Pretty dresses whenever you want them. I'd wager you think you deserve it all simply because you were born to it."

"Do I deserve it simply because I was born to it? No, of course not," Petra responded calmly. "Yet I endeavor to deserve my blessings."

Nell snorted. "'Tis easy for you to say, my lady. You were not born in a hovel, to a mother who was made with child by an aristocrat, who was only willing to allow her to remain his kitchen maid until she showed. You did not have your mother then die before you were nine years of age, leaving you to be on the streets as not even the hovel's landlady was willing to feed you for more than one additional meal."

The girl was breathing hard by the end of this, her cheeks pink with anger, and yet seemed a bit surprised at the same time to have said so much.

"No, you are correct," Petra said, and did not mention that she, herself, had lost her mother to consumption before she could walk. For her loss was little in comparison to Nell's. Her heart went out to the girl, yet she knew it would do her no good to say as much—not at this moment, at least—so she forged on. "Lady Vera said you had a benefactor. Who was he?"

"He did not tell me," Nell said, then rolled her eyes and offered more information when Petra merely lifted one eyebrow and waited.

It seemed as Nell neared her tenth year of life, and her first year living as a street urchin, she'd been hired as a young maid-of-all-work by some men who met in rooms down by the docks. She saw them when they arrived, served them tea, and then cleaned the room after they left, never being privy to their discussions. One of the men, a gentleman by his appearance and manner, spoke with her a few times, eventually discovering she was an orphan. A fortnight later, having successfully petitioned the governors, he placed her in the care of Mrs. Huxton at the Asylum for Female Orphans.

"I never saw him again," she said with a shrug that did not quite hide the hurt that had washed over her face.

"And is this gentleman responsible for the inheritance you supposedly will have once you come of age?" Petra asked.

"I believe so, yes, my lady," Nell said. "It is what Mrs. Huxton said, though she never explained why. She kept telling me she would explain once it was over."

"How did she mean, *once it was over?*" Petra asked, pouring both of them more tea. She went to add milk and sugar to Nell's cup, but she was stopped. "Only sugar, please, my lady. I like milk in my tea, I do, but I can only have a bit before I earn a dickey tummy."

This time, it was an embarrassed pinkness that spread over her cheeks, and she looked down at her lap.

"Of course," Petra said smoothly. "Why, my friend Frances is much the same. As is my Aunt Ophelia, and my late fiancé, in fact. All to various levels, you understand. It was my aunt, who stayed with my papa and I for a while when I was a little girl, who taught me to love tea for its very flavor, and not for how it tastes when altered. She could take no milk and disliked overly sweet things, and thus, I take my tea just as it is, just like her. I am teased quite regularly for it—though when it comes to sweet treats and puddings, well, that is where my darling aunt and I diverge."

Nell looked up at her sharply, and Petra expected to earn the girl's anger once more, for she had sounded quite silly, and rather spoiled. And talking about family to an orphan was most insensitive. *Badly done, Petra,* she thought to herself.

Somehow, though, Nell did not seem to take offense. Upon accepting her cup of tea, she even answered Petra's question without further prompting.

"I do not know what Mrs. Huxton meant, my lady. Though I believe whatever it was might have been the reason why she was killed. And I could not tell you whether it was Mrs. Yardley or Lady Vera who delivered the second blow, but I do promise you it was not I."

EIGHTEEN

"IF WE TAKE A TURN ABOUT THE GARDEN, MAY I TRUST THAT you will not attempt to escape?"

Nell eyed Sable through the windows, who was sitting like a princess next to Teddy's side on the garden steps, tilting her head toward him to direct his hand into the best places to scratch.

"I expect that hound would trip me up again before I could. And Teddy would only find me again in a trice, even if I did manage to leg it." She paused, then added, "I remember him, you know. From my own time on the streets. He was but a little tyke then."

"Did you know his mother?" Petra asked, her hand on the French doors to the garden. Teddy turned with those smiling blue eyes of his, and she immediately felt terrible that she was attempting to betray his trust. Nell was already nodding, but Petra said, "No, please do not tell me. Teddy will do so in his own time, and I respect him and his decision to wait."

Nell went quiet at this, and Petra sensed a stab of jealousy from the girl. Teddy, too, seemed to sense something and darted off with Sable into the wisteria tunnel, its purple flowers having just had their season, only the masses of featherlike leaves upon its winding vines remaining.

But as she had hoped, the quiet garden seemed to calm Nell. The girl looked around at the sculptures of Greek and Roman deities, and the gardens bursting with flowers, including fragrant roses, tall, spire-like lupins, globe-like alliums, and vibrant irises, all bordered by cheerful dianthus and violas. Petra watched her bring in a great lungful of air, and she did the same. Then she led the way toward the western side of the garden, where they were hit by a wall of fragrance and a veritable field of peonies in hues of pink, white, cream, and buttery yellow. Nell's eyes, nearly the color of the wisteria, went wide.

From the pocket of her dress, Petra pulled out her little dagger, unsheathing it from its scabbard and trying not to think of Duncan as she did. Nell eyed her warily until Petra handed it to her.

"Why don't you choose some blooms as you tell me what happened? Enough for a medium-sized vase—yes, would be perfect in the room where you shall sleep. For I think it best that you stay here with me at Forsyth House until this matter is resolved. Would that be acceptable?"

Nell stared for a long moment, then nodded, taking the dagger gingerly. Petra's gardener was always leaving flower baskets about, and she found one easily enough. Nell took her time in choosing her blooms, beginning with one in a pale pink that looked like it was on the precipice of unfurling into its glory.

Nell began talking haltingly at first of the events from one week earlier, when Mrs. Huxton, whom she described as kind and caring, if tough, was found dead.

She spoke of awakening earlier than normal, at five o'clock, due to feeling unwell in her stomach.

"We had a new orphaned girl taken in the night before, round midnight—a young thing of four who was crying and quite frightened. Mrs. Yardley said I could sit with the girl and have a cup of hot chocolate with her until she fell asleep." Nell touched her stomach with a wry grimace. "But the milk, you know. It normally does me little harm when in a hot chocolate. But this time? Well, I awoke needing the chamber pot with some haste."

Choosing the next peony she wished to cut seemed to stave off any embarrassment she might have had in relating this. Nell then explained that she'd ensured the girls' dormitory was locked as it should be, and chose to exit through the kitchen doors to use the outdoor chamber pot. When she returned, she thought she heard something in the front room and went to check, but found it empty. When she went back through, that was when she witnessed Mrs. Yardley, standing with her ear to the doors of the chapel.

"She did not see me, and I held back. Then, suddenly, Mrs. Yardley all but leapt away and ran for her room. A moment later, Lady Vera hurried out of the chapel, looking like death itself was after her. Her ladyship went toward the kitchens, and I went into the chapel, where I planned to pretend to enter through that door if someone questioned me."

It was then she'd seen Mrs. Huxton on the floor, but confirmed the matron was still alive and breathing. She saw the tassel from Lady Vera's celadon-hued reticule and picked it up. Then she heard a noise coming from the chapel's main doors. Thinking either Lady Vera or Mrs. Yardley was returning, she'd rushed outside once more, intending to enter the chapel again a few minutes later, claim surprise at finding the matron unwell, and offer her help.

"Forgive me, my lady, but I didn't want to have to explain that I'd seen either of them. Mrs. Yardley is too suspicious and high in the instep by half, and Lady Vera—well, I quite like her, but she does rather act as if she owns the orphanage. Always sending us older girls out on errands, and borrowing us if she needs more scullery maids for a party she hosts. I don't rightly feel as if she should be able to do that without paying us, see?"

"I would have to agree, yes," Petra said, and considered asking what type of errands Lady Vera would require of Nell and the older girls. In truth, she was beginning to have questions about her dear friend Lady Vera, though she disliked even entertaining such a notion. Still, was it possible Lady Vera asked Nell or another girl to collect letters with a particular wax seal on them from a member of the Bellowers? Yet, before her mind could truly mull over this question, she was compelled to give her attention back to Nell.

"I waited no more than five minutes, and then I walked back into the chapel," Nell was saying. She used the dagger to slice off another bloom, its sharp blade cutting through the stem with ease, and then looked as if she would drop the bloom as she paled.

"I saw Mrs. Huxton, dead, on the floor, with the candlestick all bloody next to her head. I ran down the aisle to see who might have done it, who had been such a coward as to kill her like that, but there was no one. I heard nothing. No footsteps, or doors closing, or anything. In truth, except for thinking I'd heard something coming from the front parlor, all was quiet from the moment I awoke until I went back to the chapel. Then I heard Lady Vera sobbing, but I did not go in."

"Why not?" Petra asked, but mildly. And when she sensed hesitation, she said, "You may speak freely, Nell. By my estimation, all three of you could have delivered the blow that killed Mrs. Huxton. However, you had every reason to keep her alive if she held the key to you learning of, and receiving, any monies left to you."

Though Nell had continued to retain a bit of her prickly demeanor, Petra was surprised to see the girl's eyes well with unshed tears. But after one sniffle, Nell chose another peony and quickly cut it.

"Well, like I said, I do like Lady Vera, but her ladyship is most formidable. If she had killed Mrs. Huxton, and she was so willing to use us girls as her unpaid help, who was to say she would not use me as an easy person to blame?"

It shocked Petra to hear Lady Vera being described in this way and she wished to defend her friend, but she tamped down those feelings. And part of her felt proud of this girl, who had lost her mother and lived on the streets of London before being taken in by the orphanage. Nell had grown up having some education, her intelligence, and her sense of self-worth. It was more than a lot of girls, privileged or not, walked through life with, and at any other time, Petra would encourage the girl and her endeavors. Yet, for the time being, she knew she must simply learn the facts.

"I cannot find fault in that supposition," Petra said. "What then?"

Nell said she tiptoed back to her room, where she pretended to be asleep until Mrs. Yardley came to fetch her to harness the cart pony and drive out to Jermyn Street to fetch Miss Frances Bardwell at her rooms over Bardwell's Apothecary.

Petra knew the details from there, having heard them from Frances herself, and so she asked, "What, then, happened between you and Mrs. Yardley? Why did you attack her and then leave with the box that had once belonged to Mrs. Huxton? And what is the significance of this box?"

Nell, who had chosen another peony bloom, suddenly whirled, pointing at Petra with the little dagger.

"I did not attack her, my lady. She attacked me!"

Petra did not back up, but she did smile. "I am aware."

"How do you mean, my lady?" Nell said, lowering the dagger, her hand shaking a little as she did.

"Because, whilst it took me some time to realize what I had noticed, Mrs. Yardley only had one wound on her—at her temple, from you striking her with the box. Yet when she first touched her temple after coming round from her faint, her fingernails were already dark with blood—though I now know it was not her own. It was *she* who scratched *you*, was it not? And I would wager if you push up your right sleeve, I shall see the proof."

Carefully, Nell did so. Indeed, she had not been smartening herself earlier, but attempting to keep the sleeve from touching her scratches, which looked inflamed.

"Teddy?" Petra called out. In a flash, the boy was there, his grin bright and open, Sable bounding alongside him. She asked him to go inside and collect the tin Frances had given her containing items for wound care.

Nell began to protest, but Petra shook her head. "We will get those wounds cleaned, but right now I must know: What is the significance of the wooden box?"

The girl's eyes welled, but she kept her composure. "Mrs. Huxton said she would keep the proof of my inheritance safe. She would not tell me where, but one night, I saw she had not closed her dressing room door, and I was able to see in. I saw her take out the wooden box, and then pull some papers from her pocket. She'd folded them into a small packet." Nell then frowned. "Of course, Mrs. Yardley began calling for me, and I had to scamper out through the front room in order not to be seen. I'm certain Mrs. Huxton put that proof into the box, though." Then a hitch came into her voice. "Only I didn't find anything in the box except for a few buttons and this."

From her pocket, she reached in and pulled out a small miniature portrait of a child of possibly four years of age or so and handed it to Petra. With quite fair hair that curled at the ends, light eyes, and laughing smile, Petra said, "Why, this could be me, though I know it is not."

Painted from only the neck up, Lady Vera had been quite right in that it was impossible to determine the child's sex. For both small boys and girls wore dresses when they were that young, and many boys did not get their first haircut until they were breeched, which sometimes did not happen until they reached the age of six.

"It might also have been me," Nell said. "My hair was that color until I was three or four, or so said my mum. She claimed my father was fair, and that's where it came from." She canted her head. "But I believe this painting might be of a boy . . . "

"Do tell me why you would say so," Petra said, peering closely again at the child in the little painting and wishing she had the quizzing glass from her reticule. "Do you see something in this painting I do not?"

For one moment, Nell flashed a lovely, youthful smile, much like the child's in the painting. She seemed to delight in being asked to display her intelligence, though her countenance sobered again quickly. "No, my lady. That day I saw Mrs. Huxton putting papers into that box, she took out the miniature, sighed, and I am fairly certain she whispered, 'Oh, my sweet boy, I fear I failed you,' before putting it away again."

Petra recalled the story of how Mrs. Huxton, when she was still a governess, had been forced to flee and leave her young charge in the care of his angry and potentially abusive father. Petra felt she could understand that Mrs. Huxton might have continued to feel enormous guilt and worry, even years later.

There came a polite cough, and Petra and Nell both looked up to find Teddy had already reappeared.

"Mrs. Ruddle is wondering if you asked for a delivery, my lady," he said, handing her the tin of wound-care supplies.

"I don't believe so," Petra replied, then instructed Nell to sit on a nearby bench and pull up her sleeve. She soaked some cotton wool in a solution Frances had concocted that smelled strongly of gin. "This is likely to sting," she warned Nell, whose face had already screwed up at the smell. Teddy waited until Nell's hiss of pain had been emitted and then spoke again.

"Well, my lady, Mrs. Ruddle says there's a delivery man claimin' you ordered some of the same wine Lady Elizabeth and Lady Sloan served last night, and he's insistin' on talkin' to Lady Petra herself."

Petra, remembering all that had happened the night before at Sloan House—including the interlude in one of its darkened doorways—concentrated on cleaning Nell's scratches so she would not flush scarlet.

Duncan had managed to release every muscle in her body with his attentions and she had felt practically weightless by the time she slipped back into Lady Sloan's dining room, her lips unable to keep from their upward curve.

To give herself some credit, she left Duncan looking thoroughly drunk on her and muttering that he might have to sit down for a bit before returning to the Bellowers. As he'd leisurely kissed her goodbye, he added that he would not even have to invent a story of the pleasure he'd just enjoyed, for the truth was infinitely better.

Once back in the dining room, Caroline had taken one look at her and known immediately, clapping her hands together in glee, and then insisted on knowing every detail.

Even the sight of the dowager marchioness sending an icy glare in their direction as she clung possessively to the arm of her son, James—who appeared to be his unruffled, roguish self once more—did not manage to dim the feeling Petra had of a lightness blooming within her.

But then Petra and Caroline had been found by Lady Sloan, who charmingly demanded to know what they were laughing about. Petra, knowing she needed to answer before Caroline said something naughty, had rather shouted, "The wine! I do believe it was the best claret I have had in quite some time, and Lady Caroline and I were scheming on how to get the two of you to confess where you obtained such a fine spirit."

Much food, and indeed several glasses of the excellent claret later, Petra had a vague recollection of Lady Elizabeth saying something to her about wine. And thus, it was highly possible there was a cask of it being delivered at this moment.

"Blast," she muttered beneath her breath as she wound a bandage about Nell's arm after applying some of the salve Frances made that smelled like lemon drops. But then it struck her that the delivery man might be Mr. Fife. If so, she would finally be able to ask him if he had delivered any transparencies containing gardens.

"Didn't see who the delivery bloke was, my lady," Teddy said with a shrug when she asked if Mr. Fife had brought the wine. "I was fetchin' the tin."

"Of course," Petra said, then addressed Nell. "Would you stay here with Teddy whilst I assist my housekeeper? Yes, I am asking that you do not run off. And Teddy, Nell is not guilty of any wrongdoing that I can see, so I hope the two of you shall be friends by the time I return."

A few moments later, she heard the angry voice of Mrs. Ruddle saying, "Sir, I do not care if you were told by the Queen herself to deliver this wine, I shall not accept it without Lady Petra's approval."

"I am here, Mrs. Ruddle," Petra called out as she approached. The delivery man turned, and she said, "Why, Mr. Fife, how wonderful. I was hoping to see you."

Mr. Fife pulled off his cap and sketched a bow, his sideburns unruly and his stubble growing once more. He did not look as almost-handsome as the night before, with bags beneath his eyes. Mrs. Ruddle, her own narrowed eyes taking him in with marked disapproval, clearly did not look as if she would ever find him appealing. But Mr. Fife's smile was as easygoing as ever.

"Ah, Lady Petra, it is a pleasure to see you again. Please forgive me my lack of proper appearance. The celebratory events of last night went, ah, much longer . . ."

"No need to explain, Mr. Fife. I witnessed some of it myself," Petra said, then hastened to add when both Mr. Fife and Mrs. Ruddle looked at her curiously, "from Lady Sloan's window, of course. It was quite the momentous occasion, and everyone was celebrating, so I quite understand." She craned an ear out toward Berkeley Square and beyond. "I am simply glad the din has not started up again quite yet. The Prince Regent was in attendance last night and said he would be declaring three days of celebrations at nine o'clock this morning."

"'E already done so, my lady," said Mr. Fife with a sudden smile that was charming and slightly lopsided, leaving Petra oddly wanting to smile in return. "Not an hour ago, from the windows of St. James's Palace. Surprised us all, he did. Made the announcement, an' sent off 'bout twenty or more boys to be yelpers, cryin' out the news all over London. There're to be celebrations all over London, in the Green Park, Hyde Park, and others. There's to be everything from concerts to theatre, to the King's archers givin' a demonstration. Prince Frederick's also plannin' ta do a military demonstration in St. James's Park, I believe. No, I ain't tellin' no porky pies, my lady. 'Tis true!"

Petra turned to Mrs. Ruddle. "How exciting. Do you not agree, Mrs. R.?"

Her housekeeper merely sniffed. "It shall be a very loud three days, if last night was anything to go by, my lady." Then her stern face softened. "However, I do believe it shall also be a momentous occasion, like you said." She then raised her eyebrows to Mr. Fife and he cleared his throat.

"I have the cask of wine you requested, my lady. May I have my boys bring it inside?"

Petra heard a small intake of breath, and turned to find Nell, but no Teddy. The girl had cast her eyes politely downward, however, and Mr. Fife merely tipped his hat to her, then turned his attention back to Petra.

"Yes, of course," she said, conceding to herself that it was her fault she was now out the cost of a cask of wine. "But I should also like to ask some questions of you, Mr. Fife."

"Oh?" he said, one eyebrow raising in a rather imperious manner. Then when both her eyebrows inched upward, he hastily added, "My lady," and lowered his gaze.

"Yes," she said, "I have questions about the transparencies at Bardwell's Apothecary."

"Pardon me, my lady," said Mrs. Ruddle, who, upon hearing Petra accept the wine, had turned to tell the rest of the staff. "But where did Miss Nell go?"

Petra turned again. Nell was gone, the basket of flowers on the ground, fragrant peonies spilling out onto the grass, the handle of the little dagger glinting up at her, its blade having landed directly in one of the fat blooms.

Quickly, she moved to scoop it up, and a moment later Teddy came running up, blue eyes wide. "My lady! It is Nell!" He pointed out the servants' entrance to the street near Berkeley Square. "She ran, she did, but some blokes 'ave grabbed her!" As he turned toward the door, where Mr. Fife and Mrs. Ruddle still stood, his arm slowly lowered.

"Show me, Teddy," Petra said, already moving off. "Mr. Fife, please help us!"

"Of course, my lady," came Fife's voice after the briefest of surprised pauses.

Petra was running, with Teddy out front, but within a few strides Mr. Fife had passed them, running at quite a surprising speed for a man so burly. Out into the street, which was still quiet in the morning, he stopped. Petra caught up with him in a few more strides and gasped at what she saw.

Four men with hats pulled down low over their eyes were bundling a fighting and kicking Nell into a carriage. She managed to kick one man between the legs and with an enraged sound, he swung his right hand back to slap her, until another man caught his wrist just in time, yanked it down, and shoved him onto the back seat of the carriage, which was already moving. By the time Petra stopped running, too, the carriage had swung around the corner, and Nell was gone.

Teddy had put on a last-minute burst of speed, and slowed when it was clear he had no chance. He turned and pointed emphatically at one of the men, saying anxiously, "My lady!"

With a gesture for Teddy to return, she demanded, "Did you see them, Mr. Fife? Did you recognize any of them?"

"Four men," he panted, sweat blooming over his collar. "Never seen 'em before. Carriage looked hired. What could they want with that girl from the orphanage?" Hands on his hips in a way that somehow looked comical, he looked around, and so did Petra, panic blooming in her heart. Then she spun a circle, eyes searching all over. Charles and Allen had run out after her, with Mrs. Ruddle and Smithers hurrying out of Forsyth House as fast as they could. Even Annie, walking out a bit more slowly on Enid's arm, had emerged, thankfully with Sable on her lead.

"Teddy?"

Petra called his name twice more, but he, too, was gone. And she could only wonder what spooked him more: the abduction of the girl he had pledged to find and watch over, or the fact that Duncan had been one of her abductors.

NINETEEN

PETRA'S BAND OF CAPABLE SERVANTS AT FORSYTH HOUSE WERE in a very rare uproar.

"I must insist you be silent!" Petra was forced to shout.

Instantly, there was quiet in the kitchens. Smithers, speaking for the staff, said, "We are all terribly sorry, my lady. We are simply concerned for young Teddy and the girl. To be kidnapped from Berkeley Square in broad daylight? It is truly shocking."

"Of course you are worried," Petra said calmly, "as am I. However, whilst I am afraid I cannot explain as much as I would like, I wish to tell you what I can so that each and every one of you will remain vigilant. I do not know precisely what is going on, but you should be aware that one of the men today was Mr. Shawcross."

There was a chorus of shocked gasps and then Annie broke in.

"Be sensible, everyone, if you please. We here are all aware that Mr. Shawcross handles situations of a clandestine nature for Their Graces, the Duke and Duchess of Hillmorton. Lady Petra is saying we must assume there is a reason for his involvement."

And then came the chorus of relieved sighs and nods. Petra gave Annie a grateful look.

And then felt chagrin at herself, wishing she had said those very words to her own reflection yesterday instead of thinking the worst of Duncan. *Alas,* she then thought wryly, *I shall never have Annie's calm thinking, will I? No, indeed, but I must forgive myself for it, too. Besides, if Duncan wished for someone perfect, sweet, and lacking in impetuous behavior, he would have gone off me long ago!*

"I shall also take his involvement as a sign that Miss Nell Parker will not be harmed whilst in his care, and that he will send word as soon as he can," Petra then said aloud to the group. Further sounds of relief were heard. Then she asked if anyone had seen Teddy, or spoke to him before he ran off.

Everyone shook their heads, but Mrs. Ruddle screwed up her face for a moment. "He did give that Mr. Fife a bit of an odd look, my lady. No, not as if he were frightened of him. More like he knew the man, and did not care for him."

"I will have to believe Teddy is safe, then, and is possibly attempting to locate either Mr. Shawcross or Nell," Petra said.

"He did bring Sable to me before he ran back out, my lady," said Enid. "Told me to put her lead on, handed me a message to give to you, and then whispered something right diverting in my ear. Can't think on why he did any of it." From her pocket, she produced a piece of paper that had been rolled into a small scroll, and offered it to Petra.

Unrolling it, Petra read the words in Duncan's untidy scrawl, further proof that it was his hand—and that he was under stress— being that he reversed a letter in one word, writing a *q* when he meant a *p*.

By the time you read this, she will have escaqed with T.

"Duncan is letting me know all is well," she said, her hand going to her heart in relief. Though she still did not understand why Nell would have run to begin with, or why Duncan would have wished to kidnap her, she could not but shake her head in brief amusement. Teddy was clearly working with Duncan, and had pretended to be shocked to see him abducting Nell. *Those two should be an act at Drury Lane*, she thought, before announcing, "Teddy is with Miss Nell, and we must trust that he will keep her safe." At the happy exclamations, Petra looked at Enid. "Now, what did Teddy say?"

"Get the *feòragan*," Enid said immediately with a little shrug.

Out of nowhere, Sable leapt up from where she was lying at

Enid's feet and began running around the girl's legs at such a speed she was but a brown blur. Enid would have fallen over had it not been for Allen catching and quickly righting her. As Charles leapt to unravel the lead, Petra hurried to make certain Sable's neck wasn't being pulled, and found the metal snap-like contraption Lottie used for her custom-made leads had released itself with the intense pressure.

"Lottie, you are brilliant," she said under her breath, holding up the hasp.

And then she remembered her youth back at Buckfields with Duncan teasing her in Gaelic when he wished to make her angry, and grinned. He'd often call her *feòrag,* and, thinking it something mean or naughty, she would then attempt to chase him, ordering him to recant his words. He'd laughed every time, and it wasn't until much later she'd learned a *feòrag* was nothing more than the Gaelic word for a cheeky little creature Duncan always found to be quite adorable and excessively amusing—a squirrel.

"So that's the command," she said, rubbing Sable's ears. Teddy no doubt wanted to make certain Petra knew it, in case Sable's newest trick was needed for reasons other than amusement. "In English, it means 'get the squirrels.'"

This was a favorite phrase of Sable's, too, but for a different reason in English. Her ears perked up and she dashed to the door, begging to be let into the garden. Smithers complied and she raced to the nearest tree, circling it and looking up in hopes of spotting some of the cheeky, chattery red squirrels. None of whom, despite her speed, she had luckily ever been able to catch.

This little scene helped put the servants of Forsyth House back to rights. Petra then declared that, because of this strangeness, and because of the impending three days of celebrations, Forsyth House was to have every door and window locked and bolted except for those rooms that were commonly used, like Lady Petra's drawing room.

A few minutes later, however, she had another idea. Yanking upon the bellpull in her drawing room, she called Enid and Annie, who rushed in, looking relieved to find Petra unharmed.

"The wooden box that Nell had, and Teddy presented to me," Petra began. "Where did it go?"

"It is nearby, my lady," Enid said with a sudden smile. "When Teddy brought Sable to me, he also told me to hide the box. He didn't say why, only that he felt it might be the best thing to do. I put it in the secret compartment in the fender of your fireplace."

Annie lifted the rectangular cushion from its metal framework and extracted the beautifully carved wooden box. "I do not think it is a secret compartment, Enid. Just an extra space between the metalwork and where the cushion fits."

Enid shrugged. "I prefer to think of it as a secret compartment. It seems more romantic than just a fender."

After a quick look at the box to find it empty, a thought came to Petra.

"You may very well be correct, Enid, well done. I think that is the secret to this box as well—that it may have a secret compartment somewhere. And if something Nell told me might be true, then it is possible what is in this compartment might be of importance. We must endeavor to discover it."

There was a knock on her drawing room door, and Smithers entered, looking uncharacteristically surprised. In one hand was a silver salver; atop it was a small rectangular package wrapped in a piece of vermilion paisley silk, its ends tied in a knot. Both a letter and a folded note were next to it. In his other hand, he held a calling card.

"My lady, three deliveries have come for you, almost all at once. An invitation has come for you . . . from the Dowager Marchioness of Langford. Your presence is requested with immediacy."

Petra scoffed, and she felt little need to be civil. "Her ladyship's request is denied."

Smithers's graying eyebrows shot up, then he was once more

her stalwart butler. Clearing his throat, he said, "Of course, my lady. I shall let her footman know." Then he held out the salver. "Then this letter with a seal I have never seen before came for you at almost the same moment as a package from Lady Caroline. And there is a note for you to read first."

Using the letter opener, she slit both the note and the letter. Smithers may not have recognized the seal upon the letter, but she did.

It was the seal of a gentlemen's sporting club not far from Lambeth. The club was a small one, and allowed for men who wished to meet other men to do so in private as they practiced boxing, fencing, and other sports. And the letter itself was in response to the one Rupert had delivered for her yesterday, which she had sent to her friend Juddy Bellingham, whom she hoped would provide unobtrusive watchmen for the orphanage.

She read the short missive with relief. Juddy had readily agreed, though cautioned that even one gentleman walking regularly past an orphanage full of young girls could be considered hazardous to the gentleman if he were reported. But it was promised he and his cohorts would do their utmost, as they would be celebrating the news of victory at Waterloo at the club itself.

Tucking it in her pocket, she then read the note from Caroline.

Dearest, after an interesting evening last night, after which I exhausted my adoring Whitfield—I could not let you show me up, you understand—I once more read through my diary. I think it might behoove you to read the entries as marked. But you should stop there unless you feel I have not already been forthcoming enough about my former liaisons . . .

I shall collect my diary from you at tea this afternoon. Do lock it up until then.

TWENTY

PETRA RETIRED TO HER BEDCHAMBER, ASKING ENID TO GIVE
her one half hour before coming to help her dress. Settling onto
her reading chair next to the windows overlooking the gardens,
Petra carefully chose the pages marked by pieces of red ribbon and
began reading—for she certainly did not need to know more than
she already did about Caroline's boudoir activities.

However, a second, hastily scribbled note inside the diary directed her toward one section marked with a purple ribbon. *Just in
case*, Caroline had written. It was the account of her dinner party
the night before Emerson's murder.

And reading Caroline's words that reported Duncan's actions—
as well as their conversation later in Caro's drawing room when
Duncan was recovering from being cup-shot from too much
wine—was cathartic indeed. Finding Caro's written statement to
be exactly as she had professed at Sloan House allowed a little sigh
to escape Petra's lips. It was as if the last remaining thread of question her heart had foolishly held on to had been proven unneeded.

Then she began at the first entry marked, noting it was some six
weeks before Emerson's death. The place was Evermark Manor, the
lovely estate near Westhumble, in Surrey, gifted to Caroline by her
father upon the occasion of her marriage. One and twenty guests
were present, including the companion of Lady Vera's ward.

"I had forgotten Lady Vera briefly had a ward that season," Petra
said to herself as she confirmed through the guest list that Lady
Vera had not attended the house party, only the ward and her companion.

And indeed it had been a brief wardship. The young woman

had been presented at court by Lady Vera, effectively putting her on the marriage mart, and had needed but two balls after Lady Caroline's house party to secure herself a husband. Caroline's later notes reminded Petra the gentleman was an Irishman, and Lady Vera's ward had been wedded and off to Donegal before anyone in London had even really learned her name. But it was not truly the ward who had been the subject of Caroline's ink usage. It was the companion.

Miss Dodd was her name and Caroline had noted in the margin that Miss Dodd was a "led captain." This simple slang phrase told Petra volumes. That Miss Dodd was a spinster, and not nearly as lucky a one as Petra herself, with her own fortune and independence. Miss Dodd had no inheritance or house of her own, making her a poor dependent of her family. In all likelihood, Miss Dodd hired herself out as a companion for young, unmarried women like Lady Vera's ward in exchange for a small amount of money in her pocket and a chance to briefly escape the drudgery of her life.

Yet it seemed Miss Dodd and Petra had something in common, in that they refused to believe they could not have romantic liaisons of their own simply because they were not married. And Miss Dodd's partner of choice, it seemed, was one Mr. Phineas Rushton.

It was through Caroline's diary entries that Petra's memories of Mr. Rushton finally began to somewhat return, and she could only blame her state of being a besotted, newly engaged woman for hardly noticing him at the time. That house party had been her first as the future Viscountess Ingersoll, and because Caroline had been hostess, and married, Petra had been allowed to attend with only Annie as her lady's maid and not with a chaperone in tow as well.

Those days had been her first true taste of freedom, and Petra mused on this as she turned the diary page. With Annie only seeing to her needs in the mornings and evenings, it had been a time of being quite thoroughly without anyone to watch her movements. It had felt so freeing that Petra now wondered if she knew even then that her independence would later become of the utmost importance to her.

"Thank you, Caroline," she murmured with a smile as she kept reading.

In the end, however, she found that Caroline did not write much about Mr. Rushton, a sure sign that he had not been a diverting guest. Evidently, he had been invited at Emerson's behest solely for the reasons that he was Emerson's and Duncan's friend from Oxford, and sorely in need of some fresh air in the countryside.

Petra saw the notation that indicated Mr. Rushton was rather portly, and that he had a pleasing countenance and charming smile that Caroline quite appreciated—as did her captain, from the amusing comment Petra read.

To see Mr. Rushton and Ingersoll standing on either side of Shawcross makes for quite the display of handsome men. My captain agreed, saying it is rather like seeing Apollo bookended by two matching cupids, though greatly differing in size.

Petra also found notations that indicated Rushton became a bit petulant whenever Petra spent time with Emerson, so much that Caroline's Captain Smythe wondered if the jealousy were of a romantic nature. Several entries later, Petra saw that the captain clarified the jealousy.

Rushton is not jealous of darling Ingersoll for having Petra. No, quite the opposite!

Petra's brow furrowed. So Rushton had wished for an attachment of his own with Emerson?

She struggled to recall anything that indicated as much and

could not, even though little bits and pieces of that house party were returning. This included Duncan seeming occasionally out of temper, and her laughing at him every time he was forced to evade Lady Vera's ward. Caroline flirting with a baron who would become one of her first true paramours was another. And then a moment when she and Caroline went for an early morning walk only to stumble on Captain Smythe and his handsome lieutenant in a rather sweet embrace under the canopy of a tree.

Yet her memories of Rushton were becoming clearer, too. She was recalling that Emerson teased him because Rushton kept attempting to tame his rather wild hair by a liberal application of pomade. Emerson had finally taken pity on the man and offered his valet to Rushton for a morning to demonstrate. Sometime later, Rushton had emerged with his hair in such similar style to Emerson's that upon standing on either side of Duncan, the two men had indeed looked like two smiling blond cherubs bookending a scowling, dark-haired, green-eyed god.

Whisking open her fan, Petra cooled her thoughts on that particular memory, stopping only when she found an entry in Caroline's diary about Rushton and Miss Dodd, the companion. It seemed that Caro's lady's maid had discovered Rushton in a mutual flirtation with Miss Dodd, with Caro writing, *I'm told they were quite keen on one another and were found together several times, though there is no evidence—yet—that she has visited his room at night, or vice versa.*

This was the last page that Caroline had marked with a red ribbon, but Petra flipped through a few more pages, just to see if Caroline had forgotten anything further. She did so with a bit of amused trepidation, however. For reading details of Caroline's tryst with the dashing baron might be more than she bargained for.

Indeed, for a few pages, she felt like Teddy from the previous morning as she clapped a hand over both her eyes, splitting two fingers just enough to be able to make out the writing as she searched for key words, giggling and exclaiming "Heavens!" more than once.

Then, just as she thought Caroline's diary might begin smoking with all the scandalous content, she saw the entry. It was but one page, and contained so many references to naughty whisperings from Caroline's baron that Petra could forgive her friend for overlooking it. She read the pertinent parts two more times, feeling quite unnerved. For Caroline's casual recollections from three years earlier of her enjoyable house party had created unintended repercussions for the present.

Doubt and suspicion were once again vining their way around Petra's heart, and question after question filled her mind. But this time they were not about Duncan. No, instead her queries were for four others. Two she knew not where to find, and one she did—though that third person might very well help her find the two others.

As for the fourth, she could ask all the questions she liked, but she would never receive an answer. But that did not vex her too much, for she did not yet feel as if she was ready to ask those questions. Not just yet.

With a sigh, Petra stood and paced her bedchamber for several minutes, thinking on how to proceed. When she finally decided, she rang for Allen, sending her underfootman to Lottie's house with a message. When he had gone, Petra did as Caroline requested and hid the diary, storing it in a locked cabinet she had not opened in some time.

This cabinet was where she kept things of a precious nature to her that she did not wish even Annie to handle, or the maids to move about when they dusted. Briefly, Petra ran her finger over the love letter from her late mother to her father, doing the same to the letter the earl had written to Petra herself on her eighteenth birthday. Then she opened a small box containing a pale green glass bead and held it up to the light admiringly. Judged to possibly be from Roman times, Duncan had found it in the ground at Buckfields when they were children and gifted it to her as a present. Returning the bead to the cabinet, her eyes rested on the two other items of importance. The first was Emerson's art portfolio. The second was the first letter he sent her—or drawing, rather, with some scribbled words that, in his mind, took the place of a letter.

She pulled it out and unfolded it gently, reminding herself that he'd had quite a good talent with charcoal drawings, especially of buildings and houses.

The drawing had been of Buckfields, and skillfully done as well. He'd drawn the long road up to the house and then had added a handful of other paths, none of which appeared on any professional drawings of the Earl of Holbrook's Suffolk seat located in Newmarket. These paths were the ones he and Petra had walked, side by side but not touching, as they became acquainted with each other. At the end of the longest path, Emerson had drawn a lovely tree, carved with a heart in its trunk. And out to the side were the ten words he'd scrawled.

Lady Petra, you have taken the path to my heart.

Tears welled in her eyes as she opened Emerson's portfolio, the one thing of his that she had not sent off to his remaining family members in Dorset.

Inside were pages of quarto-cut paper, a few of which had simple sketches of buildings and houses. St. James's Palace, Spencer House, Hillmorton House, and Carling Magna—the house belonging to Caroline's papa—which Petra decided she would gift to her dearest friend. Then there was one of Forsyth House and one very rough sketch of what would have been Ingersoll House had the remodels been completed. Each drawing then had three quickly drawn lines, stacked one over the other, that arced out from the top or one side of the building. They gave the drawings extra expression, as if the edifice were moving, or simply full of happiness.

She laid them out on the table, finding five, and began arranging them in the order of how she liked them best. Then she rearranged them again after noting that the three arcing lines on each page could connect to the page next to it and form a pathway of sorts from house to house.

As many of these houses were special to Petra, it made her smile to see how Emerson had connected them. She wondered if he did so deliberately, or if it was merely a happy coincidence.

Her smile fell away as she remembered, yet again, that she could never ask him, and that would never cease to make her heart hurt.

She checked the portfolio once more. The rest of the pages were empty, and would never see any more of his drawings. With a sigh, she slid Emerson's letter back in with the other drawings, keeping the one of Carling Magna out for Caroline.

At the last moment, she also pulled the one of Ingersoll House. Caroline was an accomplished artist with both charcoal and oil paints, and Petra decided that she would like to see Ingersoll House as it would have looked from the outside on Grosvenor Street, had she become the mistress of it.

She could describe the proposed changes to Caroline, for the house's façade had ultimately not changed when it was purchased by a banking family of good fortune out of Hampshire. They were a family who rarely chose to be in town, however, leaving the house empty except for a small group of servants who, from what her own housekeeper once observed, tended to keep themselves to themselves.

Petra recalled the last time she had been driven along Grosvenor Street and passed by Ingersoll House, which sat east of Grosvenor Square. She had been on her way home from visiting Lady Vera, whose own house was situated to the west of the square, near Hyde Park. Petra felt as if Ingersoll House had looked a little forlorn and unused, with the three arched windows on the top floor in need of a proper cleaning. It made her sigh again just to think about it.

Closing the portfolio's leather flap and wrapping the leather cord about it tightly, Petra thought that if Ingersoll House were painted the way it should have looked if it had become her house, maybe she could see it with happy eyes once more.

Then she selected a pair of garters she had purchased recently, but had not yet had the chance to wear. After that, she pulled out her little-used embroidery set before extracting from her pocket her lockpicks and her little dagger that Nell had dropped—though why the girl had fled in the first place as she did so was still a mystery.

Sitting back down in her chair by the window, Petra began sewing. For if Duncan could attach a scabbard and knife to his person in unique ways, so could she with her lockpicks.

TWENTY-ONE

Thursday, 22 June 1815
Grimley House
Grosvenor Street, Mayfair, London
The ten o'clock hour

LOTTIE'S EYES WERE DANCING AS SHE CLIMBED OUT OF A
hackney on Grosvenor Street, a shaggy gray lurcher leaping out
gracefully after her, and the two met Petra on the pavement.

While the celebrations for Wellington's victory at Waterloo had
resumed in earnest all over London, it seemed the areas with the
most concentration of revelers were Hyde Park, the Green Park,
and St. James's Park, making the streets still relatively easy to travel
by carriage.

"First, do not be concerned about Frances," Lottie announced,
seemingly anticipating Petra's question. "She has both her maid
helping at the apothecary today as well as my groom, who is
quite good with people as well as being strong and a bit menacing
looking—though he is really very kind. He took Fitz with him as
well, and thus she has ample help for the shop, and a dog who will
announce any unwanted visitors."

"I am relieved," Petra breathed.

"Excellent. And second, when your underfootman said I was
to meet you here with the dog I'd selected for the orphanage and I
should be ready to ambush Lady Vera, I thought he was having me
on. But he was not, was he?"

Petra had done quite a bit of thinking as she had worked on

transforming her garters this morning, mostly about what she had learned from Nell about the day Mrs. Huxton had died. But there were also questions that had come up from reading Caroline's diary.

"I do not yet know if I am forgiven by Lady Vera for thinking her a suspect and confining her to her house—or even if she will talk to me again. So this presented a lovely opportunity to learn which way the wind is blowing, as it were. And if she will not grant me an audience, then yes, ambushing her shall be our modus operandi." Petra grinned at Lottie's widened eyes, then leaned down to stroke the lurcher's head, who silently looked up at her with eyes the color of whisky. "And who do we have here?"

Lottie explained she recently found the lurcher outside a shop on Oxford Street. Deemed a stray, he had exuded patient calm even as the proprietor's toddler smeared linseed oil onto his fur.

"When Lady Vera contracted me, I immediately thought of this chap, that he might be the perfect dog for the orphaned girls. He's nearly impervious to chaos and seems especially keen on women, so we shall see if he is a good fit. I've named him Magnus, after my mama's uncle, who had quite the same gentle manner—and the same little gray beard, in fact."

"Don't let Caroline see you, then," Petra told the dog, "for she adores handsome gentlemen with beards and she might snap you up for herself."

"She's already tried," Lottie said as they took the stairs to Grimley House. "But she admitted the orphaned girls deserved him more." Eyeing Petra, she said, "Forgive me, but you do look rather unsettled. Are you well?"

"Well? Yes," Petra replied. "Unsettled? Also yes. Lady Vera has been like a second mama to me, and the very idea that she might have killed the former matron has me quite unable to wrap my mind around the idea. And the thought that I might not be able to repair our friendship had me wishing to cry all the way here."

Lottie gave her a gentle smile, and Petra, after emitting a sigh, continued.

"There are also some connections I have discovered as of late that I am not enjoying knowing. That is another reason why I wished you to be with me today. You are an excellent judge of character and I wish you to tell me your opinions."

"All right. What should I be looking for?"

"I feel it is important that you not know in advance, for I want you to hear what I have to say the same moment Lady Vera does. Beyond that, I shall leave it up to you to decide what you think."

"If you think me worthy, then I shall endeavor not to disappoint you," Lottie said as she took hold of the brass knocker in the shape of a Labrador's head and used it to rap upon the door.

Lady Vera's butler led them into the front parlor, looking a touch discomfited at the sight of Petra, Lottie, and a scruffy-looking dog. He told them Lady Vera was finishing a letter and would be with them shortly. Petra, however, had interacted with the butler enough times over the years to know that he was not usually bothered by hounds or unannounced calls, so it was likely Lady Vera who was still displeased with her.

To keep herself from thinking too much on it, Petra proceeded to make Lottie blush with praise over Sable's latest trick. "What made you think of it? And a hasp that breaks free? It is brilliant."

Lottie explained it was a trick she decided she would teach to all her dogs who go to anyone female. That if said woman felt she was being accosted, she would simply say the command she has chosen and her dog would run about the man's legs, causing him to become tangled and trip. As for the lead's breakaway hasp, Lottie said she had her farrier design it to her specifications, so that it could accept some pull, but will break free with effort, ensuring the dog is able to escape.

She canted her head thoughtfully. "Though my poor man-of-all-work who has been called upon to help me test the trick has declared I must find another victim on whom to practice. He has fallen on his face one too many times, I'm afraid."

Petra eyed her friend. "And may one assume Duncan came up with Sable's rather silly command phrase?"

"Of course he did," Lottie replied, beaming. "He said it would make you laugh. It was he who paid me to make certain Sable learned that trick after seeing me teaching it to a lovely spaniel, but do not confess to him that I told you. He knows you do not care for it when he attempts to protect you. So I told him, *If that's the case, then you shouldn't have used a Gaelic word, ye daft beggar.* He tried to change it after that, but it was too late. Sable had taken to that command in minutes."

This did indeed make Petra laugh. "And does Magnus know this trick?"

"He is learning it, and is fair t' middlin' so far. Do you wish to know his command word?" She leaned in and whispered "buggerlugs" in Petra's ear, who grinned. "Had to choose one the young London girls weren't likely to say."

There came a clearing of the throat from the butler. "Lady Vera will see you now."

Petra had no more walked through the door to the pretty lilac-hued drawing room, Lottie a step behind, when Lady Vera, standing near the windows, lifted her chin and boomed, "Well? Did you find Nell? Was I exonerated from this ridiculous pantomime? Tell me, Lady Petra, for I am quite vexed."

Petra's heart quickly sank when Lady Vera did not offer them either a seat or tea. The closest she came to civility was saying hello to Lottie, and quickly approving of the lurcher. Especially when he stayed calm and unruffled as Lady Vera's own pack of six dogs, all of whom were outside her drawing room, leapt at the windows, barking and growling until she commanded them to cease.

When the room was silent once more, Petra had to inwardly command herself to keep her composure. Lady Vera had always been exceedingly welcoming when Petra arrived at Grimley House, insisting she sit, fluffing up any pillows before the maid could do so, and plying her with so much tea and so many cakes that Petra fairly waddled out the door sometime later. Now, it was almost worse than if Lady Vera had given her the cut direct.

You are here to help solve the murder of Mrs. Huxton, she reminded herself harshly. *Remember that, for much larger things are at play than tea and cakes!*

"Well, Lady Petra?" said her ladyship, the way she was all but vibrating with indignance somehow making her diminutive stature seem bigger, and Petra was forcibly reminded of Teddy imitating an angry, fluffed-out cat.

Clasping her hands in front of her, Petra explained that Nell had been found, brought to Forsyth House, and then she had run off, only to be abducted before she was able to get far. Yet Petra stopped short of explaining that Nell had somehow escaped again during her abduction and was likely living the life of a street urchin with Teddy until further notice.

Lady Vera had been looking ready to shout again, but instead her eyes went wide, her hand going to her bosom.

"Is she well? Who has her? What is being done to recover her?"

Petra sidestepped this, changing the subject swiftly and purposefully.

"Lady Vera, when I met with the Queen and the Duchess of Hillmorton, I was given the impression that they made you privy to certain facts regarding a certain group known as the Bellowers."

There was an intake of breath from Lady Vera as her eyes went to Lottie.

"I was given permission to confide in those I trust, your ladyship," Petra said calmly. Lottie wisely stayed as calm and quiet as the lurcher, though Petra could feel that her friend was agog.

"Who else have you told?" It was more of a demand than a question. And when Petra replied that Lady Caroline and Miss Frances

Bardwell were her confidants, Lady Vera took a sudden step forward. "And?"

Petra blinked. "And, firstly, I believe that Nell is unlikely to be harmed, though I will not explain why at the moment. However, I have reason to think that Nell was abducted for reasons that involve the Bellowers . . . and the orphanage. I believe that Mrs. Huxton knew what this connection was, and that it did indeed have something to do with Nell's inheritance—and the inheritances of some other orphaned girls as well. What I do not yet know is how much you know, Lady Vera, and if you are involved."

Lady Vera had stood as still as a deer attempting to sense a predator. Then she gave an irritated wave.

"Of course it has to do with the inheritance monies," she cried. "I am glad you finally figured this out, my dear, even though I did my best to make you work for the connection. Oh, the duchess will be most pleased. But that is not what I was asking. What did you learn from Lady Caroline?"

TWENTY-TWO

LADY VERA WAS RINGING FOR TEA AND SAYING, "COME, SIT, and tell me what you discovered," before Petra and Lottie could do more than exchange looks of bewilderment. Hesitantly, Lottie moved to take a seat upon one of the sofas, Magnus the lurcher trotting at her heels. But Petra stayed where she was.

"I do not understand, Lady Vera. What is happening?"

A footman knocked and entered with a tea tray, followed by another holding a separate tray containing plates and cutlery. Then a third bearing a platter containing a three-tiered lemon sponge cake drizzled with crushed fresh raspberries that had been first dusted in sugar. And yet another holding a platter containing small sandwiches. Lady Vera gestured to the seat on the sofa nearest her. "Do sit down, my dear, and we shall talk."

Petra did not move, however, and noting this, the footmen worked faster than ever. The entire time, Lady Vera made polite small talk with a wide-eyed Lottie about the lurcher before exclaiming that he was sure to be the perfect match for the girls.

By the time the footmen bowed and exited the room with much haste, Petra's jaw was tight with anger and she'd crossed her arms over her chest.

"I wish to know why you are happy I told Caroline, Lady Vera. If she knew something that was helpful to you or had some knowledge of Mrs. Huxton's death, why did you not go directly to her?"

Gesturing in the direction of the windows and gardens, where the rooftop balustrades and chimneys of a fine house could be seen, she added, "Lawks, you even have a secret gate that gives access from your gardens into hers. You did not even need to have your hackney pony hitched up to pay a call."

Lady Vera calmly measured tea into the teapot, and leaned toward Lottie.

"'Tis true, you know. Before Lady Caroline and her Captain Smythe purchased that house, and when I was a young widow, I had a romance with the widower baronet who owned it, and often utilized that gate. He was a lovely man. Rather well-formed calves. But, alas, he chose to marry again. Now lives in Northumberland, though I do get a letter when he is feeling nostalgic for London." Pouring boiling water onto the tea leaves and noting Petra's irritably tapping foot, she said, "It was the duchess's idea, my dear, so you shall have to ask her once she returns from Kew. I confess I know as little as you—that is why I wish to know what Lady Caroline said. Her Grace only said it would be important to your investigation. I understand she hinted to you that you should. Did she not?"

She most certainly did not, Petra was about to retort. But stopped short when she remembered Her Grace patting her cheek, and telling her to not eschew confiding in her friends.

Petra inwardly groaned, for in fact, Her Grace had seemed to specifically mention Caroline, whilst sounding a bit worried and insistent. It was hardly the most obvious of hints, but had Petra not been so concerned on other matters, she might have picked up on the instruction earlier.

Yet why would Her Grace simply not be as forthcoming as usual and just demand that I speak with Caroline? Petra thought. *Why did she insist on an oblique approach?*

Lottie's eyes were bouncing back and forth between Petra and Lady Vera as she accepted a beautiful Wedgwood plate and chose a sandwich at her ladyship's urging.

Petra, however, was so frustrated she wanted to throw a plate to hear it crash and break. She did not, but she wished to very much.

"So you are saying the duchess has been manipulating me? To what end?"

Lady Vera laughed, though there was no malice in it.

"Manipulating you? Why that is rather Shakespearean, Lady Petra. Though, as I mentioned, I do not know any more than you. Her Grace could very well be doing just as you say."

She offered a piece of that delicious-looking cake to Lottie, whose head full of blond curls bobbed up and down in silent acceptance.

"I do know, however, that the duchess—like her favorite goddaughter—does not do anything in half measures," continued Lady Vera. "Her Grace has her reasons, and I would wager they are meant to help you, not hurt you. So, if you would please, come and sit. Have some cake or a sandwich, and let us speak."

She cut a second slice of cake, and addressed Lottie.

"She is rather reminding me of my late Lord Grimley at present. So tetchy he would become when he was hungry. And incapable of putting two clear thoughts together. And yet he always found that both his good temper and his strong mind returned after a bite or two of food."

"It is all rather good, Petra," Lottie said with a hopeful smile.

"You have had your cook make my favorites," Petra accused, then flounced down next to Lottie. "That just proves you are up to no good."

A little smile came over Lady Vera's face, and her eyes were more alight than Petra had seen yesterday. "Hm, possibly, my dear, but all in the name of what is good, I assure you."

Handing over a plate with a rather large slice of lemon cake, she met Petra's eyes.

"Though I will say this: I was not the person to deliver the final blow that killed Mrs. Huxton. It was important, however, that I not be disregarded so easily. That was not Her Grace's directive, but mine."

She went on to explain that she knew she had been seen by

both Nell and Mrs. Yardley, adding that both must think her a simpleton if they thought they were as quiet as all that. Then she modified this by saying that Nell could indeed walk as softly as any cat, but the girl had not been so soundless that morning one week earlier.

"Then it must be Mrs. Yardley," Petra said, her cross feelings—with Lady Vera, at least—indeed easing with a bite of the lemon sponge. "Yet, for some reason, I cannot see that she had the time, if I am piecing your story and Nell's together correctly. I think either you or Nell would have seen her."

"And you can rule Nell out as the perpetrator?" Lottie asked, then clapped her hand over her mouth. Petra, however, quickly assured Lottie that her opinion was welcomed, then responded to the question.

"Nell had every reason to keep Mrs. Huxton alive, both for her potential inheritance, and because she was being trained to become the undermatron—a job she wanted, working for someone she respected. It would not have made sense for her to kill the matron."

Petra did not, however, tell either woman that she was in possession of Mrs. Huxton's wooden box. For one thing, the secret compartment had not yet been breached, and while Enid had suggested simply taking a hammer to it to discover its secret, Petra had felt it was not yet time to do so. After reading Caroline's diary, she believed that if proof of Nell's inheritance were to be found in the box, yes, it might shed some light on the reason for Mrs. Huxton's death. But somehow she did not think it would name the poor woman's killer. Thus, there was no need to damage the box in order to find any documents it was hiding just yet—at least, she hoped.

"Pray, tell me, Lady Petra, what did you learn from Lady Caroline?"

Blinking her thoughts back to the matter at hand, Petra replied, "Caroline did not say anything of note, for I don't believe she has or had any knowledge of anything relating to the radical Bellowers. What exactly did the duchess say to you on the subject?"

As she said this, Petra watched as the lurcher made one circle and then laid down at Lady Vera's feet with sleepy calm. Lady Vera leaned to give his ears a scratch as she replied.

"Hm, let's see. It was at the art display she arranged at the British Museum some weeks ago, featuring all those paintings done by women. Beautiful works, especially young Miss Cole's. Stunning detail, especially in the one featuring her sister, the elder Miss Cole, playing the violin. I came for the early showing, which was much quieter."

"Yes, I was there for the afternoon showing—with Lottie, Frances, and Caroline, in fact," Petra said, nodding thoughtfully.

"Then did you not see Lady Caroline speaking with a man no one seemed to know?"

Petra looked at Lottie in confusion, wondering why this would be important. At every public event there were always people one did not know. Why would the duchess even care?

It was Lottie who finally said, "Well, I do recall Lady Caroline saying she encountered a rather rude gentleman, who professed to have an acquaintance with her. As I recall it, he kept teasing her that she already knew his name, and refused to remind her of it." Lottie shrugged. "She said he began to make her uncomfortable so she finally pretended to know him, and then he took his leave. There did not seem to be much more to it than that."

"Clearly a man in need of manners," said Lady Vera with disapproval, and began pouring out tea. "I cannot see why his interaction with Lady Caroline meant anything to the duchess."

Yes, this is quite the silly line of inquiry, Petra thought, even as Lottie said, "And why, if this man were important somehow, the duchess did not simply have Mr. Shawcross or one of his men do something about him?"

"I formed the impression that Her Grace did not wish for this gentleman to know she had noticed him," Lady Vera mused, "though why she felt that way, I could not tell you."

Petra glanced out the windows to the back of Caroline's house. She could be at Caro's in minutes and simply ask her friend if she recalled the name of the gentleman who claimed to know her, thus ending this ridiculous sidestep to her investigation.

But first, she had other questions—and after Lady Vera's sudden reveal to be all but in the pocket of the Duchess of Hillmorton, she could not help but wonder what else her friend might be hiding behind such canniness. With her ability to sound convincing about nearly everything—and with Petra being naturally inclined to trust her—Lady Vera would make the perfect person to work both for and against the Crown. Could it be possible? Combining today's charade with what she had read in Caroline's diary entries, Petra felt herself in a swirl of conflicting emotions.

Lady Vera looked at her shrewdly. "There is more you wish to know from me first. Am I correct, my dear?"

Petra nearly put her hand over her stomach to settle it. Then, remembering this was seen as a sign of weakness, kept it in her lap. Even the lurcher lifted his head, sensing something in the room, and blinked up at all three women. Lottie slowly put her tea cup back onto its saucer with a muted *click*.

"I wish to know about the companion you hired three years ago for the ward you briefly watched over until she married and moved to Ireland. The one who escorted your ward to Lady Caroline's house party at Evermark Manor in Surrey."

Lady Vera looked as if she were expecting something quite different.

"The companion? Why, I do not even recall the woman's name. I did not even meet her."

"You expect me to believe you did not make certain of the character of the companion you hired for your young ward? Why, I do not believe it for a moment."

Lady Vera's nostrils flared and Petra thought she heard the slightest squeak of nervousness out of Lottie. The lurcher's graceful head was swiveling, attempting to ascertain what was amiss.

And then Lady Vera rolled her eyes. "And you would be correct. If I had not been so very ill that week and accepted a friend's offer to recommend a suitable companion for the girl, I would have. As it was, I could barely lift my head from my pillow, I was so weak. I trusted the woman's character had been thoroughly ascertained. The only thing I recall is my ward returning home and declaring her companion not to her liking and begging me not to hire her again. I never saw the woman, not once. Why do you even ask about her?"

At this, the lurcher yawned, and put his head back on his paws again. Petra looked to Lottie, who again seemed to anticipate her question, and gave the merest nod of her head.

Indeed, Petra had already sensed Lady Vera had been truthful. But seeing both Lottie and the dog—two excellent judges of honest behavior—respond as they did made her want to emit a long sigh of relief, much like the lurcher did as his eyes closed.

"If you never met the companion, then who was your friend who vouched for her character?"

Lady Vera's lips thinned into a wry smile.

"I expect I should have called her someone I am often forced to be around, for we have never been true friends. She called upon me one day, just after my ward had the very kind invitation from Lady Caroline to Surrey. Though this lady of rank did not yet know I was feeling poorly and would need a companion for the girl, she asked if I would hire her for the house party. I felt it very odd, but I was told the woman was a spinster of good character who quite needed a few days away from her family. By the time our tea was consumed, I was wishing for my bed and agreed."

Lottie leaned forward, her eyes wide with interest. "Lady Vera, do tell us who she was—the woman who encouraged you to hire the companion."

"My dears," Lady Vera trilled, "she would be the Dowager Marchioness of Langford."

TWENTY-THREE

Thursday, 22 June 1815
Lady Caroline's House
Brook Street, Westminster, London
The eleven o'clock hour

PETRA KNOCKED ON THE DOOR OF CAROLINE'S BEDCHAMBER, and entered as instructed. Then immediately whirled around with a gasp, putting her back to the bed.

"It is only Whitfield, dearest," Caroline said blithely. "And he is quite asleep."

"I am only grateful Lottie is still at Lady Vera's," Petra said, a giggle escaping. "Yet I do not care if it is simply his bum. Would you mind covering him, please?"

She heard a rustle. "There, he is covered now. Now, come sit next to me. What is it that is so important it cannot wait until I am properly dressed?"

Petra turned back to find Caroline had taken a small pink silk pillow and placed it atop Whitfield's bare backside. She was about to laugh again when she approached the bed and saw the left side of Whitfield's face. Beneath one thick, dark brow she could see a partially blackened eye and a cut upon his lower lip. As she let her eyes travel over his muscled arms and back, she saw two bruises along his rib cage.

She'd seen Duncan naked enough times after a particularly strenuous boxing session at Jackson's boxing academy to know fists had made the marks upon Whitfield's body. And as Caroline would rather shoot someone with an arrow than strike them—plus, her knuckles were pristine and blemish-free—the damage had not come from her.

"Heavens. What has happened?" Petra asked, going to perch on the edge of the bed next to Caroline's legs.

"Did I not mention it when I sent my diary? No, I see I was not forthcoming enough when I wrote it was an interesting evening last night. It seems some of the revelers were too much in their cups and attempted to grab me for a dance as I made my way to my carriage after Lady Sloan's dinner."

She reached over and tenderly pushed Whitfield's coal-black hair away from his forehead, her touch eliciting a small sigh from his lips, but no movement otherwise.

"Thank goodness my Whitfield was there, for he saved me from the brutes. But in doing so, he was forced to engage in a bit of a boxing match before the two men ran off." Caroline's lips curled up slowly. "I was excessively attentive to him in thanks for his protection. More than once last night, and again this morning."

Petra could not smile at this, however. Her gut was telling her it was not just two overzealous revelers.

"Caro, are you certain that was what they wanted? A dance? I mean, are you certain it was meant to be harmless?"

"Well, no, but that's what one of them said as he grabbed me." She affected a terrible accent meant to mimic one generally heard on the docks. "Come on, then, love. Come and 'ave a dance with ol' Cawlen." She lifted her eyes to the ceiling. "Or it might have been Cawton. Nevertheless, his friend said something similar, and there were couples dancing all around us. I did not like it at all, but I was patient until one grabbed me too hard. He heard my scream in his ear, though, I assure you."

She lifted the sleeve of her dressing gown and Petra saw a bruise with four fingers present. "I thought Whitfield would go back out and hunt the wicked rascals down after he saw it, but I managed to persuade him to stay with me instead."

Petra put her hand over her friend's to get her attention. "Could the man's name have been Caufield, maybe?"

Caroline stilled. "Yes, I remember now. But how would you even know him?" Then she took Petra's arms, searching for bruises. "Did he hurt you as well? You left nearly an hour before I did. Oh, I should have sent my Whitfield down to ensure you—"

"I am well, dear Caro," Petra said fondly, before launching into explanations she had not had time for the night before, about Duncan having to pretend she was a ladybird to help conceal her identity when some of the Bellowers, drunken and mean, had arrived in their alley.

"I was accosted by one of these Bellowers radicals?" Caroline said, aghast. Then they both checked to make certain Whitfield hadn't noticed. The man had not so much as moved a muscle.

Petra then went on to explain her morning with Lottie and Lady Vera. Once more, Caroline was shocked. "Something I said or did may have set all this in motion?"

Petra tilted her head to one side. "You are certainly talented in so many ways. Your wit, your aptitude at the piano, your *exceptional* skill as an archer—and goodness, well done, you, in exhausting this Clydesdale of a man so thoroughly. But when listing your accomplishments, I do not think I would write *able to predict the future.* Or *practiced at accents,* for that matter."

"You think I am an exceptional archer?"

"I clearly do not tell you enough that you are, even though you are already quite aware of it." Petra's smile then faded and she explained what information Lady Vera had imparted. "I must know, did you truly not recognize the man at the British Museum? The one who insisted you knew him?"

Caroline sat back against her pillows. "I should have to think on it. I remember the interaction, yes, but thereafter I did not give it more thought than it took to tell you, Frances, and Lottie about it at the time." She looked over at Whitfield, her brown eyes going soft. "Because when he walked into the museum, I couldn't think of anything else."

Petra's heart hurt for her friend, even while it was threaded with happiness for her. She could only hope Whitfield would be kind when he met a woman who was free to marry him.

Then Caroline sat up straighter. "Wait, a bit of it is coming back. I remember offhand that he was somewhat tall—though not as tall as Duncan—and quite slender in form. Brown hair, too, but I can't recall much about his face. He was rather unremarkable, and yet familiar at the same time. But what I do remember is that he seemed very pleased that I did not know who he was. I teased him at one point, in fact. I think I said something such as, *Oh,* indeed, *you are the nincompoop I was forced to dance with at the Duchess of Hillmorton's spring ball.* Or it is possible I said Lady Oakley's house party. Nevertheless, when I did, I recall him looking quite crusty until he realized I was merely jesting. Then he seemed to go back to being right smug."

Petra and Caroline both agreed this was not only strange, but rather uncomfortably so.

"Why do you think Her Grace is so interested in this man?" Caroline asked.

"I could not say," Petra said. "But the duchess always has her reasons. The fact that she used Lady Vera to indicate I should be asking about this man makes me think that she feels it's important to me somehow. But if you do not know who he is, then it makes no difference."

"Maybe I will recall," Caroline said. "I shall continue to think on it. And ask Whitfield once he awakens if he saw the man."

"Well, then I am off with Lottie to the orphanage," Petra said, then she took her friend's hand. "Caroline, with you being attacked last night, the threat coming from this radical group, and with the knowledge we already have that something vastly wrong may be about to happen soon, I beg of you to be careful."

Caroline was quick to assure her, teasing, "Whilst you may enjoy the thrill of danger, dearest, I prefer my thrills right here in my bedchamber. And in the occasional carriage. And outside on a lovely day on a blanket. And in Whitfield's copper bathtub . . ."

Petra could only laugh. Some may see her dearest friend as merely scandalous, but Petra knew it was but one of Caroline's many facets—one that made for a diverting drizzle of tartly sweet raspberries atop the tiers of lemon cake that was her friend's long list of attributes.

As Petra stood up, she had a brilliant idea. "I know. What if I host an impromptu house party at Forsyth House for the next two nights? With you, and Lottie and Frances. You three are already coming to tea and we were planning on walking about and looking at all the lit-up illuminations—where Forsyth House is the perfect focal point. Then we can also be assured of being safe, together." She smiled. "And I insist Whitfield be a part of our merry party tonight, and stay at Forsyth House—with a room quite convenient to yours—should you both desire it."

Caroline said she would consider it, but that no one would stop her from arriving at Forsyth House for tea and the walk around London's streets. In the end, the two decided to meet at Bardwell's Apothecary before teatime. For Caroline had not purchased her own transparency, and she wished for some of Frances's excellent balms to heal her Whitfield's battered face.

That reminded Petra of something, and from her reticule she extracted the drawing of Carling Magna, which delighted Caroline immensely.

"Emerson drew this? That sneaksby! Many times I told him I wished for him to draw my papa's house and he always told me no. Of course, I knew he was but teasing me, but then he was gone too soon, and, well . . . Nevertheless, this makes me quite happy." She held it up, admiring it. "I think I shall have it framed."

Petra then handed her the rough sketch of Ingersoll House.

"Would you help me remember how it should have looked? I do love to watercolor, but you are so much better at sketching, and drawing details of houses and such."

Caroline took it with one of her rare gentle smiles. "Of course, dearest. I shall keep it in my drawing room for when you are ready, and then we shall drink wine, talk of things we love now, and make this into a lovely remembrance of what might have been."

Then Whitfield shifted, the pink silk pillow slipping off his well-formed backside, making Caroline's lips curve upward, and telling Petra it was time she took her leave.

TWENTY-FOUR

Thursday, 22 June 1815
The Asylum for Female Orphans
Lambeth, South London
The twelve o'clock hour

LOTTIE FELT A HOUSE PARTY WAS AN EXCELLENT IDEA. "I ONLY wish there would be more gentlemen than ladies. I do love Fitz and Magnus, but they are rather rubbish at dancing the quadrille."

The gray lurcher, who had done so well in telling Petra that Lady Vera was exactly the stalwart and trustworthy woman she had always known, lifted his head from the footwell and his lips pulled back in a semblance of a grin.

The pretty day was getting hotter and the streets of London were beginning to become crowded, so much so that Rupert took the carriage down several back roads on their way to Lambeth. Yet so far, the crowds did not seem to be acting ill-mannered or particularly rowdy. Still, Petra decided she would be glad when they had returned to Forsyth House for good later in the afternoon. For she wanted her horses and Rupert to be safe from any mischief-makers as much as she did her friends.

She and Lottie had to hold on as Rupert expertly guided the carriage into a left turn from Whitehall Street, away from the Palace of Westminster, and onto Westminster Bridge. Then they were jostling more than ever as the carriage began to go slowly over the Portland stone horse-way that was beginning to show significant wear.

Petra looked out the window to the Thames and the myriad of

boats navigating the river. Some were rowboats, others with sails, and a few punters—and no two boats were the same size. Nearly all, however, were in the same business, that of ferrying goods from one side to the other, and every last one was decorated with flags and streamers in celebrations of the victory at Waterloo.

"Are you going to tell me what we will be looking for once we get to the orphanage?" Lottie asked. "Or will I see a repeating of that quite diverting time at Lady Vera's?"

Suddenly, all Petra could do was laugh. "Dearest Lottie, I do wish I could tell you. My head is so full, I am simply attempting to make certain I am asking questions when and where I can. And I am keeping my fingers tightly crossed that somehow, with one of those questions, I will find the connection I need. At least I know now that whatever I find, I may send my intelligence to Lady Vera, as she has a way to send word to the duchess."

She had been wondering how to send a report to her godmother. While the duchess had told her she would be in touch, Petra had heard nothing so far. Yes, it had only been one full day, but in the back of her mind she'd been hoping the duchess would appear, simply to be certain she was on the right track.

Only now, it seemed her godmother had been manipulating her somehow. If not that, then testing her. And still the question remained—to what end? Why would the duchess feel such a need?

"Does Duncan not as well?" Lottie asked. When Petra could only blink as she attempted to clear her thoughts, her friend clarified. "Does Duncan not have a way to send word to the duchess?"

"Most certainly," Petra said. "Though it will be *finding* Duncan that is the problem."

Yet while her trust in Duncan had returned with a swiftness that made her heart glad, she still realized she did not know why Emerson had been murdered, much less who had performed the heinous act. It was something she was determined to discover, but only after she fulfilled her duty to investigate the murder of Mrs. Huxton first.

While the question of who had killed both Emerson and Mrs. Huxton was essential to know, it was also the *why* that bothered her about Emerson's demise. Conversely, in the case of the late matron, it was the *how* that niggled at her.

How was it that one of three people could have entered the chapel and used the candlestick to bash Mrs. Huxton on the head without the others seeing? Or, if there was a fourth person, how was it that no one saw or heard them?

Petra worried her lip for a moment, and then an idea of how she might test a theory or two formed in her mind. She also realized one crucial point. While all the orphans were locked in their dormitories at night for their safety and thankfully had not witnessed the murder, that did not mean they did not have any useful knowledge.

She looked at Lottie with a grin.

"Right. Let me tell you what I would like to do, for I shall require your help—both with Mrs. Yardley, yes, but mostly with the girls."

Petra explained, and Lottie approved of her strategy, and was perfectly willing to do her part.

"I am happy to show off Magnus and his tricks to the girls and see if there might be any recollections of their late matron that may have been missed." She eyed Petra shrewdly. "You have quite the gleam in your eye, Petra. What is it that *you* plan to do?"

"I am going to re-create a murder," Petra said.

Petra made introductions between Lottie and the undermatron, Miss Stebbins, who seemed to have taken to her temporary assignment as acting matron with a strong will mixed with a dose of good humor. She checked on Mrs. Yardley at regular intervals and could confirm the matron had not left her room. Her last check had been a half hour ago and Mrs. Yardley had been writing letters, looking perfectly well.

Petra thanked Miss Stebbins and asked that a maid be sent to the matron's room with some tea in twenty minutes' time. "And until then, are there two young girls who might be able to help me with an experiment? It should take no more than a few minutes and then they will be back here to meet Magnus. Yes? Excellent. Please send them to meet me in the chapel."

The undermatron had not blinked an eye. She said it would be done, then took Lottie and Magnus back to the dormitories, where the girls were doing their daily chores. Moments later, Petra found herself smiling as a chorus of delighted squeals could be heard. Then she hurried to the chapel, borrowing a vase full of summer daisies along the way, and placed it at the base of the altar.

Next, she moved to the chapel door to confirm it was unlocked. Afterward, she returned to the hallway and was making her way to the door by the staff quarters to test the hinges when she heard a young voice.

"My lady?"

She turned and there were two little girls bobbing curtsies, one being the girl with the ginger hair and the charming little lisp due to her teeth growing in. The other girl, a dark plait down her back, glanced up at Petra shyly, seemingly happy to let her friend do the talking.

"Excellent," Petra said with a smile. "Now, I should like for you two to help me with determining the parameters of a game of sorts. I shall tell you where to stand, and I want you to tell me what you see and hear, and when and how you can see the vase of daisies. Yes, that is all I wish for you to do—though we shall try it a few different ways. But for now, it must be an absolute secret between us three. Can you do that for me?"

The girls exchanged smiles, and nodded eagerly.

Within a quarter of an hour, Petra had her answer. She gave the girls each a handful of boiled sweets from the tin of them Lady Vera had purchased, and a penny each as well.

"You both did very well indeed, and I thank you for helping me."

"It was eathy, my lady," said the little ginger-haired girl. "We'd done it before."

"How do you mean?" Petra asked, then feigned consternation. "Did someone else already think of my game?"

"Indeed, my lady," she replied with a giggle. "The matron asked uth to help her in the thame way a fortnight ago. We're good at following directions—and volunteered when we heard you required help."

Petra hoped she did not look uneasy as her eyes flicked in the direction of Mrs. Yardley's rooms. "The matron? Whatever for?"

Both girls looked at each other, shrugging. "We know not, my lady."

By the time they trotted out once more, Petra could only be grateful that these darling little girls believed that Mrs. Huxton had died peacefully in her bed instead of on the cold floor of the chapel from a cowardly blow to the head—a blow Petra was now all but certain was delivered by Mrs. Yardley. Indeed, her little game had just proven that Mrs. Yardley had not only seen who had killed Mrs. Huxton, but could very well be the killer herself.

She'd just swung round to storm off to the matron's room when the chapel doors opened again, revealing the two little girls.

"Did you forget to tell me something else you did for Mrs. Yardley?" she asked, biting back her impatience to ensure a smile was on her face.

"No, my lady," replied the ginger-haired girl. "Only we forgot to thay—it was not Mrs. Yardley who we helped. It was Mrs. Huxton."

TWENTY-FIVE

"MRS. HUXTON? ARE YOU CERTAIN?" PETRA GRASPED THE back of one of the chapel's pews, feeling a bit shaken at this news.

The girls nodded in tandem, smiling with such innocence that Petra gathered herself quickly. "Well, that is most interesting," she said.

She paused, gathering her wits as best she could under the circumstances.

"Then may I ask the two of you to go to Mrs. Yardley in her rooms and ask her to come see me? Thank you, my dears. And if you would find the kitchen maid and say that tea is no longer necessary, I would be quite grateful. Do remember our pact as well, that your help for me just now was to be our secret." She held her finger up to her lips and the girls did as well.

After they'd run off, Petra found herself attempting to recall what Frances always said about taking deep breaths in order to calm oneself, finally remembering to breathe in to a count of four through her nose, hold her breath for another four count, and then breathe out slowly through her mouth.

Mrs. Huxton had worked out a way to know who could see into the chapel from various spots, and what they could see when they did? Was it possible Mrs. Huxton was not the intended victim, but the would-be killer instead?

Petra recalled Lady Vera telling her that the late matron had become agitated, even violent. So much so that Lady Vera had felt compelled to strike out at her to protect herself. But why would this happen?

Could it be that Mrs. Huxton had not eschewed her former radical ways, and was she secretly working with the Bellowers? If so, she would have known Lady Vera would flush out the truth eventually. Then had Mrs. Huxton been determined to do away with Lady Vera? Had she set up an elaborate trap, ensuring no one would see them because she was actually *intending* on attacking, and killing?

She rose from the pew, feeling thoroughly confused and frustrated even as the chapel doors opened once more and Mrs. Yardley entered.

I may not know what to believe just yet, Petra thought, *but if there is one thing I have learned in the past two days, it is the art of deception. There is nothing requiring me to tell the truth until I know more, and so I bloody well shall not.*

"You asked for me, your ladyship?"

Petra turned from where she had moved to stand, just two steps from the altar where Mrs. Huxton had breathed her last. Mrs. Yardley was walking up the aisle, clutching shaking hands together and looking nervous. Petra smiled, and told an untruth.

"I must apologize to you, Mrs. Yardley," she said. "For thinking you one of my suspects. I have proven that you could not have killed Mrs. Huxton, and I therefore am reinstating you as matron."

Mrs. Yardley's sudden smile was all happiness, lifting several years off her face.

"I thank you, my lady. Truly." She hesitated, adding, "And Lady Vera, and Nell?"

"I am still working out all that happened," Petra said smoothly. "However, as there is still something nefarious going on—not including the fact that all of London is celebrating the end of the war today and the two next days—it is quite important that the orphanage and the girls within it remain safe. My friend, Miss Lottie Reed, is here with the dog she trained—the one Lady Vera has gifted to the girls. If you agree, I should like to leave the dog here. Also, do you have anyone who might be able to come and watch over the orphanage?"

With pursed lips, Mrs. Yardley thought on this. "I do quite agree it is important to keep our girls safe. I do not know of any men of security I can call upon, but we have an excellent reputation with several of our delivery men, including Mr. Fife. I am certain I can call upon him, or hire some of his lads to watch over us until our world is set to rights once more. Regardless, of course the dog may stay, so long as he is well-behaved."

As she said this, the chapel doors opened once more and Lottie came in, with Magnus on a lead.

"He is one of the best-behaved dogs I've ever had the pleasure to know, Mrs. Yardley," Lottie said, curtsying to the matron before laying her hand on the dog's head to give his ears a rub. "I think you will be pleased with him."

Mrs. Yardley returned the curtsy, but her smile had gone stiff at the sight of Magnus. Especially when the lurcher's long nose twitched interestedly at the chatelaine full of keys hanging from her waist. Mrs. Yardley took a step back, confessing she was never at her most comfortable around dogs.

To this, Lottie enthused over Magnus's gentleness and how she had made certain he was disinclined to bite, even in chaotic moments.

Seeing the matron looking more relaxed, Lottie explained that two of the older girls had been put in charge of the dog's care and feeding. "And I shall deliver him back to his new caretakers directly. But first, I shall take him outside to use the chamber pot."

"I beg your pardon?" said Mrs. Yardley, her fingers going to the cross at her neck and her eyebrows flying up in alarm.

Lottie smiled. "Just a bit of a jest, do forgive me. I only meant that he needs a few minutes out on the grass."

"Oh, well, I suppose he must," Mrs. Yardley said on a relieved breath. "There is a small green space beyond the front doors, if you should like to take him there." Lottie thanked her and led Magnus out of the chapel.

"Before I leave, Mrs. Yardley, would you be so kind as to show me where Nell slept?" Petra asked. "I was remiss not to ask before." With a little embarrassed grin, she added, "I am quite new at this business of making inquiries for the Queen, you understand. But it is now more important than ever to make certain I am thorough in my investigation."

Mrs. Yardley agreed, and they exited the chapel. Yet instead of walking toward the dormitories, they turned toward the quarters reserved for the kitchen servants, the undermatron, and other staff.

"She did not live in the dormitories with the other girls?" Petra asked, eyeing as she did the door that led to the outside of the building. Her re-creation of the murder with the help of the little girls had told her that the killer must have somehow used this door. She had not yet fathomed how, though. The morning of the murder, the door had been locked. And had it been opened, someone would have heard the noise.

This was a fact her dark-haired young helper had innocently confirmed when Petra had asked her to open the door. The girl was willing, but had held her hands to her ears and squeezed her eyes shut, as if anticipating the horrid squeaking sound. Petra had then allowed the girl to merely throw the lock open instead, and earned herself a wide, eager smile.

Mrs. Yardley now selected a key from her chatelaine. "Nell used to live in the dormitories, yes, but she moved in here a fortnight ago. Lady Vera did not think her ready, but Mrs. Huxton and I felt it only right as she was about to begin her formal training to be an undermatron."

Petra glanced back to the exit they had just passed, recalling Nell's tale of the morning Mrs. Huxton had been murdered.

"I heard nothing. No footsteps, or doors closing, or anything. In truth, except for thinking I'd heard something coming from the front parlor, all was quiet from the moment I awoke . . ."

That meant Nell, whose bedchamber was only a few steps away from a door with squeaky hinges, would have heard it if it were opened. In fact, the door was close enough to the chapel that, in the silence of the morning, it was likely Nell would have heard it even when she first found Mrs. Huxton by the altar, hurt, but still alive.

Blast, Nell had lied to her.

Feeling nettled, Petra entered the small space, which held enough room for one bed, a chest of drawers, and a washstand. Mrs. Yardley opened the small window for some light and stood back as Petra checked all the places she herself might hide something of note. Underneath the mattress or the bed itself, within a book, or beneath a loose floorboard—though there was none of the latter Petra could easily see. The washstand, too, seemed to be just that. Lastly, she checked all the drawers. Inside the bottommost, tucked between neatly folded cotton dresses and other clothing items, were a few pages of paper that had been used by Nell for watercolor practice.

With paper being expensive, each page contained between six and ten small paintings, nearly all of flowers and gardens. One showed a peony bush full of blooms, and Petra now understood why Nell had looked as if she had stumbled upon a fairyland in seeing the peonies at Forsyth House.

She then found another painting, on its own page, of Vauxhall Pleasure Gardens. Upon seeing it, Mrs. Yardley explained that every girl, when they turned fifteen and were about to be sent to service or an apprenticeship, was gifted a half day out at either Vauxhall or at a theatre to see a suitable play. Nell had chosen Vauxhall, and had painted what she saw afterward, focusing on the green trees as much as she did the ornate and colorful orchestra pit for which Vauxhall was most recognized.

Petra's thumb ran over the page, and as she tilted the painting to get a better look at the detail, she could see there were impressions in the paper forming words or phrases. She could easily make out a few in places where the watercolor was darker—"day" and "Saint" and "His blood" were but three. It appeared Nell been writing on another piece of paper, and had pressed her quill hard enough to leave an imprint on this page. Working out something of doctrinal import, perhaps? And yet, it was the actual painting, from the particular angle Nell had chosen, that seemed quite familiar.

As she was returning the pages to the drawer, she suddenly remembered why. While at Bardwell's Apothecary yesterday morning when the transparencies arrived, one from the larger box that Frances had ordered had been a vibrant and fireworks-free painting of Vauxhall Pleasure Gardens.

Could the specific transparency desired by the man who'd attacked Annie be that of Vauxhall Pleasure Gardens? If so, what was it that made it special to him?

"My lady? Are you quite well?"

Petra turned, indignation not being very hard to convey upon her countenance, even if the words she planned to speak were meant to be misleading. She would do so in order to give herself more of what she needed, which was time to think and time to unravel all the twisted facts around her.

For while she did not quite trust Mrs. Yardley, and she was almost entirely certain the new matron had known when and how to enter the chapel and kill Mrs. Huxton without being seen, Petra could not quite convince herself of Mrs. Yardley's guilt.

In quite the opposite manner, she had innately trusted Mrs. Huxton—a woman she had never met, and who she knew to have radical ties in her past—for the sole reason that the former matron had been murdered. And yet now she had reasons to mistrust what she knew of the late matron, too.

And then there was Nell. The girl was sullen and prickly, and had more than once done things to make Petra think twice in regard to her innocence. And yet she wanted very much to say that Nell was telling the truth.

Exhaustingly, if she counted Mrs. Huxton, with her dodgy past, penchant for keeping secrets, and the possibility that she had intended to hurt or kill Lady Vera before being killed herself, Petra felt she still had three people she must investigate when all was said and done. For the only person whose innocence she was convinced of was Lady Vera's.

Petra thought of how Lady Vera had deliberately deceived her for what was ultimately a good cause, and decided to take a page from that book. For Petra felt she must continue to fool her suspects—the two who were still alive, at least—until she could work out who was guilty. This meant keeping them separate from each other was important—though she very much doubted Nell would wish to come back to the orphanage.

Still, if the girl did, Petra wanted Mrs. Yardley to turn her away.

Keeping the look of displeasure firmly on her face, Petra gamely lied. "Yes, thank you, Mrs. Yardley, I am well. It is simply that I believe that Miss Nell Parker may be guiltier than I first knew, and I think it a good thing that you should contact Mr. Fife to provide you with protection for the orphanage and its girls."

With widened eyes, Mrs. Yardley said, "I think it an excellent idea, my lady."

"Very good," Petra said crisply. "And I think that, should Nell return, she should be turned out of this orphanage immediately. For anyone who strikes a matron should not be allowed to work with children."

For a moment, Petra thought she might have overdone it, but then the matron touched the place at her temple where Nell had hit her with the wooden box.

"Oh, yes, my lady, I quite agree."

TWENTY-SIX

Thursday, 22 June 1815
Forsyth House
Berkeley Square, Mayfair, London
The three o'clock hour

PETRA DID NOT THINK SHE COULD BE SURPRISED AGAIN ON this day, but walking into her drawing room with her friends and finding Duncan playing a game of cards with his brother, both of them laughing at something so hard they did not hear four ladies entering the room—well, she was wrong on that count. Even Sable was so entranced by the sound of their deep voices that she kept watching them instead of dashing over to Petra, tail wagging.

Petra leaned toward Frances. "You did not accidentally dose my tea with Kendal Black Drop, did you? I am seeing this, yes?"

When Frances looked at her curiously, Petra made herself blink several times. And Caroline helpfully supplied more information to Frances and Lottie.

"Imagine seeing two snarling boars suddenly sprout wings, fly about, and then come together for a spirited quadrille. It would be about the same." Pulling off her gloves with a grin, she raised her voice. "Would it not, my lord, and Mr. Shawcross?"

The two brothers—only one had dark, wild waves that fell over his collar, and the other a Brummell-like coif of burnished gold— looked up at the same time, their smiles nearly identical, even if their eyes were not. Both rose to their feet with alacrity, and proved they carried the rakehell blood of their father with wickedly correct bows. Duncan even sent her a wink as he straightened. And when no one was watching, she sent him one right back.

But that only made his smile turn wolfish, and Caroline noticed, her eyebrows dancing as she looked from one to the other.

"Now, now, you two. Do behave." She lowered her voice so only Petra could hear as their friends went to be formally introduced to the marquess. "At least until there is a darkened doorway to be had."

As everyone was seated, Duncan gave some more good news in saying that Teddy had made contact as of an hour earlier. Nell remained safe, and they were all fed, watered, and would be sleeping in shifts for safety. The chances of the girl being found by the real Bellowers were minimal.

"Did they suspect that you allowed her to escape?" Petra asked, and was relieved when Duncan shook his head.

"I made certain to have that arch rogue Caufield with us," he said, "and then whispered an instruction to Nell to aim a kick at his left kneecap, which he injured recently. She did, and he fell, absolutely howling. I knew it would give her the chance she needed— though I am not certain she altogether required my help. The girl has quite some fight in her."

"And Caufield was duly blamed for having allowed her to escape," James added.

"Excellent," Petra said, surreptitiously meeting Caroline's eyes. Unless it became necessary, they had agreed not to encourage any foolhardy behavior on Duncan's part by relating how Caufield attempted to lay his hands on Caroline. Especially as they still did not know whether it was a drunken accident, or whether Caufield did so for some reason relating to the Bellowers.

It was then Petra noticed that her cook, Mrs. Bing, had outdone herself with a spread of tea things, nearly all Duncan's favorites. "If only I could charm Mrs. Bing like you can," Petra said, "I would get her chocolate fairy cakes every day."

Duncan looked smug as he stuffed half a ginger biscuit in his mouth. Petra turned to her friends, who were sharing the sofa opposite the men while she took her regular chair facing the bookshelves. "Maybe not so much boars as simply pigs at a trough."

James's lips curved up at this. "Lady Petra, you were always headstrong, and quite a wit, too, but I never knew it was such a charming combination." He glanced at Duncan. "If I were still an unmarried bachelor, Shawcross, you would have competition."

Duncan and Petra both snorted in unison, which, surprisingly, only made James chuckle. "Well, then, it is a good thing that my new wife pleases me greatly."

Now even Caroline was speechless. Again, Petra said, "Frances, darling, pinch me, for one dancing boar has just started singing an aria. Ow! Thank you, Lottie. I know to call upon you next time for proof I am not hallucinating."

Duncan leaned back with his cup of tea, a Shrewsbury cake tucked between it and the saucer. "He has fallen quite in love with his new wife, if you can believe it. I think she proved herself rather headstrong and witty, too. He has been insufferable with pining since she was sent off to Langford Hall in Shropshire for her safety."

Petra nearly snorted again, until Duncan's nod stopped her. "Truly?" she asked, astounded.

"And she is *kind,* too," James said with mock distaste. "It is rather a lethal combination on a man's heart." He added more milk to his tea, looking up at Petra from beneath his sun-lightened brows. "Though it was you, actually, Lady Petra, who forged this"—he waved a hand about in Duncan's direction, as if searching for the word—"whatever it is, between my brother and me."

"It is called friendship, brother," Duncan said with a roll of his eyes, making James nod as if the two words together were a strange, but pleasing sound to his ears.

"Me?" Petra said, then narrowed her eyes. "How?"

"Well, as Shawcross here tells me that Lady Caroline and Miss

Lottie and Miss Frances know all that he does, I shall be frank. Let us just say that, had you not been so utterly foolish and brave a couple of months ago with a certain devious physician called Drysdale, I might have been rather ruined. And Shawcross here made certain I knew it." Stirring his tea thoughtfully with a spoon, he said, "A man so rarely has the opportunity to reevaluate his life and change it for the better, and my new wife made certain I knew *that* as well."

He chose a Shrewsbury cake, dunking the flat biscuit of flour, sugar, eggs, and butter, gently spiced with nutmeg and cinnamon, in his milky brew before shoving half of it in his mouth like his brother, shrugging as he did. "And then one evening, Shawcross and I shared a bottle of whisky."

Petra's head turned sharply to Duncan. "You did not tell me this."

"I did," Duncan said calmly, using the other half of his biscuit to stir his tea. "It was the night I slept here, in the blue bedroom." He tilted his head to James. "This bastard had his coachman drop me here instead of Bruton Place."

James shrugged. "As you have no servants like the heathen you are, I assumed you would need assistance in your recovery."

Petra was nodding now. "Oh, yes, I remember that night, though it was mostly slurring on your part. In fact, all I recall understanding was 'whisky,' 'Jamie,' and 'a lotta whisky.'" She said this while mimicking his thick, drunken burr before returning to her own voice. "I thought you had been carousing at the pub with one of the men you employ." She pointed to Langford. "*He* is 'Jamie'?"

Duncan's eyes lit up with his grin, and for the second time ever that she could recall, she heard James, Lord Langford, really laugh. Damn and blast, this was all simply too strange.

Yet she could not look disapproving. In fact, what she felt was quite the opposite. Duncan had always wanted to truly know his brother, and happily, the process had finally begun.

Then not long after that drunken evening, if the calendar in her head were correct, Duncan had leveraged his newfound friendship with his brother to assist him in infiltrating the Bellowers. To make others within the association believe they both held views of reform for Great Britain that were best achieved through force.

Briefly, she met his gaze while James complimented Frances on her skills as an apothecarist, then Lottie on her brilliance with dogs, all while holding Fitz to his chest and giving him a scratch behind the ears.

The smile was still on Duncan's face, but his eyes had become worried as he glanced to James, then met her gaze. She could almost see his swirling thoughts. He was concerned he had put his brother into a more precarious situation than expected, even if it had given James a purpose he had never had in his life prior.

She felt the weight upon her shoulders as well as she looked at her friends, all who were willing to help her, to put their own safety on the line for her. With just over two full days left of the victory celebrations, and with her own investigation linked with Duncan's, if the truth was not uncovered—if they could not put a stop to whatever violence was being planned—there was the chance of so much damage. And she could not bear it if her friends suffered because of her.

By the doors to the garden, Sable gave her little whine that indicated she wished to go outside. Petra stood and went to let her out, with Fitz trotting out as well.

"That reminds me," Lottie said. "Did you not tell me that the back door at the orphanage—the one closest to the staff quarters—squeaked when it was opened?"

"That is what Nell, Lady Vera, and even the little girls who helped me said," Petra said with a shrug.

"Then did you hear me open it?" Lottie asked. "For when I took Magnus outside, that's the door I used."

"Are you in earnest? I never heard a thing," Petra said, then briefly explained to the others about Magnus the lurcher.

"That's because the hinges and lock had been recently oiled," Lottie said. "I checked to be certain. In fact, it was Magnus who knew first. I tried to go towards the parlor, but he insisted on going to that door. He then sniffed the hinges, and the door lock. Though it was faint, I could smell linseed oil. It was what Magnus had in his fur the day I met him, and I think that is what attracted him."

Petra slumped against her drawing-room windows. "Well, that does indeed settle it. I am rubbish at investigating," she said, massaging her forehead with her fingers. "I should have checked myself. Blast!"

"Does this put Lady Vera back on your list of suspects?" Lottie asked, a little worriedly.

Petra shook her head. "I think it highly unlikely. Lady Vera went to the kitchens—on the other side of the orphanage. It was clear from all my scenarios that the culprit must have come in from the door by the staff corridor. I was about to plan on giving it a good think as to how someone could have done so without hearing the door squeak, but now it is a moot point."

Duncan rose and walked to her side, handing her a ginger biscuit. "It means you just have to keep asking questions, just like I do when I make inquiries. When you reach a dead end, turn back around and find another avenue to pursue."

Petra bit into her biscuit, giving him a grateful look. "All right, then let's talk out what we know."

TWENTY-SEVEN

SHE TOLD THEM EVERYTHING SHE HAD DISCOVERED THROUGH-
out the day, from start to finish.

"Why would the Duchess of Hillmorton want you to think
about some strange gentleman at an art show?" Frances asked,
glancing between Caroline and Petra.

"I could not say," Petra said, "though I have the impression it has
something to do not only with the Bellowers, but also specifically
with me. It is as if she wishes me to make a connection, but I have
not yet discovered what that link could be. I certainly have had no
interactions with radical reformists until now."

She looked around at her friends, her eyes finally landing on
Duncan and James, who both seemed to be more interested in
their tea than seemed reasonable. *Strange.*

"What did you find when looking through Nell's bedchamber?"
Caroline asked, diverting her thoughts.

Petra explained that she'd found nothing except for some water-
colors, including one of Vauxhall Pleasure Gardens. "Do you think
that is the gardens transparency the man wanted so badly he would
attack Annie over it?"

"And left the wording with the same note that was found on
Mrs. Huxton?" Frances added.

Duncan nearly dropped his biscuit. "What? Annie was attacked?
And another message was left, with the same threat to the Queen?
Why did you not say so?"

Calmly, Petra reminded him there had not really been time yesterday as she pulled the threatening message from her reticule and

handed it off. The brothers exchanged a look, then both shook their heads.

"We don't recognize the hand," Duncan said with some disgust. "We were hoping that if another was found, we could connect it to the Bellowers. But we know the hands of the association's leader, and his top deputies."

James was examining it. "This looks almost like a woman's hand, if you ask me."

"Well, it was definitely a man who did the attacking," Petra said, and explained the events, though carefully left out Teddy's part in thinking he might have recognized the man.

"As for Vauxhall being one of the transparencies with gardens in it, yes, there was one. Though one would expect that the man wanting it so bad would have referred to it as 'Vauxhall' like everyone else," Frances said, disgust for the man coming into her voice. "For if he had—and asked politely—Annie and I both would have told him it was purchased by the housekeeper of a house on Grosvenor Street."

Petra looked to Duncan. "The watercolor I spoke of that Nell painted—I have been thinking on it, and something I noted made me realize how we might read the letter you intercepted and showed to the Queen. The one that went into the Thames with you."

"How *did* you intercept it?" Caroline asked Duncan.

He explained that it was but a simple matter once he realized that letters were being exchanged between the Bellowers and the orphanage. Whether sent to or from the orphanage, they were always delivered or collected by one of the two unknowing kitchen maids when they were sent out on errands. The girl would go to the back of a gaming hell, where either they left a letter with the man who guarded the back door, or collected one from him. Duncan only had to wait for the exchange to happen and for the girl to move on to her next destination.

"After that, I merely bumped into her, causing her basket to fall and all the contents to scatter upon the ground. I had the letter and was gone before she even saw my face, even though I was disguised quite well as a tradesman."

"Only trouble was," James drawled, "Shawcross here managed to steal the letter in the sights of two Bow Street Runners, one of which was a Bellower. They gave chase, and he had to leg it. It became a matter of being caught, removed of his disguise, and identified, or going into the Thames." With his hand, he made a diving motion. "Though I understand several ladies crossing the Thames by wherry quite enjoyed the sight of him emerging from the river. I understand one *swooned*."

As giggles erupted from Petra's friends, Duncan groaned, a bit of pink upon his cheekbones, and tipped his head back against the back of the sofa, muttering something about rethinking his decisions about brothers.

For a moment, Petra's grin stretched wide. She could well imagine the sight, for she had pushed him into the fishing pond at Buckfields countless times over the years and vividly recalled the first time he'd emerged and she realized that beneath the white shirt clinging to his wet body were the most impressive muscles. Yet she controlled herself and raised an eyebrow.

"And may I now see the letter, then?"

When Duncan's head came back up, looking at her shrewdly, she held out a hand, fingers wiggling to indicate she was waiting.

"I don't know what you mean," he said, his voice suddenly sounding rather English indeed. Yet he stopped short of saying he did not have it.

"Oh, but I am certain you do," Petra said sweetly. "And you yourself said I must figure out for myself whether or not you are the Queen's intelligence officer, and well, I have. There could not have been anyone else looking for that letter yesterday, except you and me. For even the few who knew about it did not know it was being kept in the Queen's breakfast room. And even fewer would be bold enough to break in, knowing they had but a few minutes to locate it, without knowing exactly where it was. That leaves only two people who did, Duncan Shawcross. You and me."

"Damn and blast," muttered Duncan, all while ruffling his hair from the back, like he tended to do when he was amused at being caught out.

"Did you ask the Queen's guards to pretend to storm the house, looking for an intruder?" Petra asked.

Duncan's eyes lit with an enjoyment of Petra's challenge—but, in this accusing question, she was wrong.

"Actually, no. They saw you, and then saw me following you. They knew to expect me, but I was to arrive later. As I was dressed in working-class clothes and never announced myself, they thought us both intruders." A slow grin spread across his face, presumably the memory of holding her close as they hid from the guards. "I will allow that I might have stretched the level of danger a bit, but not very much. The guards really would have used their weapons on us first, had they seen us."

"And when we were in the carriage?" Petra asked. "I searched you, so how did you hide it?"

Caroline went to speak—no doubt to make a bawdy comment about Petra searching Duncan a bit too thoroughly—and Petra preempted this by placing her outstretched hand briefly over her friend's mouth. Then she raised an eyebrow to Duncan, whose eyes were all merriment now.

"I managed to slip it under the carriage seat when you were pouting and trying to look out the window."

"You are beastly, Duncan Shawcross," Petra said with a roll of her eyes, though no one missed the amusement upon her face.

Yet when he extracted the letter from inside his waistcoat and handed it to her, it was now folded into the smallest of packets. "Where is the seal?"

"I removed it," James interjected. "I felt it best in case the letter were found on my brother's person. He could claim it was but a love letter from you that he kept close to his heart, despite it being unreadable."

"Mm," Petra said, narrowing her eyes at James first, then Duncan. They were not being truthful, that much she was certain. "Do you recognize the coat of arms upon the seal?"

When both men looked uncomfortable, she sighed. "Never mind. I recall what Her Majesty told me in wishing to be certain before a family's name is subjected to tarnish. I shall wait."

Then she unfolded the letter, which, as she'd seen before, had stiffened oddly after being in the water. Yesterday she felt as if she might have been able to read some of the words, and she was not wrong. One sentence was even still quite clear. *You must make haste, for time is short.* Could she imagine that it referred to the violent event that was to take place? Yes, of course. Did it tell her any other information? Unfortunately not.

She then showed it to Caroline. "Do you think using charcoals would help any quill marks to become visible again?"

"Excellent idea," Caro replied. "Fetch your supplies and we shall see."

A piece of charcoal was lightly rubbed over the surface of the letter, but almost no impressions had been left after its dunking in the Thames. Caroline was about to put the charcoal away when Petra said, "Wait. Rub this spot over here. What does that say?"

"One word is 'Saint,' and another is 'day,'" Caroline said after the charcoal did its job.

Petra looked excitedly to each of her friends. "I recognize these words, and the writing. And I can say for certain the letter was written at the orphanage—and possibly by Nell."

She explained that when she found the watercolor Nell had painted of Vauxhall, she noted the impressions of words from another document, most likely Nell's, too, still visible under the paint. She confirmed the words were the same as in the letter Duncan intercepted. When comparing the hand to the threatening note mentioning the Queen, however, she could not be certain they were written by the same person.

"Though I must admit I cannot see Nell as being a part of a radical group," Petra said with a frown. "That being said, I am worried I have not yet taken the full measure of her." She looked to Duncan and James. "Do you think it is possible she is somehow attached to the Bellowers, or is she being coerced somehow? And do you think Teddy could be in danger by looking after her? Should we not send someone to check on them both?"

Duncan was rubbing his face with his hand, and concern showed in his eyes as his gaze met Petra's. He suddenly looked tired. So did James, for that matter, and Frances looked as if she had been stretched to her limit after two busy days at the apothecary.

"We know there is someone at the orphanage who is active in the Bellowers, and yet she—for it is almost undoubtedly a woman— has managed to keep so thoroughly away from being seen that we have not yet determined exactly who it is," Duncan said. "In fact, excepting the youngest girls, the female we seek could be almost anyone at the orphanage."

"Truly?" asked Lottie.

Duncan nodded. "Over the various days I was conducting surveillance at the gaming hell where the messages were exchanged, I noticed not just the kitchen maids in the area, but also the cook, Mrs. Yardley, the late Mrs. Huxton, and several of the older girls. I could recognize the girls as being from the orphanage by their gray dresses, see? Each time, those I witnessed were generally visiting nearby shops, but that does not mean one or more of them were not watching to ensure the letters were properly exchanged. Whoever it is, she has managed to keep her involvement secret from everyone."

He then looked to Petra. "But to answer your question about Nell, in my short time in her presence, I found little to concern me. However, she is as tough and wily as Teddy claimed. If anyone might secretly be a young, dangerous radical, I suppose it could easily be she."

"Blast," Petra said with dismay. Despite it all, she had come to like the girl, and she hoped Duncan's supposition would be proven wrong. Still, she felt she must ask questions as if he were correct. "If Nell is working with the Bellowers, do you think she will know the exact time and day that the radicals will make their move?"

"It is hard to say," James said, sounding frustrated for the first time, "but it may not matter. What we need to find is the path that leads us to the signal."

When he noticed the confused expressions on Petra's friends, he explained, "The leader of the Bellowers said there would be 'a signal' that showed fellow comrades where and when the event will take place. Evidently, there is a 'path' of some sort that will then lead us to a signal. We will not need Nell—if she even has connections to the Bellowers—if we can correctly ascertain the path."

Petra poured herself some more tea and recited, "*A pathway to follow to the righteousness that will be doled out upon those with royal blood.* That is what he said." And when James and Duncan both looked somewhat astonished, she added, "What? I heard him when I followed the delivery man last night."

The brothers then bandied about ideas as to what the so-called path could be, and the signal. "All I know is that what Petra said is correct—that we had to follow the path that was laid out, and that those loyal to the Bellowers would understand."

"What are the symbols of the Bellowers?" Petra asked, the words springing to her lips before she really thought on them.

"A town crier—a bellower, so to speak—is one of course," Duncan said. "A piper's flute as well—signaling the Bellowers are an army regiment of sorts, going into battle. Also . . ." He picked up the piece of charcoal, turned over the unreadable letter and drew three quick, short lines, one above the other. "I was told they represent a forward movement."

Petra's heart sped up again, but this time for a different reason. And Caroline noticed it, too. "Dearest . . ."

"I will be back," Petra said. "Do not move." And she was dashing through Forsyth House to her bedchamber, Sable at her heels, startling Mrs. Ruddle and Enid as they readied the guest rooms for Petra's small house party.

She came back from her bedchamber with Emerson's portfolio. Opening it, she found the sketches of various houses, all containing the same three lines, stacked one above the other, somewhere on the page. Sometimes the three lines were vertical, going out from the top of the page. Others were horizontal, from one side of the house or the other.

Petra explained that two more sketches had been given to Caroline, but were similar. Then she laid them out at random, so that the three lines were all going in different directions. Everyone present watched her, entranced but confused.

"Now let me do this," Petra said. Once more, she shifted the sketches so that they were in an order of how she liked them, explaining where the sketches of Carling Magna and Ingersoll House would go, with the direction of their lines. Caroline helpfully had already torn in half a piece of Petra's sketch paper and had drawn from memory two simple sketches of both houses, complete with lines. When they were rearranged, the lines met.

"It forms a path," Duncan said, picking up the one at the very end. It was of Buckingham House. He looked to his brother. "Do you think this is it? Is the target Buckingham House?"

James tapped on the pages. "Possibly. But unless every member of the Bellowers were given copies of these, no one would know. How could they send out a signal with a pathway that anyone looking in the right places could see?"

Frances, yawning and looking utterly exhausted, said, "The ten transparencies I did not order," just as Petra stood and said, "The transparencies! Yes, Frances, you are correct. They are of landmarks, with fireworks, that all look like pathways."

She then explained how she had noticed when she first saw them that all the fireworks looked like a band of the Milky Way in the nighttime sky. "What if the transparencies are to be found in the windows of houses owned by those with radical reformist views? And if you found one, it would then point you in the direction of the next by following the directions of the fireworks? Meaning, if the fireworks angled eastward, then you would know to head east until you found the next house with a transparency containing a well-known landmark that also had fireworks in the scene?"

Caroline scrunched up her nose. "But why would anyone send transparencies to an apothecary? How do they know the right people will purchase them? Would it not be too great of a risk that some little girl would come in with her mama and decide that the one with the pretty fireworks over St. James's Palace was the one she *must* have?"

Everyone nodded, agreeing that this was a sound question.

"It can easily be assumed this was the idea of Mr. Rushton," Duncan said, then immediately scrubbed a hand over his face to smother a muttered curse. But Petra and Caroline had heard it.

"Rushton?" Caroline said. "Do you mean Mr. Phineas Rushton? The gentleman who came to my house party?"

James and Duncan exchanged speaking glances, then the former shrugged and said, "Cat's out of the bag, old boy. Might as well get on with it."

"Indeed," Duncan said on a sigh. "Until my sodding tongue failed me, we had been attempting to keep his name from anyone who did not already know it. We did not wish any of you to attempt to contact him or ask others about him in any way."

His eyes went to all four women, lingering most on Petra and Caroline, before he continued.

"When I briefly knew him at Oxford, he was little more than a wiseacre, and a half nib, always attempting to have others look at him as an aristocrat, and not as the scholarship boy he was. He all but invited himself to your house party, Caroline, even writing the letter to you himself for Ingersoll to sign. It was at the house party that Ingersoll and I first understood that he had radical views on the ways in which he wished to go about achieving political reform."

"What cheek!" exclaimed Caroline. "He even made himself sound so pitiable, and in need of some merriment, that I gave him one of my best rooms at Evermark Manor."

For her part, Petra sipped her tea thoughtfully. Instead of surprise, she actually could claim a modicum of satisfaction at hearing Duncan confirm the name Rushton as the leader of the Bellowers. For it proved she was making headway after all.

Indeed, earlier this morning, Caroline's diary entries had made Mr. Phineas Rushton one of the four people Petra had wished to question. The other two being Lady Vera, now since exonerated; the companion called Miss Dodd, whom Petra would need to speak with the Dowager Viperess of Langford to potentially discover the woman's whereabouts; and then one other person, whom Petra wished not to think about at present, but was compelled to do so as she recalled what she had read in the diary.

Caroline had written of the afternoon spent at Box Hill in the blithest of ways, mentioning the lovely azure skies, the ripeness of the strawberries, and how the wine and champagne had flowed, making conversation between the entire twenty members of the party quite amiable and diverting.

And then, later, between amusingly ribald accounts of the baron, Caro had mentioned witnessing Duncan and Emerson walking off together to the little copse with Mr. Rushton, talking with *a level of earnestness she had not witnessed from the three since they arrived in Surrey.* Then she had written of seeing Duncan storming away, looking furious, and of watching Petra herself walking off to find Emerson. Then Caroline followed these recollections with a sentiment Petra had found both prescient and unsettling.

Dearest Petra, she is so trusting. I do hope Ingersoll will not break her heart, for I shall never forgive him if he does. I do not even know why I have written those words! It is as if my pen is writing my innermost concerns without my first bidding it.

Then, a bit farther down the page.

My captain said he overheard Ingersoll and Rushton talking of something he did not like the sound of, and admonished me for thinking it to be a liaison. And yet, he would not tell me what he heard. I do not care for Mr. Rushton, to be sure, and sincerely hope I never see him again. I hope Petra never is forced to, either, for I did not like the way he looked at her yesterday.

Petra inwardly shook herself, looking into Duncan's handsome face for a bit of comfort, only to find him looking broody with a muscle pulsing in his jaw. As he related more details of Mr. Rushton, it was clear just how much Duncan was determined to not let Rushton succeed at whatever chaos he was planning.

"He manages to make you believe he is a much gentler soul than he is. It was quite soon after Box Hill that he began to bring in followers, and they had planned a disruption of some kind."

He flicked his eyes to Petra, an apology in them.

"It was only Lord Ingersoll's death that stopped it, and disbanded the Bellowers for a time. Mr. Rushton has since gone from a wiseacre to a dangerous man; it is important you understand this—all of you. He is secretive, and suspicious. When in his company, he rails about things that I would call perceived injustices. And what makes it worse is that he has begun more and more to believe that others are after him."

"Which we are," James drawled, but with a concerned frown.

"I have no doubt that we will find that Rushton managed to ensure that the transparencies were all sold to the correct people," Duncan said. "How, I do not know. He may even have hired someone to walk in and purchase one, only to hand it off to the intended person. We may have success in determining who bought them, but it might be better if we use the events of the evening to attempt to find them on our own."

"If you do not mind me asking, Mr. Shawcross," Lottie said, "why is it that you were not told of the time and place of the attack if you have become instrumental to the Bellowers' dealings?"

Duncan gave a dry chuckle, as did James, who was the one to answer.

"Just as Shawcross said, Rushton has become detached from what is real. To our knowledge, he has not told but three others of his plans because he is so afraid of things going awry. We know who two are, and one is not talking out of fear for his own life. The other we have not been able to approach as of yet. And the third, he is the man named Caufield, who is dangerous and quite mad."

Duncan nodded, exchanging a brief look with Petra as he gestured for James to go on. Petra met Caroline's eyes, and her friend shook her head as if to say there was still no need to tell the men that Caufield had harassed, if not attacked, Caroline and Whitfield. Not now, at least.

"We have indeed proven ourselves useful to the Bellowers, however. For instance, we have turned votes in the House of Lords," James said. "No, do not be concerned. We only did so when we were confident our interference would not unfavorably affect the outcome of the vote." He turned his palm upward in a conceding gesture. "Or, in some instances, it must be admitted that these reformists can have worthy ideas that can be accomplished without violence. In such cases, we then worked to help a good bill succeed. For instance, we are now closer than ever to having a reform bill passed to rid Parliament of rotten boroughs and ensure equal numbers of representatives that will better reflect our country's overall population."

"However," Duncan said, "I began my infiltration of the group when I was on the Continent, but I have had to bring on James at a faster pace, which has meant we are not trusted as much as we would like."

"Also, again, Rushton does not trust anyone," added James. "So whilst we have to work harder to be seen as radicals, in the end, Rushton only trusts a handful of others. And sometimes, we are not even certain he is making the decisions."

Petra was thinking on this when Caroline voiced a rather good point.

"But there are far too many houses in London. Too many for our merry band to easily discover which windows will be illuminating the transparencies we are seeking. How are we to find them in just one evening?"

Lottie spoke up again. "I think we have to assume Mr. Rushton and his men would not put the transparencies all over London. They would likely be here, in Westminster, in the streets around Mayfair—Berkeley Square, Grosvenor Square, and the like."

Petra took up the thread, holding out one of the house sketches Emerson had made over three years earlier.

"All of these houses are fashionable addresses in Mayfair, yes? If this was a plan that was to unfold three years ago and was abandoned when Emerson—Lord Ingersoll—was murdered, they likely are using some aspect of the original plan. This time I believe they are using the transparencies to be as subtle as possible. It is a visible map to be seen by anyone. But it will only have meaning to those who are members of the Bellowers. They could do as everyone in London will be doing tonight—casually walking the streets of Mayfair and St. James's, looking at the illuminations shining out of the windows of the best houses in London. And then with each house they find that contains one of the transparencies with fireworks, they will simply begin to form a path." Once again, she indicated Emerson's old sketches. "Just as I have pointed out here."

"Every one of these houses are symbols of the aristocracy and the monarchy," Caroline said dryly. "As is nearly every building and every place depicted in the ten illuminations with fireworks."

"And I postulate it will be the tenth house that will show the Bellowers where they should go—where the secret place will be for them to cause their havoc and violence," Frances said, some of her tiredness vanishing with their discovery. She looked at those who had helped her at the apothecary. "Does anyone remember all ten landmarks depicted?"

After a bit of back and forth between all four ladies who had seen them, they could agree the ten were St. James's Palace, Buckingham House, Hyde Park, the Green Park, the Palace of Westminster, Regent's Park, Tattersall's, the British Museum, St. James's Park, and the Theatre Royal at Drury Lane.

"Yet there are still too many houses around these fashionable streets," Caroline said. "How do we even know where to start? And how will we—and the rest of the Bellowers, for that matter—know the time? Much less the target?"

"Well, as for the human target," Duncan said, "we know it is one of the royal family. We must assume that once we know the location, it will become rather clear. For whilst Rushton is a truly secretive man, to the point that I believe he may be quite losing his grip on sanity, the Bellowers must be able to clearly tell where to go and what time."

"True," James said. "For if the Bellowers cannot discern the location, then they will have nothing. There will be no show of force, not enough men loyal to the cause to form a robust protest, and not enough to be called to action when he needs it."

Petra sat forward in her chair, looking between Duncan and James. "Then our ultimate goal is to find the transparencies and determine the location of the meeting place in enough time that your men can disrupt the radicals before they can then carry out their attack."

Both brothers gave a nearly identical grim smile. "Indeed, my lady," Duncan said. "You have the measure of it."

"Excellent," Petra said. "Then we will require every set of eyes we can depend upon to help us." And when James's eyebrows raised curiously, she said, "I am speaking of my trusted servants, Lord Langford. I have no doubt they will provide us with all the extra help we need."

Moments later, Smithers appeared, announcing Lord Whitfield's arrival. Luckily, Whitfield waved off questions about his bruised face as "a little tussle, nothing more" without Caroline hinting that he should.

There were then three hours until nightfall. Petra chivvied her guests upstairs—even James—to rest. When the last door was closed, she took Duncan's hand and led him into her bedchamber. She pulled him to her, resting her head against his chest as his arms came around her, kicking off his short workman's boots as he did. They fell upon the bed, and were asleep in moments.

TWENTY-EIGHT

PETRA HAD DISCOVERED SOMETHING NEW ABOUT HER LADY'S
maid as they readied to leave Forsyth House to enter the celebratory evening streets and look for the elusive transparencies. To wit,
Annie was perfectly willing to fuss over Petra about anything,
but when Petra had reason to fuss over her, Annie did not care for
it one jot.

"Are you certain you feel well enough to be walking tonight?"
Petra asked for the third time since waking from a refreshing nap
in the warmth of Duncan's arms.

True to Annie's unflappable ways, she had not so much as even
widened her eyes at the sight of Duncan in Petra's bed—which, to
date, had never happened at Forsyth House. Instead, she'd merely
helped Petra tuck the counterpane over him and let him sleep, then
whispered as they tiptoed to her dressing room, "All of us who
work here agree that it is about time Mr. Shawcross has a room of
his own here at Forsyth House, my lady. For appearances' sake, of
course."

Petra had stumbled over the threshold of her dressing room at
hearing this. Annie, however, merrily shrugged, saying it had been
a foregone conclusion in all their minds for quite some time. Yet
when Petra attempted to ensure Annie's head wound was healing,
she was gently swatted away.

"I am well. Miss Frances already looked at it and agrees," she
said crisply.

The second time, Petra had received an exasperated reply—
though only she would have recognized it as such.

And the third, when all Petra's guests and nearly all the servants of Forsyth House were assembled in her drawing room, Annie had pulled in a breath as if reminding herself to remain calm as she turned to Petra.

"My lady, I shall be with Mrs. Ruddle and Mr. Smithers, and we have been given a section around Berkeley Square so small, I doubt I would even wind myself if I took five turns about the area. Now, if you please, I should like to concentrate on my task. And you should be concentrating on yours as well."

Grinning, Petra replied, "Now I believe you," just as Duncan strode to the middle of her drawing room and looked around at all those assembled, standing in five small groups.

Petra did a quick count. Including herself and Duncan, they were fourteen people strong. All were ready to be sent out in groups to various parts of Mayfair. Of the six servants, all they were told was the most pertinent information, which Duncan now reiterated.

"Right," he said. "Please be reminded you are to act only as if you are happy the war is over, and smile whilst you enjoy the pretty illuminations. Use your notebooks to make notes occasionally of transparencies you like, and add a sketch or two. If you find one with fireworks, you will be sure to note the house where you found the painting, the building depicted, and which way the fireworks are moving. You should not unduly remark upon it."

"Mr. Shawcross, sir," Rupert said, "are there likely to be other transparencies about painted with fireworks?"

Duncan replied that yes, as several other companies produced ready-made transparencies, it was possible, but unlikely to have them be depicted in quite the same fashion as the ten that Lady Petra described.

Annie frowned. "It is eleven, my lady. There were eleven that arrived in that crate yesterday morning at Bardwell's."

Frances heard this and agreed. "You know, Annie is correct. I had forgotten one was purchased by my delivery man. But I never saw which one he chose."

"I did, but only briefly, when his delivery boy walked out with it," Annie said. "It was of a lovely house—though not as grand as Forsyth House, you understand. I must say, it looked a bit familiar, as if it might be in Mayfair, but I could not place it."

The art portfolio was still in the drawing room and Petra laid out the drawings of houses. "Was it any of these?"

But Annie shook her head as she looked them over, her finger trailing over the windows on the topmost floor of each house. "I'm afraid not, my lady. I would have recognized all of these easily, even on a glance. The house in that drawing was not one I'd ever visited. Of that I am certain."

"I think it is safe to assume it is not a house of note, then," James offered. "It may be possible the drawing was nothing more than that of a handsomely drawn dwelling the delivery man found pleasing."

Petra, too, ran her finger over the windows in one of the drawings. Something was lurking at the edges of her memory, but refused to reveal itself. "Mm, yes. I think it is quite possible. Nevertheless, we may as well add an eleventh transparency to look for on our amblings, shall we not?"

Duncan gave a surprisingly merry shrug. "What is one more to find amongst the hundreds, if not more, of those illuminations that will be shining brightly in all the windows of London?" Indeed, he looked as if the increased challenge pleased his natural hunting instincts as he addressed the room. "We shall give the endeavor two hours and no more, with each group taking their section of Mayfair and the area around St. James's. Afterward, we are to meet back here at Forsyth House. Are we agreed?"

Everyone present nodded and watch fobs were checked before making their way out to Berkeley Square.

Caroline, on the arm of Whitfield—his cut lip already looking better and the one on his eyebrow only giving him a bit more of a piratical look—asked Petra as they walked out the front doors of

Forsyth House, "I did not ask, dearest. What is in your window? No, let me guess. One with a horse."

Petra made a derisive noise, then pointed to the window of the front parlor where a transparency emitted the most beautiful illumination of a pasture scene on a summer morning. "I beg your pardon, Lady Caroline. It has *two* horses."

Then she blew Caroline and Whitfield a kiss and linked arms with Frances and Lottie, with Charles following in their wake, and they all set off from Forsyth House, each of the small groups heading in a different direction.

Duncan and James, dressed once more like gentlemen, took the farthest corners. Allen was delighted to be paired with Enid for a stroll around Mayfair, and the feeling seemed to be mutual. Caroline and her Whitfield were sent toward Grosvenor Square. Rupert and his stable lads took to the area closer to St. James's. And Petra, Lottie, Frances, and Charles took to the area around Grosvenor Street and Hillmorton House.

Within twenty steps of Forsyth House, the number of people increased to a level that Petra had never experienced. There were easily twice as many people as there had been last night by Sloan House in St. James's Square.

Bumping into one another as they walked, their fellow Londoners shouted out hellos and good evenings to everyone, the bonhomie at a level that was somehow infectious rather than unnerving. Even Frances, who had looked uncomfortable at first and had gratefully taken Fitz from Lottie's arms, seemed to relax as the night grew darker and the beautifully painted scenes glowed from windows in every house.

It was as if they had stumbled into a magical land where every street had become a museum with the most delightful paintings, almost dancing with the flickering of the candlelight behind them. Whether it was a simple still life of fruits spilled from a basket, a charming scene of two puppies tussling in a field of clover, a moody Cornish coastline with the waves rolling onto the shore, or a depiction of Royal Ascot with four stallions vying for the lead, they were all glorious and mesmerizing.

After a while, the crowd sounds had lessened in Petra's ears as she took in the sights, thinking for a moment on what a lovely thing it was for peace to have been declared. This was something she was certain would be unlikely to be repeated in her lifetime. This moment, with the streets of Mayfair alight with bobbing lamp lights and colorful illuminated screens in every window, was something to behold indeed.

She turned to smile at her friends, to tell them that they must remember this night, only to find a sea of unknown faces about her.

She whirled, panic licking the back of her throat. "Frances? Lottie?"

"Here, Petra!" It was Lottie's voice, and once she maneuvered around a family with two young children pointing up at a painting featuring a cat wearing glasses and reading a book, Petra breathed a sigh of relief.

"We found one," Frances said. With a subtle angle of her head, she indicated the window of the house in front of them. "See? It is of Regent's Park. I remember holding it up for you to see. Do you know who lives here?"

Petra stepped back to take in the address. "I do, and whilst I would be shocked to find the parents had anything to do with the association in question, I would not be so surprised to know their middle son did." She had Lottie make a quick drawing of the Regent's Park painting, saying to her friends, "Do look, the fireworks' direction is sending us farther west. Let us keep going."

They kept good track of time, yet within the next two hours, they had only found the one of Regent's Park before returning to Forsyth House.

They were one of the last of the small parties to trickle in. Everyone had a lovely outing, made all the more exciting that each group had found between one and three of the transparencies, some that overlapped when one or more of the parties had found themselves on the same street unbeknown to the others. When ten transparencies had been accounted for—no one had yet found the eleventh— Duncan congratulated Lottie. "You were correct, every one was in the bounds of Westminster. Well done."

Once the servants filed out, leaving behind the sketches and notes they had made of the transparencies they had found, all of the sketches were given to Caroline.

Working quickly, she then made small drawings depicting the landmarks, and which way their fireworks were going. With every one she finished, Duncan placed it on a very rough map he had drawn of the sections of London that comprised Westminster. Gradually, the path became visible, Duncan drawing in and labeling streets as they became clear.

"It leads to Grosvenor Street," Duncan said. His dark brows came together. "We found all those of landmarks, with the tenth being on Audley Street, at the house of a gentleman of upstanding nature with a son who has fairly recently become a Bellower. The landmark, however, was the British Museum." He gestured toward his brother, standing to his right. "James had an excellent thought earlier, which has been proven by Caroline's drawings of what everyone reported seeing. The fireworks in the paintings start off small with the first transparency, found on the west side of Curzon Street. They grow in size and strength as the 'path' of sorts is followed. Whilst the fireworks over the British Museum do look to be more intense, so to speak, it still appears to be pointing onward, as if part of the pathway. The eleventh one is the key, then, and we are still missing it. Whitfield, Caroline, you were on those streets. Are you two positive you did not miss one?"

"I did not even allow Whitfield to flirt with me even once, Shawcross," Caroline said a bit crossly. "That is how determined I was not to miss a single house."

"She speaks the truth," Whitfield said, though clutching his heart as he did with high drama as if wounded.

Then Caroline looked chagrined. "We did encounter some acquaintances once or twice. So I suppose it might be possible . . ."

But Petra was staring at the map, and recalling the brief moment at Bardwell's Apothecary yesterday morning in which she had watched Frances and Mr. Fife looking oddly at the one transparency that did not seem to be a recognizable landmark.

By their very nature, the transparency paintings were somewhat opaque so that the light from the candle burning behind it would illuminate the design. That meant Petra had been able to see the same image Frances and Mr. Fife had seen, though in reverse. Had her mind not been so thoroughly concerned about Duncan's potential duplicity at the time, she might have noticed it then.

She went to Caroline and asked her to make a drawing, whispering in her ear. Caroline blinked concerned brown eyes up at her, but did not quibble. It took but a minute or two, then Petra showed it to Frances.

"Was this the house you saw the delivery man purchase?"

Frances took the small drawing, the house's most recognizable feature being three small arched windows on the top floor. The others crowded round to look as well. As Frances studied the sketch, Duncan's eyes pinched at the corners when he saw it, then met Petra's. Her skin began to prickle uncomfortably.

"I am fairly certain it was," Frances said. "I recall the arched windows. And the number fifteen on the column. Where is it?"

"It is on Grosvenor Street," Petra said, then steeled herself to voice words she was hoping she would not need to say. "It would have been my house, if Emerson had lived, and we had married. It would have been Ingersoll House." She turned to Duncan and James. "I expect, if you will look again, you might find another transparency there."

TWENTY-NINE

Thursday, 22 June 1815
Forsyth House and Ingersoll House
Mayfair, Westminster, London
The eleven o'clock hour

"I JUST NEED A FEW MOMENTS ALONE," PETRA TOLD HER
friends after watching Duncan and James stride out. Duncan's bow
to the ladies was every bit as gentlemanly as his brother's. But when
his eyes met Petra's again, she felt the need to rush to him and hold
him close.

She did not, though. And they were gone a moment later. She
then decided she wished for a walk in the gardens. "I know my way
around in the dark as well as the day. I just need a bit of time to think.
I shall take Sable with me, if that makes you more comfortable."

She took Sable out and listened to her dog snuffling about the
flowers, looking for a hapless rabbit to chase, or, even better, a
squirrel that might have decided to be a bit more nocturnal than
usual. At first, Petra stayed within range so that her friends could
watch her from the windows of her drawing room. She picked up a
stick and threw it for Sable, even smiling as her dog sprang over a
boxwood hedge as neat as her hunter back at Buckfields, and came
trotting back, high-stepping like Lady Vera's hackney pony.

As she walked farther into the gardens, however, she thought on
the matter of truths, lies, and the often treacherous things people
do to protect others.

Lady Vera, Nell, Duncan, Emerson, the duchess, Mrs. Yardley,
and even Teddy, to a small extent, had all lied to her. If not outright

lied, they had worked to keep her from knowing certain truths. And she felt there was a large one that was within her grasp, having to do with the house she still thought of as Ingersoll House.

She glanced in the windows of her drawing room, and saw her friends enjoying tea and laughing at something Whitfield was saying.

But the house was still in her mind. She had to see it. From where she stood, it would take her less than eight minutes to walk to Ingersoll House on Grosvenor Street. She knew this from the evening walks she once took with Emerson to muse on the progression of their future home, of what was to be their future life together. That was why Annie did not recall the house so easily—it was because Petra always viewed it standing next to Emerson instead of her lady's maid.

Now, she simply needed to see if she were correct, that the transparency was indeed there. That Ingersoll House was being used as a beacon of sorts for the association known as the Bellowers.

Do not be foolhardy, a voice in her head admonished her. It sounded like a combination of the two women in London who had been most like mother figures to her—the Duchess of Hillmorton and Lady Vera. Yet both venerable women would have done as she was about to do, so Petra felt this reminder of sorts could be taken as she pleased.

Thus, when she sneaked out of the gardens of Forsyth House, her dog at her side, she aimed first for the servants' entrance at the kitchens. And when Mrs. Bing opened the door, she asked her cook to deliver a message to those in her drawing room. She said she would be taking Rupert as well as Sable with her, and would return in under an hour.

To be fair to herself, she did run to the mews in search of Rupert, and found him attempting to soothe one of her own horses, who had become overly upset with all the noise. The horse looked on the verge of bolting, and it was only Rupert's kind voice and gentle pats that were keeping it calm. Thus she did not interrupt, but dashed out the arched doorway to the mews that would take her closest to Davies Street. From there, she would turn and head north. If she walked quickly, she might reach Grosvenor Street, see what she needed, and return home before Mrs. Bing even had a chance to relay her message to her friends.

The streets were as crowded as ever. Yet while, one hour earlier, they had been full of genteel revelry, with mostly families walking about, now she saw pockets of drunken young men, guffawing and calling out to young ladies passing with their chaperones.

She saw a few shifty-looking men standing on the streets, watching people go by and looking as if they were sizing them up. Petra kept her head down and Sable at her left leg, wishing she had brought her dog's lead. For Sable's trick of tripping up a man might end up coming in handy.

"'Allo, miss," called out one man. And then he was walking next to her, keeping pace with her strides. A brief glance up said he was not much older than she. He was missing one tooth, his nose was quite red from drinking, and his eyes bleary, but Petra somehow did not think he was going to be a kindly drunk. Despite her privileged upbringing, she was no stranger to being around drunken gentlemen, and she'd found mostly that ignoring them and walking faster helped. It was speaking to them that generally made it worse.

Yet this man was not a gentleman at a ball, where she could call out to a footman, or even a friend with ease. And, when it came to any drunken man, there were those occasional few who were so intent on having their attentions recognized that ignoring them made them angry.

"You're a pretty thing," the man said, his voice growing harsher. "Why don't you have a dance wiv me?" He put one hand out to cup his ear. "Hear that, my beauty? That's someone playin' one of them waltzes. Let's have a go, shall we?"

He grabbed her wrist, harder than she expected, yanking her back to him, making her spin to face him. And then she was in his arms.

"You will release me, sir," she snapped. She stamped on his foot, already hearing Sable's rumbling growl, but it was drowned by the man's loud grunt of pain. In response, he grabbed Petra's wrist tighter, his dirty fingers digging into her skin. But then he gave a veritable howl and released her. Petra stumbled back even as she watched the man hopping on one leg while shaking the other to try to free Sable's jaws from his calf.

Petra said a command, and Sable released the man. Far from limping away, he backed up a few steps, feeling his calf, and then lunged toward Petra, hands out to grab her neck. There were screams from some other ladies who were attempting to walk by, and two men in the uniforms of His Majesty's Royal Navy were suddenly there. They grabbed her assailant and, before she knew it, one had the odious man's hands behind his back, and the other had landed a swift punch to the man's jaw.

"I thank you, sirs!" Petra called back as she lifted her skirts and ran, weaving in and out of people strolling in the street, Sable bounding at her side.

She slowed to a walk as she reached Grosvenor Street, breathing hard. She kept her eyes roaming about for any men who might wish to approach her, but she managed to find herself surrounded by strolling families.

"Are you well, my dear?" one elderly woman asked in a shaky voice as she was escorted by two wide-eyed-looking young girls of no more than seventeen, one of whom whispered to the other. Petra knew the girls had recognized her—no doubt from seeing her likeness in the scandal sheets—even if the older woman did not.

"I am well, thank you," she said with a quick curtsy. "My dog became a bit spooked with all the noise, but I have found her." She pointed in the vague direction of Ingersoll House, which she could see even from the corner. "I am just there, but I thank you."

The woman looked off toward the house. "Oh, I should hope you do not live at that one—number fifteen, I think it is. For we have let our house directly across from it for the past month and we have seen nothing but men of scarce character going in and out. And at all hours, too. Shameful, it is. I thought this would be a good neighborhood, where I would be free to let my two granddaughters walk down the street with just a maid without being accosted." She looked down Grosvenor Street, which had become even more crowded. "In fact . . . girls, we are returning to the house. It is far too dangerous out tonight."

There was a chorus of disappointed interjections from the girls, but they turned back obediently, and Petra asked if she could walk with them the rest of the way. The woman gave her a gentle smile that was also quite canny, and Petra had the distinct impression the older woman was protecting both Petra herself and her granddaughters at the same time.

The walk was short, and though the woman offered Petra some respite in her house, Petra graciously declined. "Would you mind terribly if my dog and I stand on your doorstep for a moment? I do not like what you have told me about the comings and goings at number fifteen, and I should like to see for myself."

The woman chivvied her granddaughters inside, and told Petra she was welcome to stay there as long as she wished.

Standing behind the column, Petra could see easily across Grosvenor Street to the house opposite. The one that should have been hers, and Emerson's. As she suspected she would, she saw a transparency in the window.

She watched as several rough-looking men loitered about, talking in low tones, and making glances toward both Ingersoll House itself and the transparency. Others were subtle, however. Petra noted several gentlemen strolling by, sometimes with a woman on their arm, or even as part of a family. Petra saw one man carrying a small boy on his shoulders. He stopped, gazed for a long moment at the house, and then smiled widely as he walked on.

It was then that Petra felt there must be something of note painted on the transparency, something that was a separate signal, and she must get a look at it. "It is about now that I wish I were better at wearing bonnets," she muttered to herself, thinking on how one that hid her face would be quite handy.

Still, Petra waited until she saw another group of more respectable-looking people a few houses down, walking westward down Grosvenor Street. Moving into step behind them, she and Sable followed in their wake like a spinster relation tagging along with her family as they strolled toward number fifteen.

Unfortunately for her, however, the family slowed but for a moment as they passed Ingersoll House. She heard the man say, "What ho! That house has an illumination of itself! Rather diverting, would you not say?"

The woman, who seemed to be his wife, however, was not amused. "I think it rather shows a lack of tact on the part of the owners," she said in a snippy tone.

The man blustered a bit about how he felt it was amusing, then had to catch up with his wife as she'd already moved on.

Petra, who had stopped to stare at the painting, was too transfixed to truly care that she'd been left standing alone, without the protection of others. Her eyes were scanning the transparency, desperate to see what was on the painting of Ingersoll House that could mean something. There was nothing . . . until she looked into the painted window that depicted what would have been her and Emerson's front parlor. A clock sat on a table, its hands pointing to one o'clock.

"Was it for the afternoon, or the morning?" she found herself saying aloud. "I cannot tell."

"What was that, Lady Petra?"

Petra turned slowly, her hand going to Sable's head as she felt her dog step between her and the man.

THIRTY

"I must apologize," she said, blinking up at the smiling man in spectacles, and making certain she wore a smile in return that was polite, but nothing more. "Have we been introduced?"

He removed his hat and bowed, showing curly hair and sideburns all neatly pomaded. "Indeed, we have, Lady Petra. Though it has been some years. We met a few months before the sad day in which you lost Lord Ingersoll. A fine man, he was, and I must apologize for never writing to you with my condolences. I am Mr. Phineas Rushton. We met at Lady Caroline's house party in Surrey of that year."

Shock fluttered through her, even as she recalled hearing his voice in St. James's Square. It was the same voice, but she could not believe she was looking at the man she had met three years earlier.

Her memory of Mr. Rushton had been of a man who was soft about the middle, with full cheeks and hair that was rather fair—or possibly it was merely sun-kissed. He also had not worn spectacles. She might never had recognized him had he not introduced himself. This man was tall, well-formed, and handsome, with hair that had clearly darkened naturally over time.

His face broke into a charming smile that seemed rather familiar. "I do look quite different, I know. It seems taking up the very English pastime of long country walks—and learning to be a better rider—has helped my general physique. I recall you being an excellent rider, Lady Petra, as well as an avid walker, so I know you understand."

"I do indeed, Mr. Rushton," she said, infusing warmth into her voice.

She recalled what Duncan and James had said about Mr. Rushton at Forsyth House. That he was suspicious, out of touch with reality. Yet this man seemed very clearheaded. He stood calmly, and she noted that his eyes were a light brown with a bit of hazel in them. Despite all she knew of this man, nothing about his presence was threatening to her.

Mr. Rushton asked after her father, and then Lady Caroline. He then brought up an anecdote about how Caroline had been the best whist player at the house party three years earlier in Surrey and how he had lost ten shillings to her over the course of his stay. He was quite amusing, she had to admit. She felt almost as if she were truly talking with an old friend, though that in turn began to set off a bell of warning in her head. A man who had this level of smoothness about him was not to be trusted, in her estimation.

Also, there was something oddly familiar about Mr. Rushton. He was leaning upon the stone pillar that held up the wrought-iron gate flanking the steps to Ingersoll House, looking about at all the people, and commenting on what a lively evening he'd had walking about with a friend and looking at all the illuminations. Petra was only somewhat listening, though, as her eyes darted about for Duncan or James, knowing they would be furious if they saw her here, talking to Rushton.

At the same time, however, another part of her mind—the part that kept track of members of London society—continued to concentrate. It made her wonder if Rushton might have a brother, or another relation, she knew and could ask after, much as he did Caroline, and her father. Or maybe she had seen Rushton himself recently in a crowd? Indeed, that must be the case. Regardless, her upbringing as a well-bred lady was requiring her to contribute to the conversation, and thus she spoke.

"Mr. Rushton, I must admit, I feel as if we have seen each other lately. Have you been to promenade at Hyde Park in recent weeks?

No? Was it you I saw enjoying an ice cream at Gunter's Tea Shop on Monday last, then? Do tell me it was not the Duchess of Hillmorton's recent art showing at the British Museum—"

The edges of his eyes had been crinkling with good humor as she spoke, but she stopped when she noted his entire posture stiffen.

"Why no, Lady Petra, why do you ask?" His smile grew curious, and almost flattered. Then he affected an embarrassed smile. "My apologies, I was indeed there. I had quite forgotten about it." He leaned in a bit, as if making her his coconspirator. "I must admit that my taste in art leans more toward Italianate sculpture than the paintings I saw there."

That was when she recalled Lottie telling the story of Caroline and the rude man who attempted to make Caro discover his identity. It was Mr. Rushton; it must have been. But then why was it important to him that he test his ability to be recognized?

Of course. Because if Caroline could easily point him out, if she recalled in any way that he had shown even a small bit of his radical views when he was a guest at her house party—then he could not move as freely in society as the secret head of the Bellowers. He had been testing Caroline to see if he would have to silence her.

Petra felt Sable press against her legs and she bent to scratch her dog's ears, using the moment to remind herself to keep her composure and give a blithe reply.

"Truth be known, Mr. Rushton, I do not care for sculptures, either," she said. "Now, I'm afraid I must be going. My dog here ran off earlier with all the noise, and I managed to find her. I stopped here to look up at this house. Did you know this is where Lord Ingersoll and I were to live? No? Well, when I found myself in front of its doors, and with such a pretty transparency, I decided I must stop for a moment. But it is time I get on. My friends will be waiting for me down Davies Street."

She gave him a little curtsy and then began to move off, when he moved slightly in front of her again. This time, Sable let out a brief growl that Petra felt against the side of her leg more than she heard.

"Would you care to see the inside, Lady Petra? I recall Lord Ingersoll saying how much he was looking forward to moving into his new house, but I did not realize it was number fifteen, Grosvenor Street." Tilting his head with a smile that was filled with kindness, he said, "I know the family who owns this place. They are not often in town, but the housekeeper is very kind. Shall we apply to her to see the inside?"

Petra felt a strong urge to accept. There had been a growing wish in the past year or so to see what her house might have looked like. Where she and Emerson might have slept, made love, and raised children. If her drawing room would have been as charming and comfortable as the one in Forsyth House. If Emerson had done as she had begged and made certain her drawing room had bookshelves, even though he'd teased her about it, saying bookshelves were for the library, and there was no need to have them in her drawing room as well.

As more people out for a stroll passed by the house, some stopping for a look at the transparency—and once noticing Mr. Rushton giving one man a tiny shake of his head—Petra turned to look at the house again.

Its creamy white stucco was not unlike half the houses in the area. The stairs and the iron railings that hid the steps to the servants' entrance belowstairs were quite alike as well. The boot scrape looked exactly the same as the one from the house across the street. The only outward difference from house to house in this area was the façade, and the small details that made Ingersoll House unique were its arched windows and the eight-paned transom window over the front door, double the size of the transom windows of the neighboring houses.

Petra imagined the house as she had so many times. She and

Emerson had planned to add a balustrade to the roofline, new columns to the front steps, and new iron railings with a bit of a scroll design. It would have looked lovely, and would have been just enough to give Ingersoll House a refreshed look without being showy or vulgar.

Yet beyond her curiosity for seeing what might have been, there was a part of her that was wondering if there was something she could find out about the Bellowers while inside. Would she meet some of Rushton's cohorts? Or find some sort of written document that would verify where and how they were going to pull off their violent actions? Could she find something that would help Duncan and James bring down these radicals?

"I have often longed to see inside," she began, the wistfulness coming out in her voice without having to try.

"Excellent," said Mr. Rushton. "Let us go knock upon the door and petition to see the house." Holding out an arm, he turned with a smile, giving her a look at his excellent profile. Why did she keep feeling as if she knew him from somewhere else?

"Thank you, Mr. Rushton, but I do not think so," she said slowly.

True, it was a wish she'd harbored, but she now realized she had also moved on. And there was something about being offered the tantalizing chance that made her realize she actually no longer needed it to be happy.

"Yes, forgive me, Mr. Rushton, but I do not think I, in fact, wish to see inside."

He smiled widely again. This man had charisma, of that there was no doubt.

"Oh, I think you would enjoy how lovely it looks inside, Lady Petra. There I can also tell you about something I have been working on for some time now. Your special friend, Mr. Shawcross—if I may be so bold as to call him your special friend—has become quite interested in my work, and he thought you might be so as well?"

"Indeed?" Petra said, and praised herself for sounding only mildly interested.

"I confess I think it quite magnificent of you not to pretend to be a shocked young miss when I say such things, Lady Petra," he said, and his tone was impressed, not condescending. "I am a firm believer that our rigid society rules that shame a woman for wanting to have the same, shall we say, *freedoms* as a man are quite outdated. I am also a believer that women should not lose their monies to their husbands upon marriage, much less their right to make decisions about their own life, and their children."

Petra raised an eyebrow, just enough to be challenging without looking distrustful. "And do you think women should be able to have the vote as well?"

"Oh, *truly I do,* Lady Petra," he said, and his eyes lit up with enthusiasm. "Women should have every right that men enjoy. After all, what is the difference between a man and a woman? Whilst a man may be innately stronger, is it not the woman who carries children? I have seen many a woman grow a child within her and work just as hard as any man out in the fields."

"That is true," Petra mused. Yet Mr. Rushton was not done in expounding on the virtues of women.

"And I have witnessed a woman giving birth, too. She is given nothing for the pain, which can last hours, and comes out of it contented and eager to care for her child. And then I have seen a man with a trifling bit of a stomachache from eating something he should not have, and oh, he becomes but a whiny pup of a boy!" He rubbed his clean-shaven chin, nodding thoughtfully. "Yes, whilst a man may be physically stronger in the lifting of a stone or a cabinet, he is neither emotionally nor internally as strong as a woman. So, yes, Lady Petra, I most ardently do think women should have the vote—and anything else they so choose."

"That was well said, Mr. Rushton," Petra said, and her smile was genuine. "I could not agree with you more fully. Is whatever you are doing attempting to advance the causes of women?"

"Women, men, and our entire nation," he said with an expansive gesture. "I genuinely would like to tell you about it. Are you certain you would not like to come in for a cup of tea? If the lady of the house is out enjoying the celebrations as most have, then the housekeeper is in, I am certain. She would be more than willing to chaperone the visit. I would keep you no more than the requisite fifteen minutes of a social call. It would be enough to explain what I am working toward, I assure you."

"May I bring my dog in with me?" Petra asked after a moment's pause.

"I cannot imagine the gentleman and lady of the house would say no," he said, his voice honeylike now.

She went to turn when somewhere off to her left, she heard a voice call out, "You shall not insult her, sir!" Another returned, "You bastard!" Then someone a few feet away said, "Lawks, there's two gentlemen fighting. I can't be sure, but one looks like the Marquess of Langford!"

Suddenly, Petra could hear the fight. Two men were thoroughly attempting to pummel one another, with shouted curses being hurled. Then she gasped as she saw James, landing a punch into the jaw of a tall, fit man with dark hair and a flatcap.

Petra wanted to call out Duncan's name, yell at James to stop, but she bit back the words. Something about the man in the cap did not seem right. Mr. Rushton had briefly turned to look, too, then he calmly sighed.

"Lady Petra, I think I should have to help break this up before other drunken men join in and a riot ensues. May I call upon you sometime soon? Just a discussion of like-minded individuals, of course." He was already backing away, toward the fight.

"Of course," she said, inclining her head and dropping into

a curtsy. A moment later, and from behind her, came a hissed voice.

"Psst! My lady! Do not turn around!"

Petra stiffened, and Sable's ears perked up. She had already leaned down to take hold of Sable's collar, and it was a good thing, for her dog loved Teddy almost as much as she did.

"When he is gone, turn all natural-like and take the first alley on tha left. I'll be waitin'."

THIRTY-ONE

PETRA DID AS SHE WAS TOLD, FINDING HERSELF IN A DARK cut-through. Sable's tail was wagging when Teddy met her with one of his wide, cheeky grins visible even in the absence of light, but Petra's heart beat faster when a candle was ignited from the nearly dying ember of another, and a dark figure towered over Teddy.

"What do you think you are doing, my lady?" growled Duncan as he tipped the candle into a lamp that sent a wash of light up into his eyes, making them glow yellow-green, like a long-haired black cat who was far from amused.

She was right, the man James had been fighting with had looked like Duncan, but was not. She didn't think asking why would get her very far, however, so she simply answered his question.

"I had to see for myself," she said, lifting her chin defiantly. "I had to see the transparency."

"My brother owes me a fiver, then," Duncan said to Teddy, who looked up at him with delight. This time around it was one little blond cherub with the tall, muscled, angry Apollo. Only the light within Duncan that had made Caroline liken him to the handsome sun god, even when moody, was gone. He more closely resembled Ares now in her mind, the god of war, of the lust for battle. But Ares also represented the battle for civil order, and was a protector god of those who fought to maintain order. Duncan was that very dichotomy, and she had to admit it suited him, as she suspected it did every man who worked in the shadows for the greater good.

"You did well, Teddy," he said. "Now be off with you to Forsyth House to be certain they know of Lady Petra's safety before anyone else comes out to try to find her. Take Sable with you, for she will not be welcomed where we are staying tonight."

Though she wished to ask where that was, something else was more pressing as Teddy gently put two fingers beneath Sable's collar in lieu of a lead.

"Wait," Petra said. "Teddy—where is Nell? Have you her somewhere safe?"

Teddy nodded. "My mates are looking after her, my lady. She don't like it much, though. Keeps sayin' something, under her breath like, about needing her proof before it's too late. Won't tell us what she's goin' on about, though."

"I think she means what is within the wooden box," Petra said. "Likely proof of her inheritance."

Teddy, however, looked skeptical. "I don't rightly know, my lady. I heard her say somethin' about the orphanage."

Petra looked to Duncan, who gave a nod, but in a way that indicated she needed to keep explanations short. She then told Teddy that there was a chance that Nell might be more involved with the Bellowers than first imagined, and that he must be careful around her until they knew more. She stressed she was unsure, and thus Nell should be given the benefit of the doubt until otherwise noted.

"Have to admit, my lady, that I like her now, I do, but I could see it if Nell were involved. Did you know someone taught her how to fight when she were young and on the streets? She told me she's taught some of them other girls at the orphanage. One of me mates told 'er to prove it, and befores he could but finish his sentence, she'd drawn his corker!"

Teddy demonstrated by thrusting his arm out straight, with his palm out and fingers clutched inward so that the base of his palm was angling upward in the direction of an imaginary nose.

"Blood everywhere, there was," Teddy said in awe. "Like I said, my lady. She's a wily one."

Petra, however, felt something odd—envy. She had always been tough, even intrepid—and she indeed had a few fighting moves herself, all learned as a girl by trial and error with Duncan as her constant partner. Indeed, she had proven herself still quite willing to stomp a man's foot just a few minutes earlier, had she not?

Yet, when Duncan was sent off to boarding school, and later university, Petra found herself less and less in situations where she was able to exercise those abilities to use her arms and legs in a way that might help her in a precarious situation. She was still tough. Still headstrong. And still willing to give as good as she received. But she also had been trained to do little but be a lady. And thus, when it was needed, she fought on instinct, not as one who had been taught to use their body and leverage properly.

Petra made Teddy promise he would be safe. She had been worrying about Lady Vera's safety as well, and asked Teddy if he might find a way to ascertain if her ladyship were well or not. Teddy said he would do his best, and then he was off, Sable galloping alongside him, the two disappearing onto Grosvenor Street before she could but blink. Then she whirled to face Duncan.

"When this is over, you will teach me how to do that move." She thrust out her palm, trying to emulate Teddy's hand movement. "If not, whether she is guilty or innocent, I shall contract Nell to teach me, and we shall use your nose as the corker in question."

Duncan's hand closed over hers and he began leading her farther down the alley. "No, my lady."

Petra yanked back on him. "No? How can you tell me no?"

Duncan stopped, and she slammed up against his side, which caused him not to move a single inch. He tipped her chin up with his knuckles, his thumb just lightly touching her lower lip, and said, "No, for I will teach you how to fight *properly*." He bent and brushed his lips over hers, then added while they were still touching, "Though that move might be part of your training—only with someone else's corker to be had, not mine."

Her head was spinning with a sudden wave of a thrill for her upcoming tutorial and she barely listened as Duncan asked her what she was thinking talking to Mr. Rushton in the first place, and thoroughly chastised her about her own need for safety.

She watched little as to where they were going, too, part of her wishing it would be back to Forsyth House and her bed. So when Duncan finally led her down another alley toward a garden gate, the two of them having earlier slowed to a stroll, her arm in his, through the continued crowds of revelers and back toward Grosvenor Square, Petra did not know where she was.

Suddenly, Duncan stopped, his eyes searching the surrounding darkness. Then he handed her the light and said calmly, "Petra, you must do as I say, and *run*."

From beneath his coat, he'd pulled his dagger, its steel blade glinting in the candlelight.

"I know what Rushton said," he said almost genially into the blackness as Petra began backing away, unsure of where the danger was he was sensing. "But Lady Petra will not be a threat to our cause. Leave her be and—"

Then there were four, no, six men, all coming out of the darkness, each dressed so fully in black Petra could not see their faces. While one looked to her, the others jumped almost as one onto Duncan, who was already fighting out with his knife. Horrified at the sight and fascinated at the same time, she witnessed Duncan move in ways she'd never seen. One man was felled quickly, and then another, but there were too many. Even as she backed up, she watched a linen bag being thrown over Duncan's head.

Petra heard herself yell Duncan's name, but she also heard her own being shouted.

"*Petra! Run!*"

She hesitated but a moment and then turned back toward the square, lifting her hems with one hand. She heard sounds of an angry bellow coming from Duncan as she ran. She looked over her shoulder once, and should not have.

She issued a scream as a hand was already on her shoulder. She was spinning about, falling, the lamp handle flying out of her hand and crashing to the ground as the man wrapped his arms about her waist and landed atop her. Only the chignon at the back of her head managed to keep her head from slamming upon the ground. Still, spots danced like little fireworks in front of her eyes nonetheless as, a few inches away, the candle sputtered out. She squirmed and fought, then suddenly could not breathe as a handkerchief was shoved in her mouth.

She gagged on the handkerchief as she was hauled to her feet, and another man was there to tie the handkerchief around the back of her head. In attempting to draw in a breath, she was becoming lightheaded.

Before she could do much, the first man roughly brought her hands together, binding them with a slipknot, neither saying anything other than grunts. Her bootheel attempted to find his foot, but then a rough linen bag was thrown over her head, pitching her into an even deeper darkness. She tried to shake it off, but before she could, she was being lifted and thrown over a shoulder.

And then she was moving, being carried down the street against her will.

THIRTY-TWO

Friday, 23 June 1815
Ingersoll House
Grosvenor Street, Mayfair, London
The midnight hour

IT WAS STRANGE, BUT SHE KNEW WHERE SHE WAS THE MOMENT the linen bag was lifted from her head. *I am in my drawing room.*

She was loath to admit it, but she had lost consciousness for a bit during her unconventional transport. Likely because she was fighting to breathe through her gag. She had only become aware of herself once more a few moments earlier. Then when she started at not being able to see, the bag had been lifted from her head.

And there she found herself, in the life that almost was. While she had never seen the inside of Ingersoll House, she had known her drawing room would be small, but cozy, with wallpaper of a lovely gray-green damask, thick velvet curtains in a darker green, and sofas in the softest shade of blush pink. A fireplace would be on the south side of the room—to the right from where she now sat—with a lovely fender.

It was all there, just as she had once hoped. Even the fire, which was crackling merrily, somehow not yet making the room hot.

Turning her head slowly to the right as she blinked her eyes back into focus, she could see that the mantel held on one side a medallion bearing the coat of arms of the Ingersoll viscountcy. On the mantel's opposite side, her own coat of arms, which mimicked that of her papa's, the Earl of Holbrook, in that it contained a rearing Pegasus flanked by dragons. Petra's was simpler, on a diamond-shaped charge known as a lozenge, but otherwise carried much the same heraldic elements. In the center was to be her new coat of arms as the Viscountess Ingersoll.

Her eyes went to the spot. The diamond shape was there, and it was blank. As if nothing of her life with Emerson had ever truly existed.

Someone was untying the gag in her mouth, and she spit it out, working her jaw to loosen the sore muscles even as her eyes went to either side of the fireplace.

"He did not grant me my bookshelves," she said wonderingly, sadly.

"Ah, yes. I wondered if you would know where you were, Lady Petra," came a smooth voice.

She had tried to move her hands, but they were tied behind her back. Each of her ankles was also restrained. She realized she was in a dining chair, in the middle of her drawing room. If she looked straight on, she faced east and the drawing room door. A painting she had always disliked from Emerson's personal collection was over a table against the wall.

To her left was another door—leading to the dining room, if she remembered correctly. Her drawing room's walls were mostly bare except for a couple of maps that had been pinned up. Behind her, she knew she would find the windows, and those lovely green draperies she had chosen, veering away from her normal inclination toward shades of blue.

As her hands moved and she struggled a bit, her fingertips lightly brushed something else behind her. It was a hand, but it did not move. Somehow, though, she knew it was Duncan, his back to hers, likely strapped to a chair as well, and her heart sped up.

As she turned her head once more and looked up to watch Mr. Rushton striding over to stand in front of the fireplace, she noted the large gilt mirror. It actually belonged to her. She had allowed Emerson to take it when the house was being decorated prior to their nuptials, and she had completely forgotten about it over the last three years. It was rather large, reflecting the entirety of the room, though while she could not see herself, with Rushton in front of her, she could see Duncan. As she suspected, he was tied to a chair as well, his head tipped down to his chest. He was unconscious, and his face was covered in bruises, cuts, and blood.

She felt her chest constrict with fear. She wanted to cry out to him, to see if her voice could wake him, yet something told her to keep calm. And to not ask about James, either. She wondered if James had still been down the street when she and Duncan were brought back here, sacks over their heads, to Ingersoll House.

She guessed that Duncan had been intending to take her to Langford House for safety, for she now recalled seeing a part of the house's façade just before she and Duncan were attacked. If that were the case, was there a chance James had realized something was wrong?

And then a horrible thought came to her. What if it was James who had told Rushton and his men where to find her and Duncan? What if he had been pretending to be on Duncan's side all along, but had, in fact, become indoctrinated by the Bellowers?

Bollocks! she thought fiercely, then sensed Mr. Rushton watching her.

There was something about Mr. Phineas Rushton that told her he felt more powerful the more he could tip people away from their steady rhythms. Though he did so quietly, and with quite a bit of charm, it seemed that chaos was like an aphrodisiac to him. And thus, she could not give him more. With this, a small amount of serenity come over her, enabling her to answer his question.

Looking about the room again, she said, "Indeed, it looks almost exactly as I had wished it to be. Except for the lack of bookshelves, you understand. I wished to wait until Lord Ingersoll and I were married to see my house for the first time." With a sigh, she added, "Only my one requirement, both in my drawing room and in my bedchamber, was bookshelves. Tell me, did he at least put them in my bedchamber? Where I could see them from my bed, one hopes?"

She blinked up at Mr. Rushton. And in the mirror, she caught sight of two men standing at one side of the room. She wondered if they were the men who had abducted her, or hurt Duncan, or both. One scratched his nose and she could see bloody knuckles. He also had a black eye blooming, which told her Duncan had at least got a good punch in first. She wondered if he was the man named Caufield, and thought it likely as he met her gaze in the mirror and smiled in a slow and lascivious way.

Along with the fear for Duncan now came a fear for herself. With these two men in here and Duncan unconscious, there was little she could do, even if she were able to somehow subdue Rushton, or one of his men. Duncan said these men kill, and some, like Caufield, enjoy it.

You must keep calm, she told herself as her heart felt as if it were attempting to flip over. *Try to determine first what he wants from you—and then panic, if you must.*

"I'm afraid he did not put bookshelves in your bedchamber, either, Lady Petra," Rushton said. "You see, by that time, it was important that Ingersoll not spend any more money, for it was needed for our cause."

In the silence that stretched out as she tried to take this information in, a clock upon the table by the door chimed twelve smooth times. It was midnight, officially the twenty-third of June. And in thirteen hours—if her guess of one o'clock in the afternoon was correct for the Bellowers' meeting time—the radicals were going to bring violence upon England and the royal family at a target somewhere in London.

And what Rushton is telling me is that, if my Emerson were alive—if he were my viscount, and I his viscountess, he would be joining them.

"I should like to start crying, and tell you that this could not be true, Mr. Rushton, but I cannot."

She said this as she stared at the mantel again, at the blank diamond lozenge that was to be the symbol of her intertwined life with Emerson. It was to consist of the Pegasus rearing rampant on one side, and the wyvern on the other, on a field of azure for her side, of a handsome dark red for his. There were to be chevrons, oak leaves, and other symbols, all indicating strength and constancy. Petra had liked the look of the drawing once she saw it, except for one thing. The wyvern's venomous tail had been drawn as if pointing up toward the heart of the winged horse. Emerson had told her she was being silly, but he had decided on this version of the wyvern just weeks before his death. Prior to that, the tail had been curling upward and away from the horse.

Was it a symbol? Of the wyvern—Emerson—turning against his aristocratic upbringing and seeking to pierce the heart of his wife—the Pegasus—who was the daughter of an earl, the favorite of a powerful duchess, and had never spoken against the monarchy? Or was it simply that he liked the drawing better?

"Indeed?" Mr. Rushton said, and from his waistcoat he pulled out a slim leather notebook. "I do wonder why you are not surprised. I rather understood it that you had no idea of your late fiancé's thoughts of reforming Great Britain from a monarchy to a republic. Not only did Shawcross here tell me, but so did Ingersoll himself." He slapped it lightly against his open palm, the sound somehow menacing. "What is this? Do you no longer recognize Ingersoll's journal?"

"In very much the truth, Mr. Rushton, I cannot say that I ever saw him writing in a journal, so no. My Emerson drew quite a bit, and drew well, but an epistler he was not, nor did he often journal his thoughts. That one in your hands could belong to anyone."

To this, Mr. Rushton began flipping pages in the journal, giving Petra time to study him. His face, the contours of his jaw, lips, and brow. To take in the way he stood, the tilt of his head, and all the little things that made a person unique. She bit the inside of her cheek to keep from gasping. She was not only looking at the man she knew to be Mr. Phineas Rushton . . . but also at the delivery man she knew as Mr. Fife.

Or were they indeed two men? Were they brothers, perhaps? Petra searched her memory from Caroline's house party. Emerson had known Rushton, and so had Duncan. Neither had ever mentioned him having a brother. It was still possible, but as she watched Rushton, she thought not. The two were the same man.

Why had she not noticed it before?

Because he had been in disguise, she reminded herself harshly. As Mr. Fife, he had changed his hairstyle, let his sideburns become unruly. He had also worn padding beneath his clothing, she was now certain of it. Petra recalled Caroline saying Rushton had been shaped like an egg when they knew him. Clearly, he had grown into a much leaner man in recent years—but his old clothing had come in handy when it was time to dress as a delivery man.

And then there was the biggest reason of all. It was often said that the upper classes took no notice of servants, and she sadly had to admit it was quite true. What's more, Petra, like most ladies of her station, rarely dealt with delivery men, if at all—and Rushton would not only know this, but had utilized it to his advantage.

She stiffened in her seat when Rushton brought the journal to her, along with a small candelabra, and turned it around so she could read, a smug little smile twitching at his lips.

From the past, out jumped Emerson's handwriting. She had truly seen so little of his hand as he rarely wrote long letters that it seemed almost strange—yet, she still knew it.

It was not a long passage. She read it quickly, and could almost hear his voice as she read of his finding his calling in wishing to help take Great Britain into a new era of a republic. It ended with the words, *Maybe one day I shall tell my Petra. But not until after we are married at the earliest!*

"Do you know why he did not wish to tell you?" Rushton asked quietly.

"I care not for his reasons," she said, with a little too much pettishness. She saw Rushton's lips quirk up, and even more so when she struggled against her bonds and said, "What I would like to know is what you plan to do with me, and Mr. Shawcross."

Mr. Rushton squatted down so that he was just below eye level with her. "As for what I plan to do with Shawcross, that all depends on you. As for what I plan to do with you, it depends on what you decide to do after I explain the objectives of the Bellowers—or, as we are formally known, the East London Association for Political Reform."

When he turned sideways, Petra used the mirror to glance at Duncan, finding him still unconscious. The only thing that made her feel better was seeing the rise and fall of his chest.

"If you plan to stand upon a box and preach to me, might you at least have your men tie my hands in front of me? I am rather smaller than a man, and thus the sides of the chair are digging into my arms. They have quite fallen asleep, too. If you should like me to concentrate, then I could do so much easier with my hands in front."

She thought Rushton would say no, but he merely motioned to one of the men, who warned her in a gruff voice not to try anything as he untied her, to which she snapped, "I have seen what you did to Mr. Shawcross, and I can barely feel my fingers. You have little to concern yourself with on the matter."

This made the man untying her laugh, and the stench of his breath—made worse by what smelled like copious amounts of stale ale—nearly made her gag, even without the handkerchief in her mouth. Yet soon her wrists were bound in front of her, laid on her lap. She wiggled her fingers, making a face at the tingling sensation as she spoke.

"Tell me, Mr. Rushton. Why is it that you want me to know the objectives of the Bellowers?"

"Because you can be a true instrument for change, Lady Petra," he said smoothly. "You *and* your friends. Our country needs reform, and social equality, and if we are to achieve that, we must no longer have a monarchy." His face briefly twisted with disgust. "They are no more than a boil on our society, teeming with excess and privilege. The same goes for the aristocracy in general. Both are incompatible with the tenets of a democratic nation."

He stood up and began to pace, hands clasped behind his back in a manner of deep intellectual thought.

Soon, though, he was sermonizing on the principles of the French republic and the striving toward liberty, equality, and a secular national state. Then came a fervent discourse on the excesses of Queen Charlotte and the Prince Regent, whom he declared a spendthrift of the worst sort who would most assuredly lead the entire kingdom into financial ruin. From there he spoke about the corrupt and privileged House of Lords, Parliament in general, and its need for change—including that Parliament should exercise their right to deny the crown to the Prince Regent once his father, King George III, finally died.

In truth, Petra could not fault anyone for listening to what this man had to say. Indeed, Rushton rather had a unique power to sway with his words. He was intelligent and made his points clearly, and seemed to want what was best for all Britons. She even found herself nodding along, occasionally saying, "Quite so," and "Well said, sir."

Yet, as if spurred on by her agreement, he became more impassioned. He likened a republic to a sort of utopia, as if it would solve all the country's problems in one fell swoop. As if there would be no corruption simply because there would be no monarchy, and no House of Lords.

"If we can but rid ourselves of these preening, inbred aristocrats who believe that God gave them a right to rule—if we can snuff them out like we snuff out a candle when it is of no use to us—then we will have our way forward."

When he turned back to her, his brown eyes were filled with a fiery passion and a loathing for the wealth and privilege of those in power. His voice was rising in pitch, and a vein had begun throbbing in his forehead.

"We must show the monarchy that we are willing to use force to accomplish our goals, Lady Petra. Moral persuasion shall do nothing to help our cause, our march toward a republic. Force and revolution—violence being a natural derivative of it—are the only way! We are going to take to the streets with our bayonets and our cannonballs and we are going to bring down the royal family one by one until they kneel at our feet and renounce their right to the throne!"

In the back of the drawing room, the two men cheered, their fists going in the air. In truth, Petra had not seen them respond to anything Mr. Rushton said with any great level of interest until he began talking of a show of force against members of the royal family.

This, Petra thought. *This is what Duncan had been saying. That Mr. Rushton's grasp on sanity was diminishing, and his sense of his own self-worth and his lust for violence was growing.*

And it seemed, too, that he had begun collecting followers who were more interested in a show of violence than they were of the true workings of a republic, a monarchy, or any other political system.

She clenched her hands together to keep them from shaking. She'd continuously stolen glances at Duncan using the mirror above the mantel, but he had not so much as twitched a muscle. Was he well? Had they hurt him so thoroughly that he might never regain consciousness?

In the back, one of the two men turned his ear toward the door. Rushton noticed this and signaled for them to do what needed to be done. Petra hoped both would go, but only one did.

"What say you, Lady Petra?" he said. His brown eyes were bright as he turned to her.

"I don't know," she whispered. "Your points, sir, are good ones, but I do not wish for violence." She looked down at her hands, which she had begun wringing, and let her emotions come in the form of quavering speech. "And I do not think my Emerson, my Lord Ingersoll, would have wished for violence, either. He was a kind man. If he wanted reform, he wished for it to be peaceful!"

"You honestly think so?" Rushton asked. His eyes had lost some of their passion, growing harder as he spoke. "You do not even know, Lady Petra. You were too self-absorbed to even realize the man you were about to wed only wished to marry you for your inheritance."

THIRTY-THREE

"That is not true," Petra whispered. "I knew him. He loved me."

Rushton went to speak, then snapped to the other man, "It is likely Eggerton. Go help him."

Petra hurried to speak again, for when she used the mirror to watch the other man leave the room, and while Rushton extracted Emerson's journal from his waistcoat once more, she saw Duncan's head move, just for a moment.

"I know Emerson loved me! He would not have courted me simply for my money. He had money of his own."

"Oh, but he needed that to live on, Lady Petra. *Your* money was to go to us, the Bellowers, and our mission."

"You are lying, sir!" she shouted even as Rushton snapped, "What, man?" He stalked over to the second man, who whispered to him. As she watched them in the mirror, Petra hastily used her two bound hands together to pull up the right side of her skirt, all the way to her newly altered garter. A moment later, she dropped her little dagger into the folds of her dress between her legs, her hem dropping to the tops of her half boots once more even as Rushton stalked back to her side. He shoved the journal in her face.

In Emerson's handwriting, he had written,

'Tis a good thing Petra has money, all of which will become mine as soon as we are pronounced man and wife. For the association is in dire need of funds. Whilst the earl has made me sign away my rights to her monies, the law and coverture will ultimately say it is mine to use when I like. Until then, my idea for tapping the

orphanage funds has been met with cheers. Tessa is eager to help from the inside. She claims it was her idea, but I beg to differ and say it was a collaboration between us two.

Mr. Rushton whisked the journal away and Petra did not have to try to let a tear fall down her cheek. He had been using her all this time? She could not believe it.

"Who is Tessa?" she asked, hoping she sounded like a jealous lover rather than a nosy spinster.

Mr. Rushton simply laughed. "Someone he loved more than you, I'm afraid. Lady Petra, your Lord Ingersoll was only having a bit of fun with you. Once he was your husband, you were going to be 'encouraged' to spend as much time at Buckfields as you liked riding your horses whilst he spent time with his Tessa, and we all spent time ensuring a successful march toward a revolution."

"That is not the truth!" Petra shouted, her voice cracking. "Emerson would not have done that to me!"

"Don't listen to him, Petra." Duncan's voice was weak, but angry.

Rushton's eyes lit once more, and he suddenly grabbed Petra's chair and swung it so that she was turned around and could see the left side of Duncan's face. His head rose up and then fell back down as if he was trying his best to come around and still making a hash of it.

She'd almost lost her little dagger in nearly falling off her chair, but had managed to hold on to her seat and the knife between her thighs at the same time. But she cried out when Rushton grabbed a fistful of Duncan's hair and yanked his head back, eliciting a grunt of pain from Duncan's lips.

"This man is a traitor, Lady Petra. A traitor to our cause—which, when we become a republic, will mean he's a traitor to his country. Oh, he was good, though. He managed to convince even me until last night, when Caufield saw him dancing with you outside of Sloan House, and then caught you being quite unladylike with him in the alleyway.

"Indeed, he made it part of his cover to be able to be seen in your company, as well as in society, so it was hard to prove. Until Caufield, who is rather more clever than he looks, or acts, had a hunch. By telling a quite good lie, he managed to get his lordship, the marquess"—he yanked harder on Duncan's hair—"this man's supposedly despised brother, to slip. That brawl you heard outside? It was the marquess believing that Shawcross here has been seducing his lordship's pretty new wife.

"But that was not the best of it. By using one of our other aristocrats loyal to the cause, the Dowager Marchioness of Langford was kind enough to tell us that Shawcross would be coming to meet with his brother at Langford House."

Rushton leaned closer to Petra, looking her straight in the eyes. "And then you turned up at this house, being rather too curious about it for your own good. I was called away by the ruckus with Langford, yes, but then later I saw you walking with Shawcross here. No, I would say you were following him with stars in your eyes. Indeed, I knew then that Shawcross and Langford had managed to fool me, if only for a short time. In fact, I had been feeling that something was not right, I just had not yet proven it until tonight. That was why I told only my closest allies where to meet, and who our target would be.

"That was the reason for my elaborate plan with the transparencies. I wanted only the most ardent supporters to show up tomorrow. And considering how many have found my pathway to righteousness—for I have been watching all evening, counting the numbers who passed by, looking for the signal—we shall have an army as big as Wellington's own tomorrow." He smiled and suddenly looked quite mad. "Or today, as it were. At just after midday."

Petra could see Duncan grimacing. "What do you want?" she asked as another tear slipped down her cheek.

"It is quite easy, Lady Petra, though I shall be a gentleman and give you a choice. Let you choose your own way, as you would be able to in a proper republic. You will sign your inheritance over to me as a donation to the Bellowers' cause. Every last penny of it. If you do, I shall let Shawcross here live."

"And if she does not?" Duncan growled.

From under his own coat, Rushton pulled out Duncan's dagger and held it to Duncan's throat.

"If she does not, your throat will be slit in the name of what is best for our country, Mr. Shawcross."

"Do not do it, Petra," Duncan said. "Do not give in to him."

"I will not let him hurt you!" Petra cried, leaning forward in her seat. "No amount of money is worth losing you!"

"All rather sweet this is," Rushton said, "but I am due to meet with my generals, so to speak, in one half hour at our meeting place. We must prepare for our moment, you understand."

"You mean with the stolen crates of cannonballs?" Duncan asked.

"Ah," Rushton said, nodding sagely, "someone told you. Who else in my ranks was a traitor, then?"

Duncan's Adam's apple bobbed as he huffed out a dark laugh. "If you believe there is just one other traitor in your midst, or that the thieves you dealt with to purchase the cannonballs do not do business with other *associations*, you are sadly mistaken, sir."

This seemed to enrage Rushton, and Petra recalled Duncan saying the man had become suspicious of everyone and everything. He pressed the knife closer into Duncan's neck and Petra saw a little bead of blood emerge.

"This is why I'm giving you a choice, Lady Petra," he said. "We cannot abide by traitors, or having our sources make us look the fools. We are mostly a group of working-class men, and some women. We need larger amounts of blunt to ensure we have the money to continue our forward march to revolution. We were able to secure the blunt needed for our weapons from one of the orphan girls who unwittingly signed over her inheritance recently, and it was just in time. But we need more. And the aristocrats loyal to us are all but penniless. Most are second or third sons and won't see a shilling of their inheritance until their fathers are in their graves. That leaves us with no choice." He pressed the dagger up under Duncan's ear, and smiled cruelly at Petra. "Thus, what is your answer?"

Petra wanted to snap that his own words were hardly those of someone who believed in a republican democracy, but with Duncan's neck quite literally on the line, she held her tongue.

And then Rushton's head turned toward the door. Sounds were coming from the other side. Fists upon the wood, and the anxious call of a familiar voice.

"Petra! Shawcross!"

It was Caroline. The door was jiggling, and suddenly there was the barking of two dogs. No doubt Lottie and Frances were there, too.

And then Rushton's arm swung the knife in an arc under Duncan's chin. Petra heard Duncan emit a grunt, then his head dropped forward.

Her mind went briefly blank except for the words *Rushton slit his throat.*

"*No!*" Petra screamed. But Rushton had stepped forward, teeth bared in an unholy grin, blocking her view of Duncan. He pulled from his waistcoat Emerson's journal, and then pitched it into the fire.

Petra, her little dagger between her two tied hands, lunged toward Rushton, desperate to do some sort of damage in return for killing Duncan. Yet Rushton was too quick, and her ankles, still bound to the chair, made her ungainly. He smoothly moved around her as she toppled forward, landing over Duncan's legs.

And moments later, when the door was broken down by Whitfield and her friends dashed into the room, Rushton was already through the opposite door and gone.

THIRTY-FOUR

THROUGH HER TEARS, PETRA SAW CAROLINE CLAP HER HAND over Teddy's eyes. Frances was there, trying to pull Petra off Duncan's lap. And someone—likely Lottie—was using something to cut the ropes about her ankles.

"No," she cried, clinging to Duncan. "No! He slit his throat. Fetch something to stop the blood!"

"Having you across my lap is never not going to make me happy, my lady, but I rather cannot breathe well in my current position. So, if you would not mind, maybe we can revisit this scenario again later?"

Petra froze. Her legs were now free, and with Frances's help, she stood. And then her hands were all over Duncan's chest, tipping back his head, checking his neck. There was only the trickle of blood. He opened his eyes, one of which was blackened, the other with a profusely bleeding cut. There was more blood issuing from his brow and lip than from his neck.

"You're alive," she breathed.

"Mm, barely. But first, fetch that journal from the fire, someone."

"It doesn't matter," Petra said, but Whitfield was already striding over to the fire. Using the brass dustpan, he pulled the book from the fire, stomping on it to smother the flames.

"Only a bit singed," he said merrily.

"Throw it back in," Petra snapped. "It does not matter."

"It does," Duncan said. "Read the last few entries, Petra." And when she looked at him curiously, he nodded.

Caroline had released Teddy, whose wide blue eyes looked both worried and amused, and he held the dogs while she rushed to a table where there were the remnants of tea things, including a bottle of gin. She brought them to Frances, who was already beginning to clean Duncan's wounds. As he hissed in pain and Caroline teased him that he and Whitfield looked like they'd been fighting each other, Petra opened Emerson's journal, which now smelled like smoke and had burnt edges.

She read the last few pages as instructed, her eyes blurring with sudden tears.

Written two days before his death, the words in his hand professed that his love for Petra had made him rethink how the Bellowers were going about their cause. That he no longer felt violence and force would be the best way toward political reform and that he would not be complicit in taking Petra's inheritance.

He wrote that he had already spoken with Mr. Rushton and had set an early-morning meeting with him to further discuss the matter.

She then tore out the final page and stuffed it into her pocket. It was all she needed.

She held the journal in her hands for one long moment, then let it fall to the floor with a light *thwump*. Selecting the fireplace poker, she held the handle in both hands, raised it high, and then slammed its pointed end into the middle of the journal, making her friends jump as they watched her curiously. Duncan, leaning forward in exhaustion with his elbows over his knees, watched as she used the poker to ensure Emerson's journal went properly into the fire.

"Don't rightly know what that was about, but well done, my lady," Teddy said.

"Agreed," Duncan said on a groan. Holding his hand out to Petra he said, "Now, Boudica, if you would help me up. We must leave this place before the Bellowers are sent here in larger numbers."

A voice from the doorway said, "You will all come to Langford House with me."

Petra, with Lottie and Whitfield's help, had helped Duncan to standing, but she left him as she stormed up to James.

"You bastard," she spat. "Did you really believe your brother would seduce your wife?" Using her index finger, she poked him hard in the solar plexus. "Do you know what you did? Look at him! Your brother nearly had his throat slit by a madman! And then your mother, the dowager *viperess*, she was happy to help in nearly sending Duncan to his death. And me as well! We shall not be going anywhere near Langford House!"

"Petra," Duncan said wearily, then roared, "Petra!"

She continued to glare up into James's handsome face. It made her even angrier by the second that he seemed somewhat concerned, but only truly blanched when it came to his mother. "I am listening," she growled.

"It was but a ruse, Petra," Duncan said. "At least the part about James believing the worst of me. We did so on purpose to make Caufield believe we were more divided than ever. James is not to blame."

James was quick to speak up.

"And my mother—I am at fault for not confiding in her as to our plans, and how we were working together." He looked over at Duncan. "I am sorry, brother. I thoroughly put her on the ropes for what she did in giving you up to the Bellowers." He looked back down at Petra. "She very much wishes to speak privately with you, Lady Petra. My mother—the *viperess*, which is rather apt, I must say—is requesting your presence so she may apologize. I rather suggest you take it, for we will likely never see the likes again."

THIRTY-FIVE

Friday, 23 June 1815
Langford House
Grosvenor Street, Mayfair, London
The two o'clock hour of the morning

WHEN DUNCAN WAS RESTING COMFORTABLY IN JAMES'S STUDY at Langford House, his wounds cleaned and in a set of fresh clothes borrowed from his brother, Petra finally agreed to a meeting with the dowager marchioness. It rather pleased her to make James's mama wait for nearly an hour once they'd arrived, too.

Earlier, it seemed that when Teddy and Sable reached Forsyth House, Petra's friends were already beginning their search for her. When it became clear after some stealthy surveillance from Teddy that she and Duncan were being held inside Ingersoll House, her friends had made a plan and broke in.

They'd expected to encounter a large number of men, but only found one in the servants' hall—quickly knocked out and tied up by Whitfield—and then the commotion brought out the two men from the drawing room. Sable and her lead had tripped the man up in no time, and the third, seeing his cohort trussed up and unconscious, attempted to flee, only to be felled by Caroline and Frances . . . and then knocked out by Whitfield.

"He is quite the pugilist," Caro purred after making her explanations. "What can I say?"

However, by the time James had arrived at Ingersoll House, two of his footmen at his side and all carrying daggers, the three Bellowers had been released and were gone. It was felt likely to be either Rushton himself or another cohort, but they encountered no one.

Before they had left the house for good, James and Whitfield made a quick pass through the house, looking for any bit of information they could find. Teddy found the missing transparency of Vauxhall Pleasure Gardens in an upstairs window, ready to be lit from behind by a candle to send out its signal to the Bellowers.

"The first transparency, of Ingersoll House, had the time of one o'clock," Petra said. "What if that was the time the Bellowers were to stroll back by this house to find the yet another transparency? An innocuous-looking one, without fireworks? The one that showed the target?"

Duncan had said this was an excellent thought, but said, "No, not the target. Rushton would want to wait and tell us himself. Vauxhall would be the *meeting place*."

The two maps pinned to the drawing room wall had no markings to indicate anything of use, and were thusly abandoned. Duncan said he doubted the owners of Ingersoll House even knew the house was being used, and felt it unlikely it would be utilized again.

"It was a symbol," he said. "A way to show they had support within the ton."

"The seal," Petra began, brushing a dark curl off his forehead, and wanting to leave Ingersoll House behind for now. "On the letter you intercepted, the one that went into the Thames with you. The seal was the Ingersoll coat of arms, wasn't it?"

"Was I wrong to keep it from you?" he asked softly. "And Emerson's involvement with the Bellowers?"

She thought on it, and then shook her head. "I would like to say yes simply to be contrary, but it would not be the truth. I did need to discover this on my own." She heaved a sigh, feeling the exhaustion of the day steal over her. "I still do not know who killed Mrs. Huxton, and I must discover that answer before the Queen and your grandmama return. But I think the most important issue right now is finding Mr. Rushton again. We must endeavor to stop whatever he has planned."

"We have already sent out a runner to my men and the Queen's guards. They may change their target now that we know. We shall hunt down the blackguard. And if Rushton gets away, we will find him soon enough and stop him again."

Petra bent to kiss him on the cheek, but Duncan made certain the part of his lip that wasn't bruised and sore caught hers. As she was about to leave the study, he whispered in her ear.

"If the viperess bites you, I may know someone who would be willing to suck out the venom."

"Mm," Petra said, giving him another quick kiss. "I think I shall entice her to bite, then."

If Petra thought that the dowager marchioness would be softer after having nearly inadvertently sent two people to their deaths, she was wrong.

"I sent an invitation to you yesterday, Lady Petra, which you refused," she snapped when Petra entered a drawing room done up in shades of pale yellow. "And then you keep me waiting while you tend to that . . . that baseborn man. The impudence!"

"Lady Langford," Petra said with forced calm. "I have had quite the trying morning. Therefore, if you would, please explain what it is you would like to know from me. For I am not certain there is anything I should tell you. Except this . . ." She took a step forward, though her hands stayed at her sides. Her voice was low and she looked the dowager marchioness directly in the eyes.

"I do not ever wish to hear you speak ill of Duncan Shawcross and his manner of birth ever again. And I mean what I say. Ever. Again."

Lady Langford took a step forward as well, and Petra had to admire the woman's tenacity.

"You will not tell me what to do. How dare you!"

"I dare because despite the manner of his birth, he is one of the most excellent men—no, the most excellent human beings—I have ever had the honor to know. And as I have known him longer than literally anyone in England, I may say that and everyone may know it as the truth. If you would only step off your pedestal for five minutes put together and speak with him, you would see this, too."

She held up a hand, for she felt as if Lady Langford was once again going to whinge on about the circumstances of his birth. And she took another step forward. This one larger, until she was nearly nose to nose with the formidable dowager marchioness. Who stepped back reflexively, her thin chest heaving with surprise and shock as Petra spoke again.

"I do not place blame upon you for being hurt by your husband, the late marquess, for humiliating you by bringing home a son who was so clearly a Shawcross that even the Duke and Duchess of Hill-morton took one look at him and knew it was undeniable. And no one, least of all Duncan, blames you for fighting for your own son's right to be named marquess. But you did not change once you accomplished that feat. You continued to keep the two brothers from becoming friends, and attempted to make Duncan feel unworthy at every turn."

She took another step forward, and the dowager marchioness stumbled backward, suddenly a look of fear in her eyes.

"And I, Lady Langford, am rather disgusted by it, and will not have it any longer," Petra growled. "If you should like to speak with me and Duncan is referenced in any way, you shall be respectful and call him by his name. Either Shawcross or Duncan will do, though he deserves you to call him Mr. Shawcross."

There was a moment's pause, then Petra turned to the side, gesturing to the two small facing sofas in a striped fabric the color of milky tea. "Now, would you please have a seat so that we may practice some civility when we talk?"

Petra took one of the sofas and waited. After several long moments, Lady Langford took the other sofa. Her jaw was tight, and her skin paler than usual. Petra almost asked if she would like some water, but refrained from that particular civility. She did, however, decide it was worth hurrying things along.

"I expect in summoning me earlier, you wished to know why Duncan and the marquess have suddenly come together as brothers, yes? Well, you have heard the truth from your son now, that it is for the good of the nation, and the Crown, not against it." She canted her head. "Though I can tell you that their mission is somehow overlapping with my investigation. Ordered by both Her Majesty, the Queen, and the Duchess of Hillmorton."

Lady Langford let out a brittle laugh. "You jest, Lady Petra." And then when she looked into Petra's eyes and saw she was not, suddenly her manner changed.

"My son . . . is he in danger? More so than what he has told me?"

Petra blinked. "I wish I knew the answer to that myself. Though I can tell you this much—when Duncan asked his brother, the marquess, for his help some weeks ago, his lordship found that it gave him a new purpose . . . and I expect that is something you have already discovered."

"Do you promise me upon your life that . . . *Shawcross* means no harm to my son?"

"I cannot promise that no danger will befall either Shawcross brother," Petra said, adding in a steely tone, "for as you yourself helped ensure, some already has. But, yes, that I can promise you. On my life, Duncan means no harm to the marquess." The dowager marchioness went to rise without so much as a thank-you, or a proper apology, but Petra stopped her. "However, there is one way in which you might be able to help their investigation, and mine."

Lady Langford lifted her chin imperiously, but did sit back down. "And pray tell, what would that be?"

"If you would, tell me why, three years ago, you asked Lady Vera to hire a companion named Miss Dodd to escort her ward to Lady Caroline's house party at Evermark Manor. Who was Miss Dodd to you? And where is she now?"

THIRTY-SIX

IF THERE WAS ONE THING PETRA NEVER THOUGHT SHE WOULD see in her lifetime, it was the Dowager Marchioness of Langford's brown eyes going wide with fear. For her hands to begin trembling and for her waspish voice to go to a frightened whisper. It was so disconcerting that Petra rushed to her side on the other sofa, thinking the dowager marchioness had taken instantly ill.

"How do you know I recommended that woman?" And when Petra explained that Lady Vera had told her, she nodded. "I always wondered if I would have to answer to you on this."

Petra's eyes narrowed. "Answer to me? How do you mean, your ladyship?"

The dowager stood, wringing her hands, and began pacing the short three steps between couches, up and back, up and back. "You must understand, Lady Petra. When this began, my husband had just brought Shawcross to our home from Scotland. I immediately ordered the boy out of Langford House." She licked her lips, and a hitch came into her voice. "And when he took the boy away to Hillmorton House, my husband went with him."

"Your husband left Langford House? I always understood that he left on one of his travels soon after."

"Oh, he did," she said bitterly, though without her usual snappish tone. "But he only did so to keep the ton from the understanding that he, the marquess, had left me. All because I would not accept that boy—Shawcross—into my home. My husband left me and his own legitimate son in favor of the son he'd never even known he'd sired."

There was nothing Petra wanted more than further details on

this matter, but a small ormolu clock atop the fireplace mantel chimed the half hour. It was now half past two in the morning. And while they still had over ten hours to determine where Rushton and his Bellowers were likely to cause chaos in London, she and everyone with her needed sleep. She needed to check on Teddy, too, who refused to stay in Langford House, but had accepted space in the stable's hayloft. Thus, she pressed for the details she needed.

"Your ladyship, what happened next?"

The dowager marchioness hesitated for a long moment, then seemed to steel herself.

"It was actually what happened before, shortly after James was born," she began, looking down at her hands. "There was a gentleman—one of the ton—with whom I had a longstanding flirtation. When he became widowed, with a young child of his own, and my husband was visiting other women's beds, our flirtation became an attachment."

In a shaky voice, the dowager marchioness then began to talk about how the gentleman she'd had such a strong attachment to had begun to be a different man after a while. That she found he was going to political meetings, and his votes in the House of Lords were being used to advance agendas that, as a monarchist and a Tory, she did not feel were right. And yet, she felt that his views were more than wanting simple reform. She said he began to frighten her with his passionate outbursts, and yet their attachment continued on for three years.

"And then, just as I felt strong enough to end our understanding, I became with child—and it was his."

By now, Petra could not breathe. She never would have thought the dowager marchioness would be so forthcoming, but somewhere, deep down, she suspected this woman had needed to say these words for over twenty years. And thus, she simply let her speak.

"I carried the child almost a six-month before I lost it," she said dully, and did not even respond when Petra emitted a gasp that was full of sympathy, not judgment. "Yet the gentleman was determined to make certain the entire ton knew he was the father. He was determined to ensure that he could use my rightful husband's power in the House of Lords, and with the Duke and Duchess of Hillmorton, to advance his political beliefs." Drawing in a shuddering breath, she said, "And then, less than a year later, my husband brought Shawcross to Langford House."

Petra said nothing. Before now, she had rarely felt anything but disdain for Duncan's stepmama, but now she could somewhat understand the anger that had fueled this woman's life and disposition.

It seemed that, after Lady Langford lost her unborn child—and her husband, the marquess, had returned—the gentleman agreed to leave her in peace. "He left London with his child—a son, of about six years old—and did not return to town ever again. He died a couple of years later, and sent his son to be raised by the child's grandmother."

At the mention of a son—one that would have been around Petra's and Duncan's age—and the fact that this gentleman had left his ties to London behind, certain things began to slot into place in Petra's mind. Especially how the gentleman had developed radical views before he died, leaving his motherless son to be raised by others.

"This gentleman—are you speaking of my Emerson's father? The previous Viscount Ingersoll, who died when Emerson was a boy of eight?"

A flush spread over the dowager marchioness's cheeks. She met Petra's eyes for a brief moment, and she nodded. "His lordship's name was Terrence, and I shall refer to him in that way to avoid confusion in the rest of my tale."

Petra inclined her head, and the dowager marchioness continued.

"One day, about a year after Terrence left, a young woman, Miss Huxton, arrived to be James's first governess. I received a letter from Terrence soon after, explaining that he was sending me a good reference for Miss Huxton after having discovered that she fled to London. He said he had frightened her off, and he regretted his behavior. When I spoke to Miss Huxton about this, however, she confided in me that Terrence had become even more keen on reform—and radical, violent reform at that."

"As influenced by a cousin, if I recall," Petra said musingly, the words of Lady Vera coming back to her, and the dowager marchioness nodded.

"Then, a few years later, I heard Terrence himself had died, with his son going to live with the grandmama and a new governess." She briefly lifted one thin shoulder. "And nearly fifteen years passed after that, bringing us to a time four years ago."

She went on to say that one day, "a woman appeared on my doorstep—older than you, but by not too many years. She gave her name as Miss Tessa Dodd."

Tessa, Petra's mind repeated dully. *The woman I am told Emerson loved more than he loved me.*

The dowager marchioness continued, "She was requesting an audience with me. She became loud and verbally threatening when I at first refused, after my butler said Miss Dodd seemed to be a woman of little character, refinement, grace, or accomplishment."

Upon their eventual meeting, Miss Dodd introduced herself as the cousin of Terrence, Viscount Ingersoll. The purpose of Miss Dodd's visit was to request letters of recommendation from the Dowager Marchioness of Langford because she required work. And when her ladyship first refused, Miss Dodd threatened to use what scandal she knew of the dowager marchioness and her former liaison with Terrence to bring shame upon the Langford marquessate, and the larger Shawcross family.

"In the end, as all she wished for were good references, and the chance to be a companion in certain circumstances, I felt that agreeing to her demands would be of little issue. Until I began to understand that she was using my connections in order to forge her own. And they involved helping to sway members of the ton to her radical reformist point of view."

The dowager marchioness paused, then her expression briefly became pained.

"This included a young man of consequence at Lady Caroline's house party who was cousin to Miss Dodd and her nephew. He— the nephew—would also be a guest there, even though this young gentleman did not know either as kin, having lived in the shelter of his grandmama's sphere for so long."

"My Emerson," Petra whispered. *And that blackguard Rushton had deliberately lied to further pain me, trying to make me believe Emerson was having a liaison with Tessa. They were cousins, and that is all.*

"Yes, sadly. And your Lord Ingersoll would go on to become so imbued with radical reform like his papa that he became a danger-ous man indeed."

"Miss Dodd was recruiting others to her cause, then?" Petra said, numb at hearing those words spoken so plainly. "Who was her nephew? I do not recall anyone else at Lady Caroline's house party with the name of Dodd."

The dowager marchioness lifted one thin shoulder in a shrug. "It does not necessarily follow that the nephew's last name was Dodd, too. Nevertheless, Miss Dodd later married. And when she did, she seemed to go quiet in her reformist zeal. And, thus, I would not have even recognized her, but for—"

Petra's mind was still determined to understand who Miss Dodd was related to, however. "So, this Miss Dodd was Emerson's cousin. Then who was the other young man—Miss Dodd's nephew?" she interrupted, her voice tinged with exasperation. "There were some twenty guests there that week at Evermark Manor. Half were men, and all save two were peers."

"I had not taken you for a simpleton, Lady Petra," said the dowager marchioness, a bit of her usual caustic tone reappearing. "Miss Dodd's nephew, and your Emerson's cousin, is Mr. Phineas Rushton."

"No," Petra whispered. It was difficult enough to believe that Emerson had become so radicalized—at least until just before he died. Emerson had not just been a reformist, for that would have been but a trifle. Reform was needed. Reform was a good thing. Bloody hell, she and all her friends wanted better things for their country, and most of all, for women. But Emerson had been an advocate for force and violence in the desire to remake Great Britain from a monarchy to a republic, and had become radicalized into such behavior through the efforts of his cousins.

"I am sorry," said the dowager marchioness. And when Petra's eyes went wide, she said, "I am, Lady Petra. For it was quite clear, even to me, that you loved him. And I know his true affiliations were kept from you. I am sorry to be the one to have to tell you after these three years."

The dowager marchioness explained what little she knew beyond that, with rather more tact than Petra had ever expected from her ladyship as well. That while the association Emerson had belonged to had existed since the late 1790s, it had only become known as the Bellowers in the recent years, when Emerson had been brought into the fold.

And it had been Emerson and his cousin Mr. Rushton who had given the association its name. Emerson, Lord Ingersoll, had been the handsome, upstanding, boyish-looking viscount who gave the Bellowers the clout they needed with various others in the peerage and the gentry.

It was because of those in the upper ranks of society that the Bellowers had so much secrecy until relatively recently. The peers had demanded it, for they had not wished to be known as traitors in society until it was clear the Bellowers' objectives could be accomplished.

Indeed, the dowager marchioness explained that the only reason she knew of the association at all was because of her attachment to Emerson's father, the previous Lord Ingersoll.

"I only discussed my knowledge somewhat with Her Grace after I heard the news about your Lord Ingersoll," she told Petra. With a sigh and a look upon her sharply planed face that said it made her quite uncomfortable to speak with such candor, she added, "I know you and I have never cared for one another, Lady Petra, but I did believe you should have known the truth when it happened. It was a consortium of those closest to you who decided you were not yet ready to understand. In the end, I rather agreed with them."

She then looked Petra up and down with a little exhale through her nose that indicated she was admitting to herself that she no longer saw Petra in the unfavorable light she once did.

Nevertheless, there was one thing Petra understood that Lady Langford did not. Despite the fact her ladyship was a patroness of the Asylum for Female Orphans, she did not know that Mrs. Huxton had been murdered, or that there was a connection between the Bellowers and the late matron's death. That fact was still a secret known only by a handful of people. Even the men who governed the orphanage did not yet know.

Still, it became clear very quickly to Petra that Duncan's stepmama also had no idea that the orphanage, through the embezzling of inheritances that should have belonged to the orphaned girls, was the source of the Bellowers' funds. The dowager marchioness knew that Emerson's title and influence had been what had taken the Bellowers from a small association to one that was gaining in power and influence, but nothing else.

And Petra believed one thing without having to convince herself of it—that the dowager marchioness would not have allowed it to happen if she had known. And she felt Lady Langford proved it by what she told her next.

"I also feel it right to tell you something else the Duchess of

Hillmorton told me regarding the late matron, Mrs. Huxton," she said. "In fact, it was Mrs. Huxton herself who told the duchess."

"Indeed?" Petra said.

The dowager marchioness nodded. "As I understand it, Mrs. Huxton was once visited by Emerson. She was most glad to see him looking so well. But as they talked, she realized he had taken up his late father's radical ways, and then some. In hoping to deter him from further going down that path, Mrs. Huxton went to the Duchess of Hillmorton for assistance, knowing she was the confidant of the Queen. Mrs. Huxton also knew that Emerson and Shawcross were like brothers, having been told by Ingersoll himself."

Petra felt a chill going down her arms, but said, "Please, do continue, your ladyship."

"Then one night, Lord Ingersoll took that tumble down the stairs. His death helped disperse the Bellowers for a time. Recently, I heard my James talking, saying they were gaining strength again, but I did not know how swiftly, or what they were using as a show of strength from the peerage. Nor did I know my son and Shawcross would become so involved."

"They are but traitors to the Bellowers, not to their country," Petra snapped. And this time, the dowager marchioness held up a hand in acquiescence. She repeated, however, that she knew no more than what she had just confessed.

"Oh, but you do indeed," Petra said. "Tell me, who is Miss Dodd now?"

"Why, Mrs. Yardley, of course," the dowager marchioness replied, blinking in confusion when Petra's mouth gaped in a most unladylike way. "I thought you knew. Miss Tessa Dodd became Mrs. Yardley."

It was then Petra remembered the way Lady Langford had looked at her when she had arrived yesterday at the Asylum for Female Orphans. It was such a withering look, and yet she had glanced at the new matron as well. It was now so clear. The dowager marchioness had already thought Duncan had recruited his brother James to the side of the Bellowers, and seeing Petra be so friendly with Mrs. Yardley—someone who had once been a radical and could possibly be one again—had been too much for her to bear.

"The last time Miss Dodd—that is, Mrs. Yardley, forced me to help her with a letter of reference, it was to obtain the post of undermatron at the orphanage," her ladyship explained. "She explained to me that, while she still wanted reform, especially for the rights of us women, she had lost her inclination for violent aspects of it. Whilst she had been a quite terrible companion to young girls wishing to marry, I did recall her being rather sweet with children. As I had not heard anything of her radical leanings in so long, I thought she had changed her ways, like Mrs. Huxton had. It was possible, you understand. I genuinely thought it possible."

"Yes, one can come to understand they have been small-minded, and one can work to change their way of seeing the world," Petra said, looking pointedly into her ladyship's eyes as she said, "For some, I genuinely hope it will be possible."

Yet before her ladyship could fully grasp her meaning, Petra said, "Though I must thank you for doing what others have not, your ladyship. For you told me the truth. And so I shall do the same for you in kind, with information I have learned within the last two days. Neither Mrs. Huxton, nor Emerson, died by accident. No, indeed, they were both murdered. Emerson when an unknown man snapped his neck whilst at Duncan's former town house . . ." A realization struck, and she added, "Which I now believe was in retaliation for Emerson's last-minute change of heart, of his understanding that reform should hopefully come without violence."

The dowager marchioness was holding her hand to her heart. "And the late matron?"

"Mrs. Huxton was murdered in the chapel at the Asylum for Female Orphans, and I have yet to discover the culprit." But Petra said it almost thoughtfully as another understanding came to her.

She knew where Mr. Rushton—and likely some of his Bellower cohorts—would be. In fact, she had all but sent them there herself, and in doing so put so many young lives in danger.

"I must go," she said. And without so much as a brief curtsy, she turned and rushed from the room.

THIRTY-SEVEN

SHE STOOD IN JAMES'S LIBRARY, AFTER HAVING ASSEMBLED her friends once more.

"I know it is very late, and we are all in a state of exhaustion. Should you wish to stay here, I cannot blame you. But instead of being foolish again, I am telling you where I shall be going. Now. This very minute, in fact. I have already ordered a horse saddled, for there is no possibility of a carriage getting through the crowds, which have likely become more filled with ruffians."

"And ones in their cups," Caroline said darkly.

Duncan was already on his feet. Just moments earlier, she'd breathed a sigh of relief when she dashed into the library to find his color had returned after rest and some beef stew from the kitchens. She herself had accepted a bowl and made herself eat a few bites while the others were being roused from their beds.

Petra took in everyone in the room. Petra, Frances, and Lottie were yawning, if alert. James and Duncan had similar intent looks on their faces. Then there were Teddy, Whitfield, James's two footmen, and three other men introduced as two of Duncan's trusted men of security, but no other names were offered.

Petra gave everyone a brief history of her investigation. This included a quite bland version of what she had learned in Caroline's diary entries regarding her house party three years earlier in Surrey. How Mr. Rushton had been invited, and how he had been seen in what seemed like a flirtation with Miss Tessa Dodd, the companion of Lady Vera's ward. Without being overly specific on what she had learned from both Lady Vera herself and the Dowager Marchioness of Langford, Petra explained how everything connected to her investigation at the orphanage.

"Miss Tessa Dodd, as was, married and became Mrs. Yardley—the new matron of the Asylum for Female Orphans. It seems Mrs. Yardley is the aunt of Mr. Rushton . . . and they are both cousins to Emerson, the late Lord Ingersoll."

Duncan and James exchanged looks, and her other friends gasped. Teddy, Whitfield, and the other men merely looked politely interested, looking at Petra to continue.

"Mr. Rushton—who we know to be a tall, thin gentleman with perfectly combed hair and speaking the King's English—goes by another name and identity as well. He is also Mr. Fife, the genial, burly delivery man with bushy sideburns who sounds as if he just walked off the docks in the East End."

This elicited a rare exclamation from Frances. "*Mr. Fife?*" she repeated in outraged tones. Yet Caroline gently reminded her that time was of the essence and encouraged Petra to go on.

She did, explaining that when Annie was attacked at Bardwell's Apothecary, she had not seen the man, but had heard his gentleman's accent. Petra went on to tell them about her attacker calling her an abigail—a lady's maid—even though Annie was dressed as a shopgirl.

"Then, when I eventually thought back to my earlier meeting with the so-called Mr. Fife, he had bowed to me and called me 'my lady.' Understandable if I, too, had not been wearing a Bardwell's apron and thus all but dressed as a shopgirl as well. I didn't think much on it at the time, for my mind was occupied elsewhere. But eventually I realized he would not have referred to me as such—not dressed as I was—unless he was certain of my identity. Unless proper introductions had been made between us, and he *knew* me."

Duncan, looking frustrated, said that they knew Rushton would don disguises—much like he himself did. "But he was always so secretive, so paranoid, about what he did and where he went, that

while we knew he would often play the part of a tradesman or delivery man, or even the gentleman, we rarely knew where he would
utilize those disguises."

With his glower deepening, Duncan explained that, from what
little they could tell, Rushton had never interacted with anyone
but servants when he became Mr. Fife, so he never thought Petra
would come across him. "We knew he delivered to places in Jermyn Street, but he was never reported at Bardwell's. I apologize,
my lady, and to you, Miss Frances. I should have confided that in
both of you as well. I should have warned all of you."

"Do not concern yourself," Frances was quick to say. "I was never
impressed with Mr. Fife as a delivery man, I must admit. And, I
have just now realized that he lied to me about having a little boy
experiencing teething pains! An odious creature for many reasons,
he is!" And this was agreed by Petra, Caroline, and Lottie alike.

"How did you come to understand the two men were one and
the same?" Duncan asked Petra.

"I noted when I saw Mr. Fife that he seemed quite a burly man,
and the one time I bumped into him, his arm was quite soft—
almost like touching a quilt. Teddy, too, gave me a good clue in
mentioning an angry moggy." She smiled at Teddy. "It made me
think of something deliberately puffed out. Mr. Rushton used to
be a larger man, but lost weight. Yet he kept his older clothes, it
seemed, and found some way of padding them out."

"His trousers," Teddy piped up. "That was why they were so
baggy that day when he attacked Miss Annie. Because he wore an
old pair that weren't padded."

"I agree, yes," Petra said. "But when I saw him at Sloan House,
there was something else. He seemed strangely unwilling to inter-
act with the servants—as if he were above them in station. And
then once, I saw him smile, and it seemed familiar to me somehow.
As if I had seen it before." She paused and said, "It reminded me of
Emerson's, to tell you the truth. But it was when I truly had reason

to watch him—when he had us tied up, and he was taunting me with Emerson's journal—that I finally saw how much he looked like Mr. Fife. At first I thought they might be brothers, but it became more plausible that they were one and the same man."

She gave her friends a wry smile.

"With Rushton's accent, overall physique, and entire demeanor changed, he was hardly recognizable, especially when his hair darkened from blond to brown as he aged." She glanced at Duncan. "And I expect he chose the name Fife to represent the instrument a piper plays when marching into battle."

Duncan cursed. "One of the symbols of the Bellowers. Indeed, I was a damned fool not to confide in you sooner."

Petra wrung her hands. "Not as big of a fool as I, however. Yesterday, I suggested to Mrs. Yardley that she contract some men to help keep the orphanage safe. Having not yet realized Mr. Rushton and Mr. Fife were one and the same—and that he is the nephew of Mrs. Yardley—I specifically told her to contract Mr. Fife for added security. I believe he, and some of his men, will be at the orphanage now, deciding on how and when to carry out their plan that will commence in a matter of hours."

Duncan was already pulling on his boots and Petra stepped up.

"You will not leave me here. As I said, a horse is already being readied for me. Thus, you may either allow me to accompany you, or I shall go on my own. You have those two choices."

The muscle in Duncan's bruised and battered jaw was still alive and pulsing beneath a small contusion.

"You must at least have ways to protect yourself."

"She shall have my flower bombs," Frances declared.

"Do not ask," Caroline said to the men's confused faces. "And be certain to bring a handkerchief to cover your face."

"And you will take Sable and Fitz," Lottie said. "And their leads, of course."

The other men looked curious as to this until Teddy informed them of the dogs' tricks.

"I shall be coming with you," Caroline declared. "And it is as pointless to argue with me as it is with Lady Petra. Langford, where is your bow and arrows? Have them fetched for me immediately. I will do nothing but stand outside in a hiding place, and use my arrows to stop anyone needed."

Again, the other men looked taken aback until Teddy said, "A shilling says Lady Caroline can hit anything with an arrow you point out, dead center." To which Whitfield added proudly, "I would just give the lad your money, for it is quite true."

Duncan's hands were on his hips, but he did not argue, only saying, "And you, my lady? How will you defend yourself? That little dagger will do you just as little good, I'm afraid."

At this, Petra carefully pulled up the left side of her dress to the top of her garters. More than one man in the room pulled in a breath. Duncan, however, moved closer, his voice astounded, and a bit hoarse. "Ye fastened your lockpicks to your garters?"

Petra, her talents at embroidery minimal but serviceable, had devised a way to attach her four most used picks into her garters without them poking either her or catching on her dress.

"It was easier than having them in my reticule," she said. "And my pockets, whilst my favorite thing about my dresses, are a bit roomy, allowing my picks to bounce about uncomfortably. This way, the chances of them being found by someone else is quite minimal. Though I do know I need a better system as, whilst I can easily remove them for use, putting them back in their little slots is a bit more difficult."

"And then on my other leg . . ." Dropping her skirts on one side, she pulled up those on the opposite side.

"That is my dagger!" Duncan thundered, then his voice went hoarse. "Strapped to *your leg*." He added a Gaelic curse word that did not need to be translated by anyone in the room.

"Scandalous, dearest," drawled Caroline. "Brava."

"Teddy found it after Rushton dropped it," Petra said blithely. "And I think it is mine now. It is small enough to be strapped to my leg. And, besides, James has already given you another one."

"One that belonged to our father," James added, and Duncan turned to him in surprise. But being men, all that was exchanged was a look, and a nod.

"Right," Frances said. "What shall we do whilst you lot are riding to the orphanage? Lottie and I refuse to sit here and drink tea."

It was decided that while some of Duncan's men had already been alerted, there were other pockets waiting for news. Frances and Lottie would set out at first light to alert others, accompanied by more of James's footmen.

Dark cloaks and bonnets were then borrowed from the Dowager Marchioness of Langford to help conceal Petra's and Caroline's identities, and soon, everyone was riding out, Sable on Petra's saddle—though looking quite unnerved by the experience—and Fitz in Caroline's arms. They took back roads, and decided upon Lambeth Bridge instead of Westminster in hopes of encountering fewer issues. Over the Thames, the boats below were lit up with lanterns, and people sang as their boats bobbed in the water. With the warm, clear night, it should have been a thing of glory for Petra to behold. Instead, her stomach was roiling.

What would they find when they arrived? Would the Bellowers be holding the orphaned girls hostage, terrifying them? And what of Mrs. Yardley? She had never fully trusted the woman, but was the matron a murderer too? Had she been the person to sneak into the chapel and deliver the killing blow to Mrs. Huxton's head?

And if so, was it simply because Mrs. Huxton was a barrier to Mrs. Yardley and the Bellowers gaining access to any more inheritance monies from unsuspecting orphans? Or had there been another reason?

Then her mind turned to Nell. Had the younger girl been in-doctrinated into the Bellowers as well? Or had they attempted it and Nell had run in order to save her life? Petra felt strongly for the latter, but Nell somehow remained an unknown.

While the outward riders—the footmen and Duncan's men of security—were forced to beat off a couple of drunken men, they encountered few issues. And by the time they could see the orphan-age, with several delightful homemade transparencies glowing in the front windows, the crowds had thinned to almost nothing.

Teddy offered to run ahead as scout as they neared the orphanage.

When he returned, breathing heavily, everyone had dismounted. The darkness, with only one lamp for the entire group, did not diminish how Teddy's smile lit up the night.

"Lady Petra, you were right. They're in there! Rushton as well, dressed as Mr. Fife. Saw five men and one woman. Only problem is, there's a bloke on guard at the front door. I gots lucky—he were taking a piss with his back turned when I got my look-see. No, I did not see any of the orphans. Saw a kitchen maid serving tea. The woman was an older lady sittin' by the fire with her arms crossed."

"Mrs. Yardley," Petra said, nodding. "And I am glad no orphans are about. Nell told me that they could be locked in their dormitories. Let us hope they are in there and safe."

Whitfield had opened the satchel brought by Frances, lifting out one of the flower bombs. "What are these, may I ask? They smell like lavender and sage."

"Until you throw them and they break," Caroline said dryly. "Then there is a powder inside that smells like . . . well, it will cause havoc with the eyes, the nose, and the throat."

"Ingenious," Whitfield said, holding one up and looking at it as if wishing to know how Frances made it.

But another of Duncan's men came back, who had followed Teddy as a scout for the back half of the property. He delivered the bad news that there were about twenty scruffy-looking men out in the gardens, laying about and drinking. He reported they looked fairly soused, but that could only make them meaner.

From Frances's bag, Petra fished out a bottle of laudanum. "If we can douse their drinks with this . . ."

"Excellent idea," James said, "though it would take some minutes to really help. And we cannot guarantee all will drink it."

"Better some than none," Duncan said, and Teddy stepped up again. "Mr. Shawcross, Nell told me the name of the cook here at the orphanage. I may be able to get her to let me in. If she can offer the men more drink, with this . . ."

Petra, suddenly frightened, put her hand on Teddy's cheek. "Be careful, dearie. All right?" Then James dug in his pocket and produced two shillings. "This ought to help persuade her."

Teddy had disappeared into the darkness before they could say anything. One of the stable lads who had ridden with them took charge of the horses, leading them away to a more darkened place.

Then Teddy was back, his eyes wide. "Couldn't do it, my lady, Mr. Shawcross." He gulped. "The men, they were up and readying themselves. They're looking like they're about to be on the move." He switched his eyes to Petra. "Even worse, when I looked back into the front parlor, I did see one orphan. It's Nell, and she's tied up, my lady I don't know how they found 'er."

"Knowing Nell," Petra said, "I think it likely she escaped."

An idea occurred to her. "I know where we may find extra help. Even if it be only a handful of men." She told Teddy where to go, and what to say, and he disappeared into the darkness once more.

There was no more time to waste, however. If these Bellowers were to be stopped, they must be stopped at this very moment.

"I am the only one here who knows the layout of the orphanage," Petra declared. "Those of you who plan to take care of the men outside, Mr. Shawcross will give you your orders. As for those inside, this is what I think we should do."

THIRTY-EIGHT

Friday, 23 June 1815
The Asylum for Female Orphans
Lambeth, South London
The three o'clock hour of the morning

DUNCAN'S MEN WENT FIRST, WALKING WITH QUICK, SOFT STEPS through the side gate and to the back garden, easily disappearing into the inky night despite their size. Petra heard a grunt and then a body fall quietly to the ground. He was dragged away. She then heard her signal. A fairly authentic sound of a hissing cat.

She took a breath, knowing Caroline was hidden somewhere behind her and had excellent aim. Then she straightened her bonnet and ran up to the front door of the orphanage, knocking frantically on the door, calling out, "Help! Please open up!"

A quite frightening-looking man answered the door, holding a short wooden club that he smacked in his palm. "What d'ya want, miss. Orphanage's closed for the night. I'm keepin' these little girls safe." Petra saw his menacing smile and had to force herself to play her part.

"I am here to warn Mrs. Yardley!" she said. Then called out, "Mrs. Yardley! You are in danger! It is Lady Petra!"

The guard advanced on Petra, causing her to step back, but it had worked. The door flew open wider, and Mrs. Yardley appeared.

"Why, Lady Petra! What is it? Is everything all right?" She glared at the guard, who gave a nod and stepped back.

"You are in danger, Mrs. Yardley," she said, pretending to be breathing hard. Her eyes were wild and her hair was windswept.

"A man named Mr. Rushton will be coming here. He is a member of a radical organization and intends on holding the orphanage hostage! We must get the girls out, Mrs. Yardley, before he comes here." She craned her head over Mrs. Yardley's shoulder, but could see little except the entrance hall. "Did you have Mr. Fife come? Is this guard here part of his contingency to protect the girls? If so, we may be able to fend them off."

Mrs. Yardley had gone still at the sound of Rushton's name, but then seemed to relax at the sound of Fife's.

"Of course, your ladyship. Mr. Fife has been protecting us all night. Why don't you come in and explain what is happening?" As Petra hurried to follow her in, Mrs. Yardley turned with eyes that held a bit of amusement. "You will be pleased to know we found Nell, too. She came back, attempting to collect something she lost. You were right, Lady Petra, she is quite dangerous. I think she may have even killed our poor Mrs. Huxton. That is why we made certain to tie her up."

With one graceful arm gesture, she indicated Nell, who was sitting upon a chair next to the arched doorway that led from the lobby to the matron's quarters. She was gagged and with her hands and feet bound, much like Petra had been just hours earlier. She had a bruise blooming on her cheek and her violet eyes were hot with anger as they swiveled to meet Petra's.

"You struck her?" Petra asked, moving closer to the girl as she untied her bonnet. Then her voice hardened. "Good. This girl has been nothing but trouble, and she kicks and hits like a man. I want to protect these other girls, but should this one be a casualty, I care not. You will hold my bonnet, girl, for being such a pest." Then she dropped the bonnet in Nell's lap, staring into Nell's eyes and then giving the inside of the bonnet a pointed look as the girl's eyes filled with hurt tears.

"Yes, she has rather been a pest, and for far too long," Mrs. Yardley confirmed from behind Petra. "This way, your ladyship. Mr.

Fife will be pleased to see you, of that I am certain. My, you smell delightfully of lavender and sage. Do you keep your dresses in a drawer with scented sachets? Yes? Oh, I must try that sometime."

Petra's ears had been trained to hear a prearranged sound, but it had not yet come. Fear tightened her throat for Duncan, James, Whitfield, Teddy, and the rest of the men. What if they had been overpowered? Or, heavens, please, no . . . what if they were killed?

She walked into the lobby, in which sat three men. Next to them was Mr. Rushton—dressed in his padded clothing as the bulkier, burlier Mr. Fife. And it truly was amazing how he had transformed himself. Everything from his look to his build to his hairstyle, and even the way he held his jawline and smiled. He was a master of a simple disguise.

"Mr. Fife," she gushed. "It is so good to see you here, looking after these girls until the danger has passed. Thank you, I am most grateful."

She expected him to be his genial Mr. Fife persona, to smile and doff his cap. Instead, he rose slowly, as did his three men.

"I rather think you can drop the act, Lady Petra."

"Mr. Fife?" she said, eyes widening and blinking innocently. "Whatever has happened to your charming accent?" She let a thread of fear come into her voice. "Mrs. Yardley? Is something amiss? Are these men threatening you?"

"Oh no, Lady Petra," Mrs. Yardley said with a cackling laugh. "It is we who are threatening you. You see, you are standing between us and our ability to set a long-held plan in motion. One that started with me, my nephew Phineas here"—she nodded toward Mr. Fife—"and your own late Lord Ingersoll, also known to me as my dear cousin Emerson. Until, that is, Emerson decided to come pay a visit to his old governess."

It wasn't hard for Petra's lip to tremble. "How do you mean?"

"We had everything planned, we did," Mrs. Yardley said. "I'd married a stupid half-wit of a man who gave me a new name and enough money to help begin a new and more powerful association for reform than we have ever known. Phineas and I both managed to be invited to Lady Caroline's house party—though of course you would not remember me. I wore spectacles and made myself look the epitome of the sad, unwanted spinster. But it gave us time to reintroduce ourselves to Emerson, who I'd known when I stayed with his papa from time to time, when Emerson was a boy. He was so easy to manipulate as a boy, and even easier as a man. We had him converted to our side by the—"

"By the picnic at Box Hill," Petra said. "Yes, I am now recalling."

"Ah, so you have finally recalled the things I'd hoped you never would," said Mr. Rushton. Then with a sickening smile he added, "And how is Mr. Shawcross feeling?"

"He is poorly, if you must know," she snapped. "Unconscious, and does not even know I am here." Trying her hand at an East End accent, she added, "And that ain't no porky pies, Mr. Fife."

Yet all this did was make the man and his cohorts laugh, confound it.

Petra gathered herself and continued playing her part. "As there is clearly no chance of me escaping again from you, I shall allow you to use me to lure out the royal family—or whatever it is you plan. After that, we shall discuss you having my money. I confess I am not yet willing to give my inheritance over to you quite yet, but if you will give me your word you will never hurt Duncan again, I shall consider it. But in the meantime, I wish to hear the rest of Mrs. Yardley's story. I feel it is quite short, so there is no need not to grant me the wish of hearing what I do not yet know."

Mr. Rushton smiled. "Very well. Go on, Tessa. Tell her what she wishes to know. It will not make a difference one way or the other."

Mrs. Yardley seemed pleased to have the stage.

"Emerson was instrumental in so many ways," she said, clutching at the silver cross hanging from her necklace. "Money, influence, connections. And then one day, he discovered his old governess—one his father had adored as much as he—was the matron here at the orphanage. That she had once been as loyal to our cause as his father. He came to visit her, rejoicing in how well she looked, and how kind she still was.

"As they talked, she mentioned how most of these girls here are the unwanted and illegitimate daughters of soldiers, the gentry, and even some of the lofty ton. He then discovered that any monies these girls had coming to them are kept secret from them until their fifteenth birthday. At which time, they are given some papers to sign that release them to their sad life as a servant for some privileged aristocrat, or as a likely just as sad life as an apprentice somewhere. Or even to a worse fate as the wife to some penniless man who just wants a drudge to clean his house, and a body who cannot refuse him when he wants his pleasure. But Emerson learned how extraordinarily simple it would be to get these girls to sign away an inheritance they never even knew they had, and would never miss."

This time, Petra let her hand come to her stomach, for she felt quite ill. Yet she urged Mrs. Yardley to go on.

The woman let out another laugh, this one much harsher. "Oh, but it worked for a while, until Emerson found out that Mrs. Huxton went to the Duchess of Hillmorton with her worries about him and his choices. She also spoke to him another time or two. And, sadly, it seemed to work."

"I beg your pardon?"

"Yes, Lady Petra. Our Emerson was so easily swayed by one person or another that Mrs. Huxton was able to sway his mind again, to make him believe the Bellowers were unworthy of his time and patronage. And, well, we were days away from the biggest show of force we'd had to date when he said he'd changed his mind. When he said he wanted us to pursue peaceful reform." She shrugged. "And, well, after that, we simply could not trust him anymore."

Mrs. Yardley then looked to her nephew, Mr. Rushton, and he shrugged, his face breaking into a terrible grin.

"Thus I snapped my cousin's neck and laid him out on the stairs for his pretty, young, and infinitely silly fiancée to find," he said.

THIRTY-NINE

IF IT HAD NOT BEEN FOR THE SOUND OF A CROSSLY YELLING cat, and the shattering of the front room's glass by an arrow, Petra would have unsheathed Duncan's dagger and run at the smugly smiling Phineas Rushton. She would have done it for herself, for Duncan, and, yes, for Emerson. For the life she had lost, and for the love she had nearly lost just hours earlier. She would even have done it for Mrs. Huxton.

Instead, from the pockets of her dress that were hidden by her traveling cloak, she pulled out four flower bombs and threw them as hard as she could at the floor, yelling, "Nell, cover your nose and run!"

Suddenly, there was chaos. Another arrow came through the window, and Mrs. Yardley screamed. Then there was the sound of gagging and retching. Petra had turned, running back toward where Nell had been tied, and was gone. And then she felt someone grab the back of her cloak, making her stumble and go down just as she made it into the hallway by Mrs. Yardley's room. But she already had grabbed Duncan's dagger from beneath her skirts.

She whirled to see Mr. Rushton, eyes alight with madness, hair flopping forward into his face, and a handkerchief over his mouth, as he pulled a knife himself. She was coughing and beginning to gag as Rushton lunged.

Instinctively, Petra did not use the dagger, but instead twisted, thrust out her left arm toward his face, palm forward and fingers curled downward. She barely felt the pain as it connected with his nose. She saw blood and heard his yell.

And then came a blur of cotton skirts, exposed legs, and a guttural scream in a higher pitch. Rushton was flying forward in an arc. He landed with a *fwump* on his back by the lobby desk, at nearly the exact place where Petra had seen him yesterday. Through her watering eyes, she saw Nell standing over him, Petra's little dagger in her hand, ready to strike if he moved.

Petra scrambled to get up and kicked Rushton's dagger away. There were sounds of men rushing in from the back of the orphanage. And quick shouts of, "Three here, Mr. Shawcross! All secure!"

"Petra!" someone called. *Caroline.*

Choking and coughing, she called out. "I am here! With Rushton!"

The main door to the orphanage was opening, and fresh air coming in. Caroline rushed in, bow at the ready. She took one look at Rushton and said, "Goodness, dearest, did you do that?"

Petra smiled over at Nell. "No, Miss Nell Parker did, and she was *brilliant.*"

For the first time since meeting her, Nell smiled. A wide, slightly lopsided smile that made those violet eyes glow. That defined her chin, and showed a bit more teeth on one side than the other.

And somehow, some pieces fell into place. Nell might have her mother's surname of Parker, but Petra would bet more than two shillings that the aristocrat father Nell had never known was named Terrence, Lord Ingersoll. The same man who gave Emerson that same lopsided smile. And that would make Nell an Ingersoll, too.

"Where did you learn to do all that?" Petra asked. "I am amazed, truly."

"Thank you, my lady," she said. "I learned it from the gentlemen's sporting club around the corner. One of the gentlemen saw me watching, and after talking to me, told me he felt young girls should learn to defend themselves. A kind man, Mr. Bellingham is."

In exchange for prison time and not the gallows, Mrs. Yardley gave up not only the time and the place that the Bellowers' show of force was to take place—that afternoon at St. James's Park during Prince Frederick's military display—but she also sent official word to the Bellowers that the attack was to be called off.

It was in a letter sealed with wax containing the Ingersoll coat of arms, from the very signet ring Petra had sent off to Emerson's remaining family. When it came time to seal the letter, Mrs. Yardley produced it from a chain that hung around her neck and was tucked beneath her higher necklines. While hidden beneath her clothing, it fell just below the cross she wore for all the world to see, and Petra realized the times she had seen Mrs. Yardley touching her cross, in truth, the woman had been clutching at the ring that had become a rallying symbol for violence.

The letter was then delivered to the gathering place—the orchestra pit at Vauxhall Pleasure Gardens—where the Bellowers would learn their target and instructions. Mrs. Yardley confirmed that one of the wild theories bandied about in Petra's drawing room was correct, that Rushton had paid unsuspecting citizens to purchase the correct transparencies, including the one of Vauxhall Gardens. Yet it had been innocently mislaid for a time by the housekeeper of Ingersoll House herself, leading a paranoid Rushton to storm over to Bardwell's Apothecary and attack Annie in an attempt to retrieve it.

As to why Rushton—in disguise as Mr. Fife—allowed them to be put on sale at Bardwell's Apothecary at all was down to his ever-growing sense that he was being watched and targeted. He felt that if transparencies were to be sold legitimately, then no one would be able to connect their sales to a signal to other members of the Bellowers.

Yet as she was led away by Duncan's men, Mrs. Yardley spat, "If my nephew had not been so secretive about everything—always seeing conspiracies left and right and thinking others were going to usurp his power—the Bellowers would know who to attack and it would have been done!"

Later, Duncan and his men orchestrated a raid on the Bellowers at Vauxhall Pleasure Gardens. While some of the radicals did manage to escape, by the time Prince Frederick—one of the first targets within the royal family—and his men marched onto the grass of St. James's Park for their planned military display, a full orchestra playing a song of victory with gusto, most of Rushton's followers had been arrested and were off the streets.

Mrs. Yardley had even given up the location of the cannonballs, rifles, and other weapons to be used in the attack. They had been stored in the unused mews stables of Ingersoll House. Prince Frederick, and indeed London itself, had been saved from a deadly attack.

For their part, Lottie and Frances had done an excellent job at locating Duncan's and the Queen's men. Sable and Fitz, too, had helped in tripping up or biting the arms of no fewer than two men each out in the back gardens. One turned out to be Caufield, whom Teddy recognized by his coarse language as the shadowy, rusty-guts man. And once he saw his face, Teddy was able to confirm to Duncan that he had witnessed Caufield stealing cannonballs, making Teddy just as much an intelligence officer as Duncan.

And once the orphanage had been cleared of every semblance of the Bellowers, Petra had used her lockpicks to unlock the dormitories and let the girls out.

Miss Stebbins calmly and quickly took control of the orphanage, and praised Magnus the lurcher for doing an excellent job of keeping the girls calm during such a frightening time. And later that afternoon, and with the assistance of several gentlemen from Juddy Bellingham's sporting club as extra guardians, the girls all received a day out to enjoy the celebrations at St. James's Park. Nell would be there with them, as the newly appointed under-matron.

But Nell would meet with her young charges after a trip to Forsyth House, where Enid helped her to bathe and let out the hem of one of Petra's cotton dresses in a pretty lavender that complemented her eyes. Afterward, Petra took Nell into the dressing room of her bedchamber. She pointed up at the portrait on the wall, near the bath.

"Is that the gentleman who helped you find a place at the orphanage?"

Nell's lips parted. "It is indeed, my lady. Who is he?"

Petra smiled. "That is Emerson, Viscount Ingersoll, and the man I was going to marry."

"I confess I had hoped to see him again," Nell said quietly.

"I quite understand that feeling," Petra said, slipping her hand in her pocket to feel the crumpled page of Emerson's journal she had torn out. Where he had had a change of heart, both about violent political reform, and taking her inheritance. She remembered the last four words he had written.

All will be well.

After a pause to gather herself, Petra removed from her pocket a small packet of papers. "Annie and Enid managed to find the way into Mrs. Huxton's box. There was a secret drawer that opened when you simultaneously pushed two carved birds, one on each side of the box." She handed over the packet, saying, "However, I think you know there is another place where you can find proof of your inheritance. Let us go back to my drawing room and we can see it."

She'd asked Nell to bring along the watercolor she had painted of Vauxhall Pleasure Gardens. Upon careful inspection of the words etched onto the page from a previous letter Mrs. Yardley had written to her nephew, Phineas Rushton, they were able to write out all that could be read. Petra explained that, at first, she had only seen the words "day," "Saint," and "His blood," and that she thought the letter had been religious in nature. Instead it had been a letter not written by Nell, but written by Mrs. Yardley about Nell. In the letter, Mrs. Yardley related proof that Nell was an Ingersoll.

"See," Petra said, pointing to the words. "It reads, *The girl was born on the day of Saint George, nearly five months after that hall* maid Terrence had seduced began showing." Then the words are, "*His blood is her blood, there is no doubt.*" Petra did not continue to read aloud, however, as the next words proclaimed that they, as Ingersoll relations, then felt that they were duly within their rights to claim Nell's inheritance.

Petra looked at her as Nell sat, completely shocked, upon her sofa. "It seems she knew you had seven thousand a year coming to you from your father—through Emerson's own inheritance, that is. And that your father was her own cousin—"

"Terrence, Lord Ingersoll," breathed Nell. "I had hoped I had read it correctly when I was painting and saw the words emerge, but I could not be certain."

"You have some of the hallmarks of an Ingersoll," Petra said, looking fondly at the girl. "Your inability to take milk is one, yes, but I see him in you especially when you smile. Your half brother, my Emerson, had much the same smile, and it is a lovely one."

"Your Lord Ingersoll—my half brother," she grinned shyly in saying the words, "he did mention that I resembled someone who worked in his father's house. He did not say who, though. I never thought he truly meant it, or that he would be recalling my mother."

"Sadly, the late Lord Ingersoll—Terrence, that was—had a habit of seducing his female staff. However, I know that Emerson had several governesses before his father died. With how well you speak, read, and write—much of which is learnt in earliest childhood—I would not be surprised if your mama was also his governess for a time as well."

"Before she was seduced by my father, you mean."

"Yes," Petra said. "And I shan't tell you how to feel about that. You must determine on your own how you feel about your father, and Emerson as well. I simply hope that you confide in someone and not let any feelings fester."

Nell's eyes welled a bit, but she did not cry, only nodding.

"Then I think there is something else you are due, Nell." From her pocket Petra extracted a signet ring with a crest carved intaglio, a wyvern at its center. "And I think the reason that Emerson helped you, and ensured you would have some of his own inheritance, is that he was a good man deep down. Too easily swayed, yes, but good in the end."

"You wish me to have it, my lady?"

Placing the ring in Nell's hand, she said, "Indeed. I think Emerson would have wanted it to go to you. For while Mrs. Yardley confessed that she discovered your paternity from looking into your intake paperwork after noting those Ingersoll traits you shared, Emerson had attempted to arrange it that no one but Mrs. Huxton would ever know who you were. He tried to protect you, and keep you from becoming embroiled in his family in the wrong way." As Nell's fingers closed slowly over the ring, Petra said, "The Ingersoll name has been all but tarnished, yes. But with you at its helm now, I think it can recover and shine once more."

Several days later, when Nell had decided to continue on at the orphanage despite the fact that she was now an heiress, Petra packed up the portrait of Emerson and sent it to the girl with a note, addressing it to Miss Nell Parker-Ingersoll, the name Nell had chosen for herself.

Nell—I hope you will look at our Emerson when you need to be reminded that everyone deserves a second chance. And though I never became his wife, I hope you will look upon me as your sister-in-law, and come to me if you are ever in need. Or simply if you would like to have tea (no milk) and talk—just two women who are endeavoring to deserve their blessings.

—Petra x

FORTY

Monday, 26 June 1815
Buckingham House
The ten o'clock hour

"It is rather lovely that some men are not such rotten creatures, is it not, Lady Petra?"

"It is indeed, Your Majesty," Petra said, smiling.

"But look at them. Both their handsome faces, black and blue," the Queen then said, fluttering a bejeweled ring toward the sofa where Duncan and James sat. It appeared they were in a contest to see how much of one biscuit they could each stuff in their mouth before their grandmama, the duchess, noticed and admonished them. "I am glad Sir Bartie's girl is such an excellent apothecarist that her balms have helped them heal." She then cocked her head and said, "Though it does make them both look rather roguish, I must say."

"I do believe they both look like heroes," the duchess said proudly. She had not stopped smiling and casting proud glances their way since her two grandsons walked into the Queen's red drawing room, side by side, then gave two of their most correct bows.

"Grandmama, does that mean you will tell us which one of us is your favorite?" Duncan asked, a cheeky challenge in his voice.

"She does not have to, for I know it is I," James added, popping the rest of his biscuit in his mouth.

The duchess gave one of her throaty, cackling laughs.

"And they are back to being as incorrigible as ever—though now in tandem," Petra said. "Please, Your Grace, make certain to put them in their place as often as possible, for their bond grows by the day and they are rather teasing me within an inch of my life."

"And I rather think you can handle yourself, Lady Petra," the duchess returned, but with a little wink when the Queen allowed herself a chuckle and sipped on her tea.

A bit later, when the men, full of biscuits and the compliments of the Queen, were told to go outside and stop being naughty after they made Her Majesty laugh so hard that she actually snorted, Petra was left alone with her godmother and the Queen. At that point, a third person was admitted, curtsied, and came to sit where the men had vacated.

Lady Vera's smile was like Petra thought her own mother's might have been when Petra had done well. She was full of pride and spun tales of Petra's intrepid investigative skills to the duchess and the Queen that Petra was forced to claim only half were true.

"She accused me of being the killer, Your Majesty, Your Grace!" Lady Vera said. "That was how much she wished to make certain she found justice for Mrs. Huxton. It is quite commendable indeed."

"It is only what should be done when someone has unjustly lost their life," Petra said, but returned Lady Vera's fond smile. It was lovely to have her friend once more.

This, however, was where the Queen seemed to have not understood. "Was it Mr. Rushton, or Mrs. Yardley who delivered the final blow to the poor matron's head?"

"In a way, it was both of them, Your Majesty," Petra said. "Mrs. Huxton had proof that she was planning on giving to the orphanage's governors about how some of the girls' inheritances were being stolen by the radical group called the Bellowers. Unfortunately, she was so frightened of the Bellowers that her abilities to think in a rational manner were compromised."

"Poor Mrs. Huxton." Lady Vera sighed. "She will be missed. Do go on, Lady Petra."

Petra smiled and did as requested. "Well, Mrs. Yardley confessed to sending Mr. Rushton to threaten Mrs. Huxton. He met with the late matron just before Lady Vera arrived at the orphanage chapel. He was evidently disguised as Mr. Fife and was able to arrive soundlessly after making sure the hinges to the door by the staff quarters were duly oiled. Nevertheless, by the time Lady Vera arrived, Mrs. Huxton was quite unnerved and not thinking clearly. Then she attempted to attack Lady Vera—out of fear, of course—and was knocked unconscious."

"Something for which I will never forgive myself," Lady Vera said with a sniffle, then accepted a handkerchief from the duchess with watery gratitude. The Queen, however, gestured for Petra to continue.

"When Lady Vera ran for help, that was when it happened. Mrs. Yardley saw her opportunity and let Mr. Rushton back into the orphanage via the side door. I am afraid he committed the horrible act in a matter of seconds, and then put the threatening message referencing Her Majesty beneath Mrs. Huxton's head."

Petra looked to the Queen. "We found a whole sheaf of those notes, written by various members of the Bellowers. They had planned to fling them out into the crowds if they had succeeded in their attack—and leave them beneath the bodies of those they killed, of course. It was a tactic meant to instill fear, and they nearly succeeded."

"Fear-mongering will never triumph in the long run," said the Queen sagely. "Not when there are good and strong people about like you and the Shawcross men, my dear."

Petra's cheeks turned pink from the compliment, but she quickly returned to explaining what she had discovered.

"Mr. Rushton was able to walk away from the orphanage disguised as Mr. Fife—someone whom no one would think twice about if they saw him. Yet, it seems no one even did, and thus he nearly got away with murder. And as for Mrs. Yardley, she was able to be convincing of her innocence because, despite assisting in every way possible, she did not, in fact, kill Mrs. Huxton."

"But why did she stay—Mrs. Huxton, I mean?" asked the Queen. "Why did she not leave when she was threatened?"

"She was protective of those girls, Your Majesty," Lady Vera said softly. "She protected them up to her last breath."

The Queen then asked for a listing of the girls whose inheritances were stolen. She said in the name of Mrs. Huxton, she would do what she could to make it right. That the girls might not end up with all they had originally been due, but she would ensure they all at least had enough to put away, and just maybe, buy themselves a new life.

"And as for the radical reformists," she said, "Lady Petra has told me of the things that Mr. Rushton said about his motives. His wants for our country. For the common man, and for women. That they were often sane, sound ideas that were simply implemented by an unsound man who felt force and violence over proper discourse was the best way to go about it. Nevertheless, I do not know if it will do any good, but I will be speaking with my son, the Prince Regent. We must at least listen to the needs of our citizens and see how we can make their lives better." She set her mouth, and did not even look at her snuffbox. "Yes, it must at least be attempted."

"Whilst the celebrations we witnessed were glorious and something that we may never see again in our lifetimes, I am rather glad they are over."

Duncan said this on a yawn as he and Petra laid on a blanket in the Queen's Gardens, the private park for members of the royal family. The Queen had insisted that Petra be allowed to use them whenever she liked, and could even ride her horse about the nearly forty acres of land. She had then privately hinted that it was quite a romantic place for a ride, and then a picnic, "and other things, as well," she'd added with a knowing smile.

The Queen had not been wrong, either. Duncan on his mahogany bay stallion and Petra on her chestnut gelding, Arcturus, spent an entire morning just riding around, before choosing a spot with a lovely tree and a bit of water sounding from an offshoot of the Serpentine. Letting their horses graze, Petra and Duncan ate a lovely lunch prepared by Mrs. Bing, then just laid back on the blanket and let the world be itself without their help, just for a little while.

It was only when Petra went to kiss him, and he hissed with pain as she laid her hand over his heart that she sat up. "What is it? What is the matter?"

"I had forgotten how much they hurt afterward," Duncan said, squeezing his eyes shut.

Panicking that Duncan had been hurt again, she straddled him and began pulling up his shirt.

"Oh, it is the hands again, my lady?" he said, his grin coming out. He put his own hands up by his head and said, "I have rather been waiting for you to finish what you have so cruelly started—twice." He closed one eye, the bruise about it having faded to that sickly green, yet somehow the color only complemented his eyes even more. "Well, there was that darkened doorway, so you were only cruel once."

But Petra only gave him a light swat as she searched for what was ailing him. She stopped when his shirt was pulled up to his throat. Five small stars were tattooed over his heart. Red and inflamed at the moment, marking them as having been done sometime between the moment he left her bed yesterday morning and their ride today, they looked like five little fireworks exploding over his heart.

But they weren't fireworks. She made him sit up as she pulled off his shirt completely.

"It's Cassiopeia," she said wonderingly, gently tracing the almost W-shaped line of stars, the same shape that could be found on the freckles on her nose.

"You've put your mark upon my heart, Lady Petra," Duncan said, his eyes never leaving hers.

"And you've given me the room to walk my own path to your heart," she replied.

And then she kissed him, her hands and her whole heart very happy to continue what they'd started.

AUTHOR'S HISTORICAL NOTE

The Asylum for Female Orphans was a real orphanage for girls in Lambeth, South London. During the Regency, it was housed in a former inn called the Hercules Inn, and was located near Westminster Bridge and Vauxhall Pleasure Gardens. It was an open secret that most of these girls were the daughters of soldiers, the gentry, and even the aristocracy. While some did come into inheritances left by their benefactors (or, likely, one of their parents), many did not. They aged out at fifteen and often went into service or into an apprenticeship.

The scene in this book that ends chapter fourteen, with Major Percy arriving in a post-chaise and four to deliver the news of Napoleon's defeat at Waterloo to the Prince Regent—who was the guest of honor at a dinner in St. James's Square—was also real. It was borrowed (and only slightly fictionalized) from the actual account written by the hostess of that momentous evening, Mrs. Edmund Boehm. This includes the words Major Percy said to the prince as he knelt and offered His Royal Highness the French standard as proof.

Afterward, the three days of celebrations that gripped and enthralled London were very much as I described, with Londoners of all classes and ranks celebrating in the streets with (temporary) abandonment of societal rules. Making the occasion even more magical, from the research I read, were the painted transparencies in every window, lit up from behind by a candle to make the painting flicker and almost come alive. Indeed, it must have been akin to walking through a fairy-tale land for the delighted citizens of

London who strolled the streets reveling in victory after so many years of war.

At the same time, however, there were some groups (often called associations) that were beginning to ramp up their calls for the abolition of the monarchy. While this was not a new idea by any means, and their followers were inspired by the French Revolution and the American Revolution, some of these associations felt that reform through violence instead of peaceful protests and discussions was the way to accomplish their goals. As evidenced by history, these radical groups failed in their missions and eventually disbanded, with overall support for the monarchy intact.

There were, of course, real-life intrepid women in the Regency era making waves in everything from society to politics to women's rights, despite everything in place to limit them. And I would like to believe that there were also women like my fictional Lady Petra, who had some hand in secretly routing threats like those in my book while encouraging the political reforms that began to come about thereafter. The more I read of how tough and clever the women of the Regency era were, the more I'm certain there were just as many we'll never read about as those we luckily can.

ACKNOWLEDGMENTS

Thanks doesn't quite cut it for those who have been patient with me as I made my way through Lady Petra's second mystery. (I'm looking at you big-time, Hannah O'Grady!) Book two of a series is, to me, exciting and so much fun to write, but it's also a wee bit terrifying. Every author wants each of their books to be better than the last, and when you have a team around you that gives you the space and encouragement to make a book (hopefully) a worthy follow-up to the first, then the gratitude that is already present is sent into the stratosphere. So, thank you stratosphere-levels to my wonderful editor, Hannah; my amazing agents, Christina Hogrebe and Jess Errera; and to my incredible Minotaur team, including Sara Beth Haring, Sara LaCotti, the production team, and my diligent copy editor and proofreader. Thank you again to David Baldeosingh Rotstein, for another gorgeous cover that blew my mind. And to Liane Payne, for working with me to create such a charming illustrated map for Petra's London. Last but never least, thank you to my wonderful parents, for all your continued love and support. Indeed, you all are the best!

ABOUT THE AUTHOR

Annie Hewitt Photography

Celeste Connally is an Agatha Award nominee and a former freelance writer and editor. A lifelong devotee of historical novels and adaptations fueled by her passion for history—plus weekly doses of PBS Masterpiece— Celeste loves reading and writing about women from the past who didn't always do as they were told.